About the Authors

Maisey Yates is a *USA TODAY* bestselling author of more than thirty romance novels. She has a coffee habit she has no interest in kicking, and a slight Pinterest addiction. She lives with her husband and children in the Pacific Northwest. When Maisey isn't writing she can be found singing in the grocery store, shopping for shoes online and probably not doing dishes. Check out her website: www.maiseyyates.com

Maya Blake's hopes of becoming a writer were born when she picked up her first romance at thirteen. Little did she know her dream would come true! Does she still pinch herself every now and then to make sure it's not a dream? Yes, she does!

Feel free to pinch her, too, via Twitter, Facebook or Goodreads! Happy reading!

Susanna Carr is an award-winning author known for her contemporary romances. Readers throughout the world find Susanna's stories a delightful escape that has often helped them through difficult times. Reviewers frequently describe her work as 'fun,' 'sexy' and 'a must read.' When she isn't writing or spending time with her family in the Pacific Northwest, Susanna enjoys reading romance and connecting with readers online. Visit her website at susannacarr.com

The Greek Mavericks

COLLECTION

July 2019

August 2019

September 2019

October 2019

November 2019

December 2019

Greek Mavericks: At the Greek's Pleasure

MAISEY YATES

MAYA BLAKE

SUSANNA CARR

MILLS & BOON

First Published in Great Britain 2019
By Mills & Boon, an imprint of HarperCollins *Publishers*
1 London Bridge Street, London, SE1 9GF

GREEK MAVERICKS: AT THE GREEK'S PLEASURE
© 2019 Harlequin Books S.A.

The Greek's Nine-Month Redemption © Maisey Yates 2016
A Diamond Deal with the Greek © Maya Blake 2016
Illicit Night with the Greek © Susanna Carr 2016

ISBN: 978-0-263-27565-0

0819

MIX
Paper from
responsible sources
FSC® C007454

This book is produced from independently certified FSC™ paper to ensure responsible forest management.

For more information visit: www.harpercollins.co.uk/green

Printed and bound in Spain
by CPI, Barcelona

THE GREEK'S
NINE-MONTH
REDEMPTION

MAISEY YATES

To Jackie, Megan and Nicole for listening to me say 'this is weird. I'm not doing it right. I don't think this is good enough!' every time I work on a book, and who help me through it. Every time.

CHAPTER ONE

SOMETIMES ELLE ST. JAMES imagined taking a pen and stabbing it straight through Apollo Savas's chest. Not to kill him of course. He didn't have a heart so the wound would hardly be fatal. Just to hurt him.

Still, other times she fantasized about crossing the boardroom, wrenching free the knot on his tie and tearing the front of his shirt open, scraping her fingernails down his heated skin and feeling all those hard muscles beneath her hands. Finally. After nine long years of resisting him, resisting the heat that roared through her body every time their eyes met.

That one was *way* more disturbing than the stabbing thing.

It was also far too frequent.

They were sitting in a crowded meeting and she should be paying attention. But all she could think about was what she would do to him if she had five minutes with him, alone, behind a locked door.

It would either be violent or naked.

He was talking about budgets and cuts. And she hated those words. It would mean scaling down her team again. As had been the story of the past twelve months, ever since he'd bought her out from her father's holding company. A company that had since sunk into bankruptcy.

Just another moment in a long line of Apollo undermining her. Finally, her father had been forced to give her responsibility. Since his stepson had finally proven to be a viper in the nest, so to speak.

She'd been installed as CEO. Then Apollo had come down like a hammer.

It was his fault. At least in part. And nothing would convince her otherwise.

She had a plan. A plan he seemed intent on thwarting at every turn. She knew she could rescue Matte without all of these sweeping staff changes, but he wouldn't give her a chance.

Because—just as he'd always done—he was making it his mission to undermine her. To prove he was better even now.

But that didn't stop her eyes from following his hands as he gestured broadly, from wondering what those hands might feel like on her skin.

She could write what she knew about sex on a napkin. The sad thing was, it would be two words.

Apollo Savas.

He'd been sex to her from the moment she'd understood what the word *sex* meant. From the moment she'd understood why men and women were different, and why it was such a wonderful thing.

The dark-haired, dark-eyed son of the woman her father had married when Elle was fourteen. He had been fascinating. So different from her. Rough around the edges, a product of his upbringing in a class of society Elle herself had had no contact with. His mother had been a maid prior to her marriage to Elle's father. The culture shock had been intense. And very, very interesting.

Of course, since then he'd grown into a dark-hearted

man who'd betrayed her family and put her under his boot heel.

Still, she wanted him.

The Big Bad Wolf of the business world, huffing and puffing and blowing your dreams down.

"Don't you agree, Ms. St. James?"

She looked up, her eyes locking with Apollo's, her heart thudding a dull rhythm. The last thing she needed was to admit she'd missed what he was saying. She would rather admit to having fantasies of killing him than the alternative.

"You'll have to repeat the question, Mr. Savas. My attention span for repetition isn't infinite. This is the same song you've been singing for months, and it isn't any more effective or logical than it was last time."

He stood, his movements liquid silk. She could see from the black glitter in his eyes that she was going to pay for her words. The thought sent a shiver down her spine. Fear mingled with unaccountable lust.

"I am sorry you find me boring. I shall endeavor to make myself more interesting. You see, I was speaking of the fact that for a company to be successful it must be sleek. Well oiled. Each cog functioning at top capacity. Extraneous cogs are unnecessary. Sluggish cogs are unnecessary. I was attempting to be delicate with my metaphor." He began to walk down the length of the boardroom table, the postures of each person he moved behind straightening as he did. "Perhaps I would have held your attention a bit better if I would have simply said that if I identify a portion of your company functioning at less than optimum capacity I will start slashing and burning your employees like they were dry brush."

Her entire face felt like it was on fire, her heart pounding harder now. She clenched her shaking hands into fists. "Everyone in this company—"

"I'm sure your speech is about to be inspiring and truly emotional, but since this is not a feel-good underdog sports movie, you should perhaps save your breath, Ms. St. James. You can say what you will, but I have seen the numbers. Conviction doesn't equal profits. I will be reviewing everything closely and making cuts at my discretion. With that, I think the meeting is adjourned. Ms. St. James has a very low tolerance for my droning, I hear. If it is the same for the rest of you, you should be pleased to be sent on your way."

The collective surge of bodies making their way out of the room reminded Elle of a herd of wildebeests fleeing a lion.

A big, bored lion who wanted nothing more than to scare them by flashing his teeth. He wasn't going to give chase. Not now.

No, now his focus had turned to her.

"You are in rare form today, Elle."

"I am in exactly the appropriate form, *Apollo*," she said, reverting to the use of his first name.

They were *family*, after all.

Not that she'd ever seen him as a brother. A sexual fantasy she didn't want. Her biggest competitor. Her darkest enemy. He was all of those things, but not a brother.

"I own your company," he said. "I own *you*." Oh, dammit all, why did those words make her…ache? "You never seem to show me the proper amount of fear."

"Real leaders don't rule with an iron fist," she hissed. "They understand that intimidation isn't the way to gain respect."

She shouldn't be talking back to him, but she could never control her tongue around him. They'd known each other for too long. Had spent too many years in the same household.

And she had spent too many years tearing strips off him when she'd felt like she had the upper hand. When she was the blood daughter of her father, the one who held a rightful place in their upstate mansion.

Things changed. Oh, how things changed.

"Says the woman who is no longer in a true position of leadership." He smiled. Showing his teeth.

She wouldn't scatter. She would not. She was not a wildebeest.

"Oh, but I am. As long as Matte is an independently operating entity beneath your large corporate umbrella, I am here to run it as best as I can. I am here to stand in the gap for my employees and give you the information black-and-white printouts can't."

"You're being ridiculous. Everything is electronic now. I'm not wasting resources on printouts."

He turned and started to walk out of the office. "You know what I mean. A flat, two-dimensional report reducing everything to statistics and cold numbers is hardly the be-all and end-all."

"That's where you're wrong," he said, taking long strides down the hall.

Elle had to take two steps to his one, her high heels clicking loudly on the marble floor as she hurried after him. "I am not wrong. It doesn't offer the whole picture. You can't possibly know how the company is really functioning. How each worker impacts the creative process. Matte isn't just a magazine. It's a line of cosmetics, a fashion brand. We have books and—"

"Yes," he said, stepping into an elevator, "thank you, I am very familiar with how my assets function."

"Then you should be aware of the fact that I have strategies in place that require all of the manpower I possess. Initiatives that take time to launch but will catapult this brand into worldwide recognition."

"Yes. So you said last time we met. And, unlike you, I don't drift off in meetings."

She growled and charged into the elevator after him. "I did not drift off."

He pushed the button to the lobby and the doors slid closed. Then he turned that dark, unsettling focus onto her. The air around them seemed to shrink, rendering the already crowded space impossibly tight. "No. I don't believe you did, Elle," he said, his voice as silken as his movements. "You were looking at me with a great deal of intensity. Too much to be on another planet entirely. What was it you were thinking about exactly?"

"Driving a pen through your chest," she said, smiling.

Because she would be damned if she'd say, *Tearing your clothes off and seeing if you're as good in reality as you are in my dreams.*

Even though she felt like that reality was written all over her face, across her skin in the red stain of a blush.

He offered her a wry smile. "You know I can't be killed like that. You have to cut my head off and bury it in a separate location to my body."

"I'll let the hit men know." She turned and smiled at him again, and he offered one in return.

The doors slid open, revealing the rather vacant bottom floor. Matte shared its offices with many other businesses, and with penthouses on the top floor. At this hour of the day not many people were coming and going.

"Where is it you're staying, Apollo?" she asked. "A crypt somewhere in Midtown?"

"The one just next to yours, Elle," he said, his tone light. "After you."

He extended his hand, waiting for her to step out of the elevator. She swept past him, moving through the lobby and going through the revolving doors. She stepped on to the busy Manhattan sidewalk, put her sunglasses on and stood there, tapping her foot.

Apollo emerged a moment later, straightening his suit jacket and standing across from her for a moment.

"Care to continue shouting at me while I walk?" he asked.

"I'm not shouting at you. I'm calmly explaining to you why you're wrong in your methods of handling my company."

He turned away from her, walking down the crowded street, his broad back filling her vision.

"Apollo!" Okay, she was shouting now. "We are not through with our meeting."

"I think we adjourned it."

"The general meeting," she said, upping her pace. "But *we* are not done."

"I'm just here," he said, gesturing to an old boutique hotel only two buildings down from the Matte offices. "Since I'm in town primarily to deal with Matte I thought I should stay close."

"Congratulations. How sensible."

"I have my moments. Judging by the fact that I'm a billionaire who successfully staged a takeover of your father's company, I've had several moments, actually."

"If you were as clever as you think you are you would listen to my plans for Matte. The answer isn't to reduce us down to nothing. You have to let me try and expand it, otherwise we really will die."

"You're assuming I'm trying to save you, dear Elle. Perhaps I just want to pull the plug."

"You… You…" She was sputtering now. She never sputtered. She blamed him.

"Villain. Scoundrel. I answer to any of those really."

"You have always been a competitive son of a bitch, but this is above and beyond."

"You're assuming this is a competition."

"What else could it be? You're ungrateful. For everything my father gave you. And for the fact that he didn't give you everything."

He chuckled, a dark, humorless sound. "Oh, you mean that he didn't give me his corporation, or Matte, in the first place? Why do you think he installed you, Elle? Your competence? No. He gave you the position to keep a foothold once I bought him out."

The words landed hard, hollowing out her midsection. Leaving nothing but a crater behind.

Like you didn't suspect that already.

She had. Of course she had. But the fact he knew it meant it was obvious. Possibly to everyone.

The doorman opened the golden door for them and Apollo paused to tip him before continuing on. Elle opened her purse and produced her own dollar, handing it to the man before going in after Apollo.

She was not allowing him to do her tipping for her.

"I am in the penthouse suite. It's very nice."

"Why am I not surprised that I just got out of a meeting where you were discussing tightening belts for my company, and yet you're staying in the penthouse suite."

He pushed the button for the elevator and the doors slid open. She followed in after, starting to feel slightly out of breath.

"I am not in need of money, *agape*, if that's why you thought I was mentioning cuts."

Agape. She hated that. He'd started using that on her

sometime when she was in high school. Just to make her angry. And some small part of her grabbed hold of it every time, holding it near. *Love.*

Oh, what a ridiculous, stupid…

She really hated her hormones.

"Why else would you mention cuts?" she asked, keeping her tone sweet.

The doors slid shut and she had the uncomfortable feeling of being trapped in a closed-in space again.

"Because *you* need the money. Matte needs the money. In a digital world your print publication is lagging and while you have certainly come up with innovative ways to compete, you haven't leveled out yet."

"But if you have enough—"

He chuckled. "I don't run a charity. I run a business. My corporation turns profits. That's what it does. I make money hand over fist, and I'm comfortable admitting that. I'm proud of it. But that won't continue if I don't refine my assets. Refining is a hot and painful process. It takes fire. And people being fired."

"Ha-ha. You're far too funny for your own good."

He frowned. "Was that funny? It wasn't meant to be."

The elevator stopped and the doors opened on a narrow hallway. Apollo stepped out and walked down a few doors, pausing to open it. "Come in," he said.

She very much had the feeling of being a small, vulnerable creature invited into the lair of a predator.

You are not a wildebeest. You are just as scary as he is. You are a lioness.

She stepped over the threshold and into the room. It was lovely, he was right. Ornate moldings and trim framing the space, the windows looking out over Central Park.

There was a large seating area with a bar, and off to

the left an open door that she could see led to a bedroom with a very large, dramatic bed.

She imagined, as tall as he was, he took up most of the mattress. That thought made her picture him—long, tanned limbs sprawled out on the bed. Would he look more relaxed in sleep? Would he seem less...lethal out of that custom-fit black suit that conformed to every line, every muscle in his body?

He closed the door behind her with a finality that made her jump.

"My team is the best there is," she said. "They have some of the most creative minds in this—or any—industry. You have to admit the fact that the Matte Guidebooks have been hugely successful. And the makeup guide actually helped to increase sales of the cosmetics. It was specific to the brand and that—"

"Again you are telling me things I already know. I didn't get to this position in life without paying attention. I understand that your team is important to you. But if I don't do what must be done, if I don't make the hard cuts, none of you will have a job."

"But I—"

"You seem to be under the impression that this is a democracy, Elle. Be assured, absolutely, that this is a dictatorship. I am not negotiating with you. And it is only by my good graces that your pretty ass remains in the CEO's office."

Heat and fury washed over Elle in a fiery baptism. "And here I thought it was because I'm good at my job."

"You are," he said, taking a step toward her. "But there are a great many people who would be good at your job. People who didn't get handed their position from their daddy."

"Oh, that's hilarious, Apollo. As if you didn't get a leg

up from my father, you Judas." She took a step toward him, rage propelling her now. "My father treated you like one of his own children. He put you through school."

"And I excelled on my own."

"Then you stabbed him in the back."

"I bought him out for much more than thirty pieces of silver, little girl. Perhaps what really hurts is the fact that you were betrayed by your father, not by me. He put you in this position knowing you would fail."

She gritted her teeth, doing her best to shake off his words. To not allow them to take hold. All of this reached down deep. To old wounds. To the way she'd felt she couldn't measure up to Apollo, the son her father had always wanted. To her own fears of being eternally inadequate. And he knew it.

She would not let him win so easily. "He trusted you. When you offered to help he didn't imagine you dismantling everything."

Apollo lifted one broad shoulder. "He made a mistake in trusting me."

"Clearly. You would betray not only the man who set you on the path to success, but your own mother."

"She's fine. Your father is hardly financially ruined. She continues to enjoy her status as his wife. And again, Elle, need I remind you your father sold Matte, and some of his other holdings, to me of his own free will."

"You had him in a position where he couldn't say no."

Apollo took another step toward her. He was so close now that she could see his eyes weren't completely black. She could see a faint ring of gold that faded to copper, then to deep brown. Could see the dark stubble beginning to grow in at his jawline.

Could smell the scent of his aftershave and skin.

"Interesting you put it like that. If dire financial straits take away choice you could argue my mother had little choice in marrying your father in the first place."

"That's ridiculous," Elle said. "She wanted to."

"Did she?"

"Of course."

"A cleaning lady offered the chance to live in luxury after years barely making it in the US? After years of homeless poverty in Greece?"

"That isn't… It has nothing to do with this."

"Maybe," he said. "Or maybe the point is that you can always say no, Elle." He leaned in. "Always."

She could barely breathe, her head swimming, her entire body on high alert. She was almost certain she had no blood in her veins, not anymore. It was molten lava now, heating her from her core.

She remembered so clearly feeling this way every time he brushed past her in the halls of the family estate. Every time she caught sight of him at the pool—his lean, muscular body so fascinating to the girl she'd been.

Only once had they ever come so close to each other. Only one other time had she ever thought he might feel the same forbidden desire that she'd felt from the moment she'd set eyes on him.

Apollo is going to be your new stepbrother.

Everything in her had rebelled at that, immediately. Because she had seen him and wanted him in a way she knew would be wrong once their parents were married. So she had distanced him. She had been…well, sometimes she'd been terrible. But it had been for her own survival.

It was even worse now. He was still her stepbrother. But now, any affection she'd ever felt for him had been twisted by his betrayal. She should have stopped obsessing about him a long time ago.

But she hadn't. She couldn't. She was a slave to this, to him. Always.

She hated it. She hated *him*.

And she had spent nine years resisting him. Embracing the anger, the annoyance and everything else she could possibly use as a barrier between her desire for him and her actions.

Giving in would be a failure. In terms of her self-control. In terms of her relationship with her father. What would he think if he knew she wanted Apollo? What sort of scandal would erupt if the media knew she was helplessly attracted to her stepbrother?

So she had denied it. Pushed it down deep. But she had been aware of it every time she saw him. Every glance. Every accidental brush of his hand against hers. Every time she went to bed at night, hot and aching for something she knew only he could give her.

But he had bought out her father's company. He was gunning for Matte. Her father had installed her as CEO to keep some connection to the company—just as Apollo had said. And she'd failed spectacularly.

She could feel everything slipping out of her grasp. The company. Her control. Everything.

And she'd never tasted him. Never had him. This man who was destroying her whole life. Who commanded her fantasies and called out the deepest, darkest desire from deep inside of her.

For what? For appearances. To triumph.

There would be no triumph here. She was losing. Utterly. Epically.

Why not have this? Why not have him?

It was all going to burn to the ground. She might as well go up in flames with it.

She could see his pulse throbbing at the base of his

throat. If only she had a pen in her hand. It would be so easy from this position to stab him clean through with it. But she didn't.

So instead, she reached up and grabbed hold of the knot in his tie, and wrenched it free.

CHAPTER TWO

APOLLO SAVAS DIDN'T entertain daydreams. He was a man of practicality and action. When he wanted something, he didn't sit around fantasizing about it, he took it.

That was the only reason he knew that it was no hallucination that Elle St. James, his stepsister and mortal enemy, was currently stripping his clothes off, her eyes bright, glittering with rage and desire.

He had resisted her, this, for years. Resisted her. Out of deference to the man he considered a father. Out of respect for all he'd been given.

But all of it had proven to be false, had proven to be a lie. And still he had roped Elle off. Had kept her separate—in many ways—from his plans for revenge.

And David St. James had known he would. Because whether she knew it or not, he had always protected Elle. She had always mattered.

But things had changed. And now she was tugging at his tie. And he was tired of restraint.

He reached out and wrapped his fingers around her wrist, holding her hands still. "What the hell are you doing?" he asked, his voice a growl.

She looked up at him, her green eyes round, those soft, sassy pink lips shaped into a perfect O. "I…" Color flooded her face.

"If you were thinking you were going to take my shirt off, either stop now and walk out that door, or keep going and understand that I will have you flat on your back and screaming my name in a very *different* way before you can protest."

Her color deepened, her eyes growing even wider. He thought she would run. Because Elle was a *good* girl, by the standards of her father. Though, she was stone-cold, aloof and fancied herself far above him.

It had made him want to destroy that facade from the first. He hadn't. Because he knew that she was innocent. Knew that she was nothing more than a cosseted rich girl who would be completely out of her depth with a man like him. A man who had grown up on the streets in Athens, who had learned the hard truths about life early on. About loss. About the true nature of people.

He had known that if he ever touched her it would violate the trust he had built with her father.

But if she was going to touch him now, if she was going to remove that barrier that had always loomed between them, then he wasn't going to put a stop to it.

Apollo Savas was a man who took what he wanted.

With one exception.

Elle.

He had wanted her from the moment she'd transformed from a girl to a woman. A haughty, rude woman who walked by him with her nose in the air half the time. Perversely, it had always made him want to have her even more.

She thought his hands were dirty. Thought he was beneath her. It made him want to put his filthy hands all over her. Made him want to pull her right down with him.

His biggest betrayal had never been buying St. James

Corp's most valuable assets and breaking them off piece by piece.

No, his biggest betrayal had started long before he'd discovered David St. James's true nature. It had begun long before he'd discovered the dark secrets surrounding just why he and his mother had been brought into the St. James home.

His first betrayal had been in the way he'd looked at Elle.

But everything was shot to hell now anyway. Every allegiance broken with his "family." Why not this, too? Why not slaughter the last sacred cow?

He had destroyed everything else. He might as well destroy this, too. And he would relish it.

Her hand was still frozen, holding on to his tie. Then, her eyes took on a determined glitter, her lips curling into a snarl as she yanked hard on the silken fabric, pulling it free from its knot.

He growled, grabbing ahold of that sleek high ponytail that had been taunting him from the moment he had walked into the boardroom today. He wrapped his fingers around her coppery hair and pulled hard, tilting her head backward. Her nostrils flared slightly, her lips parting.

They held their positions for a moment, staring at each other, clearly waiting to see what the next move was.

He had waited too long. He was not waiting another moment.

He would have her now. Strip away every prim and proper layer. Punish her with his kiss as he should have done that day she'd dared him at the pool. The only time the anger between them had given way and revealed the layer beneath.

Of course, she had acted as though nothing had happened after. And so had he.

But he would make sure this time she would not be able to act unscathed after he was through with her.

He wrapped his arm around her slender waist, drawing her up against his body as he backed them both toward the wall. It stopped their progress ruthlessly, her shoulder blades pressed firmly against the hard surface. He bent his head, kissing her neck, his teeth scraping her skin.

The sound that escaped her lips was raw and desperate, her hands clutching his shoulders, her fingernails digging into his skin through the fabric of his suit jacket. Then she slid her palms down flat, grabbing hold of the front of his shirt and tugging hard, sending buttons flying as she wrenched it open. She pushed his jacket from his shoulders, grabbing hold of his shirt and shoving it down, too. He unbuttoned the cuffs, helping her and her progress, and untucking it from his pants and throwing it down onto the floor.

She looked completely shocked, and wholly satisfied by her actions as she regarded his body. Then she pressed her palms to his chest and slid her fingers down to his stomach, her fingernails scraping him lightly as she did. She grabbed hold of his belt, making quick work of that, as well.

"Greedy," he said, taking hold of her wrists and drawing her arms up over her head, holding her there with one hand as he set to work on the buttons of her silk blouse with the other.

She fought against him, the color in her cheeks deepening, her breasts rising and falling with the shallow gasps of her breath. He chuckled when her shirt fell open, revealing an insubstantial red lace bra and he imagined she thought it made her seem daring.

She arched her back, thrusting her breasts into greater prominence. He tightened his hold on her, pressing her hands more firmly against the wall. "You don't get to set the terms," he said. "Not in the boardroom, not in the bedroom. I am in charge in *all* things."

"Always a competition with you, isn't it?" she asked.

"Oh, *agape*, it has never been a competition. How can it be when I always win?"

For the first time, he saw a slight flicker of doubt in her eyes. But it was quickly replaced by a challenge. "So insecure that you have to exert your dominance in such a cliché fashion? You are exactly the same here as you are in the office."

He leaned in, his lips a whisper away from hers. "You're going to pay for that."

"I hope this isn't an empty threat, Apollo," she said, the words throaty, enticing. "You seem to be full of those."

He closed the distance between them, closing his teeth around her bottom lip and biting her. She gasped and he pulled away. The flush in her cheeks had spread to her neck, had down to the full swell of her breasts. She might be angry, but she was aroused, too.

"One thing you need to learn, *agape*, is that my threats are never empty. It's simply that the consequences might be delayed in coming."

She looked down, then back up. "I do hope the coming isn't terribly delayed today."

Those words, coming from Elle's lips, seemed shocking. From any other woman it might have been commonplace dirty talk. Not even all that dirty when it came down to it. But from Elle? It had the desired effect.

He was so hard he thought he was going to burst through the zipper on his pants. His heart was raging, his hand shaking as he undid the last button on her blouse and pulled it from her shoulders.

He couldn't remember the last time a woman had affected him in such a way. If one ever had. But then, he had never been in a situation quite like this. His partner had never looked at him with lust and rage burning from her eyes all at the same time. She'd never looked quite like she wanted to strangle him and have her way with him in the same moment.

And, he had never been with Elle.

"I didn't realize you were a dirty talker, Elle." He scraped the edge of her ear with his teeth. "If you had been negotiating this way all along you might have been a lot more successful."

"You're a bastard," she bit out, turning her head and tracing the line of his jaw with the edge of her tongue. "A complete and utter—"

"And you want me," he said, releasing his hold on her and drawing his face back, pressing the tip of his nose against hers and meeting her fierce gaze. "So what does that say about you?"

"Oh, I know that all of this is the final nail in the coffin of my decency." She grabbed the end of his belt buckle and yanked it through the loops, then set about working on the closure of his slacks.

"Go out with style, I say." He slid his hands down her slender waist, to the full curve of her hip, and down farther, gripping the hem of her skirt and shoving it up roughly over her hips. No surprise, her panties were the same red lace as the bra.

Not that he was complaining.

"I took you for a white cotton kind of girl," he said. "Who knew that you had so many secrets?"

"You're never going to know my secrets, Apollo," she said.

"So venomous," he said, his lips touching hers now as he spoke the words. "And yet, you're dying to have me."

She put her hand between them, pressing her palm against his hardened arousal. "Same goes."

"I'm tired of talking."

And then, he crushed his mouth to hers, claiming the kiss he should have taken years ago.

Elle had no idea what she was thinking. She wasn't thinking. She was feeling. Feeling everything. Rage, need, arousal like she had never known existed.

She would like to be confused about this. About how this could happen. About how she could be doing this with a man she hated so very much. But lust and anger had always been twisted up together where Apollo was concerned. Well, maybe not always. But in the past few years. And that was when her desire for him had turned from a girlish crush into a woman's need.

She wasn't sixteen anymore. She knew what men and women did in the dark. She didn't need her own hands-on experience to be aware.

But somewhere, during all of that, Apollo had gone from being someone she trusted and admired—a member of the St. James family—to their bitterest enemy. And somewhere, as that change had taken place, her desire for him had changed, as well.

And now it was this strange, twisted thing that she couldn't begin to untangle. And there was no other man who made her feel anything near what he made her feel.

It didn't matter that it was sick. It didn't matter that it was wrong. What Apollo made her feel was pure adrenaline. Pure excitement. Even if it wasn't all good.

He made every other man she had ever gone out with seem like a bland, beige substitute.

That was why this was happening. Really, it was why it *needed* to happen. When this was over, she would finally be cleansed.

Her need for him would go down in one fiery ball of pleasure and rage. And when she looked at him she would feel…nothing.

Oh, she wanted that more than anything.

She kissed him back with all of that. All of the anger, all of the lust. His tongue swept against hers, his hold on her hips firm, blunt fingertips digging into her skin. Then he shifted his position, putting his hands between her thighs, stroking his fingers over the thin lace that concealed her desire for him.

She gasped, everything inside of her shaking. She had never been this intimate with a man before, and yet she wasn't afraid. She wasn't experiencing any virginal nerves. She was more than ready for this. It was the combination of years of fantasies. An explosion of… Well, of everything.

His fingers slipped beneath the fabric, gliding through her slick flesh. If he'd had any doubt about how much she wanted him, he couldn't doubt it now.

"Yes," he said, the word a growl.

The way he said that, the absolute, incontrovertible evidence of how much he wanted her in return radiated through her. Spurred her on. She grabbed hold of the waistband of his pants and underwear, tugging them down his lean hips. There was no place for tenderness here, no place for hesitation.

She reached between their bodies, wrapping her hand around his hardened length. It was her turn to shudder, her turn to growl. She had never touched a man like this. She had no idea he would be so very big. She was nearly weak with wanting him. This was why she felt hollow. This was what she needed to be filled.

He slipped one finger inside of her and her breath hissed through her teeth, the unfamiliar invasion shocking and immensely pleasurable.

She took hold of his arms, clinging onto his rock hard biceps as he continued to tease her with a preview of what she really wanted.

She looked up at him, her heart hammering in her chest. He was beautiful. There was no question. And she wanted him. She wanted him more than she'd ever wanted anything in her entire life. It was important that she know it was him. As if it could be anyone else. As if anyone else could ever make her feel this way. This exhilarating mixture of destructive anger and impossible need.

She kissed the corner of his mouth, tracing his lower lip with the tip of her tongue. He moved his hand from between her thighs, lifting it, grabbed hold of her bra and pulled it down, revealing her breasts to his gaze. He lowered his head, drawing one tightened nipple deep into his mouth.

Sensation shot through her like an arrow, hitting her low and deep. A low, harsh sound escaped her lips and she let her head fall back as she laced her fingers through his hair, tugging hard as he continued to pleasure her.

"Please," she whimpered, "please."

He moved away from her, then bent down grabbing ahold of his pants, pulling his wallet out of the pocket before producing a condom.

Her breath gathered up in her chest like a ball and held there, a heavy weight she couldn't move. She could only watch him. Look her fill at his beautiful, masculine form. He was even more beautiful than she had imagined.

He returned to her, his bare chest pressing against

hers as he flattened her against the wall. She looked at his face, his gorgeous, thoroughly despised, utterly beloved face.

She grabbed hold of him, bracketing his face with her hands and tugging him forward, kissing him hard and deep. He put his hand back between her thighs, this time pushing two fingers into her, stretching her gently. She was so ready for him. Beyond ready.

"Do it," she said against his lips.

He moved his hand, gripping hold of her hips, sliding one hand down her thigh and lifting her leg, opening her to him. He tested her slick entrance with the blunt head of his arousal. Then he thrust deep inside.

The pain was sharp, swift. Tears stung her eyes, and she shut them quickly because she didn't want him to see. She didn't want him to know. She had felt powerful a few moments ago, but this made her feel a lot more vulnerable. Vulnerable was not what she wanted. She wanted pleasure, she wanted her desire satisfied. She wanted to rid herself of this toxic, intense feeling she had for him once and for all.

But, she hadn't anticipated this. Not just the pain, but the feeling that she was breaking apart. The feeling that they were connected, closer than she had ever been with anyone.

Somehow, she had imagined the fact that she hated him might buffer against any other emotions.

But it didn't.

So she kept her eyes closed.

If Apollo noticed, he didn't comment. Instead, he fused his mouth to hers and flexed his hips, a flash of pleasure slowly overtaking the pain.

Slowly, all the discomfort began to recede. And she just wanted him. There was nothing else. There was no ugly history between them, there was no anger, no hatred. Nothing but an intense, burning need to be satisfied. She clung to him, to his shoulders, her lips pressed to his as he established a steady rhythm, pushing them both toward the brink.

He thrust hard and she let out a hoarse cry, raking her nails down his back. He growled, his rhythm faltering. And then, there was no more steadiness. There was nothing but a frantic race to the finish, his movements rough, intense. And she took it all. Every last bit.

He gripped her chin, tilting her face up, forcing her to meet his gaze. And she did. She didn't look away, unwilling to flinch in the face of his challenge. She shivered, tension growing more and more intense in the pit of her stomach, her internal muscles gripping him tight as her orgasm began to build.

He slowed his movement suddenly, withdrawing slowly before pushing back in hard. White light broke out behind her eyes, release exploding inside her like a bomb, a wild burst of aftershocks radiating through her, leaving her shaken, weak. And then he followed, his entire body going stiff as he shuddered out his own release.

He lowered his head, his teeth digging into her collarbone. She let her head fall back against the wall, a sigh escaping her lips.

They stood like that, for just a moment. And then slowly, reality started to creep in.

She had done it. She had given her virginity to Apollo Savas.

And suddenly, horrifically, all she wanted to do was curl into a ball and cry.

She pushed at his shoulders, and he withdrew. She began to look around at the ground, realizing that only her shirt had been entirely discarded. Everything else was simply askew. That was—frankly—slightly more embarrassing than the alternative. She hadn't even waited for him to undress her completely.

He would think she was completely desperate. He would think that she had been yearning after him for years.

It was the truth. Which was what made it particularly horrifying.

She straightened her clothes, tucking her skirt back into place, fixing her bra as she pulled her blouse back on. He said nothing. He simply watched her with those dark, unreadable eyes.

She smoothed her hand over her hair.

"Too little too late, *agape*," he said.

She froze, her hand still poised over her undoubtedly wrecked ponytail. "Excellent," she said, her voice so brittle she thought it might break.

"I am leaving in the morning."

"All right," she said, the words hollow, echoing in her head.

"I will not see you. I will not make any decisions about staffing changes until the next time we meet."

"I'm relieved to hear that."

"I'll be back in town on the twentieth. Make sure you keep your calendar clear."

With that, she could see she was dismissed. With no more fanfare than if they had simply finished a meeting.

And he was still naked. It was absurd. But she wasn't going to highlight the absurdity. Not when she simply wanted to get out of there as quickly as possible so she could have a complete and total meltdown.

"Then I'll see you on the twentieth."

She collected her purse, drawing the strap over her

shoulder and clinging tightly to it. To keep herself from…
Slapping him? Kissing him again? She wasn't certain.

"Excellent. Should I call you a cab?"

"No," she said, checking her watch. "It's… It's only
three o'clock. I have to go back to work."

She had to go back to work like this. With the impression of his hands still on her skin, her cheeks burning
from the brush of his whiskers against them.

"So it is."

"Goodbye," she said.

He tilted his head. "Goodbye, Elle."

CHAPTER THREE

ANTICIPATING THE TWENTIETH had become something of a reverse Christmas countdown. In that she hoped it would never come. It might have been nice to have an Apollo Advent calendar though. So that every time she thought about him arriving she could eat a piece of chocolate to try to deal with her stress.

When she arrived at the office that morning it was with an industrial-strength coffee, a bottle of ibuprofen and a very fake smile plastered to her lips.

Because Apollo was due to arrive—who knew when—to start handing down edicts from his high horse. And she was going to have to face him for the first time since they had… Since that day in his hotel room.

The very thought of that made humiliating color wash through her face. That day had been an aberration. Something that would never be repeated. She had, after all, gone the first twenty-six years of her life without sex. She should be able to happily get through another few weeks. Then, maybe when everything settled down, when Apollo stopped coming in and poking at her employees, reshuffling her business and in general upending her life, she would contend with the fact that she needed to find a relationship.

That was the problem. She had simply waited too long.

She had allowed Apollo and her desire for him to become so large in her mind that nothing else could compare.

Well, now she'd had sex. With Apollo, as it happened. So, question answered, tension diffused.

She was a modern woman. She wasn't going to allow him to make her feel ashamed about her actions. Even though, considering he was a relic of a man, he would attempt to make her feel ashamed. If for no other reason than he would be actively attempting to assert his dominance over her.

Well, no thank you. She was…indomitable.

She gritted her teeth, opening the door to her office and nearly dropping the coffee in her hand when she saw who was already sitting at *her* desk. "That's my seat," she said, the words coming out crisp and harsh.

"It's lovely to see you too, *agape*."

"Now, Apollo," she said, deciding that she was going to be the one to address the elephant in the room before he got a chance. It was there, she might as well be the one to name it. "Don't try to sweet-talk me just because we had sex."

"I wouldn't dream of it," he said, his lips tipping up into a smile.

"No, I suppose you wouldn't. That would require you to know how to sweet-talk."

"You rocked my world. I saw God. You have ruined me for all other women."

She gritted her teeth against the strange, ridiculous warmth that flooded her when he spoke. He was being a jerk, and she knew it. So his words shouldn't make her… anything. She took a fortifying breath.

"What you said," she said, waving her hand. "Substitute 'men' for 'women', 'slightly disorganized' for 'rocked', and 'God' for… I don't know, maybe 'a really good cheesecake'? Not exactly divine, but adequate."

"You are in *typical* form today."

"I try for consistency, Apollo. It's part of my charm."

"I have rarely seen evidence of your charm. Your *charms* perhaps, but I'm not really speaking of your personality."

"Right, well, for some reason things have been especially difficult between us lately, haven't they? Though, I imagine not as difficult as things have been between you and my father. Have you spoken to him since you rammed that knife into his back?"

"Oh, yes. Of course we have."

"You're sick. How could you do that to your own—"

"He is not my own anything. I am not your blood, *agape*. And a good thing to or what happened between us would be off-limits. Both in the past and in the future."

She gritted her teeth, trying not to blush. She was definitely playing at being slightly more blasé and experienced than she was. But he hadn't called her on it yet. So she was going to carry on. "I would rather run my new Jimmy Choos through the shredder, thanks."

"Is that what the kids are calling it these days? I admit, that doesn't sound very sexy."

"It wasn't meant to be."

"Right. Tell me, Elle, how is my mother?" he asked.

Elle arched a brow. "How long has it been since you've spoken to Mariam?"

He shrugged. "Months? She doesn't approve of my betrayal any more than you or your father do."

"And yet you don't feel any guilt over it?"

"I have my reasons," he said, his tone so cold and hard it could cut glass.

"I'm sure you do, but none of them are compelling

enough for me or my family. I don't care what your reasons are. And your mother is well," she said. "I just talked to her last night."

It had been difficult to talk to her stepmother when memories of what had passed between her and Apollo had lingered so persistently. She had felt...guilty and completely transparent. Thankfully, Mariam had her own topics to discuss and hadn't seemed to notice Elle's general silence.

"Well," she said, clearing her throat, "as charming as this little detour has been, let's get down to business."

He reached up, touching the knot on his tie. "Oh, you meant *actual* business."

"You're a pig."

"I'm wounded. Now, I've been going over projections for the quarter. You have to either increase profits soon or you need to start cutting expenses. I can guarantee one, but I can't guarantee the other." He stood, placing his hands on the desk. *Her* desk.

She tried to cling to her anger. Anger that would hopefully be much more powerful than the attraction that was still surging through her. What was her problem? She was supposed to be cured. She was supposed to have inoculated herself to all future Apollo encounters. Cure yourself from a snakebite with snake venom, and all that. But she didn't feel cured. She did not feel at all inoculated. In fact, she felt a little bit dizzy.

"Of course you can't," she said, the words coming out harsh. "No one can guarantee a profit increase. But trust me, if we keep on going in this new direction—"

"This isn't about trust. It's about the bottom line. I have a great deal more experience in business than you do, Elle."

Those words rankled. In part because they were true.

In part because they dug beneath the suit of armor she had worked so hard to put into place today. It hit the wound beneath it that twinged every day. That she was her father's second choice through and through. When she failed at this, she would prove that she never should have been here in the first place. That if her father had had his way he would have put someone else in her position. That if Apollo weren't too important for it, if Apollo hadn't turned against them, it would likely have been him.

You decided failure be damned, remember?

Yes. She had. But it was difficult to feel committed to that now.

"But I care about this company."

"As do I. It's a part of my bottom line, and there is nothing I care about more than my bottom line."

"Well, Matte is only part of your bottom line because you set out to acquire it when you saw that it was floundering. You knew what you were getting."

"And without my influence this company would probably already be six feet under. Like the rest of the holdings I bought from your father."

"You fired the final shot into them."

"A mercy killing," he said, his tone hard. "Don't oppose me, Elle. I am not doing this for my own amusement. If I succeed, you will succeed along with me. I am not the enemy that you set me up to be."

She didn't know what to say to that. Except, it was a disagreement they were not going to settle. Not without blood anyway. "Yes, but you said you were standing there ready to pull the plug, so let's be honest. You aren't a savior, either."

"I never claimed to be."

"Well, don't stand there and pretend that you aren't the villain."

"Oh, did you think that's what I was doing? You're wrong there. I know full well that I'm the villain here, *agape*. If I had a mustache I would twirl it. Alas. You will have to settle for the assurance that I know full well where I stand in this little play. However, we do not have to oppose each other. I know that my presence is sinister. However, there is nothing you can do to fight it. But understand I will save Matte if it's at all possible."

"You're here to announce cuts today, aren't you?"

"Surprisingly, no. But I did come to discuss something with you."

"What?" she asked, feeling suspicious.

"I would like for you to come to my European headquarters. To get a little bit of an idea for how things run, to attend to some meetings there, and to attend a certain number of charity events."

"What?"

"What I would like to do is help revitalize the image of Matte. I would like to bring you into the public eye. Have you as the public face, so to speak. With a little bit of help you could provide a facelift all on your own. And then, maybe we would be able to avoid cuts."

She hadn't expected this. She was, in fact, struck dumb by the fact that he was extending a hand out. That he was offering her a chance to not only save the company, but to do it in such a public way.

She had been prepared to be the one left standing in the ashes. A phoenix who was not poised to rise. She had been prepared to go down in flames, with her hands on Apollo's naked body.

And now…now he was changing things. Again.

"You just expect me to pick up and go to Europe with you?"

"Yes. And I don't exactly expect you to have a major issue with being asked to spend some time in Greece with me."

"Your headquarters are in Greece still? Are you the last remaining corporation in the country?"

"I am successful. Worldwide. It would be a poor thanks to my homeland to remove the jobs and revenue I provide simply because there's been some unrest."

"Please, don't tell me you have a heart. Only a moment ago you were telling me that your decisions were based on the bottom line."

"I *don't* have a heart. I simply have a strong liking for dolmas and ouzo."

"That I can believe."

He smiled, and for a moment, she felt like she was looking back at the boy he had been. The boy she had known all those years ago. The one who had captivated her from the first moment she had laid eyes on him.

The boy she had proceeded to snipe at and torture with flippant remarks every chance she got. Reminding him that he wasn't really a St. James. Because she'd been nothing more than a little girl with a crush and she'd handled it like they were on the playground.

But though things had never been easy between Apollo and her, he'd been very close with her father. But as close as Apollo and her father had once been, they were just as distant now.

And she had been thrown into the middle of that divide. Tossed into a storm she could never hope to weather. Between two alpha males locking horns. One defending his turf, the other intent on destroying it.

So take control. Do this.

"Well, I'm not going to complain about a free vacation," she said, trying to keep her tone light. She wasn't going to show her hand. Not to him. Wasn't going to let him see that this mattered to her. That she was going to use this—whatever it was to him—to gain a handle on things again.

To redeem herself.

"Oh, this isn't going to be a vacation," he said, rounding the desk and making his way toward the door. "We will go to Greece and work. Additionally, there is a charity event in Athens that we will attend together."

"As business associates," she said, "I assume."

She couldn't even imagine her father's reaction. If he had any idea that she and Apollo— He would be furious. Disgusted.

The idea of disappointing him like that…of losing him altogether, was something she couldn't fathom.

Her mother had left when she'd been a child. She could barely remember her. But she remembered the hole left behind, because it was still there.

She couldn't go through that again.

Apollo gave her a dismissive glance. "What else would we be? The entire idea is to strengthen the brand. Should there be any suspicion that the two of us had—"

"There's no need to keep bringing it up."

"You're the one who seems to persist in bringing it up."

Elle crossed her arms, shaking her head, her ponytail swinging back and forth. His eyes followed the motion.

"You should wear your hair down," he said.

She abruptly stopped shaking her head. "I didn't ask you for fashion advice."

"And yet, I'm giving it. Because you desperately need it." He looked at her, his expression critical. "Yes, you need a slightly younger look. One that isn't quite so… ironed."

"Well, my clothes are ironed. Would you have them look rumpled?"

"I would have you look slightly less like a matron."

She frowned. "I do not look matronly. I have a very classic sense of style. It's chic."

"You certainly know how to flatter your figure." He didn't bother to hide that he was looking. "But you need more than that to be the kind of brand that people remember."

"I'm not a…brand," she sputtered, "I'm a woman. Where are you going?" He had walked past her, heading for the door.

"I thought I might go and speak to some of the staff."

"No," she said, hurrying after him. "I do not wish to unleash you on them. I don't want you talking about how their jobs may be in jeopardy when you make final decisions."

"Their jobs may well not be in jeopardy if you don't fight me every step of the way. People like a public face. You can provide that. You can be strongly associated with the brand, and in effect, become a brand yourself. A young, professional woman. Brilliant, fashionable. You can be that woman."

She rolled her eyes. "That does not sound like—"

"It isn't a negotiation. Either you comply with my plan, or you are subject to Plan B, which is making sweeping cuts and doing my best to lift profit margins that way."

She made an exasperated sound, following him down the hall. "I wish you wouldn't keep walking away from me."

"I have places to be. I want to take a look at the different departments. Get a body count. So to speak."

"We are *talking.*" She scampered after him. "Of course I will agree to go."

He pushed the button for the elevator. "I'm glad to hear that. I get the feeling sometimes you're just opposing me for the sake of it."

"And I get the feeling that you're an ass to me just because you enjoy it."

He chuckled and she stepped in just as the doors began to close. "Well, you are possibly correct in that assessment. Anyway, you spent a great many years being an ass to me simply because *you* enjoyed it."

She let out a harsh breath and watched the numbers on the elevator as it moved. Suddenly, she was very aware of the fact that she and Apollo were alone again. She looked at him, just a quick glance out of the corner of her eye. She tried to ignore the restless feeling between her thighs. Tried to ignore the restless feeling in her body.

After what seemed like an eternity, the doors opened again, and they were on the floor that housed the marketing department. He stepped out of the elevator and began to sweep his way through the space like a destructive wind. As he whipped by, heads turned, expressions went from relaxed to terrified.

"See that? Your mere presence lowers morale. I hope you're happy."

"I don't care about morale." He paused by one of the desks. "Hello," he said, clearly attempting to be charming. "My name is Apollo Savas. I'm the owner of this company. What is it you do?"

The girl, a blonde who could barely be twenty-five, blinked rather owlishly. She seemed to be struck dumb by his presence. Either by the fact that he was the owner of the company, or by the fact that he was just so damn good-looking. Truly, it was a problem. Elle felt a moment of sympathy for her.

"I'm on the marketing team for the makeup line," she said, looking a little bit thunderstruck.

"Have you been satisfied with the performance of those products?"

"Well," she said, shuffling the papers on her desk around, "we have seen an increase in revenue this past quarter. And our relationships with vendors—"

"How do you plan to continue the increase? What do you think attracts consumers to this product? Why should they buy this instead of say…any other brand of lipstick? I am a man, I know, but I'm not certain why one sort of cosmetic might be more attractive than another."

"I… I…"

"Enough," Elle said. "You do not need to prod at my staff."

He turned toward her, an amused expression on his face, and suddenly she felt like they were the only two people in the room. That little blonde might as well have evaporated into thin air.

There was no question, she was not remotely as immune to Apollo and she would like to be.

Apollo would question the purity of his motives if his motives were—in fact—ever pure. They weren't, so he was certain there was something self-serving and wretched behind them now. Even if he didn't know precisely what.

He had wanted to impress upon Elle the importance of her complying with his plan. When he had left her after… After the appalling lack of control that had occurred in his hotel room, he had formulated a plan to try to improve things for her company. A foolish thing, perhaps. He didn't know why he should care about the fate of her magazine. Beyond the fact that it was a potential profit machine for him.

Perhaps it was the fact that she had become collateral damage in a war he'd never intended to bring her into. But David had placed her in direct line of the firing squad.

Apollo wasn't a kind man. At least, no one ever accused him of being so. And he had never made it a goal to be seen that way. He had cared about very few people growing up, and it had turned out those he had cared about most had betrayed him long ago.

And so he had stolen his stepfather's empire, started dismantling it. But he had left Elle at Matte. God knew why. He'd known in the end he would destroy it, destroy her.

Perhaps it was because he knew what it was to be caught in the consequences of the sins of the father. Hers and his. Perhaps because he knew that—whether or not Elle had been kind to him when they were younger—she was innocent here.

But now…now it was as though a veil had been stripped away from his eyes. He would have to use her. There was no other choice. There was no preserving her. That much had been made clear when he'd taken her against the wall.

It had been symbolic in many ways of that protection being destroyed. That desire to keep her safe from himself being completely and utterly ripped away.

He could no longer ignore Elle. Could no longer dance around the fact that he would have to destroy her along with her father.

He would use her. And he would discard her.

It had nothing to do with his desire to strip her naked again. To watch her pale skin flush with pleasure once more. It had nothing at all to do with that, because he was not going to allow himself the indulgence.

Indulgence was unacceptable. But revenge? That was sweet.

"Perhaps you would like to give me a tour of the rest of the department, Elle?" he asked, ruthlessly cutting off his train of thought.

"Of course."

They moved away from where they had been standing, and she continued on down the role of desks. "Just don't *talk* to anyone," she said, her voice hushed.

"Why is it that you think you can tell me what to do when I am in my own company?"

"Because I am the boss," she said, her tone sounding slightly petulant. "That has to count for something *somewhere*."

"Sadly for you, I am your boss. Being boss of a lot of other people doesn't give you extra clout. I am the final word. So let it be written, et cetera."

She swept through the little space quickly. "There you have it. And now, I expect you want to be going."

"No," he said, crossing his arms across his chest. "I'll head back up to your office floor and set up for a few hours, get a few things done. I do like to familiarize myself with my acquisitions."

Elle looked livid. Her jaw set, her lips in a flat line. "Can't you do that in your hotel room?"

The mention of his hotel room brought back illicit memories. "I could. But I want to get a greater sense for how things are running here. It is in your best interest to keep me around. I might grow attached. I might yet see the importance of this team you keep talking about."

She said nothing, but her expression took on a rather long-suffering edge. They walked back through the office space and toward the elevators again. She pushed the button, then pushed it again when the elevator didn't immediately appear.

"If I didn't know better I would say you were in a hurry to escape my presence."

"I *am*," she said, flashing a smile. One he very much wanted to kiss right off her pretty face. But he was still calculating. When. Where. What. He wouldn't touch her until he made those decisions.

If he touched her at all.

"I do admire your honesty," he said, instead of kissing her.

"What is taking so long?" She scowled, hitting the button again. Then suddenly, the doors slid open.

"Tenth time's the charm," he said, stepping inside.

She gave him a withering glance before moving inside after him.

The doors slid shut and he had the impression that all the air had been sucked out of the space.

The tension between them was unlike anything he had ever known before. Likely because she was the only woman he had ever bothered to resist. He could remember well the first time he had noticed her as a woman, rather than a girl. Sometime after her seventeenth birthday, when all of her snubs and cutting comments had begun to arouse even as they enraged.

When they'd given way to fantasies of him showing her how base and beneath her he truly was.

His attraction, swift, sudden and abhorrent to him, had hit him low and fast in the gut, so quickly he had not had the chance to guard against it. He had not expected to have to guard against an attraction to his chilly younger stepsister.

He had nearly acted on it back then.

He could well remember the time he'd come home from university to see her getting out of the pool. Sleek curves barely concealed by a hot pink bikini that should have clashed terribly with her red hair, but rather was all the more enticing for how incongruous it was.

And he'd gone over to her, and she'd said something snotty, as she usually did. Then he'd grabbed hold of her arm, and pulled her to him. Her green eyes had gone wide, those pink lips parting gently. Begging to be kissed.

But he hadn't. He'd watched the water drops roll over her bare skin, over her breasts, had imagined lowering his head and slicking up the slow-rolling water. But he hadn't done that, either.

He'd waited. Waited until her eyes had darkened with desire. Until he'd seen her breath speed up, the pulse in her neck beating at a rapid rate. He had held her arm until he'd been sure he'd turned her on. Until he'd been sure the little ice princess was hot all over.

Then he'd let her go, and turned away, hard as iron and fantasizing about what he might have had.

And now… Well, now he'd had her, hadn't he? He had answered the question he'd never meant to ask.

He looked at her now, at the sleek ponytail that begged for him to grab hold of it, to wrap it around his hand. Her long, elegant neck. The soft curve of her pale lips. His stomach tightened. Clearly, his lust for her was not so easily dealt with via one quick screw up against the wall.

"I wish you wouldn't do that," she said, pressing the button that would take them to the floor that housed her office.

"Do what?"

"I wish you wouldn't stare at me."

"I'm trying to unlock the mysteries of your mind," he said. "Or rather, I'm attempting to remember what you look like underneath your clothes." He knew that taunting her was the wrong decision. Knew that it would only push them back to the place he was so desperate to stay away from.

You don't want to stay away. You want her naked and panting in your arms again.

"Stop it," she said.

"You're so desperate to forget what happened between us."

"Nobody likes to remember rock bottom, Apollo. I consider having sex with you my own personal walk through the valley of the shadow of death."

"I'm honored, I'm sure."

"Honored isn't what you're supposed to be." She arched one finely groomed brow, her lips twisted into a sneer. She was so self-righteous when she was just as guilty as he was. So sure she was above this attraction that burned between them when she was just as enslaved.

He wanted her. The angrier he got with her, the more he wanted her. Whatever this thing was, the sick, twisted desire that was exploding between them, he couldn't measure it or assign a number to account for it. He couldn't parse it the way he could a business acquisition. It wasn't the simple desire he felt for the sort of woman he usually picked up to spend a few hours of fun with. It was much, much darker.

It was forbidden. Something he had told himself he couldn't have.

Perhaps that was why it was coming to bite him in the ass now. He didn't typically practice restraint. Maybe by creating forbidden fruit, by placing it in the middle of his personal garden and telling himself he could not eat it, neither could he touch it, he had created temptation.

That made the most sense. Since Elle looked like original sin. A brilliant, shining apple he wanted to bite into.

And why shouldn't he? His reasoning for resisting her didn't matter now. He didn't want to honor her father. And he still wanted to kiss that puckered expression off her face. So why the hell not?

"You don't like me," he said, that darkness compelling him now. "And yet, you do want me."

"Come now, Apollo, don't tell me you like every single one of your bed partners. We both know that sex isn't love," she said, tilting her chin upward, a faint blush spreading across her cheekbones, adding a kind of dissonance to her bold words.

Elle was certainly playing the part of experienced woman. She had gone up in flames in his arms, an equal participant in the conflagration. And yet, it didn't all ring true. Didn't quite piece together in a way that made sense.

He wasn't sure he cared to analyze it. It wouldn't change his actions either way.

"Perhaps. But sex and hate don't typically go together," he said. "And you claim to hate me."

"I do," she said, green eyes flashing. "I hate you for what you've done to my father. To me."

"Not enough to leave the company."

"That would be abandoning it altogether. What he built. What he's trying to keep hold of, in spite of you. I won't do that."

"I do admire your dedication. Your loyalty."

"Why do you admire my loyalty? You don't possess any of your own."

"We admire the things in others we struggle with ourselves, do we not?" he asked.

"I wouldn't know. I certainly don't admire anything in you."

He chuckled, turning to face her, closing some of the distance between them. Her eyes widened and she backed against the wall. It reminded him a little bit too much of what had happened the last time they had been alone in an enclosed space together.

"I think there are a few things you admire about me," he said, moving in a little bit closer. Her eyes widened, her pupils expanding, the green in her eyes reduced to a thin ring. Her mouth dropped open, soft and round, and begging to be kissed. To be explored. "You most certainly admire what I can do to your body. I think we both know that."

"I *do* possess some restraint," she said, her voice trembling.

"Do you?" he asked, his voice sounding rough, ragged even to his own ears. "Perhaps we should test it."

He reached out and hit the stop button on the elevator, his stomach tightening, feeling as though a fist had closed around it.

He reached out and took hold of her arm, mimicking that day out by the pool.

"You want me," he said. "Admit it."

"I will not," she said, reaching out, shoving him. But then her hand lingered on his chest, her breasts rising and falling with her rapid breathing. She looked up at him, her eyes wide, terrified.

"You want me even now," he said.

And it felt imperative he make her admit it.

She tapped against his chest with her fingertips before slowly curling her fingers around the material of his shirt.

Then she pulled him to her, kissing his lips hard, deep.

He tasted anger, and a hint of shame on her tongue. And he knew just how the two mixed together, because he felt it, too.

She groaned, pushing away from him suddenly, but he wrapped his arm around the back of her head, holding her steady, working his fingers through her thick, red hair. "You want me," he growled, "don't deny it."

"Wanting isn't the same as having."

With his other hand, he opened the top button on her blouse. "It's the same for us."

"It doesn't have to be," she said, sounding desperate.

"I think it does," he said, his voice rough. He didn't know himself. Not at all.

She reached between them, pressing her palm over his hard length, stroking gently through the fabric of his dress pants.

"I dreamed about you," she said, her voice hushed, her words rushed. "About this."

"So did I," he said, placing his hand over hers and increasing the pressure of her touch. "Every night."

"Have you had another woman since you had me?" she asked, her tone fierce.

"No." He suddenly thought of her touching some other man like this. "Have you had another man?"

She shook her head, curling her fingers around his arousal. "No."

He growled, pulling her into his arms and kissing her, rage and relief burning through him. The very idea of another man putting his hands on Elle made him angry. He wanted her. It had been too long. Nine years. Nine long years lusting after Elle St. James, even as he hated her family. Even when he was overtaken by the desire to see their destruction, he wanted her. It was unacceptable.

He would burn it out. He would burn it out and then it would be over. Afterward, he could discard her if he wished, but this would finally end.

He stripped her clothes from her body as quickly as

possible, nearly tearing the delicate fabric of her blouse in his haste. Definitely tearing her panties.

She didn't protest. Instead, she made a sweet little sound of pleasure as he wrenched the lace fabric away from her skin, as he stroked his fingers over her wet flesh, so slick, so perfect. She wanted him. There was no denying it, no faking it.

He could feel the evidence for himself.

He stripped all of her clothes from her body this time, leaving her completely bare to his gaze. He had spent so many years fantasizing about what she might look like. The size of her breasts, the color of her nipples. That beautiful thatch of curls at the apex of her thighs.

Yes, he had woken up from a deep sleep many times thanks to a dream about Elle's naked body. He had been—for so long—consumed with the curiosity of what lay beneath her prim clothes.

Now, he didn't have to wonder. Now he knew. But he had a feeling she would still haunt his dreams.

No. Because you will have her until you are finished with her.

Yes, he would. Even if burning it out meant reducing them both to ash.

He stripped his suit jacked off and cast it onto the floor, spreading it as wide as he could. Then he swept her into his arms, and lay her down on the fabric.

He didn't have time to worry about anything. He was too needy. Too desperate. Two more things to add to her list of sins, because ever since he had made his fortune, ever since he had pulled himself up from poverty he had ensured he was never needy or desperate.

He pressed a kiss to her inner thigh and she shuddered. Then he kissed her again, gratified to feel her tremble beneath his lips as he moved closer and closer to the heart of her desire.

"I am desperate to taste you," he said.

She bit her lip, closing her eyes and turning away as he flicked his tongue where she most wanted it. "Apollo," she said, "you don't have to…"

He planted his palms firmly on the soft globes of her ass, pulling her more firmly up against his mouth, tasting her deeply in response to her protest. She wiggled beneath him, and he wasn't certain if she was trying to get away, or if she was trying to move herself closer.

Either way, he didn't care. Either way, he was going to get what he wanted.

He brought his hands into play, stroking her with his fingers, thrusting one deep inside of her, reveling in how slick, how ready she was for him.

She was sweet, like dessert. A flavor he had never realized he craved until he had her on his tongue. And now, he knew that this was the thing he had been missing. This was what he had craved all this time.

He stroked her deeply, adding a second finger to the first. And she shattered beneath him, her internal muscles tight around him as she shuddered out her release.

"Oh, Apollo," she said, leaving no doubt that she knew exactly who she was with. Leaving no doubt that she wanted him. No one else but him.

"Are you ready for me, *agape*?"

She didn't speak, she only nodded.

He freed himself quickly from his slacks, not bothering to undo the buttons on his shirt, not bothering to move his hands any lower than his hips. And he thrust inside of her, the breath hissing through his teeth as she closed around him.

Yes, restraint was for other men. For better men.

He was going to conquer. Conquer his desire, his rage.

He would seize what he wanted. The only question was why he hadn't done it sooner.

He brought his hips against hers, his pelvis coming into contact with her clitoris every time he thrust deep inside of her warm, willing body. And he was lost, lost in this, in her. In Elle. And he didn't give a damn that they were in an elevator, he didn't care that he was using her. Nothing mattered but this.

He gave himself over to it completely, lost himself in the rhythm of her body, the slow, slick glide of their flesh, the soft, sweet sounds she made. The words that poured from her lips, hoarse whispers begging him to continue. To take her harder, faster, just please, *please*.

Inside, he was begging himself to hold off on finding his pleasure. He didn't want to go over the edge without taking her with him.

He wanted to do more than that. He wanted her screaming. He wanted her just as lost, just as obsessed as he was. Just as desperate to burn out the flame before it consumed his entire being. Utterly. Irrevocably.

He refused to be alone in this, in this destructive obsession. He would destroy her along with him.

That thought crystallized, clear and sudden in his mind as his release washed over him in an uncontrollable, endless wave. And then beneath him, she arched her back, crying out her own pleasure, her fingernails digging into his back, even through the fabric of his shirt. And he relished the slight bite of pain that came with the unending onslaught of pleasure. It was the only thing rooting him to the earth. The only thing keeping even part of himself under control.

And as she shuddered out her release beneath him, as

he skinned his hands over her bare skin, he realized exactly what he would do.

He would have her until he was through with her. Would build her up as the public face of the company. And when the time was right, he would drop the blade on the guillotine.

He would remove her from her position as CEO, and with that final move, remove the St. James family from his life. Close the chapter forever.

He would not simply burn out their desire, he would destroy her along with it.

He leaned forward, brushing his lips against hers. "Now there, *agape*, I'm not so bad, am I?"

CHAPTER FOUR

ELLE HAD OPTED to keep her mouth shut from the time she had slowly collected her clothing off the floor of the elevator. She stayed silent as Apollo's driver took them to her apartment and all while she packed her bags, with Apollo looming in the corner of her apartment, until they made their trek to the airport and boarded his private jet.

She attempted to keep the awestruck expression off her face as she gazed around the aircraft. She knew that he was rich. She just hadn't quite realized that he was *private jet* rich. She had been raised in very fortunate circumstances but, even so, her father didn't own his own plane.

Well, he certainly wouldn't *now* even if he had before. Because of Apollo. And it would do well for her to remember that.

The problem was she did remember. While they had made love or…whatever it was you called what the two of them had done, she was aware of who he was. How much he had done to destroy her family's legacy.

Still she wanted him.

She felt… She felt completely and totally frazzled. Somehow, she had ended up kissing Apollo again. And the moment they touched, it didn't stop there. It never stopped there. It *couldn't*.

Apparently.

"Do you approve?" he asked, sinking into the plush leather chair next to one of the windows that looked out on the tarmac. "Or am I to take that expression to mean you are terrified of your surroundings? It's very difficult to say."

"I like the plane. I'm a little bit afraid of being alone at thirty thousand feet with you."

"Afraid you'll join the mile high club?"

Dammit, *yes*. "I think we can both agree that whatever has been going on between us is not a good idea."

"It's a terrible idea. Take your seat so that we can ready for takeoff."

She looked around, elected to sit in the chair farthest from his. "For the record, I still hate you."

"Oh, I'm well aware," he said. "I think that was what you screamed in my ear only a few hours ago. Oh, no, I think what you actually screamed was 'more' and 'harder.'"

"It isn't like you weren't complicit."

"Complicit. *Explicit*."

"What exactly is your goal here, Apollo?" she asked. She didn't trust him. Not one bit. She was not in a position to refuse his command that she fly with him to Greece. Neither did she entirely trust his explanation.

"That depends," he said, leaning back in his chair, his body all leashed power and tension. "Are you speaking of business—" his gaze raked over her body "—or pleasure?"

"I thought we both agreed that the pleasure angle is a poor one for the two of us to take."

"It is. It's a terrible idea, *agape*. We hate each other. As you have stated many times. Or, more to the point, *you* hate *me*. I have no such strong feelings about you."

"No," she said, her tone biting, "you don't feel anything for me or my father. You simply destroyed us for your own pleasure."

"Your father's company was hemorrhaging money long before I came by to deal with it."

"So why didn't you help him?"

"That's a complicated issue, Elle," he said, his words hard.

"I don't have any trouble understanding complexities. Go right ahead and explain."

"There is more between your father and I than you know."

"Enlighten me," she said, the words escaping through clenched teeth.

"Not now. But understand what I'm doing is for a bigger purpose."

"Your ego? Honestly, you're unbelievable. He gave you everything. He loved you best from the beginning," she said, voicing the words that she never had before. Words she had long believed. "And now you've betrayed him for money."

"Love," he spat. "What is love, Elle? Tell me that. Is it what your father feels for you? As he moves you around like a pawn, desperate to put you between me and his queen? Did he love me, or did he see me as another tool he could use? I don't put any stock in love. It has never done anything for me, so I will hardly defer to it now."

Her heart was pounding hard, her throat tight. And she knew what she wanted. She hated herself then, more than she had ever hated him. "What do you want from me?"

"In the short term? I intend to burn this thing out between us. A fire can't keep on forever, can it?"

"Are you suggesting we sleep together while we are away from New York?"

"I'm doing something much stronger than suggesting."

Rage turned to excitement, flickering at the center of her being and radiating outward. The idea of being with him again, of touching him again, made her hands shake. "I didn't realize you got off on coercing women into your bed."

"We both know I didn't have to coerce you into it at all. Also," he said, his tone pointed, "we have never made it to a bed."

The thought of being in bed with him seemed…luxurious. The chance to explore his body at her leisure, rather than finding herself at the mercy of the explosion that occurred between them every time they touched. The force of it propelled her, made it impossible for her to think, impossible for her to resist. What would it be like to make the *decision* to have him? To give herself all night to indulge in that long-held desire for him.

She had always wanted him. And she had hated him for it. She'd been so angry that he was so…untouched. So utterly uninterested. So she'd pushed at him, tried to make him angry if she couldn't make him want her. She'd taunted him. And finally, she'd decided to taunt him sexually.

She could remember very clearly choosing the smallest, brightest bikini she could possibly find—one that absolutely clashed with her red hair, but one she felt would get her the attention she desired—to try to catch Apollo's eye when he came home to the family estate over break.

He had approached her as she'd gotten out of the pool and she'd felt… Naked. Alive. Afraid. So she'd defaulted to her usual position.

She could remember turning to him, her lips curled. *They'll let anyone into the estate, won't they? How my family's standards have fallen over the years.*

His eyes had blazed then. With anger. And he'd grabbed hold of her arm. She hadn't been afraid, though. She'd been…electrified.

He had held her there, looked at her hard, and for one moment, one desperate moment, she had imagined that she had seen lust in his eyes. That she had seen interest. But then, he had released her and turned away, leaving her there as though nothing at all had happened.

But now, somehow, for some reason, he wanted her, too. *This is your chance. To put it behind you once and for all so that you can move on.*

"All right," she said, ignoring the thrill of excitement that shot through her. "I agree. We have to get back on proper footing so that we can deal with each other as business partners."

"You are not my partner."

"Whatever. Terminology aside I am agreeing to the idea of an affair. But it has to stay a secret. Can you imagine the scandal? Me. Dating my wicked stepbrother who stole my family legacy after he wormed his way into my father's good graces."

"Of course. I have no interest in parading my intimate association with you in front of the world. As I already said."

His words, his *tone*, rankled. "I find it funny that you speak of it as though you find it distasteful. Of course *I* do. Everyone who moves in business circles fears you. I can see why I would want to disassociate from you. But not why you would wish to disassociate from me."

He arched a brow. "I have a type, Elle. It is not buttoned-up redheads. As you know, gentlemen prefer blondes. Or, in my case, scoundrels prefer blondes, brunettes or redheads so long as they're willing to part their thighs. I like women who know how to smile. Who know how to have fun. I do not like little harpies who claw at me even as they tear my clothes off."

"You like it when I claw at you."

Heat flared in his dark eyes and she took that as a win. "I consider this a unique circumstance."

She wanted to ask him why he thought heat was exploding between them the way it was. She wanted to ask him if it was ever like this for him and the other women he had sex with. But that would betray her inexperience. And that was something she wasn't willing to do. She wanted to protect her vulnerable places. Wanted to shield everything she didn't know from him.

That was an old defense, and one that she employed daily. She hated asking for help. Hated appearing ignorant.

Her father was a hard man, and she had always had the impression that he was standing by waiting for her to disappoint him. So she never let him see when she was floundering. Never let him detect one bit of uncertainty in her. She had wrapped herself so tightly in her ironed-on exterior, so careful to never show a wrinkle. She had difficulty letting go of it under any circumstances.

And if she was determined to never let her father see her sweat that went even more for Apollo.

That meant she couldn't ask the questions that were gnawing a hole inside of her. They would just have to go unanswered. It didn't matter anyway. Nothing was going to come from her association with Apollo. Nothing except freedom from the bizarre hold he had over her—and her life.

She had spent far too long being preoccupied with him. She would just be glad to have it handled.

And if she was a little bit…giddy over the thought of some time to deal with the attraction…well, that was normal. People acted ridiculous when it came to sex. History was filled with examples. Wars were started over sexual desire. She could hardly expect herself to be above the kind of insanity that captured almost all of humanity.

She spent the rest of the plane ride musing about restraint and dozing on and off while Apollo continued to work. Every time she opened her eyes and looked at where he was sitting, he was maintaining the same position, his focus never broken from his laptop, or the spreadsheets in front of him.

It was strange, watching him from across the darkened cabin. He had changed so much in the past few years. The lines on his face becoming more pronounced, as though each year had left a mark behind, evidence of the living he'd done.

And as a teenager, he had never worn a suit. He had always kept his hair slightly longer back then, too. Now it was cropped ruthlessly short, as though he was trying to look like he had sprung out of the ground a very conservative billionaire.

She wanted to find that boy again. Strip off the layers and layers he'd put over the person he'd been. The one she had… Well, the one she had felt so many things for.

She let her eyes flutter closed again, and when she opened them, they had landed in Greece. Customs and passports and the like were handled in an efficient manner involving people coming to them and apologizing for any delays. After that, they were ushered into a limousine, all their bags packed quickly into the trunk as they departed straight from the plane to the highway.

Athens was an incredible sprawl she hadn't accurately pictured in her mind. The rolling hills were capped with white, not from snow, but from the stone houses packed tightly together, flowing along with the landscape.

The downtown wasn't anything like the glass-and-steel jungle of Manhattan. Ancient structures mixed with more modern buildings, the history and heritage of the nation evident in the intricate stonework, the massive pillars and marketplaces scattered throughout.

"Where are we going?"

"I have a villa just outside the city."

"Of course you do," she said. "But I thought we were going to your offices?"

"We will. At some point. But some adjustments have been made to accommodate some of our new goals."

"Meaning what?" she asked, tearing her eyes away from the scenery to look at him.

"I don't think it's that difficult to guess."

They drove out of the city, winding up the steep, packed hillsides. They escaped the sprawl, moving to an area where trees were more plentiful. Where houses were a little bit less common. Until they reached the top of a completely vacant hill that overlooked the sea. There, behind a secure set of wrought-iron gates was a white stone house that was even more imposing than the St. James family estate in upstate New York.

"Is this your primary residence now?"

He lifted his shoulder. "As much as any place, I suppose. It is my home, after all."

"I *do* know that. You were born here. You left here when you were eight."

His focus sharpened. "Have you been reading unauthorized biographies?"

"No," she said. "I just paid attention when you used to speak around the dinner table. I used to know you, Apollo, as difficult as it is to remember back that far."

An emotion she couldn't put a name to flashed through

his eyes. "I did not realize such memories were worth saving."

"Know your enemy, and all of that."

"I suppose so."

The limousine pulled closer to the house, and the driver put the car into Park. Elle opened up her own door, stepping out and looking up at the house. To her, it looked like a lot of cubes of varying sizes stacked on top of each other, large windows on all sides looking out at the hills behind them, and the ocean before them.

"It doesn't seem like you're afforded very much privacy," she said.

"Are you concerned that the village will see you naked? Because make no mistake, most of the time spent in this house will be spent without clothes."

The dark, sensual promise should have frightened her, offended her. Instead, it excited her.

"The thought crossed my mind," she said. No point in playing the prude now. Not when he knew full well she wasn't.

"Never fear. I can tint the windows at the flick of a switch, and we won't even have to sacrifice the view. But good to know you are on the same page as I am."

"I have great concern for my modesty." And her sanity.

"Well, I hope you don't concern yourself much with it in my presence." He walked ahead of her, moving to the front of the house. "Our things will be brought in momentarily. Come, let me show you around."

She followed him inside, her heart hammering, her mouth suddenly dry. She didn't know what might happen next. If he was going to strip her of her clothing immediately and press her up against a wall again. And if he did, what would she do? She would capitulate. She knew that from experience.

But he didn't make a move to touch her. Instead, he paused in the expansive entryway. "I think this is self-explanatory," he said, indicating the living area with the low-profile couch that was up against the wall, curving around to another. "Beyond that is the pool." He walked ahead, up the open staircase that led to the second floor. She followed him. "My office," he said. "The library, kitchen and dining area. I felt the second floor made for a slightly better view." He continued straight up the stairs, to the third floor and she quickened her pace to keep up. "That way is my room," he said, pointing down to the left. "And then here you will find yours." The opposite direction from his. He began to walk to her room, and she followed, feeling a little bit like a lost puppy afraid of losing sight of her master.

He pushed the door open and revealed a light and airy space. Everything was white. The bedspread, the gauzy curtains that hung around the bed frame. There were no curtains on the windows, just as with the rest of the house. The square, unobstructed glass pane afforded a brilliant view of the jewel-bright sea, and let in the pale, sun-washed light.

"There are several settings for the windows. One is a blackout setting. That way the sun won't disturb your sleep," he explained.

She nodded. "I'm not sure I understand," she said, looking around the room. "I thought we would be sharing a room."

He chuckled. "I don't sleep with my lovers, *agape*. I have sex with them. We don't need to share a bedroom for that."

Dammit. He managed to make her feel completely gauche and out of her depth even though she was doing her best to appear like all of this was commonplace for her. She'd been feeling like she was succeeding. Until this moment. She gritted her teeth. "Of course. How could I be so silly?"

"I imagine you typically date nice boys who like to spend the evening making love before they pull you close and cuddle you."

His mocking tone burned her down deep. She was starting to feel at a disadvantage again. She would not allow it. "Do I seem like the type of woman who enjoys cuddling?" she asked, arching a brow. "You cannot possibly guess at the sort of man I typically associate with. You don't even know me. Not even a little bit. You know what I've bothered to show you, and that's all."

"My mistake. If you will excuse me, I'm going to get ready for this evening. And I have a bit of work to catch up on."

"You worked the entire time we were on the plane."

"Impatient for me?"

She swallowed hard. She swallowed her honest answer, which was most definitely yes. "Just concerned you're going to fall over at the age of twenty-nine from high blood pressure or something."

"Your concern is touching. I will see you this evening for the charity gala."

He turned and walked out of the room, closing the door behind him.

She turned and looked out the window, gazing at the view. For some reason, this time, she had the feeling of being inside of a terrarium, but it didn't feel quite so open. Once that thought entered her mind she felt as if she were some kind of creature he was keeping in a cage until he was ready to take her out and play with her.

Somehow, back in New York this had all felt equal, like they were in the same space, wanting the same things. But not now. Silly, because he owned her company. She should not have felt equal with him in the workplace. Should not have felt like they were on the same footing at all. And yet, for some reason—her pride, her intense dedication to her business persona—she had felt like they were.

But not here. In his house, in this show of his incredible wealth, she felt vulnerable. Powerless. She was in his home country, a place where she didn't even speak the language, trapped in his house on the hill.

She wondered, for a moment, if this was what he had felt. Walking into her family home as a teenager, his mother engaged to a powerful man so far above her station. And he had been greeted by a stepsister so consumed with her own feelings, her own issues, that she'd been nothing but horrible. Had done nothing but try to make him feel completely unequal to the place.

She blinked, pushing back an unwanted wave of sympathy. That was in the past. What she'd done had been out of girlish fear of the strength of her feelings.

Apollo was not acting as a boy, reacting to fear. He wasn't reacting at all. He was a man on the warpath, and God help her if she got in his way.

CHAPTER FIVE

WHEN ELLE APPEARED at the top of the stairs that evening wearing the silk gown that he'd had sent up to the room earlier, Apollo wasn't sure he had the strength to attend the gala. No, most of him wanted to grab hold of her and drag her straight into her bedroom and strip it off her.

The emerald green silk gown seemed almost demure in the front. It had a high neckline, the delicate, shiny fabric skimming her curves. It rippled when she walked down the stairs, flowing over her body like water.

But it was the back he couldn't wait to see. He had selected the dress for that very reason. True to his word, he was intent on raising her profile in the company. All the better to make her family's humiliation more apparent. If no one knew who the St. James family were, if they were only aware of the companies, while the family itself remained faceless, his disgrace of them would not carry the impact he required.

In a few weeks he would cut ties completely. He would let her drown along with her father and the rest of the St. James family.

It was cruel. But what David St. James had done to Apollo's father, the way he had manipulated Apollo's mother…

He forced himself to smile at her. To practice some

form of charm. He did possess it, after all. Though he didn't often exercise it when dealing with Elle. He could have any woman he wanted, and had, even before he had become the man he was now.

The girls he had associated with from nearby all-girls institutes back when he had been a teenager had found him fascinating. None of them had ever intended on taking him home to meet their parents. But a great many of them had taken him to nearby gazebos, backseats of cars and vacant dorm rooms. He might not be the kind of man they could proudly claim, but they had certainly found him attractive enough for certain uses.

Of course, Elle had already proven she had no issues using him for her physical satisfaction while she despised him on a personal level. So, he supposed that there was no point in attempting to be charming now.

All thoughts of charm or anything else were completely emptied from his mind when he saw the side of the gown as she reached the bottom of the stairs. He could think of nothing more than the possibility of stripping it from her body now.

"Turn around," he said, his voice hard.

"Why?" she asked, turning to face him, her hands clasped in front of her, demure, as though she had no idea what she was doing to him.

"Turn around," he said, deciding that he would forgo charm completely.

A flash of color spread up her neck, into her cheeks. Clearly, even if it made her angry, she quite enjoyed it when he gave orders. She turned slowly, teasing him by taking her time. And when she revealed her back fully, his stomach tightened, his blood pooling in his groin.

The back of the dress was a deep V ending just above the curve of her rear, exposing her entire back, the edges glittering with delicate beadwork. The seams over the silken material served to enhance the round shape of her backside, creating an even more dramatic shape to her curves.

He wanted to take her back upstairs, not just so he could have his way with her, but so he could keep any other man from laying eyes on what he thought of as his.

"It does not matter how many men have come before me," he said, not realizing he was speaking the words out loud until they had already escaped his mouth. "You are mine now. You have always been mine, Elle." The words were more raw, more real than he'd intended.

But then, this feeling was more raw, more real than anything that had ever come before it.

He saw attachments for what they were. Saw clearly how easily feelings could be manipulated. But what he felt for Elle was beyond him. It could never be distilled into one neat emotion. Could hardly ever be defined.

He needed it gone. Needed to burn it out. So that in the end he could walk away from the St. James family and never look back.

Walk away from her.

She turned to face him, her signature red ponytail swinging along with the movement. "That's quite possessive," she said.

"I'm kind of a bastard. You have agreed to be my mistress until such time as we have burned out the attraction between us. That means you are mine. And mine alone."

"I hardly make a habit of overlapping lovers."

He took a step toward her, closing the distance between them. He wrapped his arm around her waist, planting his hand firmly at the center of her back and drawing her close to him. "I would not permit it."

"You might own my company, Apollo," she said, her voice low, sultry, "but you do not own me."

"That's where you're wrong, I think," he said, sliding his hand up the center of her back, cupping the back of her head. "Because for now those two things are the same. I own both the company and you."

"You're a caveman."

He wrapped his fingers around her ponytail, tugging hard. "Shall I drag you back to my lair?"

She gasped, the sound one of arousal, not fear.

"You can pretend to hate this thing between us all you want. You can pretend to hate my commands. But we both know that no matter how shocked and appalled you pretend to be, you want this. You want me."

She leaned in slightly, and he kept his hold tight on her hair. Then she pressed her lips gently against his before biting him hard. "I might want you," she said, "but it is not the way a woman *should* want a man."

"Take your hair down."

"I refuse to give in to your every command."

He shifted his hold on her, grabbing the bobby pin that was buried in the ponytail that wrapped one coppery strand around the rubber band that secured her hair, concealing it from view. Then he grabbed the rubber band itself, pulling it free.

Her red hair fell past her shoulders in soft waves, extra full because of the way it had been restrained.

She frowned, her brows locked together. "I can't go like this. My hair is a mess."

"It is perfect."

"I do not have to wear my hair to please you."

"Your hair pleases me however it is fixed," he said. "But this way, this way, all I can think about is burying my fingers in it. Pulling you toward me. Kissing you deeply. With it like this, I want nothing more than to take you straight back upstairs and make you scream my name. And so, I leave the final decision on how you wear it up to you."

She tilted her chin upward. "Well, it's already down."

He chuckled, the soundboard of satisfaction. "I thought you might come to that conclusion."

She narrowed her eyes. "I prefer you without a tie."

"It is a formal event."

"Without the black tie, with the first button on your shirt undone, so that I can just see your chest hair, all I can think of is you tearing the shirt open the rest of the way so that I can put my hands on your hard muscles. So that I can feel your heartbeat raging against my palms. I can think of nothing but leaning in, running my tongue over your skin. And so," she said, arching her brow before turning away from him. "It is up to you."

Apollo smiled and began to loosen his tie.

No matter that they were pretending to be merely business associates at the gala, Elle could not help but think the two of them looked like they had been engaged in sexual intimacy in the car on the way. Her hair was down, looking very much like he had already run his fingers through it. His shirt was undone, his tie long discarded.

And yet, they had not had the benefit of engaging in any kind of intimate activity.

When they had gotten in the limousine she had scooted as far away from him as possible, telling him she needed space, time to collect her thoughts. She did. She was exhausted, jet-lagged, and the nap she'd had earlier had only helped a little bit. Beyond that, she was still raw from their last encounter. And if they were supposed to appear in public together in a platonic fashion, she did not want the feeling of his touch lingering quite so strongly in the forefront of her mind.

Now though, she was regretting it. Now she sort of wished she had climbed onto his lap in the car and satisfied her desire for him. Anything to take the edge off the extreme arousal that was pounding through her even now.

The gala itself was beautifully appointed, held in one of the oldest and most sophisticated hotels in Athens. When she arrived, she was surprised to see that Apollo's name was on everything.

"You didn't tell me that it was *your* charity gala we were attending."

He shrugged his shoulder, taking a glass of Champagne off the tray of a passing waiter. "It did not seem important."

"I think it is rather important. I wasn't aware that you had founded the charity."

"It's very boring. Press junket stuff. The kind of thing that one says to improve their reputation with the media. It's a game I scarcely have the patience to play at the best of times. I did not see the point in trying to convince you that I was somehow a paragon of virtue simply because I donate money to impoverished families."

"You do?" In spite of everything she knew about him, in spite of her feelings about him, she could feel herself softening.

"Yes. Do not look at me like that. I am a businessman. Believe me when I tell you this benefits me in financial ways."

"Why are you so resistant to being seen as good in any fashion?"

"I do not like to raise people's expectations."

She blinked. "Why?"

"Because they will find themselves disappointed."

She looked around, taking in the beautifully appointed marble interior of the hotel, the impressive pillars, the glittering chandeliers. Couples dressed in the finest couture were already making their way out to the dance floor. She wished she could dance with Apollo. That he would take her into his strong arms and pull her up against his chest, hold her...just to hold her. So that she could relish his strength, his heat, if only for a moment.

She shook her head. That was extreme foolishness. She wanted nothing more from Apollo than for him to leave her alone and allow her to run their business as she saw fit. Well, that and sex for the sake of sex, until they had burned out the attraction between them.

She did not want him to hold her. She did not want to press her head up against his chest and listen to the sound of his heart. Did not want to spend an hour kissing him, just kissing him. *No*, she didn't want any of those things.

"I shall introduce you to some of my associates," Apollo said. "And to some of the members of the press who are in attendance."

"Oh, you're too kind," she said, keeping her tone light.

He pressed his hand lightly on her back, guiding her toward a group of people who were standing there conversing. He made introductions, and dropped his hand quickly back to his side, bringing a great deal of distance between the two of them as he shifted his position within the group.

One of the men was a businessman from Italy, another a Greek, who had his business in the United States. They started to make conversation about staying relevant in the age of the internet and online superstores, and she was so lost in the discussion that it took her a while to notice that

Apollo was no longer standing next to her. She frowned, searching the crowd quickly. And then she spotted him, out on the dance floor with a blonde woman wearing a dress with a hem that fell just beneath her butt cheeks. Rather nice butt cheeks too, Elle was loath to admit.

She fought to keep the scowl off her face. She knew that they were supposed to be playing the part of business associates but she felt this was taking it a bit far.

"I see Mr. Savas has abandoned you," the Greek man, Nikos Vardalos, said.

"Not at all," she said, taking a deep breath. "We are not here together. Mr. Savas is able to dance with whoever he chooses."

"Then I suppose you are free to dance with whoever you choose?"

She could always tell him she had a boyfriend. She often did that when confronted with men she wasn't attracted to in these kinds of situations. But Nikos was handsome enough, and Apollo was dancing with someone else. Really, it seemed rather silly for her to stay hidden away in a corner.

"Absolutely," she said. "I am always free to do whatever I want."

He laughed, treating her to a smile that she had no doubt often made women go weak in the knees. Sadly, not her. Not now.

But she pretended. She offered a smile in return.

"I like a woman who knows her mind. And does your mind tell you that you might want to dance with me?"

"I would be delighted."

He extended his hand, and she accepted it, wrapping her fingers around his. His touch was warm, but it did not light her on fire, not the way that Apollo's did. It was sort of comforting, to have a man touch her like this, and for her to feel so very little.

Every interaction with Apollo, every brush of his skin against hers, was so layered. Was so hot, so intense, she couldn't ignore it, or pretend it hadn't burned. It was never simple. It was always hate spread over lust, spread over a strange attachment that stemmed from all of the years they had known each other. And betrayal. The betrayal that was unique to what she felt for him because of how well they had known each other. Because of how she had felt about him for so long.

Because of the way she had trusted him.

And you betray your father by sleeping with this man. By wanting him.

Still, she couldn't help herself. Still, she could feel nothing as Nikos pulled her into his arms and swept her onto the dance floor. Still, she felt more when she looked across the crowded room and locked eyes with Apollo, who was glaring at her and her dance partner with dark rage.

Fine. He was welcome to be murderous. She didn't particularly care. They were here separately. He was dancing with another woman, and she would be damned if she would play the part of wallflower.

She shifted her hands lightly on her partner's shoulder, tightening her grip on his hand.

"I think Savas wants to kill me," Nikos said, his tone tinged with amusement.

"Oh, I don't suppose he wants to kill you," she said, her tone dry. "Anyway, he and I are associates, as I said before. And neither of us believes in mixing business with pleasure."

"Excellent. Then I shall never do business with you."

She laughed. "Well, that would be a shame. Since

you are in retail, I would very much like to do business with you."

"Perhaps it is crass of me to discuss this during a dance," he said, "but tell me more."

They spent the next two songs largely ignoring the music and discussing the various ways in which they could marry their two brands. She decided that she liked Nikos quite a bit even if he did not make her heart beat faster.

She only wished that he could.

He was Greek, he was wealthy, he had a hint of a gorgeous accent. Truly, if she had a type, this was it. If any other man was going to start a fire in her loins quite the way that Apollo did, this man would. But there was nothing. Absolutely nothing. It was an extreme disappointment.

Still, though she had not found a way to encourage desire toward another man, she had come away with a very promising business contact. They parted at the end of the song, and he did not try to make any sort of romantic overture. He must've sensed the lack of chemistry as profoundly as she did.

She was making her way toward a waiter to get herself a drink when she was all but accosted by Apollo. "Having fun?"

"It's a charming party," she said.

"Yes. I told you already that you would be with me and me alone while we work out the attraction between us, did I not?"

"I'm sorry, I was not aware that a waltz was on par with intercourse."

"You are playing with fire," he said.

"Then you are, too. Don't think I didn't notice your lovely blonde partner."

"It is expected of me."

"And you want my face in the paper. Therefore, I had better do something newsworthy. You put me in this dress that leaves me essentially naked, and now you're going to act as though my getting attention is not somehow essential to your *plan*?"

"All you have to do is simply walk into a room to gain attention, *agape*. Trust me on this."

"I find your assessment flattering, if slightly ambitious."

"I don't care whether or not you find it ambitious. It is the truth." He looked around them. "Even if you have not noticed, I have. Every male eye—and many of the female eyes—have been on you from the moment you walked in. You are absolutely the one to watch here."

"Is that so?"

"Yes. And when you make a large charitable donation in the name of the company, you will become even more of a conversation piece."

Her mouth opened, then snapped shut. "I did not know you were going to make use of my money."

"Of course I am. Anyway, it is a good cause, on that you can trust me. As I said, I provide housing and other necessities for families who have fallen below the poverty line. Surely you can find no fault with that."

"I suppose not."

"You sound so distressed. It must be terrible when I don't rise to the part of blackguard when it suits you."

"Sincerely awful. I can see why you prefer to pretend you're terrible. For consistency."

"I am nothing if not consistent."

She laughed. "If only that were true."

"What is that supposed to mean?"

"Exactly what it sounds like. You are not consistent,

I don't care how you frame it, I don't care what you say. You were a friend of my family, and then you betrayed us. There is nothing consistent about that."

His expression turned dark, fierce. He leaned in and her breath caught in her throat. She thought, for a moment, that he might kiss her. She hoped that he would. He did not. "From the moment I understood there was better than the circumstances I existed in I was determined to find better. When I went to a private school, knowing full well that I didn't belong there, I was determined to rise to the top of the class so that no one could question whether or not I had the ability to succeed in the realms of society into which I had been thrust. I have done nothing but hold myself up from the bottom with my brute strength from the moment I understood it could be done. If that's not consistency, I don't know what is."

"Yes, I know you pulled yourself up quite a bit. But it's quite convenient to forget that my father's money provided a ladder to help you out." She turned away from him and he grabbed hold of her arm, holding on tightly to her and pulling her back to him.

"I was willing to advance myself using any means necessary. Again, I claim consistency." He released his hold on her, straightening the cuffs on his shirt. "Go off and have fun. We will meet again at the end of the night. Do not forget to make your donation."

"Of course not."

"I imagine Luka would like to dance, as well."

"Are you off to find him?" she asked.

"No, but I suggest you should."

"Now you're encouraging me to dance with other men? There's that legendary consistency."

"No, I believe you're right. You should do what you

can to get your photograph in the news. And I shall do what I have to to get attention of my own. I will see you at the end of the evening."

CHAPTER SIX

BY THE TIME the car pulled back up to Apollo's house later that evening he was in a violent temper. Elle had done exactly as he had demanded and had danced with every businessman within fifteen years of her age. And she had charmed every single one of them. She had no doubt delighted the media.

She had done exactly as he'd asked, and he was incensed. Spending the evening *not* touching her had been akin to torture. But he was ready to move ahead with their agreement. He was ready to claim her. To remind her exactly why she was here, and who she was with.

They had not spoken in the car on the way back to his villa. She was vibrating with indignation next to him, but he didn't care.

When they got out of the car and walked into the house he turned to her. "I want you to go to your room and open up the top drawer of the bureau there. You will find some other items that my staff has procured for you. Make yourself ready for me."

He stormed off to his office then, pouring himself a glass of scotch and downing it in one desperate gulp, relishing the burn as it slid down his throat.

He paced the length of the room, trying to figure out exactly what happened to make him so agitated.

Jealousy.

He could not remember the last time he had ever felt jealous. If he ever had.

He closed his eyes, allowing an old memory to wash over him. Hell, the bikini. Yes, he had been jealous then in a strange way. Of the fact that she was young, with her entire life ahead of her. Of the fact that men had not yet discovered her, and he would not be a part of that discovery. He would have given everything to have been the first man to touch her. To have been the one to awaken her sensuality. Her every sigh, her every moan.

To have been the one who gave her that first climax.

Yes, he would have given anything to be that man at one time. He had been jealous then. Of a man who had not existed. And somehow tonight every man who had danced with her had become one of those nameless, faceless men who had come before him.

He hated them, even without knowing who they were.

He tossed his suit jacket onto the floor, stalking out of his office and going up the stairs toward her bedroom. She had better damn well be ready for him. Because he was not waiting another moment.

He threw open the bedroom door without knocking, and she turned to face him, still wearing the dress she had been wearing to the gala.

"I thought I gave you instructions to change," he said.

Her green eyes glittered with anger. "Yes," she said. "You did. But I have no desire to dress up like some strange interpretation of a fantasy that you have, brought about by your magnanimous staff."

"Expensive underthings offend you?"

"The idea that I might not want to choose my own? The idea that I might be interchangeable with any of the other women you consort with? That offends me."

"What do any of my other lovers have to do with this?"

"Everything. You are treating me exactly as you would any of them."

He clenched his hands into fists, his heart beating so fast it burned. "And you want to be special? Is that it?"

Her cheeks flamed. "I don't want to be the same. I don't want to be just one warm body of any of the ones you could have."

"Still you doubt my desire for you?" He undid another button on his shirt, then another, stripping it off as he walked toward her, feeling every inch a predatory animal. "What must I do to show you that I am your servant, *agape*? What must I do to show you that you own my body?"

The color heightened in her cheeks. "I own your body?"

"Do you think I want this? Do you think I want to be a slave to the desire I have for a St. James? If you think you hate me then just imagine how much I hate you. Your family. Your family name. Everything you stand for."

His words were coming out hard and fast. He was saying more than he had intended. He had never intended to bring this up with her at all. Had not intended to speak any of this to her until he was giving her her marching orders and ordering her to pack her things and vacate her office. He had not intended to reveal any of this until he'd unleashed his ultimate betrayal on to her.

But he couldn't stop it now. He could not stop himself. "If any woman at the party tonight had made me feel even a fraction of what I feel for you I would have taken her into the nearest hallway and pushed her skirt up. Sadly, I only respond to you. You have me on a leash, Elle. I hope you are happy with this revelation."

Her eyes were round, her lips parted slightly. "I don't

understand. You were part of our family. How can you possibly feel that way?"

"Easily. You don't understand what manner of man your father is, you don't understand what manner of man I am. When you were seventeen years old, parading around the family estate in your bikini, I would have liked nothing more than to put you flat on your back. I was a man of twenty, and I would have had you, sweet little virgin that you were. And even knowing how wrong that is, I hate every man who came before me. I regret not taking you then. Such wasted years, Elle. I could have rid myself of my hunger for you then. But I didn't. For what reason? To preserve some semblance of a conscience we both know I don't have? Pointless. But then, I still harbored illusions that I might be good."

"I… You wanted me then?"

"Did you not know? Of course not. You were blind. A little virgin."

"Stop saying that. I wasn't ignorant. It's just that you seemed angry…not…"

"As it always is with us."

"Either way, I'm not ignorant."

"Did I have the wrong end of it then? Please don't tell me you weren't already experienced or I truly will hang myself for being so foolish that I didn't have you."

"Why are you acting like this?"

He didn't know. He damn well had no clue. All he knew was that he was enraged. Over tonight. The other men who'd touched her. The orders she was refusing to obey. Over his behavior nine years ago. Over his behavior now. "Why are you refusing to wear the lingerie I provided for you?"

"Because I will not be one of your whores," she said. "Because I *was* a virgin when you had me at your hotel room. Your jealousy is misplaced while mine is certainly not."

Her words hit him like a punch to the gut. "A virgin?"

"Apparently it matters to you. Apparently you are quite proprietary and possessive, though you have not earned the right to be."

He growled, pulling her into his arms, grabbing hold of the sides of the delicate fabric of the dress and wrenching it down over her shoulders, tugging the bodice down low, revealing her breasts to his hungry gaze. "I am the only man to ever have you?"

"Yes," she said, her voice breathless.

"This pleases me much more than it should," he said, gripping her chin between his thumb and forefinger and tilting her face up to him. "All during the ride back to the villa I was contemplating the different ways I could kill each and every man who danced with you. In my mind, they had become your previous lovers. And I discovered that I felt rather violent about them. About the missed opportunity I'd had. You see, I wanted to be the one to teach you about pleasure."

She bit her lip, as though she were holding back a litany of words. Either curses, or the confirmation that he had indeed been the one to teach her about pleasure. He had a feeling she neither wanted to yell at him at this moment nor give him anything pleasant to latch onto.

"I did teach you about pleasure, didn't I? Against the wall in a hotel room. Dammit, Elle, you didn't tell me."

"Would it have made a difference?"

No. It made no difference at all. Not to anything. Not to what had gone before, and not to what he must do now. The fact that Elle had been a virgin changed nothing. She had been innocent of the wrongdoings of her father before he knew that, and she was innocent of them now. The fact he was her only lover might fill him with a sense of masculine pride, a sense of conquest, but it didn't change the fact that he would betray her in the end. That he would make an example of her and use her to wound her father.

The way her father had wounded his father. The way he had devastated his mother. The way he had devastated Apollo himself.

Whatever sins his father had committed, the rest of them had been nothing more than collateral damage. And so would Elle be. It was not fair. But none of this was fair.

It wasn't about fairness. It was about justice in the way that only he could obtain it.

"Yes," he lied. "It would have made a difference. I would have been much gentler with you." Except he knew he would not have. He would not take that fiery encounter in the hotel room back for anything. When Elle had unleashed all her rage on him. All of her desire. It had been the most singular experience of his life. He would trade it for nothing. It was a moment that belonged to him, one that could not be stolen no matter how low he sunk.

He was a villain, and now, he was embracing it fully.

He leaned in, kissing her, keeping it soft, keeping it light. She grabbed hold of his face, deepening the kiss.

He picked her up, carrying her to the bed and laying her down on the soft mattress, tugging the gown from her body. There would be no more talking tonight.

If he had his way, there would be no more talking until he was through with her. And if that meant spending the next two weeks in bed, then they would spend the next two weeks in bed.

CHAPTER SEVEN

THE PAST TWO weeks at Apollo's villa had gone surprisingly smoothly. It was strange to coexist with him and not fight. It actually reminded Elle of a different time. A simpler time. Back when they had actually liked each other. When she had looked up to him. When he had—apparently—had some sort of attraction to her that he had buried.

Of course, maybe they had coexisted so peacefully because their lives had been essentially separate. Unless they were making love. Which had not been confined to evenings, or to bed. She was certain that at this point, Apollo had taken her on every surface in the entire villa.

She was not complaining. It had been... Well, it had been the culmination of her most heated fantasies. It was strange. Like she was living a life borrowed, one that she could not possibly have in the long term, but one that was in many ways preferable to the one she had been living. She was still seeing to her responsibilities. Sometimes working in his office, sometimes from the office in his home while he was out.

She couldn't complain about the vacation. Of course, it was also difficult to justify the fact that she was sleeping with the enemy. Though, not literally, since they didn't sleep together. They had sex, and then he left.

"It's how I do things, *agape*," she said, amusing herself with her poor imitation of Apollo's voice as she paced the length of her bedroom.

A knock on her bedroom door startled her. She wondered if she had summoned him just by thinking about him. But he had just gone out to work a couple of hours ago, so she doubted he was back already.

She opened the door, to see one of his servants, Maria, standing there holding a package. "This is for you, miss," she said.

"Oh," she said, her whole body getting warm when she realized what it was. "Thank you."

After Maria left, she closed the door and opened the package hurriedly. Inside was a hot pink bikini. She had been planning this for the past few days. Maybe it was juvenile. But she wanted a chance to recapture the moment that both of them had missed. One that seemed to linger in both their minds.

She didn't waste any time getting into it, examining herself in the full-length mirror, watching as her cheeks flooded with color. She didn't make a habit out of wearing things that were so revealing. Though, honestly, after spending so much time naked with Apollo, she shouldn't feel self-conscious.

Still, she did.

That was different. That all happened during the heat of the moment. This was…premeditated. She had never staged anything quite like a seduction with him. And that's what this was. But she was aching for something, searching for something more. She couldn't deny that what she felt for him wasn't hatred at this point. It would be so much easier if it was.

She felt… Well, she felt a lot.

She took a deep breath, opening her bedroom door

and heading down the hall, down the stairs and outside to the pool. She was intent on being there when he got back. Intent on giving him the chance to make a different decision this time when he saw her in the bathing suit.

She slipped beneath the warm water, paddling over to the edge of the infinity pool, looking out over the view of the ocean. It was beautiful here. She hadn't thought it was possible to feel so at peace in Apollo's lair. Certainly not when she had first arrived.

She couldn't say they were growing closer, not exactly. But…it was more than it had been. For one thing, they could be in each other's presence for a full five minutes without screaming at each other. Sometimes they could go that long without tearing each other's clothes off, too. But only sometimes.

The thought made her smile, she lifted her face up to the sky, bathing herself in the warmth of the sun.

"What are you doing out here?"

"I finished work early," she said, turning, her heart slamming hard against her breastbone when she saw Apollo standing there, still dressed in the suit that he'd worn to work.

"Come here," he said, his jaw set, his dark eyes intent on her.

Elle draped her arms over the back of the infinity pool, arching her back slightly, thrusting her breasts up out of the water. "I'm enjoying the water."

"Elle," he said, his tone warning. "Do not make me come in there and get you."

"I think I would like for you to come in and get me. It's what you should have done nine years ago."

He smiled, a genuine smile. It wasn't one that was tinged with cynicism, neither was it mocking or laden with barely contained rage. It made her heart turn over in her chest, made it expand.

He began to remove his suit, starting with his jacket, then his tie, then slowly undoing the buttons on his shirt. There had been ample time over the past couple of weeks for her to become familiar with that gorgeous male physique, but familiarity hadn't made him seem commonplace. Not in the least.

He arched a brow, slowly placing his hands on his belt buckle, working the leather through the loop. Her mouth went dry and she fought to keep herself from moving closer to him. She was going to hang back. She was going to force him to come to her.

He undid the closure on his slacks, pulled the zipper down slowly, his eyes never leaving hers. He pushed his pants down his narrow hips, exposing himself to her. He was everything. Absolute perfection. Everything she had wanted a man to be and then some. No, there was no chance of him ever becoming commonplace in her eyes.

Slowly, he made his way to the pool, climbing down, the water rising up and concealing his body from her.

"You took my show," she said, just as he leaned forward, his sleek, athletic body slicing through the water effortlessly.

"I thought I would bring it to you," he said, approaching her, wrapping his arm around her waist and drawing her up against him.

"Oh," she said, "I guess I can appreciate that."

"I think you can more than appreciate that," he said, looking pointedly down at her breasts, at her tightened nipples, pushing up against the thin fabric of the bathing suit.

"I make it too easy for you," she said, not sounding even remotely regretful.

"I'm not complaining," he said, sliding his hand down her waist, resting his hand on her butt.

"Of course you're not. You're so certain of yourself, and all I have done is make you even more certain."

"I was named after a god. I came into the world with a rather inflated view of myself."

"Of course you did. How could I forget?" She lifted her hand, resting her palm on his chest. "I ordered this bathing suit for you."

Heat illuminated the darkness in his eyes. "I thought you might have."

"We have a chance to make a different decision." She traced the water droplets that were trailing down his chest, rolling into the grooves of his muscles. "I wish that I had done something differently then. Been a little bit bolder."

"You were young. You shouldn't have done anything. I shouldn't have done anything."

"I was young, but I knew what I wanted. And it hasn't changed." She looked up at him. "I still want you. I wanted you all this time, even when I was angry at you."

He wrapped his fingers around her wrist, lifting her hand to his lips, pressing a kiss to her palm. "Yes, I know you did. Believe me when I say the feeling is mutual."

Those words, those husky, delicious words, sent a little shock of pleasure through her. It wasn't strictly physical. It went deeper than that.

Unfortunately, all of this went much deeper than the physical. Much deeper than she wanted it to go.

"I do."

A smile curved his wicked mouth. "Listen to us. We have managed to converse for several minutes without fighting."

"A miracle."

"Perhaps. Though, I imagine we are skirting the edge of sacrilege assigning anything divine to the nature of things between us."

"Perhaps."

He had a point. What they shared was carnal, lustful.

No, not only that. Beautiful. Altering.

Impossible.

He was her stepbrother, he was her enemy. Truly, it was the enemy part that made it most impossible. The stepbrother issue would hardly mean anything. They hadn't been raised together. They shared no blood.

There's no affection, either. Not from him.

She squeezed her eyes shut, unable to look at him while she had thoughts like that. He closed the distance between them, pressing his lips against hers. And she just let it wash over her, warmer than the sun, more refreshing than the water they were standing in.

Desire assaulted her, her stomach tightening, a pulse beating low and hard at the apex of her thighs.

It had been just over a month since their first encounter in his hotel room in New York. Just over a month since she'd been with a man for the first time. It hadn't taken long for her to grow accustomed to it. For her to know exactly what she wanted. For her to learn his body, and to learn what hers desired of him.

He slipped his hand beneath her bikini bottoms, taking hold of her with his large palm. She loved his hands. Loved the feel of them on every inch of her. Loved looking at them. Spent a great deal of time fantasizing about them.

But then, it was like that with every single inch of him.

So many things did not live up to the promise. Did not live up to the hype. Apollo was not one of them. He took her every fantasy and superseded by leaps and bounds.

In comparison with the reality her fantasies of what sex with him would be like seemed childish. Simple.

She had known it would feel good, she had known she would find him attractive. She hadn't realized it would be so raw, so exposing. Hadn't realized it would strip her bare of everything, not just her clothes. She had thought it would just be physical.

That was such a simplistic thought. His body was the missing piece of hers. He was everything she ached for in the dead of night, the reason that she felt hollow sometimes. It was because she was desperate to have him inside of her. Only him.

She parted her lips for him, expecting him to conquer, expecting him to invade. Instead, he was gentle, his tongue sliding slowly against hers, the slick glide sending a sharp pang of need through her. So acute it was almost painful.

She forked her fingers through his hair, deepening the kiss, pressing her body as firmly against his as she could. She knew that if any of his staff members walked out now they would get a bit of a show. But honestly, her brain was too foggy with desire to really get a handle on that reality. She couldn't care. Not for her modesty, not for anyone's sensibilities. There was only this. Only him.

She lost all sense of propriety, all sense of loyalty, all sense of…everything when she was with him.

She became a new person. A different version of Elle.

She had to wonder what might have happened if she had taken the steps to close the distance between them nine years ago. If they would have forgotten about decency back then.

It didn't matter. They were doing this now. She tried to shove aside the thoughts of everything else that had happened in the ensuing years. The wedge that had been driven into the family.

Her father, his mother and her, all on one side of the gulf, with him on the other.

She didn't want to think about them. Not now. Didn't want to think about the father she could never be good enough for. The father who had preferred her stepbrother to her.

Probably still did, in truth. Even though Apollo had taken a chunk out of David St. James's empire, he probably privately celebrated his stepson's ruthlessness.

Apollo might have betrayed them. But Apollo never acted like he wished she were someone else. Apollo never made her feel like she wasn't good enough. He gloried in her body, in the attraction between them. It was more than she had ever had from…anyone.

The thought filled her with a sudden, intense swell of emotion. Whatever they had, whatever this was, it fed her soul in a way nothing else did. Because it was about her. It wasn't about the business. It wasn't about performing to his satisfaction. He cared about performing to hers. They were in this together. They wanted each other.

For once she wasn't striving for approval. Wasn't trying to live up to an expectation she simply never could.

Her father had seen Apollo as his hope. The son he never had. The heir she could never be.

Then he had trusted Apollo to bail him out, never speaking to her about anything. Never consulting her. He had always trusted Apollo above her.

And Apollo had betrayed him.

But that didn't stand in the way of her and Apollo. He didn't look at her and see the unfulfilled promises of someone else. He wanted her. In spite of everything.

It was balm for her soul.

He swept her into his arms, lifting her as though his arms were created to cradle her close. As though she was the perfect weight and size for him. As though this moment had been fated from the beginning.

He carried her up from the pool, striding right into the house, clearly just as unconcerned as she was about being seen. She had a feeling his staff was paid to look the other way when he was conducting affairs in his home. She shoved that thought to the side. She wasn't going to think about other times, other women.

Right now, she was the only one. That would have to be enough.

He started up the stairs, and she put her hand on his cheek, tracing the fine lines on his face. Additions to his features, new and fascinating. She remembered his face so clearly as a teenage boy. Smooth, pretty. Full perfect lips, amusement in his dark eyes, a kind of irreverent quirk to his brow.

He was no longer smooth. Dark stubble covered his jaw, his chin. Deep grooves bracketed his mouth, marred his forehead. The face that had once been pretty was now more rugged, more distinguished. The laughter in his eyes was gone, replaced with a kind of intensity that burned her from the inside out.

The irreverence was still there, though. It was one of her favorite parts of him. That dry, sardonic humor that would make her laugh in the strangest moments. That would take her from anger to entertainment in only a few moments. That would see her kissing him instead of screaming at him thanks to one well-timed comment.

He was one of the few men who had ever stood up to her. Who had gone toe to toe with her and made her feel like she just might lose.

Not for the first time she wondered at the ground

they had covered since then. Wondered about what had happened.

But she didn't have time to turn it over anymore, because they had reached the top of the stairs, and only a second later, her bedroom.

He set her down, water dripping down her body, pooling down around her feet. "I'm going to get the carpet wet."

"I can't say I am very concerned about that."

"Well, it's your carpet."

"Yes, it is," he said, one side of his mouth curving upward.

He regarded her for a moment before taking a step toward her, tracing the line down the edge of her bikini top, the tip of his finger only barely delving beneath. "This is the stuff of my darkest fantasies."

"A fluorescent bikini?"

He chuckled. "You. In this bikini. So much of that beautiful, pale skin on display. Your hair… It should look ridiculous with this color. Instead, you're simply everything bright. I wanted you then. I consider this my reward for good behavior." His smile turned wicked. "You know, I only wish I had known you were a virgin."

"Is that so?"

"Yes. Had I known you were a virgin I would have relished my prize all the more. I was obsessed with having you first. With teaching you about pleasure."

"You did," she said. She had held the words back from him two weeks ago. Because she had not been ready to share that with him. Had not been ready to confess just how much he had meant to her. What it had meant that he was her first lover.

Or why he was.

But there was no use in protecting herself now. She didn't want to.

"It was always you that I wanted," she said. "That was why even though I said I hated you, even though I was so angry at you the first time I kissed you, it went as far as it did. Because it was always you for me, Apollo. No matter how many years have passed, no matter what ugly words were spoken between us, it was always you."

Apollo knew he did not deserve the words that Elle had just spoken. He was using her. For these past two weeks he had been using her. To satisfy his need for her. Biding his time until he could get his revenge, filling the hours with the pleasures of her body knowing that in the end he would betray her.

There was nothing else to do. This thing between them could not last. And he could not deviate from his course of revenge against his stepfamily. Not now.

He had made up his mind. There would be wreckage. Collateral damage.

But he wouldn't think of it now. Instead, he would take that unearned compliment. Savor it. Hold it close. He would consider this the satisfaction of a desire born years ago. The revenge would be a satisfaction of a different desire, but it was a separate issue. In his mind, she wasn't a St. James. Not now. Now, she was his lover. As he had long fantasized.

When he was finished he would end his association with her and continue on, viewing her again as the daughter of his enemy, rather than his mistress.

He could barely tear his gaze away from her, away from her pale, delectable curves, so effortlessly displayed by the flimsy material of the bikini.

That she had done this for him… It was strange. It

created a shifting sensation at the center of his chest, made him feel as though the earth had tilted slightly. This shared memory that they had of this time when they had wanted the same things... It was strange to have it here in the present.

Just take it. It is a gift.

He would. Whether he deserved it or not. Because, as he had already told her, he was the villain here. Nothing would change that.

Slowly, ever so slowly, he untied the top of the bikini, peeling it away from her luscious breasts, baring them to his gaze. She was pale everywhere except for here. Here, she was pink. Pink and perfect and everything he desired. He leaned in, tracing the edge of her puckered nipple with his tongue before sucking her deep into his mouth.

"So sweet," he said, his voice rough and unrecognizable to his own ears. "Better than honey."

She shivered beneath him and he recognized his pleasure coursing through her body. He was learning to read her. Learning to understand what made her moan, what brought her close to the edge. Had learned how to tease her. How to hold her on the brink of climax without giving it to her completely.

He had never kept a lover for this length of time before. Always, he was finished with them after a couple of nights. A couple of weeks was unheard of. There was something...intoxicating about it. Something singular. To know one particular woman's body in such an intimate fashion. Of course, he was well-versed with the female body, but that was different. This was...

Well, this was Elle.

He imagined it would never be the same with another woman, no matter how long he was with her. Elle was a fiery, living fantasy come to life, everything he had ever imagined she might be and more.

It was a damn shame. He wished she was a disappointment. Wished that she was something he could despise. Wished that she could have done something, anything to confirm that he was right to carry out this revenge plot, and use her as he'd planned.

He wished he had left her as the brittle, buttoned-up woman she had seemed in his mind only a couple of weeks ago.

But now he knew her. Knew her body. Knew her soul.

That's ridiculous. You cannot know someone's soul. You haven't one of your own.

He pulled her close, taking hold of the tie on her swimsuit bottoms and tugging the thread roughly, then the other side, letting it fall to the ground. Trying to break the spell that she had cast over him with this bright, insubstantial piece of fabric. It was insane. And yet it was so...

He had advanced no further with her than where he had been nine years ago. He was still a slave to his desires. And now he was old enough to know that going out and getting any redhead at any bar would not suffice.

Now that he had had Elle, he knew that there was no substitute. Ever. There had never been another woman like her, and there never would be again.

He dropped to his knees in front of her, suddenly overwhelmed with his desire. He buried his face between her thighs, tasting her, deep and long, relishing the flavor of her desire as it spread over his tongue. He was insatiable for her. Desperate for her. He pushed one finger deep inside her slick channel, then another, loving the way that she bucked against his hand, the needy cries for pleasure that escaped her lips.

She was desperate. Like he was. She was in this with

him. He needed it proven. Needed to know for sure. He felt like he was losing his mind. He did not know himself now. Never in all his life had a woman made him shake. Never in all his life had a woman owned him in such a way. Never had a woman successfully erased visions of any other.

But she had.

He gripped her hips, holding her tightly against his mouth as he continued to pleasure her, until she shook just as violently as he did. Until she was on the verge. Until she was whimpering, crying out for release. Begging for it.

He loosened his hold on her, sliding the flat of his tongue over her as he rose upward, tracing a line to her belly button, up farther, until he was standing. Until he could capture her mouth with his. He pulled her up against him, let her feel the hard, insistent thrust of his arousal against her stomach. Kissed until he was dizzy. Until she was pleading with him to take her.

He rocked his hips against her, relishing the raw sounds she made, the feeling of her fingernails digging into his skin. It was always like this with her. Desire tinged with violence.

And he loved it.

He backed her up against the bed, and they fell onto it. He positioned himself between her thighs, pressing the head of himself to her slick entrance. He pushed into her easily, her arousal easing the way. She was so hot, so tight. She was made just for him.

As he seated himself fully inside her he had the strongest sensation that he was home. That he was complete for the first time in years.

A deep, strong emotion tugged at his chest, a sense of déjà vu that he didn't want to place. This was new and familiar all at the same time. And he rejected it. Didn't want it. But as his arousal built, as she flexed her hips beneath him, meeting his every thrust, he found he could not hold on to his control and keep the emotions at bay.

She wrapped her legs around his hips, and as she gave herself up to her own release, as his own climax crashed over him like a wave, those feelings crashed through him, as well.

And as he was tossed violently in the surf, he could think of one thing. Elle. That she was the port in the storm. That she was the constant. The North Star by which he had been guided for years. A star he had turned away from.

The realization left him feeling like his chest was full of broken glass. As though he had been wounded, invaded by sharp, shattered splinters he could never hope to remove.

He looked down at Elle, at her lips, flushed with desire, swollen from his kisses, her eyes, slumberous, satisfied. Looking at him as though he held answers.

He had no answers. At this moment, he had nothing but questions.

"Stay with me. Tonight," she said, "could you stay with me?"

And as terror tore at him like a rabid dog, he could do nothing but nod and pull her into his arms. But it did nothing to stop the hemorrhaging in his chest. Did nothing to stem the flow of pure, unmitigated fear pounding through him.

But Elle had asked him to stay. And so he did.

CHAPTER EIGHT

WHEN APOLLO WOKE, it was starting to turn gray outside. And Elle was curled up around him like a cat. He had no doubt, even for a moment, who he was lying in bed with. Who he had fallen asleep with.

He had never been close enough with a woman to even contemplate letting his guard down enough to fall asleep with her. In the past, the moment he finished making love with a woman, he left. There was no reason to linger. Sex, in his experience, could be perfectly impersonal. Sleeping with someone had seemed an intimacy he did not wish to contend with.

But he had fallen asleep with Elle, after she had asked him to stay. He had not imagined he would sleep. But it seemed natural. To hold her in his arms while they both drifted off. Bathing in the afterglow of the pleasure they had shared.

Suddenly, panic overtook him. He had a plan. A plan to make the St. James family pay for the sins they had committed against his family. To avenge the death of his father. The loss of his family fortune. The strange relationship Apollo's mother had been forced into by David St. James.

And every indignity he had suffered. Every moment he had been made to feel like he had not earned his position at the prestigious boarding school he went to. Every time he had to defend his placement in the boardroom because he had come from such humble beginnings.

She was weakening that plan. She was weakening his determination. And he could not let that stand.

He extricated himself from her hold, rolling out of bed. He forked his fingers through his hair, looking around, before remembering he had no clothes in her room. He wrenched open the door, walking down the hall completely naked. All of the staff would have gone home. Anyway, they knew better than to stare too long if they saw something shocking in his home.

Instead of going to his bedroom, he went into his office, taking a bottle of whiskey from the shelf to the left of his desk. He poured a healthy amount, and took a fortifying drink. Elle drove him to drink. This was the second time he'd turned to alcohol to deal with the effects she had on him.

Most women didn't affect him at all.

He had been determined to keep her with him until the attraction between them burned out, but he could see that something else was heating up between them, something he had no hope of burning out half so quickly.

Rage took him over. He didn't want to send her away. He could imagine it, telling her to leave. Never touching her again. Never spending another night with her. Anger overtook him, completely, dictating his next action. He took the half-full glass of whiskey and hurled it at the wall, watching the glass shatter, feeling no remorse at all.

The fact that the very thought of her leaving made him feel so helpless, so enraged was only more evidence that he had to send her away.

If he was going to take his revenge, he would have to take it now.

* * *

They had forgotten to tint the windows. That was Elle's first thought when she woke up the next morning. Her second thought was that she was alone. True to his word, Apollo had not spent the night with her. She shouldn't be surprised, but after she had confessed to him that he was her only lover, she supposed she had expected... something.

She supposed that she was foolish.

For wishing that things could be different. For wishing that something had changed between them. She didn't know what.

She sat up, clutching the blankets to her chest. And suddenly, Apollo came bursting through the door. "Good morning," he said, his mouth set into a grim line.

"Good morning," she said.

During all of the time she'd spent here, he had never come into her room unannounced. He had never come in unless it was to make love. He did not look like he had... that on his mind. Not in the least. He looked... He looked like he had come in with demons on his heels.

"I trust you slept well," he said.

"Yes," she said, a strange, uneasy feeling settling in the center of her chest. She didn't know why. She only knew that something wasn't right.

"I think it is time you left," he said, his words cold.

"But we... I don't understand," she said. "Yesterday we..."

"That was yesterday. And this is today."

She thought back to last night, to what had transpired between them. Had she done something wrong? Had he not liked her wearing the bikini and reminding him of that day? No. Yesterday he had enjoyed it. She knew he had.

"I'm not ready to leave," she said. "We agreed we needed to burn this out and I don't think it's burned out."

"A difference of opinion," he said, his tone hard. "For me, it is over."

"Apollo…"

"Also, effective immediately you have been terminated from your position as CEO of Matte."

"I… What?" She couldn't make sense of his words. She was naked, in bed, after having just spent the night making love with him, and he was firing her.

Two weeks. Two weeks she had spent with this man. In his arms. Kissing him, sharing her body with him… sharing everything.

"You heard me," he continued. His tone was flat. His eyes were flat. He was like a stranger. Only yesterday she had felt that she'd known him more intimately, more deeply than any other person on earth. And now she doubted it. She truly did. "I grow tired of the charade, Elle. Truth be told, I was planning on drawing this out longer. I was anticipating feeling a great sense of pleasure when I let you know that I was simply using you to hurt your father. I planned to set you up as the face of the company, to bring you into greater prominence so that when I made it very clear that I had taken all of your father's assets and left him ruined, the world would know exactly who he was, exactly what that meant. But frankly, I find it's just too tiring. So, I will have to be content in my revenge all on my own."

Her head was spinning. Revenge? She had been under no illusions that there was any affection between Apollo and her, but if anyone should want revenge, it was her. "You… You used me."

"Did you really think that I wanted you?"

She felt like he had driven a spike through her chest.

The cold, black words matching his cold, black eyes, making it impossible to pretend she had misheard. "Of course I did. As far as I know men can't fake…" She gestured toward the front of his pants. "They have to at least be attracted to a woman."

"It isn't just women who can lie back and think of England. What I really wanted, Elle, was to let your father know that I've taken everything from him. What would he think if he knew—?"

"Don't you dare, you bastard."

"Then I would have his company, and his daughter."

"You don't have me," she said, her throat tightening. "Two weeks, Apollo. Two weeks I gave you… I did…" She swallowed hard, panic taking over, tears threatening to fall. "I held nothing back from you! I trusted you with my body."

"A bad decision. I am untrustworthy. I have been from the beginning. You were convenient, darling, but let's be honest. Hardly more than a diversion, and one I cannot afford anymore."

"How can you say that?"

"It's true. Elle, be realistic. What could I possibly want with a near-virgin who's so cold she practically leaves icicles on my lips after a kiss?"

His words struck her like a physical blow. None of this made sense. She couldn't process it. But somewhere, in the middle of all the pain, all the anguish flooding through her like an unchecked tide, she found rage. The same rage that had propelled her into his arms in the first place.

And she clung it to it with everything she had. "How dare you?" she hissed, low and hard. "My father did everything for you. He paid for your education. He loved you—"

"No," he said. "He never loved me. He wanted to possess my mother, at any cost. And he did so. His very own Biblical fantasy where she was his Bathsheba and he sent her husband out to die."

"What?"

"Yes. My family was not always impoverished. Your father and mine were business partners, Elle. But they both fell for the same woman. My mother. She preferred my father. Your father bided his time, waited until he saw the opportunity, and then he used his sway with the board to vote my father out of the company. My father was ruined. Ultimately, he killed himself. My mother held out against your father's pleas for him to join her in the US. As his mistress. He was of course married to your mother then."

"I..."

"My mother agreed when I was eight, and we were starving. He established us in a home near his, and he came to visit often. From what I discovered later, he paid your mother off, then waited an appropriate amount of time before bringing my mother to the estate to be his wife."

"No... My father wouldn't... He didn't..."

"He did. He's a manipulative bastard who sees us all as nothing more than pawns. His actions caused my father to kill himself, it ruined my family. But I started to look into the history of my family. And when I found out why my father killed himself...why he was ruined...it all became clear." He paused. "It was your mother who contacted me."

Elle's mother who had long since abandoned the family. Whom Elle hadn't seen in fifteen years. "My mother?"

"Yes. She had seen me rising in business circles and

she…she found me one night at a bar. I didn't know who she was. Just another blonde who was after a night, I thought. But unlike most women, she didn't want sex. She wanted to talk. She wanted to tell me just what your father was."

"She came and found you? After all these years, not speaking to me for any of them, she came and found *you*? Are you that much more compelling to both of my parents?"

"In her case, I think she was compelled by revenge."

"Did she even ask about me?" Elle asked, despising the small sound of her own voice.

He said nothing, and it was his silence that spoke loudest. Of course she hadn't. She hadn't contacted her in years, why would she be concerned now? "I can't… I don't know what to think. I don't know how to process this."

His top lip curled. "Well, you will have plenty of time to process it while you stand in line filing paperwork to collect unemployment."

"Apollo… You can't do this."

His expression was granite. "I am doing this. It was my plan all along, and I am keeping to it. I am simply shortening the timeline."

Her stomach tightened, her entire body seizing up. She thought she was breaking apart from the inside out.

She had believed in him. Believed that he was the first person to see her for who she was. To want her for herself.

That was the worst betrayal of all. The fact that he'd used her. Not even because he hated her, not even because he wanted revenge on her, but because he wanted it on her *father*. Yet again, she was nothing. Nothing more than the most convenient chess piece on the board.

"Get out," she said, shaking now, trembling inside and out.

"It is my house."

"And it is my room. Leave me with what little dignity I have left." He turned away from her, heading toward the door. "I can't believe you. All the things you let me say. All the things you let me do. The bikini. As if I was… As if I mattered. But I never did. You're not any better than my father. Even if what you say is true, every word of it, you haven't risen above anything."

He turned back to her, his expression bleak. "I never wanted to rise above. I only ever wanted to drag you all into hell with me."

And with that, he walked out of the room, leaving her there, desolate and broken and certain she would never be whole again.

CHAPTER NINE

"If you don't mind me saying, Mr. Savas, you've been impossible the past few weeks."

"I know *you* don't mind saying it, Alethea," he said, his tone hard as he looked at his computer screen, ignoring his assistant.

"It's true," she said, turning on her heel and walking out of the office. Apollo didn't look up until the door had been shut firmly behind her.

Damned woman. She was always speaking the truth. He should fire her and hire someone stupid, beautiful and biddable.

When he thought the word *beautiful*, only one face came to mind. Of course, that woman was neither stupid, nor biddable. And she was persistently in his head.

Particularly in his dreams. He had woken up hard and reaching for her and she wasn't there. Because he'd sent her away.

It had seemed necessary at the time. Like he needed to put distance between them. But the longer he spent without her, the more he questioned that decision.

After all, his issue had been his loss of control, but sending her away wasn't any more controlled.

He had removed temptation from his path, but he had

not successfully destroyed his lust for her. Because of that, he was suffering now.

There was no reason to do so, of course. She had nothing to do, nowhere to go. No job. He could have her back. Make her his.

The memory of her—the warm weight of her, her sweet scent, the way she sighed and said his name—haunted him. His days, his nights.

He was like an addict in desperate need of a fix. His hands shaking, sweat breaking out over his skin at the thought of tasting her lips. Feeling her softness beneath his palms.

She was his own personal designer drug. One taste had only sent him headlong into an addiction he couldn't shake.

So maybe that was the problem. Cutting himself off completely would never work. It would only leave him wondering what it would be like to have her one last time. To lose himself inside her. To feel her delicate fingertips skimming over his back.

Just the thought sent a rush of need through him, so hot, so swift it nearly sent him down to his knees.

He had never felt like this before. Had never felt the need to keep and possess quite so fiercely.

As her father felt for your mother?

No. This was different. But one thing he knew: he had spent too many years denying this desire. He would not continue on.

He had been forced into denial, into poverty as a boy because of her father.

He would not subject himself to denial of his needs again.

He would not go one more night without her in his bed.

* * *

Elle was certain she was dying. It had been four weeks since she had left Greece. Four weeks since she had left Apollo, jobless, broken and humiliated. At least none of it had made it out into the public.

All anyone knew was that she had been replaced in her position at Matte. No one knew about her relationship with Apollo, and that was about the only thing saving her from melting into a puddle and sliding down the nearest drain, disappearing forever.

As upset as her father was about the entire situation, at least he didn't blame her. Or, maybe she didn't care. She had no idea how she felt. In only a month her entire life had been completely upended. She was avoiding her father. Avoiding dealing with that situation entirely.

Everything Apollo had said, all of the things he had told her that her father was guilty of, had settled down deep inside of her, and created just enough doubt about… everything that she wasn't sure she could deal with right now.

And then, purely selfishly, there was the issue of her firing.

She stood up, the floor pitching beneath her as she rose from the couch for the first time in hours. Being unemployed was bad for her wardrobe choices. She had been wearing sweats for three days, because there was no one there to see her anyway. Yesterday she'd worn flannels with small foxes on them. Today, her pants had owls.

"Very sexy," she said, crossing the length of the apartment and heading toward her fridge. She opened it up, immediately swamped by the smell coming from the inside. She wrinkled her nose. Something did not smell right. But it wasn't like she kept that much food in the fridge.

She dry heaved, and slammed the door shut. She'd forced herself to eat when she'd first woken up, but nothing tasted like…anything. A broken heart did that to you, apparently. But any semblance of an appetite she might have was gone now.

She felt like she had licked the inside of the tennis shoe. Okay, that thought made her stomach feel even worse.

She heard a knock on her door, and she nearly jumped out of her skin. People didn't just gain admittance to the building, so it had to be someone who already lived here. Though, her neighbors didn't speak to her, so she had no idea who it was or what it could be about.

Taking a deep breath, she crossed the apartment and undid the dead bolt and the chain, jerking it open just as she realized she should have looked through the peephole first.

But it was too late. The door was open, and standing there was her worst nightmare.

Suddenly, the vague sense of nausea intensified and she ran from the room, losing her breakfast violently in the bathroom.

"Elle?" Apollo's voice was coming from behind her.

"Stay away," she said, shakily getting to her feet. "I'm…horrifying."

"You're sick," he said, his tone vaguely accusatory.

"I…wasn't." Except she had been—though not this sick—but off her game for the past few days.

"What are you doing here, anyway?" She wandered over to the sink and splashed cold water on her face. "Who buzzed you in?"

"Some young woman who lives down the hall. Nose ring. Pink hair. She thought I looked trustworthy."

Elle laughed. Bitter, hollow. "She thought you looked like you belonged in her bed. I would give her advanced warning, but I imagine she wouldn't really care either way."

"Sadly for her. I'm not on the market."

"Okay. If you aren't here to hook up with my down-the-hall neighbor, why are you here?"

"Would you believe that I came to check on you?"

"No."

"I want you back."

"No," she said, her tone incredulous. "You can't have me back. You were awful to me. You fired me."

"And now you don't have a job. I thought you might be interested in pursuing some sort of arrangement."

She laughed, flinging her arms wide. "And here I am, vomiting as you ask me to come be your mistress. Really, there are probably more romantic settings than the bathroom."

"You need money. You certainly need a way to occupy your time."

"You're despicable."

She swept past him, trying to hold her head high. Difficult to do when the man who had made love to you then humiliated you had just seen you puke.

"Maybe," he said, lingering in the door frame, bracing his hands against it. "But it doesn't change the facts."

"Oh," she said, the world tilting slightly. "I need to lie down."

He frowned. "How long have you been feeling sick?"

"I told you, I only just… That, in the bathroom."

"You've been otherwise feeling well?"

"Not really. But then, you humiliated me and fired

me. So I don't know how well you could possibly expect me to feel."

"I'm not talking about your emotions, I'm talking about physically."

"No. I have not been feeling very well. But your emotions inform things like that."

"Have you gotten your period?"

Her mouth dropped open. "What kind of question is that?"

"The only question that matters to me right now."

Ice shivered down her spine. "I haven't," she said. "But that doesn't… It doesn't mean anything."

"You're here vomiting and looking pale, you haven't had your period in the past month and you don't think that means anything."

"We…"

"Were not very careful."

No, they hadn't been. They hadn't used a condom in the elevator, and again during that last time at his home. So really… She hadn't had a period since the elevator. "No, I guess we weren't."

"And it didn't occur to you until just now that you might be pregnant?"

"No," she said, her hand flying to her mouth, her eyes wide. "No. I'm not… I'm not."

"You have no way of knowing that."

No. She didn't. Because she hadn't taken a test. And, while she had never been particularly regular, that hadn't exactly been a problem because she had been a virgin. Now…it was a bit suspicious.

"I mean, I would prefer to wait a few days…"

He had already pulled out a cell phone. "Yes, Alethea? Find a discreet women's doctor in Manhattan who can see a patient immediately. Text me the information once you have it. When I say immediately, I mean I'm about to get in the car and start driving. They had better be ready to see us."

He hung up, and she could only stare at him. "What are you doing?"

"We are going to answer this question once and for all, *agape*. And make no mistake, if you are carrying my child there is no question that you are coming back to Greece with me. Immediately."

He could do nothing but pace outside the office at the posh, private medical facility he had taken Elle to.

He had found himself back in Manhattan for business reasons, and then he had displayed a characteristic weakness and found himself at Elle's building.

He did not know what manner of witchcraft Elle possessed that she made it impossible for him to forget her. Forget how she made him feel. Whether it was four weeks in the past, or nine years—before he had ever even touched her. She was a woman who lingered in his mind in a way that none before her—or since—ever had.

He wondered now if she had been some sort of bad omen. If the fact that he had never been able to get her out of his mind had been a warning of some kind. If she were truly pregnant with his child, he could not discount that. He had never intended to have children. But the moment the idea that she might be pregnant had entered his mind he had known that he would take possession of his child.

After his own childhood, after the way he had lost his father, he knew he would never subject his own child to such a thing. To a life without the man who was meant to protect him.

He gritted his teeth. His own father's feelings had hardly been his fault. He had been pushed into ruin by

David St. James. The fault would always lie with St. James. Apollo however was standing on his own two feet. No one was pushing him anywhere.

The door opened, and Elle emerged, clutching a few pieces of paper, her face pale. He didn't need her to speak to know what the answer was.

He had never imagined being in this situation. He supposed that any man who was sexually active could potentially face it, but he had always been very careful. So it was never anything he had considered seriously. But he had not been careful with Elle. The theme in their relationship, and the consequences of that, were now coming home to roost.

There was no panic. There was not even any rage, though he had expected it. No, there was nothing but cold, clean determination. He knew exactly what he was going to do. What he would demand.

"I…"

"Yes, I think I can guess."

"I don't know what we're going to do."

"I know exactly what we are going to do."

Her eyes widened. "You do?"

"Yes. You will be coming back to Athens with me. And then, *agape*, you and I are going to marry."

Elle was dimly aware of the fact that she was sitting in Apollo's limo, essentially in a catatonic state. But she had just found out she was pregnant with the baby of a man who despised her and her family, a man who had left her jobless and broken when he had ended their affair.

She had never really thought about being a mother. Her own mother had abandoned her early on and not bothered to keep in touch at all. Her stepmother was a lovely woman, but often silent next to her husband.

And Elle's father was so…imposing. He didn't bend. He didn't show affection. It was like loving a rock.

She had never imagined trying to re-create that parent-child relationship with herself in the parenting hot seat. It seemed…completely unappealing. It also meant she was linked to Apollo. Forever.

As if you weren't before.

She gritted her teeth. She had no idea what to say. No idea what to do next. And as far as she knew she was being shanghaied and sent to Athens again.

That thought sent her into action. "I'm not going to marry you."

He chuckled, a dark, humorless sound. "Then prepare yourself for a custody battle that will drain you of your every resource."

She blinked. "Who said I would fight you for custody?"

The moment she said it, she realized that she would. Not because her parents had been wonderful, not because they had made her long for a parent-child relationship in her own life. But because they had demonstrated in a million small ways how unimportant she was. She would be damned if her own child would walk through life feeling like their mother couldn't be bothered with them.

Just the thought made her stomach clench in agony. Her own little one, believing that she didn't want them. She wanted to apologize to the little life inside her. As though it had somehow sensed her hesitation.

"If you don't feel strongly enough about our child to stand and fight for them, then I would gladly have you step aside."

"I won't," she said, her tone infused with conviction.

The numbness was starting to wear off. And even though she couldn't quite imagine what it would be like to have a child, even though she wasn't sure if she was devastated or happy, she knew that she wouldn't stand aside.

"You just said—"

"Yes, well, I am trying to figure out exactly where I stand. It might surprise you to know this but I didn't exactly fantasize about a life with a picket fence, a husband and children."

"It doesn't surprise me. A woman with as much white in her apartment as you have doesn't seem to be planning ahead for sticky fingers."

"I wasn't. You can be sure of that. But I'm also not one to walk away from my responsibilities. And I don't want any child of mine going through life imagining they aren't wanted."

"Then, marriage it will be."

Her mind was ticking over at a million miles a minute. "I would have a few conditions," she said.

She could not believe she had just said that. She knew that you weren't supposed to negotiate with terrorists or superalpha Greek billionaires who had far too high of an opinion of themselves. So, she didn't know why she was attempting it.

"Conditions, *agape*?" He sounded…angry. But interested.

"Yes. Conditions." Now she had to quickly think of her conditions. "New York is my home. I'm not leaving New York."

"I have a villa in Greece."

"I daresay you have homes all over the world. I know you don't have a permanent residence in New York, but I do."

"Your apartment is the size of a postage stamp."

"It's big enough."

"For you. There is no room for a child. No room for a husband."

She gritted her teeth. "I did not agree to taking a husband. Not yet. I have conditions, but I won't make my final decision until I'm certain that the situation is to my liking."

"I'm not certain you want to challenge my authority. I am a well-respected billionaire, after all, and you are unemployed. The daughter of a businessman on the verge of being washed-up. If your mother hasn't spent all of his payoff money by now, she's certainly close to it. What could you possibly give a child that I can't?"

"Love. Warmth. Human emotion?"

"I'm sure the court will be more impressed with my net worth."

"I don't think so. Everyone agrees that a child needs love above anything else."

"And you feel you are more qualified to give a child parental love that I am?"

She shifted in her seat. "Yes. I do."

"On what grounds? Prior to being unemployed you were a workaholic."

"I was not."

"Did you have a single friend who was not also a co-worker?"

She didn't even have to think about that. She knew the answer to the question. But whether or not they were from work Suki and Christine were real friends. Suki had brought cupcakes after Elle had been fired. *Friendship*.

Though the thought of cupcakes made her stomach turn right now.

"You're a workaholic, too," she said.

"I'm also a man and a billionaire. No one will judge

me for the amount of time I spend working. It is irrelevant. Not so for you."

"The point is, I am the child's mother and I don't think I'm going to have an issue retaining custody."

"I disagree."

"You will have to wait, Apollo," she said, her voice infused with iron, with a strength she wasn't sure she truly felt right now. "I'm not afraid of fighting you in court. To hear you tell it your mother was manipulated into a relationship with my father and now you want to do the same to me? How are you any better?"

"I'm not," he said, his expression bleak, cold. But only for a moment. Then his walls went back up.

"Name your conditions clearly."

"I want to stay in New York. I wish to have the child here. I wish to raise him here."

"The child will be Greek. He should be exposed to his homeland."

"Exposure is fine. But I want him raised here. I want to stay here. Because that leads me to my next requirement. I want my job back."

"The new CEO has only been there for a month. If I let him go I will seem capricious."

"There is a cost to everything. And that is the cost to having me without muss or fuss. Do you accept, or not?"

She wasn't certain if she wanted him to say yes, or if she wanted him to refuse. She wasn't sure what she wanted at all.

"I accept."

A strange mixture of relief and terror washed through her. "Excellent."

He pulled out his phone again. "Alethea," he said. "I require some real estate. A penthouse, Manhattan. Something large, but secure. No rooftop balconies or anything like that. Or, if there are balconies, they need to be secure. Childproof." He hung up.

"Is your assistant finding you a house?"

"No, *agape*," he said, smiling a smile that was not friendly at all. "My assistant is going to find us a home. Now do you agree to marry me?"

Elle took a deep breath and met that coal-black gaze. "If I find the conditions are met to my satisfaction. And if I feel you won't spend my whole life making me miserable. You said I was your revenge, Apollo. Until you see me as a woman—a whole woman, not your stepsister who you harbor rage against, not an instrument of vengeance to use against my father—you will not have me. Not in your life, not as your wife. That's a promise."

CHAPTER TEN

ALETHEA WAS NOTHING if not efficient, and by that afternoon he and Elle were standing in an empty penthouse at the top of the building in Midtown. It was spacious, though hardly the sun-drenched villa he chose to call home in Greece. But it would do.

"Do you find this satisfactory?"

"I have a… I have a house," she said.

"Oh, I have already taken care of listing it for you. Unless you wish to keep it as some sort of workspace, I figured it would be best to sell it."

"You're selling my house?"

"My men have been over there packing your things."

She whirled around, her hands clenched into fists. "Apollo! I can't believe you would do something like that."

He turned to her, arching a dark brow. "Really. You can't believe I would do something like that? And here I thought it was in keeping with my character."

She pressed her fists up against her eyes, as though she was trying to use them to hold back her rage. "Everything is changing too quickly."

"Things have been changing quickly for the past two months. First, we had sex. Then you went to Greece. Then we had more sex. You lost your job. Now you're having a baby and we're working at integrating our lives. It's a fast-moving train, life is."

In truth, his life had been stagnant for quite a few years. Yes, he had more money than he could possibly spend in a lifetime. His business had continued to grow. He had fixated on his revenge plan against the St. James family. But beyond that, nothing had moved significantly in years. His life was an endless array of beautiful women, meaningless events that required him to put on a suit and smile politely at those in attendance. This was…

This was the first time in a long time he had something new.

It wasn't the revenge he had planned when he'd come back to New York, but it was…interesting. He imagined Elle would take exception to him calling her accidental pregnancy interesting.

"Fine. It's very you. But you can't just come into my life and completely reorder it."

"Why not? You have done it to me."

She looked stunned for a moment. "Have I?"

"You are going to make me a father. If that is not up-ending my life, I don't know what is."

"I suppose it depends on how involved you intend to be."

He knew nothing about how to be a good father. He could scarcely remember his own. When the other man had been alive he had all but lived at the corporate headquarters for the business he shared with David St. James. And then, after that, after the disgrace, he had sunk into drugs and alcohol. Affairs. Only a few years later he was dead.

As far as David went…the man had been an attentive stepfather. He had been… Well, none of it mattered now. Because of what he had revealed himself to be.

"I am a busy man. A wealthy man. I plan to keep my involvement somewhat limited," he said.

"Then, I suppose your personal life doesn't have to change much. Oh," she said, her green gaze turning sharp. "Except you are required to remain faithful to me."

Her words hit him low and hard in the stomach. Punched the wound he had just been examining. He could not imagine wanting a woman other than Elle. He had not taken anyone else to his bed in the month since they had parted. Unusual for him.

In fact, from the moment he had taken over her father's company, from the moment he had first taken over the magazine and brought her back into his life on a semi-regular basis, he had not been with another woman. Because the moment Elle St. James had come back into his life his body had reignited its obsession for her. Still, he did not wish for her to know that. He did not want her issuing more edicts.

He had agreed to New York, because that was simple. He had agreed to giving her the position at Matte back because it was also simple. And quite apart from that, the fact that he was providing David St. James with his first grandchild was a whole new, delicious sort of revenge.

He no longer needed to throw her out of the company. No longer required to destroy St. James in that way. He had the man's daughter. She was having his baby. She would be his wife, Apollo was confident in that.

Yes, there was a great deal he could do with that. He was certain.

"I have no experience with fidelity," he said. "I will make no promises on that score."

"Then you will enjoy the single life. If you touch another woman, you certainly won't be touching me."

"I highly doubt that."

He and Elle could scarcely be in the same room together without tearing each other's clothes off. Today was an exception, brought about by the shock of her discovering she was pregnant and by the need to see to the logistics created by that circumstance. But he knew that very soon he would have her on her back begging for his possession.

Or she will have you on your back begging for hers.

He refused to consider that. Refused to think of things that way. She was a slave to the pleasure that ignited between them every time they touched, just as he was. He was not at a disadvantage. He was not alone in it.

"The perk of staying single is that I will be free to pursue other lovers," she said, shaking her head, her coppery mane shimmering in the sunlight filtering through the large windows that overlooked Central Park.

"I don't believe that," he said, rage a hot, living thing in his stomach. The thought of another man touching Elle was anathema. But she was bluffing, and he would call her on that.

"Why is that? I may have been a virgin before you and I met, Apollo, but now that you have shown me just how enjoyable sex can be I don't think you can possibly ask me to forgo the pleasure."

"I damn well can."

She laughed. "Careful. Your desperation is showing. You wouldn't want me to understand where my real power is in all of this."

She hit too close to the bone there, cut him far too deeply.

And suddenly, he did not care that today had been an emotional one for her. He did not care that she was in a fragile state. Only than only a couple of hours ago she had been sick in front of him, while wearing sweatpants. He always wanted Elle. Always. There was never a time when he didn't crave her touch. And this was no exception.

He crossed the vacant expanse of the living area, wrapping his arm around her waist and tugging her up against him, cupping her chin with his thumb and forefinger. "Do not push me, Elle. You will not like the result."

"Do not push *me*, Apollo."

"We push each other, *agape*, that's the honest truth. And look at where it has gotten us."

"Yes. I daresay it is not the most pleasant situation."

"I could make it much more pleasant if you weren't so stubborn."

She glared at him. "The same goes for you."

"You start again at Matte tomorrow. I will give your replacement a generous severance."

He released his hold on her.

"Excellent," she said, smoothing her clothing, her voice making it sound like she thought all of this was anything but excellent.

"I have arranged for all of our things to be moved into the penthouse by tonight."

She laughed. "That isn't possible."

He lifted his shoulder. "It is possible when you pay with cash."

She shook her head. "That's the problem with you, Apollo, you have never been denied anything that you wanted."

"I don't know, Elle, I felt fairly denied of my father after he put a bullet in his brain. And why did he do that? Oh, yes. Because his dear friend and business partner betrayed him. Yes, I know a little bit about deprivation. I refuse to apologize for enjoying luxury now."

She blinked. "I'm sorry. I didn't mean…"

He waved a hand. "I am not so sensitive. Anyway, this is par for the course between us, yes? We must tear strips off each other's hides. Because if we do not, we will tear each other's clothes off instead."

She sniffed. "Maybe once. But not anymore."

"You may cling to that illusion all you want. Either way, your things will be here by this evening. How you choose to spend your time between now and then is up to you."

The next day, when Elle walked into the fully furnished penthouse she felt dazed. Her life was changing so quickly. They were going to be sharing a space while he was in New York. Living together. And he wanted to marry her.

It made her stomach tight. Made her feel dizzy.

The terrifying thing was there was some small, delusional piece of her that felt…excited. As though this were some kind of fairy tale. As though the two of them were embarking on a real relationship. Possibly, a real marriage. As though he wanted her, because she was Elle, because of the heat and fire between them, not because she was carrying his baby.

He came back. He came back before he knew you were pregnant.

She held that close. Turned it over and examined it as though it was some kind of rare treasure that she wanted to keep shielded from the world. That she never wanted to look away from. He had returned to her before he found out about the baby. She didn't know what that meant. Yes, he had said he wanted her to return as his mistress. But she knew full well that a man like Apollo was more than capable of getting any woman he desired. He didn't need her. But he had still come for her.

And the moment he had found out about the baby he had taken charge, taken everything into hand and done everything he could to make their arrangement permanent.

It was perhaps foolish to assign any meaning to that, but she couldn't help it.

At the bottom of it all, at the end of everything, she just wanted someone who wanted to be with her. Maybe that was a sad admission. But she had been lonely for so long. For all of her life. And the way that Apollo looked at her, the way that he commanded her body, so fierce and intense, at the exclusion of all else, made her hopeful that there was more to his attentions than he was willing to admit.

Of course, he would not promise to be faithful to her.

She blinked, swallowing hard, continuing to examine the modern layout of the penthouse. "Which room will be mine?"

"Any one that you choose," he said. "Though the master bedroom already has your things in it."

"Not yours?"

He lifted his shoulder. "I have several other residences. I may not always be here as frequently as you are. My headquarters will remain in Greece. That means I will only spend a small amount of time here."

The idea of him being with other women flooded her mind again. Of course. He wasn't actually planning on living with her. Not really. Not all the time. He was taking possession of her, but he was holding her at arm's length. It shouldn't surprise her. But it did hurt.

And it did nothing to remove the traitorous beacon of hope that still burned down in the pit of her stomach. She should harbor no hope where he was concerned, and still that small part of her whispered: *But he came back before he knew about the baby.*

She wasn't going to let him see her hope.

"That's fine. It will be good for the child, I think, to have us in the same house sometimes. At least there is space. I think I might go lie down," she said, heading toward the stairs that led to the upper level of the penthouse and the bedrooms.

"You're welcome to. But we have a dinner reservation in four hours. I expect you to be ready by then."

She gritted her teeth. "Is this going to be nothing more than a series of edicts?"

"You keep challenging them, I keep trying."

"Well, thankfully a meal is not a marriage."

She continued on up the stairs. Then she walked down the hall and pushed open the door to her new bedroom. In her new house. Suddenly, her knees felt like they were going to buckle. Everything was so overwhelming. The decisions she suddenly had to make. She moved quickly to the bed and threw herself down on the soft surface. And then she did the thing she allowed so very rarely. She buried her face in the pillow and wept.

Elle was always beautiful. That was part of the problem with her. No matter that she was forbidden, either because she was his stepsister or the daughter of his enemy, she was too beautiful. But tonight, in a short cream lace dress, her skin looking as waxen as a doll's, her red hair falling softly around her shoulders, she was like a particularly terrified angel. Otherworldly. Ethereal.

And all he could think of was that he wanted to drag her into the pit with him. Make her fall, as he had done.

He had not lied when he had told her that all he had ever wanted was to bring her down to his level. To somehow make it acceptable for a man like him to touch a woman like her.

What does it matter what is acceptable?

He didn't even know what was acceptable anymore. So the question, he supposed, was moot.

He had not told her what the aim of the dinner was. She would be angry at him, but he could not see her resisting once she saw the ring.

He had gone to a jewelry store today and chosen the ring for her himself. A large square-cut champagne diamond that seemed to capture her particular brand of unique elegance better than a standard sort of engagement ring.

He had also chosen one of the most up-and-coming restaurants in Manhattan to perform the deed. Because there was guaranteed to be paparazzi lurking, even if they were hiding in the hedgerows, so to speak. And, beyond that, there would be people there with cameras ready to take pictures and post what they had seen to the internet. Getting the word out had never been so easy, and since discretion was the furthest thing from his mind, it suited him.

He took her hand, running his thumb over the smooth, silken skin. Some unknown, possessive, caveman part of him relished what was about to happen. The fact that soon he would put his ring on her finger, and the world would know that she belonged to him. He gloried in that. The fact that there would be a sign of his ownership of her.

That made him think of the baby. Of the fact that she would soon grow round with it, yet more evidence of the fact that he had bound her to him, irrevocably, intensely.

He did not know who he was just now. But then, with Elle, he never did.

She looked down at his hand as though it was a potentially dangerous snake. "I don't think you brought me here simply to treat me to a nice meal. Though, it was nice."

"And we have not yet gotten to dessert."

She drew her hand back slowly. "No, we haven't. And you have been perfectly pleasant bordering on solicitous through the entire meal. And so, I need to know what's happening."

"I had planned to wait until you were finished with your cake, *agape*, but if you are feeling impatient then I am more than happy to reveal the reason why I have brought you out tonight."

He reached into the interior pocket of his suit jacket and produced a small velvet box. Though he had not imagined it possible, more color drained from Elle's face. "Is that…"

He shifted from his position in the chair, moving forward, dropping down to one knee in front of where Elle sat. This was yet another thing he had not imagined doing in all of his life. Lowering himself like this. Getting on his knees before a woman. But if the charade was going to work then he had to commit to it. There could be no doing this halfway.

"Elle St. James, I would be very honored if you would accept the offer to become my wife."

He could feel the eyes of all the diners in the restaurant on them, could sense that everyone was watching. And then he heard the sound of shutters. And he knew that it was being documented, just as he had planned. Knew that it would be a headline in the business pages by tomorrow.

"I—I told you I couldn't answer this now," she said, her tone hushed.

If Elle hesitated, she would potentially cause trouble

for him. Perhaps, in his arrogance, he had overplayed his hand.

"I wish for you to become my wife," he said. "You are the only woman I have ever imagined spending my life with. Please, do me the honor of saying yes."

It was the truth, even if it was a misleading truth. In all honesty, he had never imagined taking another woman as his wife. But then, he had not begun thinking about taking Elle for a wife until this morning. So, he supposed there was room for interpretation with those words. But they were not a lie.

Yet her expression remained set.

"Would you like to see the ring?" he asked. If he was not enough enticement then perhaps the jewelry would be.

He opened the lid on the jewelry box, revealing his carefully chosen selection.

She looked at it, her face frozen. Unreadable. She lifted her hand, as though she was going to reach out and touch it, before drawing her hand back quickly, as if the ring was a snake that might bite her.

"No," she said.

"No?" he asked. He was on his knees, on the damn floor in the damn restaurant, and she had refused him.

He felt…at a loss, and that was completely foreign to him. And along with that hollow feeling came…pain. Deep. Stabbing.

She stood suddenly, stumbling around him. "I don't think I want dessert," she said, her voice strangled.

"Are you certain?"

"Yes. I told you I wasn't sure what I wanted and you—" she looked around the room "—you did your best to make this public so that I couldn't say no. You don't get to behave this way, Apollo. I'm not your pawn. I'm not anyone's pawn."

"We will speak more in the car," he said. "There is no point in discussing it here."

"Of course not," she said, "we would not wish for me to make a scene."

He did not have to worry about the check, as the restaurant already had his details, so he took hold of Elle's hand, and the two of them made their way from the restaurant, still with the watchful eyes of the other patrons on them. A quick push of a button on his phone, and his car was brought around to the front. He opened the door for her, then slid inside, and the two of them remained silent until his driver pulled away from the curb. After issuing instructions to take them home he raised the partition between the front seat and the back, shrouding them in privacy.

"Is everything a game to you?" she asked, once they were alone, her expression fierce.

"It is not a game," he said, his voice hard. "It is a strategy. I have spent the past several years planning my revenge against your family. I was finished with it. But now, here you are, and you are pregnant with my baby. I want what I want, Elle, and I intend on getting it."

"So what? You thought you could shock me into saying yes?"

"I thought the ring might do it." It had never occurred to him it might not. Had never truly occurred to him she might refuse.

"If I wanted a ring, I would buy my own. One that did not come with a husband attached."

"Marriage makes sense," he insisted.

"I don't care about sense!" she shouted, her voice filling up the space in the car. "None of this, not ever, not from the first time we touched, was ever about sense."

"Then why pretend it matters now? Why resist me when we both know you're going to give in?"

"Because you would say things like that. Because you think me giving in to you is an inevitability. Because you do not listen, damn you!"

"You're still behaving like you have a choice here," he said, hardening his voice.

"I'm a fool. I keep expecting to discover you feel *something* for me. Anything."

Her words were raw, honest, not the shotgun shells filled with anger her statements typically were. There was a vulnerability here. An honesty he had not anticipated. They scraped at him, tore strips from his hide.

"Of course I feel something for you," he said. "I want you." The words were much more raw, much more shattered than he wanted them to be. But he was rapidly losing control. Of this moment. Of himself.

It was always so with Elle. Always.

She shook her head. "That is not the same thing."

"And yet, it is all I have."

"Because you hate my family so much?"

"Touching you was a betrayal of my father. Of my mother. I had thought to take the thing between us and twist it into something I can use."

"You're that angry?"

"Everything that I built my life around was a lie," he said, his words escaping with a force that shocked him. "I thought your father simply cared about me. Instead, it was all a part of his twisted obsession with my mother. He allowed me to care for him, acted as though he cared for me, while the whole time he knew…he knew he was the reason my father killed himself. So you tell me, Elle, in my position would you not also crave revenge?"

"It solves nothing," she said. "You had your revenge in

hand. You had it for four weeks, you thought it was finished. You had ousted me from my position as CEO. You were done with me. Done with my family, and yet still you were back at my door. So tell me, Apollo, what has revenge solved for you? What has it fixed? Your father is still gone. And you still want me. You are in fact begging me to be your wife. Where is your power in revenge?"

He could not deny it, though he wished to. Though he wished he could tell her that he had been using her all along. He had shown his hand when he had returned to her apartment. When he had asked for her to be his mistress.

And it was not only to her he had shown his hand, but to himself.

"I want you," he said. "Quite apart from any plans for revenge."

"You think that would make a marriage work?"

"It would work because we would make it work. We are attracted to each other, is that not enough?"

"I don't know. I never gave serious thought to marriage. I don't know what I want out of one." She blinked. "Except I would like more than screaming at my husband. I would like more than wondering if he is away having an affair. I would like to be chosen. Just once. Not because of someone else. You know, I'm only the CEO of Matte because it was my father's last attempt to keep hold of his empire. And you... What you really want is to make me your wife so you can lord it over my father."

"I know you don't put stock in my desire for you, because it isn't emotional. I am not capable of the kind of emotion you are talking about. But I will tell you that had I been able to want any other woman, had I had dominion over my desire for you—I never would have given in."

"I'm supposed to rejoice because you didn't *want* to want me?"

"Yes," he said, simply.

"You truly are arrogant. And you don't understand women very well."

He chuckled. "I understand parts of a woman."

"I can't deny that. But I can also tell you that it leaves you cold after, no matter how hot you burn in the moment."

CHAPTER ELEVEN

ELLE FELT DEFLATED by the time they arrived back at the penthouse. She said nothing to him as they went inside, as she walked back to her bedroom and stripped off her jewelry. How had she ever thought she could handle this man? This man who was so twisted by his desire to injure her family that he was willing to consider anyone who stood in his way as collateral damage.

If he acted like a human man, with feelings and emotions and normal connections, then it would be a simple thing to make him understand. But he didn't. She had no idea how to appeal to this enigma. This immovable rock who looked like a man but didn't behave like one.

She remembered thinking only a few weeks ago that he was heartless. She hated that she was more and more convinced it was true.

She had known him for so many years, and yet didn't know him at all. She knew his body. Knew what made him shake, knew just how to taste him, how to touch him. And she had heard that dark edge that crept into his voice when he spoke about his past, that hinted at the pain he had been through. At how he felt about it all. About what it had done to him. But she could not for the life of her imagine him as a husband. As a father. She knew fragments of him. The boy he had been, the man he was now.

The ruthless and cruel businessman, and the solicitous lover. But those things did not mesh in her mind. She couldn't marry the details together.

She sat in her room for a moment longer, not bothering to change out of her dress, checking her emails and wasting time on the internet until an hour had passed since they'd come home. Then she stood, crossing the room before she had time to fully process what she was doing. Making her way through the penthouse toward his bedroom. She paused at the door, placing her palm on her chest, feeling the raging of her heartbeat beneath her palm. Then she pushed the door open. He was in bed, naked, his blankets pushed down low on his hips, his arm flung up above his head. He was not asleep. He opened his eyes when she opened the door, arching one dark brow. "Yes?"

She crossed the room, climbing onto the bed, staying on top of the covers, lying down next to him.

He shifted, leaning over as though he was going to kiss her. She held up her hand. "No," she said, "I want to talk."

"Well, *agape*, I do not talk in bed."

"You also don't get women pregnant, and you don't ask them to marry you. Given that I already had a couple of exceptions made for me, I would ask that you make one more."

"As you wish," he said, moving back into the position he'd been in when she had come in.

"I want to know you," she said.

He paused. "There is little to know."

"I only knew bits and pieces of your childhood. Whatever you told me. But I'm curious now about all of it. With what I know now, with what you know now, I am curious about everything."

Apollo sighed. "Okay. When I was born, I lived in a

beautiful home. But that did not last. My father worked all the time, and I rarely saw him. Then when I was very young, he lost his position in the company he owned with your father. What was done to him was ruthless, as you know. From there, we lost our home. We lost everything. We lived in…modest housing, to put it mildly."

She wanted to touch him. She had just decided touching was easier than talking, that kissing was easier than honesty. Their bodies were so much easier than anything else. But putting healthy distance between them, she didn't interrupt.

"My father did not take our descent into poverty well. He dealt with his issues by taking drugs, by drinking. Eventually, what little money we had was swallowed up by his addictions. We ended up on the streets. Shortly after that, when he saw what had become of us, when he saw what had become of the family, he killed himself. I will never know why. If he felt ashamed, if he thought we would be better off without him somehow. If he simply didn't want to try anymore. I can never know the answer. And in the end it doesn't matter. The decision was made. The years passed. But one thing I do know is that he would want recompense for what happened to him. For what happened to us."

"That he should have taken himself," she said, the words coming slowly, but with conviction. "If he cared that much he would've stuck around to get revenge himself."

"He couldn't. For whatever reason," he said. "Regardless, my mother and I found ourselves on the streets, then eventually in a horrible group home sort of place. That was when we were sent for. My mother gave very few details, but she said we were going to a new home. Starting over in America. There was a house. Small, I suppose, by some standards. But clean. We wanted for nothing. Suddenly my mother was able to be home with me, instead of desperately searching for work. I had a bed every night."

"I… I can't imagine what that would mean to you in those circumstances."

"I can barely remember. Though it's something I try to hold on to. So that I never forget what it means to be hungry. When you lose the memory of your hunger…you forget why you need success."

She nodded in the darkness. "I know what you mean." She was hungry, too. Not for food or shelter. But for approval she'd never gotten before.

"Your father had come to visit us many times. Sometimes a nanny would be sent to care for me and my mother would go away for a weekend. To be with him, though, I had a boy's understanding. Your father was always good to us. To me. And when he wished to marry my mother, when he spirited us both away to your estate, I thought… I thought we had everything. Suddenly, I gained the world that I had only ever seen glimpses of before."

"I remember you arriving. I was awful to you. Because you scared me. You were…the most beautiful thing I'd ever seen and I knew I shouldn't think that about my stepbrother…like that."

"I suppose not," he said. "You were smart to hold me at a distance, Elle."

"I don't know if *smart* is the word I would use. But it was definitely a defense that worked for a while."

He chuckled. "Yes, it did work for a bit." He paused. "I never asked you… I never asked what it was like to lose your mother like you did. I suppose…your father is as responsible for that as he is for the loss of my father."

The thought made her stomach sink. "I know my father isn't perfect but I have a hard time believing he was so manipulative. But then, I guess maybe I don't… He's a man who likes control, and a man who thinks nothing of pitting his children against each other. So why wouldn't he have always done this, with every person he could? He does it to his own flesh and blood." She moved closer to him, only a bit. "My mother mostly cared about parties and handbags. Lunches with her friends. She was a trophy wife. Her identity was in who my father was, and I suppose that's why I wanted so badly to find something else. To succeed at Matte. To make my own achievements. Except…they were my father's too, really. I was living out my father's plans in my need to please him, in my need to rebel against my mother. I did miss her," she continued. "I really did. Even though I was mostly cared for by nannies. She was my mother, and she smelled of Chanel and vanilla shampoo. And I loved her."

"Of course you did," he said. "My father was distant, a workaholic and an addict, and still I loved him."

"I was happy to have your mother. Mariam has always been good to me."

"But she is not your mother."

Elle's throat tightened. "No. She isn't."

"Nothing can replace what we've lost."

"I guess in a way both of our parents chose to leave us," she said. "Though…my mother could have chosen to come back."

"Or perhaps not. Perhaps she doesn't feel like she can. Not now."

"Maybe. When it became clear the takeover of the company was…hostile… When it became clear you weren't helping…my father put me in control of Matte. And I knew why. I knew it was to use me as a shield. But still, I accepted the position. He's…all I have, really, and I wanted to please him," she said. "I wanted so badly to be accepted. I just wanted him to be proud of me. And then you came in and bought everything out. I thought maybe if I could hold on to my position he would see that I have deserved it all along. But you fired me."

"Had I known your position as CEO was such a contentious one, I might have left you alone."

"I don't know that you would have, Apollo. It isn't in your nature."

"I don't suppose it is."

"I wonder what I would have done," she said, "if he had not selected for me. If I had not been so determined to prove to him that I could be everything that…that you weren't for him."

"You can try and find out, you know. You don't have to go back to work as you. You feel trapped there… There is no reason for you to be there."

"I feel like my team is counting on me. I poured endless hours into it. So much time and energy."

"But you do not have to be there. You are the mother of my child and whatever happens, I will support you financially. You can simply stay home with our child if you prefer. You can go back to school."

She laughed. "I feel like it's too late, really."

"I hope it's never too late to change what you are," he said. "In part because I have been many things in my life. A child of privilege, a gutter snipe, a charity case, wealthy again… We can always change what we are, as long as we stay on earth to breathe one more time."

His words settled heavily on her chest. His father had stopped breathing. And so he had ended his story. "I understand that," she said.

"So if you could do anything, what would you do?"

"I would like to advocate for people who can't do it for themselves. To use the fact that I enjoy challenging people to accomplish something good. A lawyer. But for children, maybe. For women who have been abused."

"That's a very worthy goal," he said.

She shrugged. "It's a fantasy. Anyway, I feel like I was making so much progress with the brand. Really bringing it into the modern era. I know profits aren't off the charts, but the books and cosmetics and the other tie-in products have really taken us to a new level. I want the chance to fight for my staff, for my team."

"Then that is what you will continue to do," he said.

"Why are you doing all this? Saying all this?"

"The baby," he said.

"Of course."

Her eyelids felt heavy now. It was on the tip of her tongue to say that it wasn't really what had brought them together, because he had come back for her before he knew about the child. So she had to wonder what exactly really had. But she was too tired, her brain sluggish, her body even worse.

They had never had a whole conversation without it ending in them yelling at each other or sex. She was almost entirely certain she had never felt comforted by his presence. But she did now. Just being near him. This man who had walked for so long, to gain everything he had.

Everything in her possession had been thrust onto her by her father, whether she wanted it or not. And yes, that came with its own burden. But he had been forced to make the choice to succeed. Yes, her father had paid for his schooling, but if he hadn't taken it seriously, nothing would have come from it.

Had she truly understood the sort of man Apollo was she would have been more terrified of him the first moment he had walked into her company. He was a man who set his sights on things with terrifying single-mindedness. With a kind of intensity unmatched by anyone else she had ever known. If she had realized when he had reappeared in her life that he wanted revenge and he wouldn't hesitate to use her, she would have been much more afraid. Would have behaved much differently with him.

Would you?

Or perhaps, they would be in the same place. In the same moment, in the same bed. Because as much as she wanted to believe she had a bit more common sense, the fact remained that when she fell for him it had nothing to do with common sense.

No, nothing at all. It was so much deeper.

She reached out, resting her palm on his chest, felt his heartbeat beneath her fingertips.

She had dreamed of this. Of simply holding him. Of listening to him breathe. Of sharing the sweet and simple intimacy that came from being near each other. Of touching just to touch.

It felt so good. To simply be with him. Not fighting. Not having sex. Just being.

For the first time in weeks, she felt some peace. She didn't want to sleep. She wanted to prolong this, for as long as possible. If she could choose one moment to stay in, it would be this one.

But sadly, time moved forward. And as it did, she drifted off to sleep.

When they woke in the morning Apollo was still there. Elle had half expected him to have gone off again, to awaken to him standing angrily at the foot of the bed and demanding that she leave. But that didn't happen. Instead, he was wrapped around her, his legs laced through hers. He wasn't wearing any clothes. She was still wearing the dress from last night.

He was awake, and he was looking at her, a strange expression on his face. "Good morning," she said, her voice coming out a little bit like a croak.

"Good morning."

"This is a strange morning after," she said, looking around the room.

"We didn't have sex."

"Yes, that's exactly what I mean."

"How are you feeling?"

"Oh, you mean after…all of that."

He let out a long, heavy breath. "Yes, after I behaved so poorly."

"Wait a second. Are you, Apollo Savas, actually acknowledging the fact that you behaved poorly?"

"Please, don't press the issue, or I will retreat back behind my rock wall of a heart."

"Sometimes I think maybe your secret is that you are not as heartless as you appear." After being convinced of the opposite last night, this was a refreshing feeling.

"We must all maintain our mysteries, must we not?"

"Maybe. I don't think I'm all that mysterious. I think that I reveal myself to you very easily."

"If only that were the case. I should like very much for you to be easier for me to read. And yet, I can't seem to decode you."

"Then you aren't paying attention. The fact that you thought I would crumble at the sight of an engagement ring says that you don't know me very well."

"You never let me."

She let his words take root inside her. They were not untrue. She knew that.

"I know. But after last night you know why. I was afraid. If I had let you touch me at seventeen then we would have been in this position back them. And as poorly as we're handling it now can you imagine how we would have handled it if we were still that young?"

"A nightmare," he said, laughing bitterly. "Yes, it would have been a nightmare."

"I was very afraid of you. Of what you made me feel. I've always been afraid of you." He had the power to devastate her. To tear her apart from the inside out. Apollo possessed so much more dominion over her than she wanted him to know about. Than she would like to admit, even to herself. But the fact of the matter was it had always been so.

"You must not be feeling particularly wonderful, considering you slept in your dress."

She scrubbed at her face. "I suppose I do feel a bit day-old."

"Stay right here." He released his hold on her and got out of bed, crossing the large expanse of the room and heading into the bathroom. She could hear the water start running. Her heart began to beat faster. He was doing something for her. Something thoughtful. Something kind. She wasn't sure how to handle it. So she just lay there, her heart putting a dull, unsteady rhythm in her chest. He returned a moment later, standing in the doorway, naked, and thoroughly unashamed. Of course, he had nothing to be ashamed about. His body was the stuff you could write poetry about.

But she had never been very good with poetry. She would rather lick his body instead. All over. From head to glorious toe, and every muscular inch in between.

Last night, and the no touching, had been… There had been something altering in it. The fact that they had been able to lie together and neither scream at each other nor tear each other's clothes off had been something of a revelation. But that didn't mean she was ready to give up touching him entirely.

Bad idea. You don't even know what kind of relationship the two of you have.

No, she didn't. But if she wanted to move it toward a real relationship, it might be best if she maintained a physical connection with him. At least, that was a handy justification for getting what she wanted. Which was to be back in his strong arms once again. To be brought to the peak of pleasure by his talented hands and mouth.

She shivered.

"If you are cold, *agape*, I have a warm bath for you in here."

For some reason, his tender words made tears prick the back of her eyes. "Okay," she said, standing up on wobbly legs and walking toward him. She paused in front of him and he gripped the hem of her dress, pulling it up over her head. He took over after that, dispensing with her underwear quickly. Then he lifted her up into his arms and set her gently in the deep tub. The water was perfection, as though he had somehow been able to reach down inside of her and figure out exactly what her perfect bath might be like. And then—further proof that he might be reading her mind—he got down into the tub with her, positioning himself behind her, having her press her back up against his broad chest.

"We have not gotten off to the best start. And when I say that, I mean going back more than a decade, we did not have the best start."

She nodded, not saying a word. He ran his hands over her damp skin and she shivered, her nipples tightening and hardened to points in spite of the warmth of the water.

It had nothing to do with temperature, and everything to do with arousal.

"But I think things can be better between us. I'm not... I am not angry at you, Elle. I was, I admit that. I was angry at you for making me want you. For creating a desire within me that I could not satisfy. That was... That was wrong of me."

"Are you apologizing to me?"

"Yes," he said. "I am apologizing to you, because you deserve my apology. I was cruel to you in ways that you did not deserve."

"But my father deserved it," she said, her voice hollow.

"Your father has nothing to do with this. Right now, he has nothing to do with you and me. We can forget that our parents are married. That I feel a sense of betrayal where your father is concerned. We can forget about all of it. Here, right now, we have to do that. Because if we are ever going to bond with one another, if we are ever going to come together and raise this child then there is history we must erase."

"What does that mean? What does it mean for my relationship with my father?"

He reached out and picked up a bottle of shampoo from the edge of the tub, squirting a little bit into his hands. "I don't know." He began to work the lather through her hair, and her heart contracted tightly in on itself. This was what she had wanted, what she had craved all along. This attention. This wonderful, luxurious attention.

He was focused on her now, wholly and completely. In a way that no one else ever had been. It made her want to cry. She would, if she wasn't so afraid of showing that weakness in front of him. Strange how even now, while he was being kind to her, she felt like she had to have her guard up. Like something was still missing.

That made her chest ache. Because she knew it didn't have to be that way. But she didn't know what else they could possibly have, either. They had spent so many years being unkind to each other. Those were the seeds they had planted for their connection, for their relationship. He was right. Maybe all that was left to do was start over. Maybe they had to forget their family. Maybe they had to forget their prior connection. Maybe there was nothing else but this. Maybe that was all there could be. Maybe it was the only way.

She suddenly felt desperate. For him. For his touch, for everything. Suddenly felt like the world would end completely if her mouth wasn't joined to his.

She turned slightly in the water, pressing her hand to his cheek and angling her head, kissing him, slowly, deeply. Trying to make it different from the other times they had kissed. She wanted this to be different. She wanted this to be the new beginning. To be the new start to something that wasn't toxic. To something that wasn't so deadly. Wasn't so dangerous. Maybe it would even be less all-consuming. Maybe it could be something easier. Something freer.

Maybe it would never be a normal relationship, but if he didn't want to use her, and she could trust him…then maybe it could be something.

He was motionless for a moment, as though he was deciding how to react. Then, he gripped her chin with his thumb and forefinger, holding her steady as he deepened the kiss. He kept it slow, too. Tasting her deeply, his pace leisurely as he swept his tongue over hers. As though he really did have all the time in the world. As though they might in fact have forever.

She turned completely, getting on her knees between his size, leaning in, tracing a line on his chest with her tongue, all the way up to his neck where she pressed an openmouthed kiss to his skin. She looked up at him, at the feral light in his eyes, signaling his very tenuous grasp on his control. She affected him. She really did. This had nothing to do with anger, nothing to do with revenge. It was Elle and Apollo, and nothing else in between.

Oh, how she craved that. That connection that was about the two of them and nothing else at all. She moved closer, straddling his lap, bringing the heart of her up against the uncompromising ridge of his arousal. She flexed her hips, rubbing against him, sending a sharp shock of pleasure through her body. He lowered his head, sucking one nipple deeply into his mouth, those two points of pleasure on her body joining up to create a sensation that threatened to overwhelm her completely. She grabbed hold of his face, held him steady, locked her eyes with his as she rose up slightly onto her knees, then lowered herself onto his arousal, taking him deep inside, sighing heavily as he filled her, satisfied her. Completed her.

Apollo Savas had been sex to her from the moment she first met him. From the moment she understood what transpired between a man and a woman in the dark. She had always acknowledged that. Had always known it to be true. But she had missed something. She had missed the most important part of the equation. He wasn't only sex. He was something more. Something deeper. Had it only ever been about sex she would never have been so afraid. But she had known that beneath that desire, beneath that base arousal, was something much darker, much deadlier, much more dangerous.

It had never simply been desire. It had never simply been anger. It was love. It was love then, it was love now.

She loved him. The thought sent a crack of lightning

through her, threatened to split her in two with the pleasure that was building deep inside her. It created a tidal wave of emotion. Completion, satisfaction, despair. She'd never wanted to love him. She had always known that he could never love her back.

No one did. Why would he? Why should Apollo love her for who she was when her own father couldn't do that? When her own mother couldn't seem to manage it? Why should this man ever love her?

And only then could she acknowledge the fact that she had never hated him. Not really. She had loved him.

From the time she was a girl she had loved Apollo Savas. And when he had betrayed her family it had twisted into something new. Because she couldn't understand how the man she cared for so much could do that to her family. When she had thrown herself at him in the hotel room it had been the last gasp of that love, desperate to be heard, desperate to be expressed. And when she had said she hated him it was only because hate was the other side of that coin. So close to love. So perilously close, she understood now. Because it was love twisted, turned into something ugly.

She realized then, as Apollo looked down at her with his dark eyes glittering, that he had loved her father. That he had loved her family, and that was why it had been twisted into this. That was why, in the beginning, he had gone so far to seek his revenge. To use her. To harm her.

Because of how love could get twisted up.

He gripped her hips hard, taking control of their movements, thrusting up inside her, chasing his release. And she was grateful, because she had gone weak. She could no longer take control of this, no longer claim control over this interaction. No, she was now at the mercy of it. At the mercy of him, at her desire for him.

He slid his hand around to cup her bottom, gripping her tightly, his fingertips brushing up against where they joined. That added bit of contact was enough to send her over the edge. Her mind went blank for one glorious moment, pleasure stealing over her, rocking her like a crack of thunder.

And when it was over, when it all settled, when she was still straddling him, their eyes on only each other, pleasure coursing through her like an endless wave, there was only one bright, brilliant thought in her mind.

She loved Apollo Savas. She always had, she had a suspicion she always would. And she knew, with just as much certainty, that he would never love her in return.

CHAPTER TWELVE

ELLE HAD BEEN quiet ever since they had woken up that morning. Or, more specifically, ever since he had given her a bath. He could feel her slipping out of his grasp. Even as they had reached the peak together, he had felt her pull away, and he didn't know what to do about that. He didn't even know what he thought about it. If it mattered. Except that for Elle, he had a feeling emotion mattered. That it was key.

He could take or leave it. He wanted nothing more than a connection based on honesty, on a contract. It was why he wanted marriage. He wanted to have a guarantee.

He didn't trust emotions. Not in the least. Not when his mother had led such a tangled existence based on the men who had professed to love her. Not when the man who had behaved most like a father to him had revealed himself to be the worst sort of liar. How could he even fathom putting stock in emotion under those conditions?

But Elle was most certainly a more emotional creature. If only he could figure out how to read her. If only he could figure out how to connect with her. He had tried talking, he had tried kindness. And then, she had initiated sex. Neither was the magic key. He wasn't sure there was a damn magic key. He found that disconcerting.

He walked around the expensive penthouse, learning the layout of his new home. Regardless of what he had said to her earlier about how much time he would spend with her and the child, he was anticipating trying to accomplish most of his work in the States, from now on. His own father had abandoned him through suicide. His stepfather had proven to be an imposter. He would not have his child living life with that sort of cloud over them. Money only solved certain things. He knew that for a fact. Coming out of poverty and into financial gain had shown him that there were still things that money couldn't buy.

If only Elle's undying affection was one of the things money could buy. It would make things much simpler. Instead, he was left trying to untie one of the great mysteries of the modern age, or any age. Feminine emotion.

As he was brooding on this, his phone buzzed in his pocket. He picked up quickly without bothering to look and see who it was. "Savas."

"What the hell are you doing with my daughter?"

It was the voice of his least favorite devil on the end of the line. "That depends on what you've heard."

"I have seen the headline in this morning's society pages. You proposed to her last night at a restaurant. By all accounts she refused you and stormed out."

"Then I fail to see why you're calling me. Obviously Elle is up to the challenge of handling herself."

"I am calling because I feel that I have the right to know exactly what led you to a place where you thought proposing to my daughter might end in a *yes*. Do not tell me you set yourself up for public humiliation on purpose, Apollo. I would not believe it."

"It's almost as though you know me," he said, his tone easy. "I had thought she might say yes."

"After all I have done for you—"

"Yes, after causing the suicide of my father, after blackmailing my mother into a relationship, how dare I not be more grateful?"

"I hardly orchestrated your father's death, Apollo, as you are well aware. Your father made his own choices. I was certainly ruthless in my desire to push him out of the company, but what happened after that was his choice, not mine."

"In my mind, you pulled the trigger. There is nothing on earth that will convince me otherwise."

"And so you're using Elle to get revenge?"

It was on the tip of his tongue to tell him that's exactly what he was doing. To let the older man know that Apollo had corrupted his only daughter. That he had gotten her with child. That he now held all the power. It all belonged to him. But then, she walked into the room, wearing soft, baggy pants, and a loose-fitting top. Looking soft and vulnerable, not the least bit hard and glamorous. And he realized that he could not say those things. He could not use her that way. She had asked him to see her as a woman, and he did. He had been the one to suggest they put it all behind them, to start new. And so, he would choose to do so. Now, he would choose to do it for her. For them.

"Whether you believe it or not, my association with your daughter has nothing to do with you."

Elle's head snapped in his direction, her eyes rounded.

"I don't believe it," David said.

"That is inconsequential. It is the truth. I intend to win her over, one way or another. I will obtain her hand in marriage."

"Why is it so important to you?"

"Because I want her."

"And you love her?"

The question hit its mark like an arrow striking a target. Nearly made him fall to his knees. He thought about love, what it meant to him. Certainly, his mother loved him, in her way. She was a fragile woman, not unsurprising considering all she had been through. And at times he wondered if she simply had no choice but to detach in order to protect herself from further pain. After the loss of her husband, after being blackmailed into marrying a man she had not chosen.

His father, his biological father, had been so consumed with the acquisition of material things, with his status, that he had preferred death over staying and protecting his wife and child. In that sense, Apollo could not deny David's words. Suicide had been his father's choice. And not anyone else's. Though he knew that there were many complicated factors that played into that. Depression, mental torments that he could not possibly understand.

It did not stop him from retaining a boy's perspective on it in many ways. He felt abandoned. He felt angry. Whether or not his father deserved more sympathy than that was irrelevant. Apollo could only feel what he felt.

And then there was David St. James. He had truly taken him in. Truly accepted him as part of the family.

He had been a father to him. More of a father than his own had ever been. He had raised him, taught him the value of hard work, paid for his education, taught him to take nothing for granted. Though he was a hard man, though he was distant at times, he was a solid, steady figure in Apollo's life. The man he had sought to pattern himself after. Discovering the depths he had sunk to in order to obtain Apollo's mother—as though she were an item to be acquired and not a human being, as though Apollo himself and his father were incidentals—that had shown him just how deep a lie could run.

The fact that his feelings for the older man had not been eradicated overnight—if ever—showed him just what a fickle and dishonest emotion love could be.

Worse still, all of that, every bit of it, was proof that his love twisted things. Changed them in permanent and ugly ways. He was like a lit match brought up against the edge of something fragile. Making the edges curl and darken, altered beyond recognition.

He couldn't do that to her. He wouldn't.

"No," he said. "No, I don't."

"Then you don't deserve her."

And with that, the line went dead. Those words echoed in his head as he turned to look at Elle, who was regarding him with a confused expression. "My father?"

"Yes. He is unamused with me."

"Did he see it in the paper? Was it in the paper?"

"Yes," he said. "Apparently your rejection of me has made headlines."

"Well, I would apologize but it really is your own doing."

"This is true."

"What did he ask you?"

"He asked if you were my revenge," Apollo said. "I told him you're not."

"Yes, I gathered as much. But what was the last question he asked you?"

His stomach tightened, dropped low in his midsection. "He asked me if I loved you."

She closed her eyes, her face going pale. "You said no."

Elle felt as though the ground was dropping out from beneath her feet. She had been shocked, thrilled, when Apollo had not taken the chance to eviscerate her father. When he had not used her as a weapon. Had not trotted out the baby, their affair, in a crass and unnecessary way. That when he had been asked directly if he was using her, he had said no. Even if it was a lie, even in part, he had stopped using her then. He had honored her request.

But then he had been asked if he loved her. And his answer had been no.

She realized then that it was nonnegotiable for her. She needed love. She needed for him to love her. There was nothing more important. Nothing at all.

She had dressed it up in all kinds of fancy descriptions. Had tried to convince herself that all she needed was respect. That they needed to find common ground. That she simply needed someone to want her as she was, and not as a weapon in some kind of scheme. But after their encounter in the bath, after that pleasure radiated through her, after she had felt the intensity of her own feelings for him, she knew that that wasn't the case. She needed more. She needed everything. And anything else would be doing herself a terrible disservice.

She wanted more for herself. More than simply heading up a company because she wanted to prove to her father that she could. More than marriage to a man for his convenience. In truth, as much as she wanted to give her child a home with both parents she knew that if they were living together under sufferance, if she made him miserable because he eventually bored of her, and he made her miserable because her love went unreturned, their child would know. He or she would sense the unhappiness, and for them to even suspect that their presence was the cause of that kind of relationship was something she could not place upon her child.

"I can't marry you," she said.

"What are you talking about? You showed me this morning just how irresistible you find me."

"That's sex, Apollo. We have had that through everything. When I was terrible to you, you still wanted me. When you took over my business, betrayed our family, I still wanted you. Even while I was thinking about stabbing you through the chest with a pen, I wanted you. But that isn't enough for marriage. And right now? It isn't enough for me. I realized something this morning."

"That you are a contrary little thing who makes absolutely no sense?"

"That I love you. I love you with everything I have. It has always been that way. But I cannot, and will not, continue to accept this strange, leftover existence that I have cobbled together with the discarded pieces of yours and my father's manipulative plans. I'm the CEO at Matte because he wanted to play me against you, not because he thought I was suited to the position. I'm pregnant with your baby because you wanted to hurt him, and while I appreciate the fact that you didn't rub it in his face just now…that's our foundation. It's what we are."

"No," he said, his voice rough. "That is not our foundation. There was no calculation when I took you up against the wall in my hotel room, no ulterior motive when I had you in the elevator."

"How can I believe that?"

"Because it is the truth. I decided after I had you the second time that I would use what was between us to get revenge. Only because I was desperate to find some justification for what you did to me. For wanting to indulge in this thing between us."

"And why'd you come back?"

"Because I wasn't finished with you!"

"But that's the thing," she said. "I am not a thing that you can pick up and put down at your convenience. Not a weapon that you can use at your discretion. I am a human being. I have feelings. I love you and I deserve to be loved in return." She shook her head. "If you cannot give me that then I will have to go out and find someone who can."

All of the anger drained from his face, his expression turning to stone. "You are correct. If that is what you want, then that is what you must find."

Her chest felt hollowed out, her heart thundering hard in the empty space. "That's it?"

"We are at an impasse, Elle. I cannot love, and you require it. I do not wish to hold you prisoner. I see no satisfaction in making you miserable. There was a time when I might have, but things have changed."

"Maybe that means you have feelings for me?"

"No," he said, his tone hard, definitive. "I cannot."

She felt like she'd been stabbed clean through, like she would bleed out on the floor, her pain, her love, everything for him to see. She wouldn't be able to hide anymore, as she had done for so many years.

She waited for something to come, for a cutting remark to rescue her, but it wasn't there. There was nothing to hide behind. Nothing but pain and love in equal measure.

And she wanted him to see it. Wanted him to know. She was done hiding. She'd done enough damage pushing him away so that she wouldn't be hurt.

She had hidden everything for years. Her pain, her desire, her love. And she was done. Pride be damned, she wouldn't hide herself anymore.

"Why?" she asked. "Why are you doing this? There is nothing stopping us, nothing stopping this except you, and I can't understand why."

"Everything I love turns to dust, Elle. I would not have you so diminished."

"I've been diminished already!" she shouted. "All of my life. To keep the peace, to try and do what my father wanted, to try and avoid…well, exactly this, with you." She swallowed hard, shaking, all of her repressed emotion, decades of it, pouring out now. "I'm done with that. I'm making demands now."

He stared at her for a moment, his dark eyes hollow. "I can't meet them."

"You won't."

"It amounts to the same thing."

And then he turned away from her, and walked out of the penthouse, closing the door softly behind him. She had a feeling that he would not be back.

She didn't want half a life, half a love. She didn't want a future with a man who wouldn't give her what she'd just realized she so desperately wanted.

So, she let him go. And she did her very best not to cry.

Elle approached her father's office with great trepidation. She was going to let him know that she was officially resigning from Matte. She was also going to tell him about the baby, and the fact that she would not be marrying Apollo. She took a deep breath, trying to ease the knot in her chest. Then, she raised her hand and knocked on the door.

"Come in."

She turned the knob and opened the door, stepping inside quickly. "Hello, Father," she said.

"Elle," he said, gesturing at the chair across from his desk, as though she were a business appointment he was keeping. "Have a seat."

She did. "I imagine you're wondering why I wanted to speak with you."

"Not particularly. I assume it has something to do with Apollo."

"Well," she said, "you aren't wrong."

"Have you decided to marry him?"

"On the contrary, I have decided that I cannot continue my association with him."

"I fail to understand why there was an association with him in the first place. He turned against me."

"Yes," she said.

"He fired you. Then, you got your job back, did you not?"

Her face got hot. "I know what you're implying, but it didn't happen that way. Anyway, I'm stepping down at Matte. I'm going to go back to school. I'm going to figure out what *I* want to do. Quite apart from your expectations, or his. I have been caught in the cross fire for too long. I just can't do it anymore. I have to find out what I am beyond this…desperate people pleaser. I have to find out if I can be more than your shield to block you from Apollo's wrath."

"Is that what you think?"

"Why would I think anything else?" she asked.

"And yet, you have never said anything."

"Yes, well, I wanted to keep the peace. I wanted to do the right thing, be the daughter you needed. But I'm over that now. I need to be the person I'm happy with, not the person you're happy with."

"Did I force you into the position at Matte?" he asked, his tone hard.

"You can't deny that you used me to try and stand between Apollo and the destruction of the company. It had nothing to do with me. You never intended to give any of it to me. You always wanted a son, and until he went rogue, Apollo was that son for you. I was never supposed to be the one in that position. You used me."

He lifted his shoulder, the lines on his face looking suddenly more pronounced. "Yes, I did use you. But how else could I defend my legacy? I knew you could do it, Elle. I had no concerns about that. I knew Apollo had... feelings for you. Feelings of some kind, and I thought that perhaps he would modify his actions if you were in the line of fire."

"And so you used me as a target."

"I knew you were strong enough. You might think it's because I don't respect or value you, but it is to the contrary. You're strong. I would not have shielded a son from such a thing, and I did not shield you."

"Am I supposed to be grateful?"

"I could see no other way," he said, his tone uncompromising.

"Is that why you ousted Apollo's father from your company all those years ago? Because you could think of no other way to be with Mariam?"

"Yes," he said, simply. Calmly. "It was the only way I could think of to win Mariam. And so I did what I could. But she stood by him. Had his child. And for all my sins, I never held that against Apollo. That he was the product of a union I despised."

"You don't get a medal for that, Dad," she said. "Not when you were so...horrible."

"I was horrible," he said, his tone hard, his eyes ice blue. "And I would do the same thing again. Make the same choices. I didn't intend for his father to kill himself, Elle. I am not a mind reader. I could not predict the outcome. I did, however, think that it was likely Mariam would leave him when he had nothing and I had everything. I was wrong."

"She loved him."

Her father nodded slowly. "Yes, she did. But she has learned to love me, I think."

"You think?"

"Yes. I do."

"Have you ever asked her?"

Her father's face went blank. "No. I haven't. But then, I'm not certain it matters. Not now."

Elle's heart crumpled. "I think it always matters. It doesn't matter when love comes, as long as you know it's there. Does she know you love her?"

"I destroyed her world to move her into mine. I cleared my world to make room for her. If that is not love then I do not know what is."

He didn't. Elle could see that. He truly and honestly knew nothing of love being two-sided. Of giving rather than taking.

He was an unbending man. Unyielding. All arrogance and a stiff neck. Unable to truly turn and look at anyone else.

"I think perhaps love isn't destroying worlds. Or moving people around like chess pieces," she said, her voice shaking. "I think maybe it's giving more than you take. Showing it, even when someone may never show it back. Being kind even when the other person is cruel. I think love isn't always balance, but if both are willing to give more than they take…it might be a beautiful, rare sort of treasure."

"I don't know about any of that, Elle," he said. "I do know that I have you, and I still have Mariam. In that I find some success, I think."

"Do you love *me*?" She might as well ask. She had already been rejected by Apollo, so there was really no reason to protect herself at this point. She had been flayed already. She might as well allow some salt to be rubbed into the wounds.

Her father only looked at her for a moment, his gaze unreadable. "Did you not know?" he asked.

"How would I?" she answered.

"I am your father, Elle."

"That doesn't make any guarantees."

"I am a man who has built my life on a foundation made of ruthless decisions. I did not become rich by following the rules. I did not obtain my wife by playing fair. I hurt Hector. I hurt your mother. I have never known quite how to handle the people in my life. But for all of that, I do love you."

It was still indirect. Still impersonal. But she felt it was very likely the best he could do.

She also saw, for a moment, herself in the old man's gaze. Waiting to be given what she wanted, all of her conditions met. No, she wasn't being unreasonable wanting love from Apollo. But she had to consider where he had come from. What he knew.

Apollo had been broken. Battered by life. People he had trusted had abandoned him. Betrayed him. He needed someone to show him something different. Needed someone to stand by him, no matter what. To take what he could give now, and trust there would be more in the future.

She would do that for him. For her. Just because he couldn't meet her here now didn't mean he never would.

She loved him. She would love him enough for them both.

"I love you," she said, because she thought she might as well practice saying it again, to another man who had difficulty hearing it, saying it. To continually practice this new start, where she didn't hide. Where she didn't try to make herself palatable. "In spite of everything."

"I haven't changed," he said. "I am the man you have always known. You just know a bit more of the story."

"Yes, well, the whole story is important. It doesn't mean I think you made good choices."

"I never asked anyone to sign off on my choices. I made my bed, and it has the woman I love in it. How can I have regrets?"

"Well," Elle said, "I'm going to go after the man I love now. Because he's pigheaded and stubborn and scared. And I'm okay with that. As long as I can be with him. Oh. I'm having his baby, also. That might be relevant, too."

That seemed to successfully shock her father. His gray eyebrows shot upward, his mouth dropping slightly open. "You didn't see fit to mention that sooner?"

"We got philosophical. I imagine this will be the only time. But… Apollo is the father of my child. You're married to his mother, you're both the grandparents of the baby." She frowned. "It's very complicated. And you're going to have to make some kind of peace with him."

"It may not be possible. As you said, the whole story changes things. And for him, I think it transformed me into a villain. One I cannot deny I have been in years past. I tried to make it up to him by giving him all I could. But as you have pointed out to me, my demonstrations are not always clear."

"You've both caused a lot of damage. Fighting, seeking vengeance, going after what you want with no care for others…it just has to stop. If it can't be anything more than a cease-fire then let it be that. But it has to stop. I can't be in the middle. I won't allow my child to be in the middle."

"And if you have to choose between me or him?"

"It would be him," she said, not even hesitating. "Assuming he felt the same way."

Her father nodded slowly, his lips curving into a smile. "Maybe you even understand my more ruthless decisions."

"Where Apollo is concerned I have no doubt I could be ruthless. Where my child is concerned... I would shed blood."

"I fear I was too selfish to make that choice," her father said. "And that I did not have the pride that you do."

"What do you mean?"

"I did not care if Mariam felt as strongly as I did. I only cared that I had her."

"Well, I lived too much of my life that way and I won't do it now."

Her father regarded her with...pride. For the first time she could honestly say she felt it. A strange moment because she didn't feel particularly triumphant. She only felt...broken. Sad. Pride was a poor salve for a broken heart.

"I need to be loved," she repeated, for herself as much as anyone. "And I need to be assured that my son or daughter will not be used as a pawn. Not for Apollo to hurt you, not for him to hurt me. I think you will find my love for my child the most ruthless of all."

"Then go," her father said. "Tell him. Go and be ruthless for love."

CHAPTER THIRTEEN

APOLLO WAS NO stranger to despair. While he had not been terribly conscious of the loss of wealth as a boy, the loss of his comfortable bedroom, his bed, had certainly been things he'd felt deeply. After that, the loss of his father. Then, the loss of the man he had come to think of as a father.

But he had never once experienced loss like this. A loss that was, in many ways, his own doing. There had been no control in his hands when they had lost their livelihood and their money, there had been no control when he had discovered the true nature of David St. James. But here… With Elle, he'd held the power. The power to tell her what she wanted to hear, to find a way to be the man she needed. And he had turned away.

"Coward," he said aloud to the empty space in his office. He paced in front of the window, looking out over the city below. He had gone back to Greece, because he had not known what else to do. Had not known where else to go. He felt helpless, and it had been a long time since he had felt helpless. He despised the feeling. More than anything. It was one of the many reasons he had turned so sharply, so hard, on David St. James.

Because when the revelation had struck him it'd been with the force of a killing blow. It had chopped his legs out from beneath him, left him gasping, shocked. He was not a man who took kindly to such a thing.

Wounded pride, Apollo? That is a very small reason to seek revenge. A very small reason to hold on to anger.

But what his father had been through… What his mother had been through…

He knew he should speak to his mother. But the simple fact was he was afraid to hear what she had to say. He had been from the moment three years ago when the revelations about David had become clear. He didn't want to hear what she had to say. For fear that she loved him. For fear that she was happy. For fear that she supported the decisions her new husband had made because it had resulted in the two of them being together.

But he knew now that he needed to ask her. He knew that he needed to find out why she had stayed.

He picked up the phone, dialing her number, dimly aware that it was very early in the morning in New York. "Hello?"

His mother's faintly accented voice came over the line. "Hello, Mother," he said.

They had barely spoken over the course of the past three years, and when they had, it had been very carefully. Because she had known that he was actively pursuing vengeance against her husband, and while she had kept her feelings to herself, he could always sense the fact that she didn't approve. Certainly, she didn't necessarily support him, as she had not demanded he take her with him, back to Greece. He was more than capable of supporting his mother now. She did not have to stay with David St. James. And yet, she did.

"Why?" he asked, with no preamble at all. He had not meant to launch straight into it like this, but he had been unable to help himself.

"Why what, Apollo?"

"Why do you stay with him? I don't understand. The truth about David St. James was hidden from me for all of my life. But it was not hidden from you. You knew exactly what manner of man he was. And yet, you remain with him. You could leave. I could take care of you until the end of time, and you would never want for anything."

There was silence on the other end. "Yes," she said softly. "I do know what manner of man he is. I have known David St. James since long before you were born. I knew him from the beginning. I met him when I met your father. I don't know why, but I have a tendency to love hard men. Though perhaps that is a good thing for you, I think."

Apollo chuckled. "I suppose it is."

"I did love your father. And I stayed with him even when we lost everything. Even when David ousted him from the company."

"Which David did to hurt him."

Mariam continued as if he hadn't spoken. "I do believe that at the time, your father already had a bit of an issue with drugs. Though they had not yet consumed him as they did later. He was working long hours, and he needed something to help him keep up. It was competitive. He didn't want to sleep. I rarely saw him. And I would be… I would be lying if I said we were perfectly happy. But I was never unfaithful to him. I knew that David had feelings for me. But I had chosen Hector. And so I remained with him. I remained with him until the end, when everything became so twisted, and so hard. By the time he died he was not the man I had first known."

"Because of David St. James."

"Yes, and no. Business is harsh and uncompromising.

It has always been so. Many men lose all their earthly possessions and come out the other side."

Apollo was having trouble processing what she was saying. "You're saying you harbor no anger against him over what he put us through?"

"I am sorry to tell you that I put much more of the blame at your father's door than I do at David's. Yes, he ousted him from the company, but had your father taken better care of our assets we would not have been destitute. Had he not completely given up, we could have come back from it. I had no skills. I was nothing more than a village girl who knew how to do little more than sew. And while that could support us in a very modest fashion it was never going to pull us out of poverty. When David contacted me... I am not proud of what happened after that, because for all of my sins, for all of my divided loyalty, the one thing that I truly regret was any part I might have played in the destruction of his marriage."

Apollo swallowed hard. It was difficult to hear such things. To take on the knowledge of his own mother's part in all of this. "Yes, well, you had a child to take care of."

"He did not force me into an affair," she said, her voice soft. "That was my choice. When he discovered how we were living he asked us to come, he offered to buy me a house, and to care for you. A relationship was not part of that. But I... I was lonely. And I recognized what I might have had. I regretted not choosing him, I think. Because he seemed stronger. That was my mistake, Apollo. His as well, but do not blame it all on him."

"Well, his ex-wife didn't care enough about her own child to stick around after she was deposed."

His mother sighed. "No, she did not. Again, it does not excuse my actions. But I do love Elle, almost as if she were my own."

"She knows that."

"I hope so. There was a time when I thought you knew that David loved you as a son, as well."

"I did believe that," Apollo said. "But when I found out the level he had stooped to to bring you to him, to get revenge because of his love being spurned, I could not simply stay in his home, stay as his son."

"It is done," she said. "It may have been wrong, but it is done."

"I loved him," Apollo said. "What kind of a son does that make me? I cannot love without it becoming something horribly twisted. You had to care for me, and that forced your hand. I loved my father, but it wasn't enough to make him stay… David…"

"None of this, none of the tangled web, is your fault. You should not place more consequences onto yourself. We were badly behaved adults, who got our children caught in the cross fire of terrible games. Neither of you deserved it. I wish very much your father had not killed himself. But he was not simply a victim, either. Your love didn't bring out the worst in us, Apollo. Your love was the best of us."

He swallowed hard, his throat suddenly tight. "None of it is simple," he said. "None of it. So I do not understand how I am supposed to sort through it all."

"I can't answer that question for you. I do know that it doesn't benefit anyone to hold on to anger. To hold on to the past. It twists you. That's what it did to Hector. It broke him completely. All of the anger that he felt toward David… I would hate for you to suffer the same fate."

"And so…you would simply forgive?"

"I cannot make the decision for you, Apollo. I should like, for the sake of our family, for you to find it in you to forgive. But it is your journey. Perhaps I was wrong to forgive. I do not know. I only know that I had choices before me and I took the one that made me happiest."

"We can never be a family as we were," he said, "in part because while you may love Elle as a daughter, I do not love her as a sister."

That declaration was met with silence. "I know," she said finally. "I have always known."

Those words nearly broke him. Shattered him entirely. She had always known, because his feelings had always been there. Every action, every cruelty, all the anger that had passed between them over the years had been there simply to disguise that fact.

From himself.

He had never managed to hide it from his mother.

"I do not know how I can be with her."

"We can only carry so much, Apollo. I have lived an imperfect life, and if I have learned anything it's that, at some point, we must put some of our burdens down so we can pick up things we would more gladly carry. These are decisions we make. We cannot wait for the pain to go away. We cannot simply expect the anger to fade, or the grief to stop biting. We must make choices. They are the hardest choices to make. But if you want to move on, then you must begin on your own."

"That simple?"

"No," she said. "That difficult."

"I know what I want," he said. "I just don't know if I can have it."

"You're angry at David, and that is understandable. You want revenge, and that I understand, as well. But I think you can see the way that revenge twists your own life. If you deny your love for Elle simply because you want to punish David St. James, then it isn't truly him you're hurting. Then the only person whose life you've destroyed is your own."

"You stayed because you love him?"

"God help me, but I do," she said. "Though I should not. Though he perhaps doesn't deserve it. There are many days when I don't deserve it, either. Though, in his way, I believe he loves me."

He could not say he envied his mother her relationship, her marriage. And yet, he could see that they had love for each other, even if it wasn't the sort he recognized. And what sort did he recognize? That, he supposed, was the question. Did he recognize it at all?

He had. With Elle, he had recognized it for the first time. And he had run, because it had been too much. Because, as his mother said, he was carrying too much anger to accept the love that she was asking for, that she was offering.

"I suppose I have a decision to make," he said.

But it was already made. There was no question. He loved Elle. And that meant whatever the risk, whether he was able to trust himself or not, whether he truly believed he knew how to love and how to accept love, he wanted to give her what he could. What he had. He wanted to give her everything. "I will have to get her back," he said finally.

"I hope that you do," his mother said. "I hope it isn't too late."

He hung up the phone and turned back to the sprawling city before him. He would need to get the first plane out. Or perhaps he should call her. But he didn't know if apologies such as this one should be done over the phone. He had hurt her, had said terrible things. Hurtful things. He did not deserve to ask forgiveness. But dammit, if David St. James could earn the love of the woman he wanted after all he had done, why couldn't Apollo?

He turned back to the door of his office just as it opened. In strode Elle, looking red-faced, pursued by his assistant Alethea.

"I'm sorry, Mr. Savas," Alethea said. "She insisted that she had to see you."

"I do," Elle said, looking stubborn. He adored that expression. That uncompromising, demanding expression. Elle was not an easy woman. She never would be. But he didn't want easy. He wanted her. Always. Forever.

"It's okay, Alethea. I would like to see her."

Alethea shook her head. "Best you work out your problems, Mr. Savas. You have been mercurial of late, and I find it irritating," she said, turning on her heel and storming out of his office.

"That is not the sort of assistant I expected you to have," Elle said.

"Yes, well. At this point she knows where all the bodies are buried and I can't get rid of her. Sadly, she knows that."

"I had to see you," she said.

"Why is that, *agape*?"

"Because I have something to tell you."

Suddenly, his stomach plummeted. "It isn't about the baby, is it?"

"The baby is fine," she said.

"I'm relieved to hear it."

"It isn't about that. I mean, it is. But nothing is wrong."

"Well, before you launch into your speech, I must tell you, I was on my way back to see you."

"You were?"

"Yes," he said, "I was. There is something I need to tell you to. I spoke to my mother this morning."

"That's funny. I spoke to my father about… Well, I guess it must be fifteen hours ago or so. Since I am here now."

"I see. I needed to understand why she stayed with him. I needed to understand how she had managed to let go of everything that had gone on in the past. She helped clarify some things. For one, your father did not force her into a relationship. That is important for me to know. She admits they handled things poorly. But he did not force her."

Elle looked visibly relieved by the revelation. "I'm glad to hear that. That isn't something my father would willingly admit. He's such a stubborn old man. I think talking about his feelings is the thing he dislikes most in the world. But he did admit to me… He does love your mother. For all of his sins, he does."

"She loves him," Apollo said. "Somehow, she was able to let go of everything that had happened all those years ago. Somehow she fell in love with him."

"We don't have half of that baggage standing between us, and here we are unable to sort out our differences."

"There's a simple enough reason for that," he said. "I was a coward."

"You're not a coward, Apollo."

"Yes, I am. I was unable to admit my feelings for you nine years ago, and I found myself unable to admit them last week. Even to myself. But I love you, Elle. I always have."

Elle could only stand there, shocked, staring into Apollo's intense, dark gaze. He said that he loved her. He said that he always had, that he had simply been unable to admit it. That was not what she'd been expecting. She had flown to Athens, stormed into his office expecting a fight. Expecting to engage him in a knock-down, drag-out battle as she told him there would be no revenge. That they would be putting everything aside for love. Not theirs, but the love of their child. And yet, here he was…saying he loved her.

"I had a speech prepared," she said, her voice sounding hollow.

"Did you?" he asked, his eyebrows arched.

"Yes," she said. "I was… I was going to make sure you knew that our child was everything. That I would never use a child to get revenge on you, nor would I allow you to use our child to hurt me. And that under no circumstances would I allow our son or daughter to be caught in the crosshairs of your issues with my father."

"There is no danger of that."

"I… I see that. Because you… But I…" She suddenly felt a sharp pain in her chest. "I'm sorry."

"For?"

"You do love me. I knew you did. I really did. But I didn't trust it."

"Why should you take less than you deserve, Elle? Why should you take less than you deserve simply waiting around for me?"

"Because love isn't about what you deserve."

"Thankfully for me," he said.

"For all of us. We're about to have a child, and we're evidence of the fact that…parents make mistakes with their children. Even children they love."

"That is true."

"Love is…bigger than keeping score. It costs more than we could ever hope to earn. At least, it's supposed to. I need you to know, here and now, that I love you without reservations. That I believe you *do* love me. I understand what you've been through. I understand that you were used badly." She took a deep breath. "Your mother may have been able to easily forgive my father, or at least forgave him eventually, but she knew everything from the beginning. Your trust was betrayed in a way that hers wasn't."

Apollo shook his head. "The guilt that I felt over considering David a father figure to me was what truly enraged me."

"I recognized that. That what you felt was badly-used love. I did. Because I had experienced it with you. But even recognizing that, I was unbending."

"I want you to be unbending, my sweet, beautiful Elle," he said.

Her chest swelled, her heart feeling large and tender. "You do?"

"Yes. Because I want everything you are. Everything you will be. Because I want the woman you are, not simply the woman that makes my life easiest. I do not want you simply because you are the mother of my child. I do not want you because you are biddable, because you fit easily into the life I have created. I will rearrange it all for you," he said. "Somehow, I think I knew I would have to do that. And it frightened me. Again, you must understand that I am a coward."

She shook her head. "No," she said, the word coming out broken. "You are the bravest man I have ever known. Because you would open yourself up to love again even when your love had been so abused before."

"I hardly deserve a medal for accepting a gift so beautiful as your love," he said.

"Yours is beautiful too, you know."

His chest pitched sharply, his dark eyes glittering. "I was so convinced my love killed things. That it was toxic. How could I trust something that always turned into something so painful? So I denied it. What I felt for you. It was always there. I wrapped it up in anger, I wrapped it up in hate, because I wasn't ready to reach out and take it."

"I did the same," she said, her throat tight. "I told myself that I hated you, that I couldn't stand the sight of you, because in truth you were the most glorious, wonderful sight I had ever beheld. And I called my feelings something else, anything else, rather than accepting the fact that I might never have you. I pretended I didn't care rather than opening myself up and risking being humiliated. Rather than risking admitting what I might lose and how badly it might hurt. I hid my feelings, even from myself. See, I am more like my father than it seems on the surface."

"But you're here. You're here telling me now."

"If we can't learn from the mistakes of the people who came before us, then I fail to see the point of any of it."

"Yes." He shook his head. "You are very right about that. When I look at the mistakes my mother made, your father made, that my father made, in their pursuit of love, of money and success, I see nothing but a sad, tangled web. And in the end, I suppose what our parents have found is love, as best as they can have it."

"Yes," Elle said. "I think that's true."

"But I want more than that. I want deeper. None of the anger, none of the pride, none of those wasted years."

Elle laughed softly. "I suppose we already have a few wasted years."

"But no more. It is you for me, Elle. Only you. I want to make a life with you. With you and our child. I will get down on my knees and beg if I must, because my pride is nothing more than dirt if it keeps me from you."

"As enjoyable as I might find that, I don't need you to

beg. I love you already. I don't need you to do anything to gain that acceptance."

He crossed the space between them and her heart lurched, a thrill racing through her as he took her into his arms. This would never fade. It would never get old. Things had never been hotter, more intense between them because of the anger. The anger had simply covered the true intensity. It was only bigger now. Brighter, deeper. Now that she knew the racing of her heart, the intense surge of adrenaline that raced through her every time she saw him was not hate, but love after all.

"I love you," he said. "And I will lay down all of my anger, my need for revenge, my distrust and anything else that might hinder my ability to give you all that you deserve. Because if I am to be full, then I would have myself be full of nothing but my love for you."

"I was so hurt, Apollo, because I was afraid that you wanted me only for revenge. To hurt other people. And I never felt like my father loved me for *me*. I never felt like anyone in my life loved me simply because of who I am. But here you are, asking me to be difficult, asking me to be stubborn, asking for me to be myself. And I... I can hardly believe it."

"Then I will spend my every day, from this moment until the end, showing you just how much I love you, for all of the good, all of the bad and everything in between. I will do my very best to ensure that you never doubt that you are the one I love. You are the one I want. Whether you're a CEO, a lawyer, a cupcake maker, a police officer."

"I have never given any indication that I want to be a baker or a police officer."

"But you could be. You could be anything you wanted

to be, and you would still be Elle. And I would still love you."

"There is a remarkable amount of freedom in that," she said, her chest swelling with emotion. "I don't think you can possibly know what that means to me."

He pulled her closer, kissing her lips. "Then show me, Elle. Show me."

EPILOGUE

SHE DID. AND she spent every day after that showing him, demonstrating her love for him. And he did the same for her.

It was one of Apollo's proudest moments when Elle graduated at the top of her law class. One of his happiest moments, sitting there, cheering her on as she walked onstage while he held their daughter in his lap, with their new baby in the crook of his other arm. He was so proud of what she had achieved, of what she had decided to go after. Of how she had decided to use her uncompromising nature and sharp tongue.

She was, in his opinion, the best lawyer in New York City, eternally advocating for women in difficult circumstances, and for children who had had injustice done against them.

If someone would have told him when he had first married Elle that he would only grow to love her more over the next decade, he would have told them they were insane. After all, how could anyone love more than he had on the day of his wedding? But he discovered just how deep, just how wide, love could grow. Each year, each child, each achievement and each failure added a texture and a richness to what he felt for her that stretched far beyond what he could have ever imagined.

On the night of their tenth anniversary, Elle came home from work, exhausted, frowning, possibly because the case she was working on was so intense.

He took her into his arms, not saying a word. And she wrapped her arms around him, leaning on his strength.

"I'm glad you made it," he said.

"Of course. This is the only place I want to be tonight." She looked up at him and smiled. "Are the kids taken care of?"

"I believe Alethea is reading them a bedtime story. But she is not a nanny, Elle. She made sure to tell me that as she went to perform the task. This was after hovering around them at dinner trying to get them to eat their vegetables."

Elle laughed. "Of course."

"And tomorrow David and my mother will be by to take the children for the weekend. They wish to contribute to our alone time."

"Very nice of them."

"Indeed." He brushed his thumb over her cheek. "Are you ready to go out tonight?" He examined the faint shadows under her eyes. "Or would you rather stay in?"

"I would love to go out. Because I want to go show off my wonderful husband."

"You cannot possibly wish to do that more than I want to show off my wonderful wife."

"We'll have to argue about it later." She let out a sigh, a long, contented sound. "We've been together for more than ten years. It's amazing how different this last decade has been from the one before it."

"The one where we both wanted each other, but wouldn't allow ourselves to have each other?"

"Yes. I have no clue what we were so afraid of. What we were waiting for."

"The more I think about it, the more I believe we were waiting for the right time. Where we could be brave enough, give enough, love each other in the right way. Had I kissed you for the first time when I was twenty years old, I would have only messed it up later. I would not have been a man who could have given you the support you needed through all of this."

She nodded slowly. "I don't think I would have been a woman who could have gone for her dreams."

"Do you want to know a secret, Elle?"

She nodded. "Of course."

"I like everything that we have. I treasure it. I enjoy my job. I am proud of yours. But you're my dream."

Elle smiled, all of her exhaustion fading, tears filling her eyes. "Oh, Apollo. You're my dream, too."

She drew up on her toes and kissed him, and it was like the first time. Every time with her was like the first time.

"Perhaps we won't make it out after all," he said.

She smiled, her expression a little bit wicked. "Yes, perhaps it would be best if we stayed in."

* * * * *

A DIAMOND DEAL WITH THE GREEK

MAYA BLAKE

To Carly, my editor, for being the instrument that gives my words true meaning. Thank you!

CHAPTER ONE

ARABELLA 'REBEL' DANIELS stood at the back of one of the many lifts that served the giant glass and steel masterpiece that was the Angel Building, and waited for the group of four to board. Swallowing down the lingering taste of the second double-shot macchiato she'd given in to this morning, she took a deep breath to calm herself. Although she'd needed the boost very badly at the time, the effect on her nerves now prompted a bout of regret.

Caffeine and panic did not mix well, and, after two long weeks of subsisting on both, she was more than ready to ditch them.

Her heart pounded with trepidation, but, thankfully, she couldn't hear it above the loud music playing in her ears.

Grappling with what would greet her once the lift journey ended was consuming enough, although there was also the real and present albatross of having lost her biggest sponsor three weeks ago and the resulting media frenzy, to deal with. Of course, far from the wild speculation that she was using booze and drugs to cope with her problems, the media would've been shocked and sorely disappointed to know the strongest substance she'd touched was coffee.

She stared unseeing before her, the words of the letter that had been burning a hole in her bag for the last two weeks emblazoned in her mind.

Arabella,
First of all, happy twenty-fifth birthday for Wednesday. If you're surprised at this out-of-the-blue communication, don't be. You're still my daughter and I have a duty of care to you. There's no judgement on

my part for the way you've chosen to live your life.
Nor are there any strings attached to the enclosed
funds. You need it, so put pride aside and use it. It's
what your mother would've wanted.
Your father.

Steeling her heart against the lance of hurt at the stark words, Rebel shifted her mind to the banker's receipt that had accompanied the letter.

The five hundred thousand pounds deposited into her bank account was a little less than what her sponsors would've donated had she still been on their books, but it was enough to get her to the Verbier Ski Championships.

This time she couldn't stop her insides from twisting with guilt and a touch of shame.

She should've tried harder to return the money.

Too much had been said between her father and her that couldn't be unsaid. Even after all these years, the pain and guilt were too vivid to be dismissed. And nothing in her father's letter had given her cause to think his views weren't as definitive as they'd been the last time she'd seen him.

He still laid the death of his wife, her mother, firmly at Rebel's feet.

Suppressing her pain, she tried to ignore the pointed looks from the lift's occupants. At any other time she would've turned the music down, but today was different. Today, she would be seeing her father again for the first time in five years. She needed a full suit of armour in place but the music was all she had.

When another suited businessman sent her a scathing look, she mustered a smile. His eyes widened a touch, his ire rapidly morphing to something else. Rebel looked away before her attempt to excuse her music's loudness turned into anything else. Keeping her eyes on the digital counter, she exhaled as the lift reached the fortieth floor. According to what she'd been able to glean from their very brief, very stilted conversations over the last week, her accountant father worked for Angel International Group as their CFO. He hadn't volunteered any more information when she'd asked. In fact, any further attempt to pave a reconnecting road with her father had been firmly blocked. Just as he'd firmly blocked her initial attempts to give back the money he'd given her.

The deeply wounding knowledge that her father was only doing his duty to the wife he'd loved and lost so cruelly should've driven Rebel's actions, not her manager's insistence that the money was the answer to all their prayers.

But it was her father's insistence that the money was hers no matter what that had led her to finally confessing the money's existence to Contessa Stanley. Her manager had had no qualms about Rebel using the funds. Especially since Rebel had recently lost yet another big sponsor due to the continued domino effect created by the sensational reports splashed all over the media. Even her retreat from the spotlight had been looked upon negatively, with wild speculation as to whether she was finally in rehab or nursing a broken heart.

With her chances of finding new sponsorship dwindling by the day, and the championship deadlines racing ever closer, Rebel had finally given in to Contessa's arguments.

Which left her not just in a state of confusion about why her father was now avoiding her after reaching out, at last, with his letter, but also having serious qualms about using money she hadn't wanted to touch in the first place.

'Excuse me?'

Rebel started as the man closest to her touched her arm. Plucking out one earbud, she raised an eyebrow. 'Yes?'

'Did you not want this floor?' he enquired, interest flaring in his eyes as he held the lift doors open and avidly conducted a study of her body.

Groaning inwardly, Rebel wished she hadn't let impulse drive her here until after she'd gone back home to change from her yoga pants and vest top after her morning training session. Muttering her thanks, she slid through the throng.

Hitching her yoga mat and gym bag firmly onto her shoulder, she turned the music volume down as she stepped out of the lift. Plush grey carpet, broken only by a set of massive glass doors, stretched as far as the eye could see, with complementing grey walls interspersed with wild bursts of colour in the form of huge flower arrangements. On the walls along a wide hallway, high-definition images of some of the world's most gifted athletes played on recessed screens.

The whole placed smelled and looked hallowed and expensive.

Rebel frowned, wondering whether she'd walked into the wrong place.

For as long as she'd been aware her father had worked as an accountant for a stationery company, not a slick outfit whose employees flitted past in expensive suits and wore futuristic-looking earpieces. Unable to accept that the father who'd vociferously voiced his hatred of her chosen sporting career would have anything to do with a place like this, Rebel moved towards the set of glass doors and pushed.

Nothing happened. Pushing firmer, she huffed when the door refused to budge.

'Uh, you need one of these to enter,' a voice said from behind her. 'Or a visitor's pass and an escort from downstairs.'

Turning, Rebel saw the man from the lift. His smile stretched wider as he waved a matte black card. The unwillingness to prolong the stomach-churning meeting with her father dragged another smile from her reluctant cheeks. 'Damn, I guess I was a little too impatient to get up here. I'm here to see Nathan Daniels. You couldn't help me out and let me in, could you? I'm Rebel, his daughter. We had an appointment and I'm running late…'

She stopped babbling and gritted her teeth as he took his time looking her up and down again. Fingering the sleeves of the sweater tied around her waist, Rebel waited for his gaze to meet hers again. 'Of course. Anything for Nate's daughter. Awesome name, by the way.'

Pinning the smile on her face, she waited for him to pass the card over the reader and murmured, 'Thank you,' as he held the door open for her.

'My pleasure. I'm Stan. Come with me, I'll show you to Nate's office. I haven't seen him today…' he frowned '…or this week, come to think of it. But I'm sure he's around somewhere.'

Rebel couldn't stop her heart from sinking further at Stan's news. Although now she was here, she realised she'd only *assumed* her father would be at work today. The hurt she'd tried for so long to keep at bay threatened to over-take the small amount of optimism she'd secretly harboured these past two weeks.

Pushing it back, she followed Stan along a series of hall-ways until they reached the first of two brushed-metal doors in a long, quieter corridor. 'Here we are.'

Stan knocked and entered. The outer office was empty, as was the inner office once Rebel followed him in. Frown deepening, he turned to her. 'Looks like he's not here, and neither is his PA…'

Sensing what was coming, she pre-empted him. 'I'm happy to wait. I'm sure he won't be long. If he's not back soon, I'll give him a call.'

Stan looked uncertain for a moment, then he nodded. 'Sure.' He held out his hand. 'I'd love to take you out for a drink some time, Rebel.'

Rebel barely stopped herself from grimacing. 'Thanks, but I can't. My social calendar is booked up for the fore-seeable future.' She had no intention of dating anyone any time soon, either casually or otherwise. At this time of year, she had her hands full dealing with her harrowing guilt and grief.

The press liked to speculate why Rebel Daniels loved to

party hard in the weeks leading up to Valentine's Day. She'd deliberately tried to keep that façade of wild child in place. The last thing she wanted was for anyone to dig beneath the surface, find out the truth about what had happened in Chamonix eight years ago. Besides protecting her beloved mother's memory, the guilt she had to live with was monumental enough without having it exposed to prying eyes.

Now that her dreaded birthday was out of the way, her sole focus was the upcoming championship.

Smiling to take the sting out of the refusal, she breathed a sigh of relief when Stan gave a regretful shrug and left.

Rebel slowly turned and stared around the glass-walled office that belonged to her father. Exhaling, she allowed herself to scrutinise the expensive polished-leather chair and mahogany desk, upon which items had been laid out in the meticulous way her father employed. Insides shaking, she approached his desk, her eyes on the single personal item that stood to the right side of it.

The picture, set in a childish pink and green frame, was exactly as she remembered it when she'd given it to her father on his birthday twelve years ago. At thirteen years old, laughing as she rode a tandem bike with her mother in the picture, Rebel had had no idea her family was about to be ripped apart a few short years later. Or that the decimating of her family would be her fault.

She'd had no cares in the world, secure in the love from a father who'd adored his wife and daughter, and a mother who had encouraged Rebel to pursue her dreams, regardless of any obstacles that stood in her way.

It was that relentless pursuit of her dream that had shattered her family. She knew that. And yet, she'd never been able to walk away from her dreams of pursuing a ski-jump championship. Deep in her heart, Rebel knew walking away would be betraying her vivacious and hugely talented mother, who'd never been quite able to achieve a championship win of her own.

Her heart ached as she passed her hand over the picture. Her father had never understood her need to keep chasing her dream. He'd been harsh and critical to the point where they hadn't been able to stay under the same roof without endless vicious rows. But even then, Rebel had never imagined walking away would mean losing her father for this long. She'd never thought his condemnation and lack of forgiveness would be set in stone.

She dropped her hand. She was here now. She was about to undertake the most important challenge of her career. Before that happened, she needed to know whether there was a way to reconcile with her father.

Forcing the nerves down, she looked around, seeking clues as to his whereabouts. His computer was turned off, but his desk calendar was still set at a date two weeks ago. Unease spiked as she recalled Stan's words. Deciding not to read too much into it, she walked to the far side of the vast office, and set her yoga mat and gym bag down. Another half an hour of pacing, and her nerves were screaming that something wasn't quite right. After leaving yet another message on her father's voicemail stating that she wasn't leaving his office until he called her back, she put her phone on the coffee table along with her sweater, and rolled out the yoga mat.

The situation with her father, a bandaged but far from healed wound, had been ripped open by his letter, bringing fresh anguish. That anguish was affecting her concentration, something she could ill afford. Greg, her trainer, had commented on the fact today, hence the addition of yoga to her exercise regime.

She'd made it through the trials to secure herself a position on the championship-seeking team. She couldn't afford to take her eye off the ball now, no matter how unresolved her issues were with her father.

Dropping onto the mat, she plugged her earphones back in, stretched and closed her eyes. Legs crossed in front of her, she took several breaths to centre herself, then began to move through her positions.

The first few tingles she attributed to her body dropping into a state of relaxation. One she welcomed after the turmoil of the past few weeks. But when they persisted, growing with each breath, Rebel rolled her shoulders, mildly irritated and more than a little anxious that she would truly find no avenue of relief until she spoke to her father.

Then the scent hit her nostrils: dark, hypnotic, with traces of citrus and more than a hint of savagery. At first she believed she was dreaming its complexity. But with each breath, the scent wrapped tighter around her senses, pulling her into a vortex of sensation that increased the tingling along her spine.

Slowly lowering herself from downward dog, she lay flat on her stomach and extended her left leg behind her, hoping the taut muscle stretch would dissipate the strange feeling zinging through her body. She repeated the exercise with her right leg, welcoming the burn.

But the distraction wasn't sufficient. Her concentration slipped further.

Gritting her teeth, she sat up and stretched her legs wide, perpendicular to her body. She aligned her torso to one leg, then the other, then leaned forward on her elbows and slowly raised her pelvis off the floor.

The curse was thick and sharp enough to pierce the cocoon of her music.

Rebel's eyes flew open.

Sensation hit her like a charging bull. The air knocked clean from her lungs, Rebel gaped at the imposing man who sat with one leg hitched over the other and his arms crossed over a wide, firm chest.

Steely grey eyes pinned her in position. Not that she would've been able to move had her life depended on it. Frozen on the floor, she could only stare as the most arresting man she'd ever seen uncoiled himself from his sitting position and stood to a towering, dominating height. His navy three-piece suit was sharp and stylish, and drew attention to broad shoulders, a trim waist and strong thighs, but even without those visual aids, his sheer beauty was potent enough to command her attention.

Her muscles strained, lactic acid building in a body that screamed for relief, but Rebel couldn't heed it.

The man advanced, bringing the scent that had so thoroughly shattered her concentration even closer until it fully encompassed her. There was a vague familiarity about him, like a stranger she'd caught a glimpse of a lifetime ago. But the sensation passed as he drew closer.

Her chest tightened, her lungs struggling to work as he crouched down in front of her and jerked the earbuds from her ears. Flinging the wires to the floor, he leaned forward until every inch of her vision was crowded with him.

'You have exactly three seconds to tell me who the hell you are, and why I shouldn't call Security and have you thrown in jail for lewd conduct and trespassing.'

CHAPTER TWO

DRACO ANGELIS WASN'T a man overly prone to emotion or volatile impulses. And yet as he stared at the woman before him he wanted to curse again. Loudly and far more filthily than he had in a long time.

He told himself it was because the floor show she'd been giving his male employees for the last fifteen minutes was losing him money with each second her sinuous body undulated. More than that, she was drawing attention to a matter he wanted to keep under wraps by performing said floor show in Nathan Daniels' office. In a business often accused of being shady and underhanded, Draco had striven to keep Angel International above reproach. He'd succeeded beyond his wildest dreams by keeping all his dealings professional, above board and strictly private. None of his clients were permitted to publicise details of their relationship with his company save for a carefully prepared press release at the time of signing.

Draco kept that same stranglehold on his personal life.

But with the sudden disappearance of Nathan Daniels and the suspected reason behind it, Draco knew it was only a matter of time before the whispers grew to wild speculation and brought unwanted attention to both facets of his life.

And this…siren performing moves fit for a certain type of gentlemen's club right here on his CFO's office floor was the last thing he needed.

As to the pull he'd experienced in his body and especially in his groin as he'd watched her… Well, he could deal with the reminder that he was a full-blooded male.

What he wasn't prepared to deal with was her interrupting his—

'Lewd conduct?' A sultry laugh detonated his thoughts, slamming him back to the room and the sensual vision still frozen in position before him. 'I think that's a bit of a stretch, don't you?'

A thick bead of sweat trickled down her earlobe and over her jaw. He tracked it, unable to drag his gaze away as it rolled over her heated skin to disappear between small but lush breasts. He ruthlessly suppressed the growl that rose in his chest and clenched his jaw.

'You think it's a stretch to perform lasciviously in front of a window to the clear view of everyone in my company?'

Her back bowed as she flexed her hips, a smile curving her full lips. 'I wasn't aware what I was doing was so distracting. Do you mind stepping back?'

'Excuse me?' Irritated surprise held him rigid.

'I'm almost done. If I stop now, I'll have to start all over again. Sorry, I'm a little OCD like that. I need room for the last two positions, so if you don't mind…?'

Draco was sure it was pure shock that propelled him to his feet, not the secret need to see her complete her set. All the same, he stepped back, his jaw clenched harder as he folded his arms and stared down at the lithe body sprawled at his feet.

She balanced on her elbows, her torso straightened. Slim muscled legs slowly lifted off the floor, maintaining the perpendicular position for several seconds, before meeting in the middle in a sleek upside-down formation. Draco watched her stomach muscles delicately vibrate as she centred herself, her skin bathed in a sheen of sweat as her toned body achieved the perfect line.

As a former athlete himself, Draco appreciated the discipline it took to hone one's body into the ultimate competitive instrument. And while part of him approved of the level of skill being displayed before him, the greater part was eyeing the delicate, muscled perfection of her body.

And detesting himself for it.

Whoever this woman was, she had no right to be here.

About to step forward and end this nonsense, he halted mid-step as she dropped one leg to the floor behind her. The sexy agility in her body arrested him, drying out every flaying word he'd meant to deliver as he stared.

Thee mou.

Anyone would think he hadn't seen a female body before. He'd dated sportswomen at the peak of their careers and slept with more than his share of them. And yet something about this woman drew him as no other had done in a very long time.

That thought sent another bolt of anger through him. Rousing himself, he stepped forward, just as she lowered her other leg and straightened.

She wasn't very tall, only coming up to his chest. But her deep blue eyes sparked with a fire and attitude that made her appear six feet tall. Her chin, pointed and determined, and her mouth, still curved in that sultry, albeit slightly wary smile, made him think thoughts that had no room in this space.

'Now, where were we?' she asked, her voice reminding him of smoky rooms in gentlemen's clubs.

Draco dragged his mind from images of unwanted decadence to a far more appropriate ire. 'We were addressing your unsolicited presence in my building.'

'Ah, yes, you wanted to know who I was?'

'I see you've skilfully avoided my trespass charge.'

'That's because I'm not trespassing. I have a right to be here.'

'I seriously doubt that. Sanctioning half-naked women to perform acrobatics for my employees as part of their busy workday isn't part of my business model.'

'We're talking about my supposed floor show, right?'

She glanced behind her. Catching sight of the group of men staring avidly through the glass from a few offices away, she smiled and waved.

A glowering look from Draco sent his employees dispersing, although a brave buck, Stan Macallister, dared to wave back.

Deciding it was time to bring this farce to an end, Draco strode to the desk of his AWOL CFO and snatched up the phone.

'This is Mr Angelis. Send Security up to Daniels' office. I have an unwanted guest who needs to be removed from the premises. And inform my head of security that I want a report on my desk as to why this breach has happened before the day is out.'

He slammed down the phone with more force than was needed.

'Wow, was that really necessary?'

He turned to find her standing in the same position before the window, her hand on her curvy hips and her head tilted to one side. The loose knot of her silky black hair fell lopsided as she stared at him with one eyebrow raised mockingly.

'I have a client meeting in less than half an hour. I'd throw you out myself but I don't have time to take a shower before then.'

Her expression slipped at the thinly veiled insult. Draco felt childish satisfaction at scoring a direct hit. Absurdly, he'd been off balance since he'd seen her from his office next door. His need for transparency in all things had transmitted to his office layout, and with the open-plan setting and see-through glass windows across the floor he could keep an eye on most of his employees. Although he liked to believe it was unnecessary where his employees were concerned as he'd earned their loyalty, he'd learned the hard way that loyalty came at a cost.

The alternative career he'd had to choose was a cutthroat

one at best. He'd made a few hard bargains along the way to get him where he was.

What he hadn't bargained for today was seeing a decadently curvy woman on display on his CFO's floor. He'd stopped an important call mid-conversation, a move he'd never made before. Now he had an irate, egocentric client waiting for him to call back. And a snarky stranger openly mocking him.

'I hope you don't feel too silly when you find out who I am,' she said in that voice that snagged his senses, made him strain to hear her every word.

'I'm not interested in who you are. My security will furnish me with that information if I need it. What I am interested in is you being escorted off the premises—'

'Okay, this is getting ridiculous. My name is Rebel Daniels, Nathan Daniels' daughter. I'm here to have lunch with my father. I forgot to sign in downstairs so Stan let me in. My dad wasn't here. I assumed he was in a meeting or something, so I thought I'd wait for him. The yoga thing was just to relieve a little bit of stress.'

Several questions stormed through Draco's mind. Was his security so lax that someone could just *forget* to make themselves known downstairs and still make it up here? She was Daniels' daughter? Why was she stressed?

'Your parents named you *Rebel*?' Mildly disconcerted at the least relevant question that had chosen to fall from his lips, he watched a smile twitch at the corners of her mouth.

'Hardly, although my mother did wonder why she hadn't thought of that when I started using it at fifteen.'

Draco waited, wondering at the shadow that crossed her face a moment later. When she continued to stare at him, he pursed his lips. 'So your *real* name is?'

'I thought you weren't interested.' She turned and bent over to pick up her yoga mat.

He forced his gaze from her delectable behind to her bare feet, then away from her altogether when he realised he was even growing fascinated with her peach-painted toenails. 'I'm only interested in you if it helps me locate your father.'

Her head jerked up, the rolled mat held against her body as she frowned at him. 'What do you mean locate him? Isn't he here?'

'Did you have any reason to think he would be?' he countered.

'Of course I did. Why else would I have come here?'

Draco spotted two burly men rushing towards the office. His head of security looked extremely nervous. As he should be. He held up his hand when they reached the door. 'When did you last speak to your father?'

Her gaze darted from the men back to him, a tiny flash of nervousness darkening her eyes. 'Why, what does it matter?'

'Because I would very much like to speak to him too.'

Her eyes widened, again a minuscule motion that he otherwise would've missed had he not been watching her closely. 'So he's not here?' she pressed.

'I think we've established that, Miss Daniels. Now are you going to answer me, or shall I hand you over to them?' He jerked his head at the security men.

She frowned. 'What exactly is going on here? If my father's not here and you want me to leave, I will. There's no need to throw your weight about. And I certainly don't need to be escorted out.'

'But you were in here on your own for over fifteen minutes. Who knows what information you've made yourself privy to?'

'Are you accusing me of *stealing* something?' she snapped.

'Did you?'

'Of course not!'

'I'll leave them to be the judge of that. I'm sure you'll be released in a few hours once the security footage has been analysed, your belongings searched, and your alleged innocence confirmed.' Draco motioned for his men to enter.

His head of security entered, followed by his assistant. Draco ignored their contrite expressions. 'Take Miss Daniels' bag—'

'You can't be serious!'

'And the yoga mat. Make sure she's not in possession of anything that doesn't belong to her—'

'Okay, fine. I'll answer your damn questions.'

The men paused.

Draco shook his head. 'Take them. Leave her shoes. I'll let you know when I'm finished with her.'

She sent him a look filled with pure vitriol and her fingers clenched around the yoga mat as the younger guard stepped towards her. Eyes flashing blue fire, she released her hold on it, slipped her feet into her knee-high boots and propped her hands on her hips.

'Shall we get this ludicrous inquisition over with?'

Sparks virtually flew off her. In another time, Draco would've enjoyed stoking that fire just to see how high her conflagration burned. It'd been far too long since any emotion besides bitterness, guilt and the rigid control he'd put in place ruled his life. Anything beyond that was a luxury he could ill afford.

It was the same control that dictated he take hold of this situation before it blew up in his face. He'd allowed his suspicions about Nathan Daniels to go unquestioned for far too long as it was.

He straightened. 'Come with me.'

'Where are we going?' the question was snapped back immediately.

'My office.'

'Uh…sir?'

He turned to his security chief.

'We need the lady's full name in order to log her into the system.'

Draco raised an eyebrow at her.

Her mouth pursed, bringing his reluctant attention back to her plump lips.

'It's...my name is Arabella Daniels,' she muttered reluctantly.

It took less than a second for Draco to place her. Arabella Daniels had once been a promising cross-country skier until she'd abruptly changed disciplines to become a ski jumper. Although she'd remained in the top ten for the last few years, the twenty-five-year-old woman had never risen above fifth in competitions. Probably due to her off-piste antics.

His mild shock subsided into a heavy dose of distaste, but he kept his expression neutral as he dismissed his men and strode to his office.

He waited until she entered, then activated the privacy setting on his windows. Once the glass was frosted, he perched at the edge of his desk and watched her pace warily in front of him. The burn in his groin as he followed her lissom figure made him kick out a chair.

'Sit down.'

'No, thanks. I thought you had an important meeting? Or was that just a fib rolled up as an insult?'

'It wasn't a lie. But the party concerned will understand. I tend to surround myself with reasonable, rational individuals.'

She paused in her pacing, her eyes narrowing. 'Is that supposed to be some sort of dig?'

'I know who you are, Miss Daniels.'

'Well, since I told you my name, I should hope so. I wouldn't like to think you were thick or anything, seeing as you seem to be the head honcho in this glass playhouse.'

'So the rumours are true.'

'What rumours?' she asked, her expression growing more wary.

'You take pride in being deliberately offensive and exhibiting wild behaviour.'

'And you don't seem to like being told things the way

they are. In fact your actions reek of more than a touch of melodrama. Why is that? Are you overcompensating for something?' Her gaze conducted what started off as a mocking perusal. But a trace of heat flared up her cheeks when her eyes dropped below his belt.

When her gaze darted away, Draco allowed himself a stiff smile. 'I've never needed to overcompensate for anything in my life, Miss Daniels. If I had time to waste and felt so inclined, I'd give you a demonstration.'

'You assume that *I* have the time to stand around listening to your rubbish. Keep your veiled threats, ask me what you want to know and let us both get on with our lives.'

'You seem a little off balance. Is it because you feel out of your depth?' he drawled.

She jerked the hair band from her hair. Thick, silky jet waves fell over her shoulders and down her back before she started combing her fingers through the tresses.

'Why would I feel like that? Just because you're being disgustingly unreasonable—'

'Or is it because you don't find me as gullible as you do the men you like to associate with?'

'I don't know what you think you know about me, but if these absurd questions are why you brought me in here—'

'You like to dominate your men, do you not?'

She tossed her head. 'Only when they beg me to. Do you want me to dominate you? I'm fresh out of horse whips but I'm sure I can get inventive with a pair of boot laces.'

His gaze dropped to her knee-high boots. 'I'm sure you can, in the right circumstances, but I'll pass.'

She wrinkled her nose and Draco's temperature rose, along with his irritation. 'Why? Because you always wait for the right circumstances? How boring. Giving in to your impulses might just surprise you.'

Draco bared his teeth in a smile that had been described by the tabloids as his dragon smile. He knew its effect well enough to know it'd made its mark when her agitation escalated.

'I find that people like you easily confuse the reckless with the impulsive. Personally, I find the wait builds the anticipation.'

Her gaze held his for one bold heartbeat, then she glanced away. Although she engrossed herself in his office decor, Draco was certain she wasn't as bored with him as she pretended to be. The colour in her cheeks was more pronounced and the pulse beating at her throat had increased. His own blood thickened as he followed her figure. He assured himself, now he knew who she truly was, this mild fascination with her would swiftly abate.

'Well, as interesting as this all is, I'm one hundred per cent sure you know very little about me. And I have to insist you either get on with your ever-so-important questioning, or tell your guards to return my things.'

'You're attempting to compete in the Verbier Ski Championships this year. Shouldn't you be training instead of making an exhibition of yourself and taking extended lunches?'

She inhaled sharply and turned towards him, all pretence at being bored vanishing from her expression. 'You know who I am?'

'I make it my business to know people like you.'

'What do you mean, people like me?'

'Reckless athletes, who try to buy their way into the big leagues.'

She stalked to where he leaned against his desk, her whole body bristling with anger. 'How dare you? That's a ridiculous and totally unfounded allegation.'

'I know enough. The rest I don't intend to bother myself with.'

Her hands clenched. 'Just who the hell do you think you are?'

'I'm the man who intends to make sure all the sponsors

you've been chasing the last month drop you from their books. People like you paint talented and dedicated sportsmen and women in a bad light, not to mention your reckless behaviour on and off the ski slopes needs to be stopped once and for all. You have three measly sponsors left, who probably, mistakenly, think your notoriety will bring their products the attention they crave. Perhaps I'll let you keep them.'

Her eyes had been widening with each condemnation. Slowly, shock replaced her anger. And this time, when she looked around at the trophies and pictures that decorated his office, her interest was genuine.

Draco knew the moment the penny dropped.

Her lustrous hair flew as she whirled back to him. 'You're Draco, the super-agent.'

'I'm Draco Angelis, yes.'

She swallowed. 'You represent Rex Glow.'

'Your former sponsors? Yes.'

She inhaled sharply, but the next question wasn't what Draco had expected it to be. 'And my father *works* for you?'

'You're surprised by that.'

A frown clamped her brows. 'Well…yes, to be honest.'

'Why?' he fired back, his need to probe the reason behind Nathan Daniels' disappearance returning.

'Because…' She hesitated, a trace of pained bleakness flitting over her features. 'Let's just say the world of competitive sports isn't his first love.'

He folded his arms, alarm bells clanging loudly. 'Well, he was my chief financial officer up until two weeks ago, when he seemed to fall off the face of the earth.'

'And you're looking for him because…?'

'There's a small matter of a half a million pounds that seems to have evaporated from my company's accounts. I would very much like to speak to him about that,' Draco replied, his eyes narrowing at the mixture of guilt and trepidation that froze on her face.

CHAPTER THREE

REBEL KNEW SHE'D given herself away a split second before
Draco straightened to his imposing six-foot-plus height and
took the single step that brought him to within a whisper
of where she stood. His broad shoulders and the cloak of
power draped around him eclipsed her every thought and
action. But even without them, the expression on his face as
he stared down at her dried the words that rose to her lips.

This man was responsible for Rex Glow dropping her.
While a significant part of her was enraged by the blatant
admission, the greater part of her was shocked by the other
information he'd imparted.

He was her father's boss. A father who, for all intents and
purposes, had disappeared. Along with the uncomfortably
exact amount of money that had landed in her bank account.
The shock of it rendered her attempt to keep a neutral expression hopelessly futile.

'Tell me where your father is,' he pressed.

In that moment, Rebel understood why this man was
named The Dragon. His steely grey eyes were cold and
deadly enough to freeze the Sahara. And yet his nostrils
flared with white-hot anger that promised volatile, anni-
hilating fire.

'I…I don't know where he is.'

Black eyebrows clamped darker. 'You expect me to believe that?'

'You can believe what you want. It's the truth.'

'You admitted to having been in touch with him lately.
And you came here to meet him, did you not?'

'We spoke briefly on the phone a couple of days ago.
Lunch was mentioned, and I thought I'd surprise him

today…' She trailed off, unwilling to elaborate that she'd done most of the talking, while her father had remained stonily monosyllabic. Rebel struggled to hide the hurt that lanced her heart from knowing her father would've probably rejected any firm plans had he known she'd intended to come here today.

'I urge you to come clean now, Miss Daniels, before things get worse for you and your father,' Draco Angelis threatened.

The first tendrils of fear clawed up her spine. 'If you must know, we didn't make any firm plans. It was a spur-of-the-moment decision to stop by and see if he was free for lunch. I haven't seen him in a while and I thought—'

'How long is *a while*?'

'That's between my father and me, and none of your business.'

Firm, sinfully sensual lips pursed. 'You don't think my CFO's sudden disappearance and you turning up unannounced in my building is any of my business?'

'So he's taken a brief vacation. So what?' she speculated wildly, her unease growing as suspicion mounted in Draco's eyes.

'Considering he hasn't taken one in the five years he's worked for me, you'll pardon me if I find his sudden need for one, without speaking to me first, more than a little suspect. Besides, we have a procedure for absences. My employees don't make a habit of just not turning up to work when the mood takes them.'

'Because that would guarantee them an on-the-spot sacking?'

'Perhaps not on the spot. I would demand an explanation first before the sacking ensued.'

Rebel forced an eye roll, which was far from the nonchalance she tried to project. 'So you're not just a dragon to work for, you're an ogre as well? Congratulations.'

Sharp grey eyes, surrounded by the most lush eyelashes

she'd ever seen on a man, lasered her. 'You find this subject amusing?'

Anger surged through her. 'About as amusing as discovering that you seem to have a personal vendetta against me when we've never even met before.'

His face tightened, his expression growing even more formidable. 'We didn't need to meet before I knew exactly what sort of person you are. Your antics in the last half an hour have only confirmed it.'

'Really? Would you care to share it with me or should I take a few wild guesses?'

'You've barely scraped through into ski finals for the last few years because your work ethic is average at best. You're more concerned with headlining in the tabloids with your extracurricular activities than putting in the hard work to secure yourself a position in the championships.'

She swallowed hard before her temper got the better of her. 'I'll have you know I was an under-twenty-one record holder for two years.'

'But you haven't placed higher than fifth in the last six years. Your position in the rankings has fallen in direct proportion to the rise of your notoriety. It doesn't take a maths genius to work out where your true interests lie. Which is why I wonder why you even bother.'

Anger gave way to bewildered hurt, but Rebel locked in her emotions, determined not to show him how his words affected her. 'I'm still at a loss as to how all of this or anything in my *private* life concerns you.'

'If it concerns my client, it concerns me. Besides, it's only a matter of time before your reckless actions have a direct impact on another athlete,' he retorted pithily, his gaze boring harder into her, condemnation stamped in every pore.

Draco Angelis' reaction was too strong for Rebel to believe his motivation stemmed from concern for his client alone. But she was too busy struggling not to react to the accusation of recklessness to pay it much heed.

The only thing Rebel wanted was to leave his office and his oppressive presence. She needed the head space to ponder exactly what her father was up to. And whether the money he'd sent her was indeed embezzled funds as her every instinct shrieked it was. The enormity of what that would mean struck cold dread inside her.

'I think we're done here, Mr Angelis. Rex Glow is no longer my sponsor, so I don't have to listen to you or your groundless accusations about my life. If you choose to believe whatever nonsense you read in the papers, then that's your problem, not mine.'

He made no move to stop her as she headed for the door. She knew why the moment she tried to pull it open and found it unyielding.

'Open this door now.'

Cold steel eyes pinned her in place. 'I'm not finished with you.'

'But I am with you,' she replied, a vein of panic rising in her belly. She rattled the door harder, but the reinforced glass didn't budge an inch.

'You can leave once you tell me where your father is hiding.'

She whirled at the hard demand. He was less than a foot from her, his stance even more imposing than before. His scent attacked her senses a second later, once again cutting a dangerous swathe through her thought processes.

The man wasn't just a dangerous dragon. He was a precariously beautiful creature, his face and body an alluring, breathtaking combination designed to trap helpless prey.

Not that she was one!

'Do you jump to conclusions about every single subject or are my father and I being singled out for special treatment?'

'You think I want my company exposed to the fact that my CFO has embezzled from me?'

Renewed panic gripped her insides. 'Where's your proof that he has?'

'The evidence isn't concrete yet, but what I've found so far doesn't look good. It's only a matter of time before we trace where the funds ended up. His not answering my calls or emails doesn't exactly look promising.'

'What…what would you tell him if he answered?'

Draco's narrowed eyes scoured her face. 'He's served me well for five years. I'd be prepared to listen to his explanations.'

'Before throwing the book at him?'

'You think I should let him go scot-free if he's guilty?'

Her heart lurched. 'Since we haven't established that he's done anything wrong, I think this is a moot point.'

'Sadly, your poker face isn't as flawless as you think. You know where he is. Tell me now and I'll consider not pressing full charges.'

'I don't know where he is. I swear,' Rebel answered.

Draco took the last step that separated them and grabbed her bare arm. The hand still clutching the door handle dropped as raw electricity raced across her skin. Intense tingling tightened her every cell, straining towards the point of contact with a severity that stole her breath. Her lips parted as she fought to get air into her lungs.

Above her, Draco inhaled sharply. The expression on his face reflected her bewilderment for a second before the cold façade slid back into place.

'You may not know where he is, but you know something. I suggest you come clean now.' He repeated his earlier threat.

Rebel shook her head. If her father had truly embezzled the money he'd deposited in her account from the Angel International Group, there was no way she could get it back. And right now, Rebel couldn't be sure which was worse—confessing her suspicion of her father's guilt, or informing Draco Angelis that she had used the funds to secure her place in the Verbier tournament. From Draco's censorious reaction to her as an athlete, Rebel knew he wouldn't hesitate to condemn her as an accessory to the crime and have her thrown in jail.

'Arabella, this is your last chance.'

The sound of her name on his lips sent shafts of disconcerting fire through her belly. The sensation was so powerful it weakened her knees, and the secret place between her legs was dampening with each second his hand remained on her.

God, what was wrong with her? She'd heard her girlfriends confess to growing wobbly at the knees when some hot guy glanced their way at a nightclub. She'd secretly rolled her eyes at that implausible statement, knowing she'd never be one of those women. The shocking sensation ramming through her right now filled her with horror and more than a touch of anger.

She parted her lips, but Draco shook his head, his other hand rising to clamp her other arm.

'Think carefully before you speak.'

She pulled in a deep, sustaining breath. 'No,' she stated firmly.

'Just so we're clear, to what exactly are you saying no?' he breathed softly, dangerously.

Rebel ignored the warm breath washing over her face and raised her chin. 'To answering any more of your stupid accusations. To being kept prisoner in this office. To you having your hands on me. No to everything. Now, let me go before I scream this place down.'

'Scream all you want. This room is soundproof.'

'How very convenient. Do you do this a lot, then?' she taunted.

'Do what?' he sliced at her.

'Drag women in here and hold them against their will?'

A muted curse in a language she didn't understand

spilled from his lips. 'No woman has been in here who didn't want to be.'

The images his words conjured up jarred her into squirming before she forced her muscles to lock tight. 'So you admit to seducing women in your office during the workday?'

A chilled smile parted his lips. 'You assume that I do the seducing.'

'So women not only stage floor shows in your offices, they also seduce you behind closed doors into the bargain. Your poor thing. How on earth do you get any work done?'

'You have a reckless, smart mouth, Arabella.'

Another zing went through her, but she fought it tooth and nail. 'Along with a smart brain. So if you think anything's going to happen here other than me walking out the door in the next minute, think again.'

'You set too high a premium on yourself, I think.'

'Ah, so if I were to strip right here right now, you'd turn me down?'

'You won't. You like to pretend otherwise, but I'm willing to bet, deep down, you're less Lady Chatterley and more Miss Prude.'

The droll observation brought heat to her cheeks. Dear God, he was making her blush *again*?

'Well, sadly for you, you'll never find out.'

'I will. If I wish it, you'll get your chance to strip for me in the very near future. At a time and place of my choosing when I know we won't be interrupted in any way.'

'Wow, you must tell me where you acquired your crystal balls. I'm running out of ideas for Christmas presents.'

Dear Lord. Was she truly standing in front of him, discussing his balls?

He freed one arm. Rebel was about to exhale with relief, but her breathing stuttered as he curled his long fingers over her nape and tilted her chin with his thumb. She'd never imagined the skin along her jaw was sensitive until experiencing Draco Angelis' branding touch. Now every nerve in her body screeched as her heart raced and her blood heated.

His head lowered a fraction and his gaze dropped to her lips. He was about to kiss her. And she couldn't move.

Rebel grew frantically aware of every desperate breath that passed between her lips, her own gaze unable to shift from the mouth drawing ever closer to hers.

'I don't need crystal balls. My human ones are more than adequate to deal with challenges from the opposite sex. But we're straying from the subject. Tell me what you know, Arabella.' Again that smile peeled back a layer of her skin and exposed her to sensations as alien as a distant galaxy.

'For the last time, take your hands off me. I don't know where my father—'

The buzz of an intercom from his desk froze her words. Draco tensed, the flex of his jaw exhibiting his displeasure at the interruption.

'Mr Angelis, I'm so sorry to disturb you, but I have Olivio Nardozzi on the line again. He refuses to leave a message or be put on hold. He says you promised to call him back fifteen minutes ago.'

He raised his head, but he didn't let her go. Nor did his gaze move from her lips as he answered, 'Tell Olivio I'll speak to him in two minutes. Tell him he can either hold or wait for my call.'

'Yes, Mr Angelis.'

The intercom clicked and silence once more engulfed them. Draco didn't seem in a hurry to speak, or do anything but hold her prisoner.

Rebel knew she had to move, but for the life of her she couldn't get her legs to work. So she employed her best defence. 'Another one of your angelic, perfectly reasonable, *high-maintenance* clients?' she mocked.

With a slow, deliberate movement, his thumb rose from her chin to pass lazily over her lower lip. 'There will come a time when this delectable mouth will get you into trouble you won't be able to escape from,' he drawled in a low, dark voice that resonated deep within her.

'Tick tock, Mr Angelis.'

His grip firmed, the fire branding her deeper. Then he released her with an abrupt move that spoke of barely leashed emotion. Before she could escape, he caged her in by placing his hands on the glass door either side of her.

'You have until six o'clock tonight to tell me what you know about my money. Trust me, you don't want me to come after you.'

She wanted to dare him to do his worst, but Rebel bit her tongue. Draco Angelis had already demonstrated that he had the power to strip her sponsors from her with nothing more than a hatred of her vivacity. Sure, she'd taken a few risks on the ski slope that had earned her a name in the sport. But they'd all been carefully calculated and had taken into account the injury she'd sustained when she was twenty-two. Without those risks, she'd have fallen even further down the rankings and lost all her sponsorship long before now.

As much as she wanted to tell Draco to take a running jump, if she wanted to get to the bottom of her father's actions, or have a last chance at securing the Verbier championship and laying a few ghosts to rest, she needed to retreat and regroup.

A tug on her Lycra training bottoms drew her thoughts away from her mother and her errant father. She gasped as Draco slid a business card into her waistband. The backs of his fingers brushed her skin and her muscles jumped at the contact.

Before she could form an effective comeback to his audacious action he stepped back. A moment later the frosty glass cleared and a click released the door.

'I assume I'm free to go now?'

He lifted the phone and punched in a series of numbers. 'Provided you're not held by my security, then yes, you may leave. But we both know you're guilty of something, Arabella. Make the wise choice and use my private number. I guarantee you won't like the consequences if you don't.' He sat down behind his desk. The infinitesimal twitch of his chair away from her was as definitive a dismissal as any as he spoke into the phone, 'Olivio, my apologies for keeping you waiting. I hope you're chomping at the bit to speak to me because you've given further consideration to my offer?' His voice rang with charming familiarity, not at all like the ire he'd demonstrated towards her.

Rebel could barely recall stumbling from Draco's office and summoning the lift that raced her back down to the ground floor. She assumed she was free to leave when the Angel head of security met her on the ground floor with her belongings. Thankful that she wouldn't be required to answer any more questions, Rebel took her bag and yoga mat and hurried out into the weak February sunshine.

The light breeze that whispered over her skin brought a little clarity, but her senses were too focused on the card burning against her skin, and the grave certainty that the money she'd used to secure her place in the Verbier tournament was indeed money stolen from a man who seemed to have the lowest, blackest opinion of her, to feel the cold.

Plucking the card out of her waistband, she stared at the black and gold inscription and the private number etched into it.

Rebel wanted to rip it into a dozen pieces and scatter them to the four winds. But deep in her heart she recognised the foolhardiness of doing so.

She might not understand why her father had chosen to help himself to money that didn't belong to him and then pass it on to her. Their last few rows had been awful enough for her to imagine he was done with her as long as she chose to keep competing. For him to have followed her career closely enough to know when she needed help at once lifted her heart and plunged it into despair. Not in a million years would she have wanted him to help in this way.

Jerkily, she searched for her phone and dialled as she hurried away from Draco's building. The moment the line connected, she rushed to speak. 'Contessa, have the cheques we paid out to the tournament organisers cleared?'

Her manager snorted. 'Well, hello to you too. And the answer to your question is yes, the cheques cleared this morning, so did the money we paid for your travel, accommodation and equipment. We only need an extra fifteen thousand for incidentals, but I'm sure your remaining sponsors will front you that. I was going to pop round to your flat tonight with a bottle of champagne to celebrate. I know you don't like to drink during training, but I thought a sip or two wouldn't hurt…' Her voice trailed off for a moment. 'Rebel? Is something wrong?'

Rebel exhaled shakily, her vision hazing as she fought panic. 'And there's no way we can get any of it back?'

'*Get it back?* Why would we want to do that?' her manager demanded, her voice rising.

'I…I just…it doesn't matter.'

'Obviously it does. Tell me what's happened.'

Unwilling to drag Contessa into her problems until she confirmed the depth of the trouble she was in, she forced lightness into her voice. 'Ignore me. Just last-minute nerves. You can come over, but can we give the champagne a miss, though?'

'Of course…are you sure you're okay?' the older woman pressed.

'I'm sure. Talk to you later.'

She hung up and immediately dialled her father's number, already suspecting it wouldn't go through. When the mechanical voice urged her to leave a message, Rebel cleared her throat. 'Dad, it's me…again.' She paused, a new fear chilling her heart. Draco Angelis wasn't above having her father's phone traced. Until she got answers for herself, Rebel didn't want to lead the man who made her spine tingle with dread and other unwanted emotions straight to her father. 'Call me. Please. I need to talk to you.'

Feeling helpless for the first time in a very long time, she hung up. Plugging her earphones in, she ramped up the volume and hurried to the Tube, all the while willing her focus away from the card she'd tucked back into her waistband, hoping against hope she wouldn't be forced to use it.

CHAPTER FOUR

DRACO READ THE bullet points in the report for the second time and closed the file. He spared a thought as to why his CFO hadn't bothered to cover his tracks, then dismissed the useless thought. The *why* didn't matter.

The inescapable fact was that a crime had been committed. By Daniels and his daughter.

Draco didn't doubt for a second that she was neck deep in this theft. Her guilt had been written all over her face, despite her trying hard to hide it. Her racing pulse had condemned her just as definitely, no matter how much her smart mouth had tried to distract him.

A muscle ticced in his jaw as he remembered the velvet softness of that mouth…the smoothness of her skin. Arabella Daniels didn't use just her mouth to distract. She used her whole body. The need to remind *his* body hours later of that potent tactic irritated Draco as his car raced through the wet, lamplit streets towards the Chelsea address his investigators had supplied him with.

Another bout of irritation welled inside him.

He'd known Arabella wouldn't honour the deadline he'd given her. Six o'clock had come and gone three hours ago, and, despite the conclusive, almost cynical evidence of theft he held in his hands, the daughter of his CFO had remained silent.

Closing the electronic file, he opened a thick manila envelope that held a completely different set of problems. While Draco was satisfied that months of hard work were poised on the edge of finally reaping rewards, he couldn't believe the seemingly inescapable strings Olivio Nardozzi had attached to the contract in his hand.

But he hadn't come this far to lose.

Carla Nardozzi, champion figure skater, number one in the world, was a prize every sports agent wanted. Hard-working, charismatic, almost virginally shy, she would be the jewel in his agency's crown…if her father weren't leveraging an unthinkable condition to signing his daughter with the Angel International Group—

'Sir, we're here,' his driver interrupted his thoughts.

Draco alighted from the car and stared at the two-storey Victorian façade. While he hadn't been surprised Arabella lived in Chelsea, he'd expected her to inhabit a glitzy condominium, not a homey dwelling on a leafy suburban street. Mounting the shallow steps to the door, he pressed her intercom.

The door released half a minute later. Draco told himself he didn't care if she didn't bother about her security, but by the time he arrived in front of an open doorway on the first floor irritation had given way to anger.

Loud music pumped from what seemed like a hundred speakers, although he couldn't immediately see them as he went down a short hallway and arrived in a sizeable living room painted snow-white, and decorated with splashes of purple and pink.

He didn't have time to be offended by the jarring decor because he was once again confronted by a scantily clad Arabella Daniels, who didn't bother to look up as he walked into the room.

Draco dragged his gaze from her cross-legged figure enough to take in the fact that she was packing for a long trip. Escaping with the proceeds of her ill-gotten gains, perhaps?

He gritted his jaw and waited.

A moment later her head snapped up. Blue eyes met his, widened, before her mouth dropped open. 'You're not Contessa,' she shouted above the pumping rock music.

'No, I am not.'

Her eyes darted from him to the darkened hallway and back again. She set aside the sleek, specialist, lightweight skis that Draco knew cost several thousand pounds, and rose lithely to her feet. 'You…I wasn't expecting…what are you doing here?'

'Do you always answer your door without checking to see who you're letting in?' he bit out.

She shrugged. 'I thought you were Contessa, my manager. She's the only one who knows where—' She stopped and waved her hand. 'Let's get back to *my* question. What are *you* doing here?'

'If you insist on playing this game, I'll give you one guess, *after* you turn that racket off.'

Her pointed chin tilted and she folded her bare arms. 'No. If you don't like my taste in music, feel free to reuse the front door.'

Stopping his gaze from conducting a full scrutiny of her body, clad in vest top and hot pants, Draco stalked to the entertainment system set on top of an artsy-looking vanity unit and stabbed the off button.

'Hey, you can't do that!'

He turned and faced her, willing himself not to react to the mingled scent of peach shampoo and delicate perfume that infused his senses now his eardrums weren't being shredded.

'Did you forget the time, Arabella? I'm willing to give you the benefit of the doubt on the off-chance that my deadline escaped your notice because you don't possess a watch?'

Her frowning gaze slid from the silent music system to his face. Her arms tightened and her stare grew bolder. 'I have a watch. Several, in fact. I know exactly what the time is.'

The cold blaze of anger chilled his insides. He welcomed it far more than he welcomed the lick of fire that had flamed in his groin at the sight of her bare, shapely legs. 'I can only conclude, then, that you thought my last words to you were a joke?'

She made a humming, almost accommodating sound under her breath. 'Not quite. You don't seem the joking type. I don't imagine you'd appreciate a joke if it reared up and bit you hard.'

'So that's how you live your life? On the edge of reckless jokes?'

She shrugged. 'You know what they say…if you're not living on the edge, you're taking up too much room.'

The urge to grab her, drag her close, just as he'd done in his office, assailed him. He stabbed his hands deep into his pockets to curb the impulse. Arabella Daniels took pleasure in flaunting her risqué behaviour. Draco wasn't here to be riled. He was here to do the riling. To let her know she wouldn't be getting away with stealing from him.

'But if you insist on a definition,' she continued, 'I'd say I considered your words more of a suggestion…perhaps an invitation? As you can see, I opted to reject both.'

Draco drew in a breath, unable to accept that anyone could have so very little self-preservation. Back in his office, he'd considered her careless attitude a front, but now he wasn't so sure. But then why was he surprised? He knew first-hand the sort of person he was dealing with. Wasn't such a creature the same one responsible for reducing his sister's dreams to dust? He'd trusted his precious Maria's well-being and burgeoning talent to someone he'd thought would treasure and harness them. Instead, his sister's life had been irrevocably destroyed.

The rock of guilt and bitterness that resided in his gut pressed hard and punishing. He'd taken his eye off the ball, relentlessly pursued his own dreams, and his sister had suffered for it. Continued to suffer for it. Draco absorbed the expanding pain he'd become used to bearing. He was grateful for it, in fact. The reminder of the past was as timely as it was bracing.

He looked past her to the suitcases, clothing and equipment strewn on the living-room floor. 'Going somewhere?'

'Yes, as a matter of fact,' she replied. 'And you're interrupting my packing, so…'

Draco sauntered forward, his gaze narrowing on the two skis already wrapped in protective binding and the third one that she'd been wrapping when he walked in. 'Your equipment looks new. Expensive. Have you come into a windfall perhaps?' he enquired.

She tensed. 'It's none of your—'

He slashed his hand through the air. 'Enough. I have irrefutable evidence that every single penny your father misappropriated ended up in *your* bank account. Whatever his motives were for taking the money, he didn't seem inclined to cover his tracks. I've already given you enough time to come clean, but it looks like you prefer to wallow in lies and snarky banter. My time is valuable, Miss Daniels. I refuse to waste any more discussing your guilt. Now, are you prepared to take this seriously or shall I cut my losses and let you explain to the authorities how you came to be in possession of half a million pounds belonging to me?' He took his phone out of his pocket and gripped it, fingers poised over the buttons.

Her arms dropped from their belligerent position. As he'd spoken she'd grown paler, but there was still more than enough fight in her eyes for Draco not to be under the misconception that she'd seen the light of true contrition. 'I wasn't lying. I don't know where my father is, and I didn't have anything to do with the taking of the money.' Her brows clouded. 'Are you sure this isn't just some misunderstanding?'

He bared his teeth, cold amusement making him shake his head. 'I'm not in the habit of *misunderstanding* the whereabouts of my company's funds.'

She paled further. 'I told you, I don't know where my father is.'

'Have you tried calling him?' he fired back.

'Several times.' Her fingers spiked into her loose hair, and for the first time Draco witnessed her undiluted distress. Satisfaction lanced through him. He was finally getting through to her. Herding her into a position where she couldn't fail to see that he wouldn't be swayed from seeking restitution. 'He hasn't answered my calls.' The tiny note of bewilderment in her voice suggested she wasn't lying.

'Be that as it may, the funds ended up in your bank account.'

Her full lips firmed for several moments before she nodded. 'Yes.'

He exhaled. 'So, are you willing to answer my questions now?'

She nodded again.

'The championships don't start for several weeks. The training grounds in Verbier won't be open for another month. So where were you going?'

'I have a friend with a chalet in Chamonix. I was going to stay there while I train.'

'You mean you were fleeing the country with your ill-gotten gains?' he sneered. 'Perhaps meet up with your father and celebrate getting one over on me?'

She flinched. 'No.'

'Just…no? You're not going elaborate?'

'What more is there to say? You say you have evidence that the money ended up in my account. Will you believe me if I say I didn't know it was coming in the first place? That when it arrived I tried to return it?'

He lifted a brow before staring at the expensive items on the floor. 'Really?'

'Look, I know what you're thinking—'

'I seriously doubt that. Picking up the phone and instructing your bank to return the funds was too much effort, but spending it wasn't?'

'I didn't spend it. Not immediately.'

He placed the phone back in his pocket and stared at her until her gaze dropped. 'I'm sure you're going to explain that.'

'The money arrived after Rex Glow and the rest of my sponsors started dropping like flies, thanks to you, I'm guessing.' Her white-hot glare threatened to thaw the edges of his icy anger. 'My father must have realised what you were doing...' she paused...but it was already too late.

'So you're saying your father not only took my money, he also breached my company's confidential secrets?' He couldn't stop the growl that accompanied the question.

'No! I don't know.'

'You keep saying that, and yet all signs point to you hiding something.'

Her mouth worked for several seconds, before she blew out a breath. 'Fine, if you must know, I hadn't spoken to my father in years before I heard from him two weeks ago.'

He tensed. 'Why not?'

'*That* is definitely none of your business,' she snapped, her fingers spearing into her hair again and tossing the heavy tresses over her shoulder. 'But I did try to find out about the money the few times we spoke afterwards. He assured me there were no strings attached. That it was mine to use. And when a few more sponsors dropped me...'

'You went ahead and used it, without a single thought as to its true source?'

'You might automatically suspect everyone you meet to have nefarious motives, but the father I knew before we... lost touch was hard-working and *honest*. I don't know what you did for him to—'

'Excuse me?' Her audacity stunned him. 'Are you trying to wheedle your way into somehow blaming me for this?'

'My father isn't here to account for what's happened, is he?'

'No,' Draco muttered, a daring solution to the conundrum he'd been toying with taking root and firming in his mind. 'He's not. But you are.'

Her eyes widened. 'What's that supposed to mean?'

He stared into the clear depths, unable to pull his gaze away. 'It means the sins of the father will have to be paid for by the daughter. Especially when she's turned out to be a direct beneficiary.'

'Right. Hold that thought for a second.' She turned and walked to the sound system. She toyed with a few buttons before pressing one. About to warn her against restarting the ear-bleeding music when they weren't finished talking, Draco stopped when low, sultry, Middle Eastern fusion music flowed into the room. He stared, his gaze compelled by the sinuous movement of her body as she returned to where he stood. 'I'm afraid I'm not interested in whatever plans you've concocted, Mr Angelis.'

His fists balled harder in his pockets. 'By all means refuse if you feel you're in a position to. I'll bring myself to wait.'

Her mouth curved in a ghost of a smile. 'No need to wait. I have a plan in mind for how you can get your money back.'

Not what he'd been expecting. Or what his new plan entailed. But… 'I'm listening.'

'My manager has received a request for me to star in a reality TV show after the championships are over. I wasn't going to accept, but, since I now have no choice, I'll hand over the proceeds from the gig to you—'

'No.' The word shot out of him with a brevity that rocked him.

She blinked. 'Umm…what?'

'I said no.'

'I heard you. I just don't understand why you'd refuse, seeing as it's my life and I can do what I want with it. Also, I thought all this posturing and threatening was so you'd get your money back?'

'Not in three months' time. And not after you'd whored yourself in front of a camera to repay me.'

She inhaled sharply. 'You did not just say what I think you said.'

'Isn't that what it amounts to? You opening your life to intense scrutiny until every dirty scumbag out there knows what brand of toothpaste you use and what you wear to bed at night?'

'It isn't that type of show—'

'They are all *that type of show*. If you think otherwise, you're naive as well as stupid.'

'And you're an arrogant ass, who's under the illusion he can dictate to me. I don't doubt that you wield a lot of power in the sports world.' She laughed self-mockingly. 'You've already shown you can strip me of my sponsors, although I'm still not completely sure why, but I'm damned if I'm going to give you power over my personal life. You don't agree to my proposal, then fine, have me thrown in jail. Although how that gets you back your money is beyond me.'

Draco looked down at her, a small part of him unwillingly intrigued by her relentless fire. It spoke to a part of his nature that wasn't relevant any longer. These days he harnessed his cold passion to controlling his empire. And to ensuring Maria wanted for nothing. Any other emotion was superfluous.

The reminder of his sister brought him back to reality.

'You're bluffing. People like you love the good life too much to bravely accept a jail term, but before you deny it, tell me, are you willing to risk your father going to prison for his crimes?'

She froze, her eyes widening. 'My father? I thought you said *I* would repay the money?'

'That doesn't absolve him of wrongdoing. My company is being audited at the end of the month. Regardless of who repays the funds after that, the crime will be discovered.'

'But…I can't pay back half a million pounds by then,' she blurted.

'I know,' he replied with more than a drawl of satisfaction.

The shadow he'd glimpsed earlier settled over her face, her eyes darkening as she stared at him. 'You have the power to stop this. If you want to. That's what you've been hinting at all along, isn't it?'

'That depends on whether you're prepared to meet my demands.'

She shook her head. 'If you expect me to pull out of the championship, then the answer's no.'

'You want to compete that badly?'

She bit her bottom lip, then released it. Her mouth trembled slightly before she exhaled. 'Yes.'

Draco wasn't aware his hands had left his pockets until they cupped her shoulders. Delicate bones and soft, silky skin registered along his senses, even as he spoke. 'Are you willing to can the bravado and listen to me for five minutes?'

'If you insist.'

He drew her closer. He told himself it was because he needed her close so she didn't misunderstand what he planned to say to her. 'I insist.'

Her gaze dropped to his mouth for a moment before sliding away. 'Fine. I have training at five in the morning, so if you don't mind, can we just get on with it, Mr Angelis?'

'Draco.'

Her eyes flew back to his. 'What?'

'For what I have in mind, you'll need to start calling me by my first name. Try it.'

'Umm…no—'

He slid a finger beneath her chin to hold her steady. 'Say my name, Arabella.'

Her nose wrinkled. 'I prefer Rebel.'

'I think we've established that what you prefer is low on

my priority list. I will call you Arabella. And you will say my name, without the snark or the attitude.'

'Fine… Draco.'

His fingers tightened. 'Once more, with feeling.'

'This is *truly* absurd… *Draco*.'

The sultry decadence of his name on her lips arrowed straight through his rigid control, reminding him unequivocally that his libido was alive and well. For a hot second, Draco spied himself from the other side of the room, observing the unfolding scene with growing astonishment.

Was he really contemplating this insane course of action?

Then he reminded himself why he was doing this.

For Maria. For the sister he'd let down so severely. For the sister whose eyes filled with pain each time she looked at him, and yet was determined to rise above bitterness. To *forgive*.

Draco hadn't quite mastered that particular technique. Wasn't sure he wanted to. Bitterness and pain were his correct penance for letting his sister down, for ruining a life that had once held so much unbridled potential.

If he could get back even a shadow of joy for his sister, he would do whatever it took.

'Earth to Draco?'

The sinful drawl brought him back to himself. To the room where low decadent music thrummed to a sensual rhythm, and where a reckless siren in hot pants could well be the answer to what he needed.

He really was going crazy…

He jerked as soft fingers grazed his jaw. The touch was gone a second later, but its earthy power streaked fire across his senses.

'If I haven't turned you into a zombie, can you tell me why me calling you by your first name is necessary in this grand plan of yours?'

He stared into her flawless face. With her wide eyes and parted lips, she perfectly emulated innocence. Except he knew she was duplicitous to the core. She was wild, totally remorseless and disturbingly reckless with well-documented antics both in her professional and personal lives.

Those heinous traits would guarantee that he would remain sexually and emotionally detached—not that the latter was in doubt—from the plan he intended to carry out.

This was for Maria. And Maria alone.

'If you want to keep your father and yourself out of jail, I need you to pretend to be my fiancée for the next three months.'

CHAPTER FIVE

REBEL'S FIRST THOUGHT after the shocked laugh that erupted from her lips was, 'I'd rather skydive naked. Twice.'

She knew the words hadn't remained mere thoughts when Draco's features tightened with formidable displeasure. His mouth twisted in a cruel yet fascinating line that drew her gaze to the sensual curve she'd warned herself not to keep staring at.

'If you think that's your worst nightmare, then you haven't experienced hell.'

'I'm sorry…were you serious?'

If anything, she succeeded in angering him more. Although he barely moved, his overpowering presence filled the room with an oppressive aura that strangled the breath in her lungs. 'Did you not guess that I wasn't the joking type?'

'Yes, but…why on earth do you need a fake fiancée? And why me?' she tagged on, stunned that the absurd questions were falling from her lips.

Again his mouth twisted and he shook his head, as if he was having trouble accepting the very subject he'd initiated.

'The *why* will be explained after you accept my proposal. The *why you* is because you happen to be in the position of being in my debt, literally. And because your reputation fits what I need.'

She couldn't stop the lance of hurt that stabbed her. 'My reputation?' she asked, even though she knew she was inviting further hurt.

'You have a loose relationship with the truth, and you steal. Why not add pretence to your repertoire?'

Rebel jerked away from him. Or she tried to. Draco held on easily, taking firmer hold of her shoulders. Despite the sensations shivering through her at that contact, she forced herself to speak. 'Because not even a million pounds and a dozen acting awards could make me pull off *pretending* to like you. Let me go.'

Grey eyes gleamed dangerously. 'I'm not a man you want to cross, Arabella. So I suggest you give serious thought to giving me what I want.'

'And I suggest you give serious thought to what you're asking me to do. In what universe would anyone believe we're even remotely *attracted* to one another, let alone engaged to be married?'

He didn't answer her immediately. Instead his hold loosened until his fingers merely brushed her skin. Slowly, they left her shoulders and trailed down her arms. Light. Barely whispering. Electrifying. Rebel had thought his forceful grip was bad enough, but the light caress of Draco's fingers along her skin started fires in places that stunned and alarmed her.

The pads of his fingers grazed the inside of her wrists. Rebel couldn't have stopped the wicked shiver that raced through her any more than she could've stopped breathing. Despite telling herself to step away, to stop this disturbing assault on her senses, she remained rooted to the spot as he traced her racing pulse.

A half step closer and one scant inch separated them. This close, she could see the tiny gold flecks in his eyes that added an extra layer of dynamism to Draco Angelis she wouldn't have thought impossible. His rich scent blanketed her with dark, dangerous promise as the music she'd stupidly thought would clear her thoughts added to the thick, sensual pool she was drowning in.

He stared down at her, eyes piercingly direct, reading every emotion she desperately tried to hide. Then he lowered his head.

Her breath lodged in her lungs as, for the second time that day, the belief that Draco Angelis was about to kiss her shook her. Wild anticipation roared through her, shocking her with its intensity. Surely she couldn't want this?

The brief, superficial liaisons she'd had in the past had always left her cold. To the extent that no man had been allowed to go beyond a few kisses, despite the tabloids' wild speculations about her sexual antics. She'd been content being a virgin with no thought as to what her first sexual encounter would be like simply because it hadn't been a concern.

Now with every atom in her body screaming at the mere thought of being kissed by this man, the reality of her sexual innocence hovered like a time bomb above her head.

Would he think her some sort of freak? Would he laugh his head off?

Pull yourself together!

What on earth did it matter what Draco Angelis thought? He would never place high enough in her life to ever find out. Just as she would never allow this kiss to happen...

About to step away, Rebel found herself captive once more when he shackled her wrists. The mouth tantalisingly close to hers drifted past. His breath warmed her jaw, then the sensitive skin beneath her earlobe.

'You don't think we have chemistry?'

'N-no,' she forced out.

'Then why is your pulse jumping? Why does your breath catch every time I swipe my fingers across your skin?' he husked in her ear. 'You've been staring at my mouth for the last minute and licking yours in anticipation of my kiss. Do you want me to kiss you, Arabella?'

'No. No!' This time when she jerked out of his hold, he let her go. Striding to the other side of the room, she crossed her arms over her chest, keenly aware of the tightness in her breasts and the telltale pearls of her nipples. 'I don't know where you're going with this—'

'You doubted our ability to pull off an authentic attraction. I've just proved you wrong.'

'You've just proved that we're both half-decent actors. I'll grant you that much. It still doesn't answer my question as to why I'd ever think of indulging you in this absurd caper.'

His eyes darkened dramatically. Coupled with his glare and the stubble gracing his firm jawline, Draco's 'fallen angel' demeanour ratcheted up her already racing heartbeat. He clenched his fists at his sides, his nostrils flaring briefly before he inhaled control back into his body. The whole process was fascinating to watch and Rebel found herself following every subtle movement.

'It seems you were right. I wasted my time coming here.' With an arrogant shrug, he cast another condemning glance around the room, then strode to where she stood. 'I'll be reporting you and your father to the authorities the moment I leave here. I suggest you save yourself a few hours of unwanted attention, and don't try and make a run for it. No doubt the press will get hold of the story by morning anyway. I'll also be pursuing civil charges to recover the stolen money so make sure you hire a good lawyer.'

He was leaving. Just as she'd wanted.

He would be pressing charges against her and her father. Killing her chances of reconciliation or putting her nightmares behind her so she could finally lay her mother's ghost to rest.

Just what she didn't want.

As he walked past her and disappeared through her living-room door, Rebel knew she needed to stop Draco. But what had happened between them minutes ago had struck a vein of irrational apprehension in her heart. Whatever his ultimate plan was in seeking a fake fiancée, she was instinctively convinced she would come out the worst for it.

But the alternative...

Ice drenched her as her front door was pulled open.

The alternative for her father was unthinkable. She'd already deprived him of the love of his life. Could she sit by and watch him be deprived of his freedom as well?

'Wait!'

He froze in the doorway. The hand gripping her door handle tightened, but Draco didn't turn around. Fear climbed up her throat, the thought that he might carry on walking a live wire snaking through her.

'Can we talk about this some more?' she addressed his silent frame.

He released the door and faced her. 'No. You're under the impression that you can bargain with me. You can't. Either agree to my demands or face the charges.'

She swallowed. Leaning against the hallway wall, she speared her fingers through her hair, seeking rationality in a world gone wildly askew.

'I don't even know what I'm agreeing to exactly.'

'I've given you the broad parameters of what I want from you. The finer details will be ironed out once I have your agreement.'

She chewed on her lower lip. 'So I agree to be your pretend fiancée for three months and you call off the search for my father and drop all charges?' she verified.

His jaw flexed for a moment. 'Provided you play your part right, yes.'

'And nothing I agree to will interrupt my training programme?'

'Your training will proceed as you wish, but you have to be prepared to accommodate a travelling schedule. Considering you were attempting to relocate, that shouldn't be a problem. I assume you're doing your dry-land drills at the moment?'

She gave a surprised nod. 'Yes, I've been alternating the on-site training and dry-land training. I return to the snow next month.'

'We'll work out a different schedule when the time comes.'

'I...okay.'

They stared at each other, Rebel unable to believe what she was a hair's breadth from agreeing to. Draco's expression remained shuttered, but he stared at her with an intensity that pierced her to the soul.

'I think you'd better tell me exactly what you want from me. I can act it up with the best of them, but I'm not sure I can pull off wide-eyed innocent if that's what you require.'

Draco stepped back into the hallway and she released a breath she hadn't known she was holding. With an agile foot, he kicked the door shut. Sauntering back, he leaned one shoulder on the opposite wall. 'Since that's the type of woman I'm trying to avoid, my suggestion is that you be yourself with one or two modifications.'

'Just so we're clear, what do you think I am?'

'A reckless pleasure seeker with very little regard for anyone's feelings but her own.'

Rebel wasn't sure why her stomach dropped and rolled or why disappointment cut so deep. She had nothing to prove to Draco Angelis. His opinion of her didn't matter. All that mattered was her father was safe from whatever hellhole had been intended for him. She still had a chance at closure, might even dare to seek absolution for the wrongs she'd done.

'And the modifications you seek?' she asked past the hard lump lodged in her throat.

He straightened from the wall, his height and breath dominating the space so she was aware of nothing else but him.

'You will not see any other guy while you're with me. Any past liaisons are officially over as of tonight. As far as the public is concerned, you're mine and mine alone.'

The possessive throb in his voice rammed home his acting ability. 'Is that all?'

'For now. We'll discuss any further addenda as and when they come up.'

'How democratic of you,' she murmured under her breath. 'Who exactly are we faking all this for?' she asked curiously.

He thrust his hands in his pockets and rocked on the balls of his feet. 'Do we have an agreement?'

Rebel swallowed hard, a chasm opening up before her she couldn't see a way out of. 'Yes.'

Draco gave a single nod before he strode back into her living room. By the time she followed him in, he'd taken a seat on her small white sofa. The sight of him, dark and imposing, on her dainty sofa sent another fissure of alarm skittering through her. But there was no backing out now. She'd agreed to this.

'Sit down.'

She curbed the snarky comment that tripped on her tongue and sat down on the armchair opposite him. Draco had nearly walked out and doomed her father to criminal prosecution. While she didn't know why her father had done what he'd done, she wasn't about to risk dicing with Draco again. Instinct warned he wasn't prone to giving second chances.

'Do you know of Carla Nardozzi?'

Rebel frowned. 'The three-time champion figure skater? Of course. Everyone knows who she is.' The twenty-four-year-old was stunningly beautiful, with a talent that had seen her soar up the figure-skating rankings halfway through her seventeenth year. She was the darling of the sports world, with sponsorship deals that had made her one of the richest sports stars by the time she was twenty-one. Her talent and success, coupled with her shy and innocent demeanour, had given her an unattainable, almost royal-princess allure that only added to her appeal.

'I want her.'

An unpleasant zing jerked Rebel in her seat. Viciously unwilling to examine the feeling, she stared back at Draco. 'Then I'm at a complete loss as to why you're sitting in my lowly Chelsea flat when you should be somewhere on the Upper East Side in New York courting her. That *is* where she lives, isn't it?'

'She divides her time between there and her training facility in Switzerland. But at the moment, she's at her father's estate in Tuscany.'

'Even better. You could be reunited with her in less than two hours. I'm sure she'll eventually see past your… interesting traits to a happy ever after with you.'

A dark frown clamped his straight brows. 'Happy ever after? What the hell are you talking about?'

She shrugged. 'You just said you want her…oh, is she playing hard to get? Is that what this is about? You want to use me to make her jealous?'

His frown deepened, then he shook his head. 'You misunderstand. She's playing hard to get, but not in the way you think. I want her as a client, but her father's standing in my way.'

Rebel despised the relief that poured through her. It pointed to an interest in Draco's private life that shouldn't be piqued. In any shape or form.

She straightened her back and cleared her throat. 'Right. I'm still at a loss as to why you need a fiancée.'

Draco sat forward and planted his elbows on his knees. 'During our last few meetings, Olivio Nardozzi hinted heavily that he'll let me sign his daughter only if I brought something…more to the table.'

'More? He wants you to date his daughter in order to secure a business deal?'

A whisper of disdain crossed his rugged face. 'I suspect he has something more permanent than dating in mind.'

That unpleasant zing returned, harder than before. 'So you intend to beat him at his own game, all for a business deal?'

Disdain morphed into something darker. Bitterness edged with pain. His features cleared a second later, but the image lingered in Rebel's mind, sparking a different interest altogether.

'I have other reasons for pursuing this.'

'Such as?' she asked before she could stop herself.

His eyelids dropped. The hands dangling between his knees slowly clenched into fists and bleakness settled over his face. Rebel was certain he wasn't aware he was exhibiting such a strong and telling reaction to her question. Her breath stalled in her lungs as she watched him battle to get his emotions under control.

By the time he raised his head, his expression was once again formidably neutral. 'My other reasons are private.'

She shook her head. 'I don't like surprises. I heard you on the phone yesterday. There was familiarity between you.'

'And your point is?'

'I hardly think Papà Nardozzi would be hell-bent on pairing you with his daughter if you two hated each other's guts.'

His eyes gleamed. 'I've known Carla since she was a teenager.'

'And…?' she pressed, disconcerted by the need to probe deeper.

'And our past bears no relevance to this deal. Your role is to help me convince Nardozzi that I'm already taken.'

Pushing aside the burning need to know more about his past with Carla, she asked instead, 'Will he sign his daughter with you if you don't give him what he wants?'

'He's on the brink of achieving the biggest endorsement deal any sports personality has ever acquired, through my company,' he replied. 'Javier Santino, the sponsor, is growing tired of the unnecessary delays. Nardozzi needs to be made aware of where I stand once and for all.'

'A simple *no* to him won't suffice?'

His eyes turned hard. 'Some people don't understand the word. They believe it's their right to have what they want simply because they want it.'

The direct taunt stabbed her deep, but she managed to

keep her composure. Standing, she folded her arms. 'Okay, I get it. So we're talking a few outings with me on your arm to convince Papà that he needs to find another suitor for daughter dearest?'

'It requires a little more than that. Nardozzi is hosting a charity gala in Italy this Sunday. He's invited me to stay at his Tuscany estate the day before the gala. He's made it clear he won't be discussing the deal, which means he intends to push his personal agenda instead.'

'So I'm expected to come to Tuscany with you this weekend?' she asked, feeling a curious dredging in her abdomen at the thought of sharing her private time and space with Draco Angelis.

'Yes. We'll fly out on Saturday and return on Monday morning.'

Rebel paced the short distance to her window and settled her agitated body against the sill. 'I still don't get why you're humouring him if you don't think he'll walk away from a deal he clearly wants.'

Draco remained silent for a full minute, prompting her to think she'd misstepped without knowing. When his face tightened again, she was sure she'd hit a nerve somewhere.

'I don't just want to represent Carla for this deal. I want her to change training teams. I want to be in charge of her training.'

The sense that she was missing a key element in this scenario nagged at her. The idea that it might be far from platonic was another notion she couldn't dismiss. But Draco had made it clear he wasn't prepared to share that side of his plan with her. 'I wasn't aware agents had a say in which training teams their clients took on.'

'They don't. Not normally,' he said abruptly, before rising to his feet.

About to ask him to elaborate, she bit back her words when he swerved towards her. 'Before we leave for Tuscany, we need to ensure our relationship attracts the appropriate public attention.'

'Won't it raise suspicion for us to be suddenly engaged?' she queried.

'I'm an intensely private man. I'm not in the habit of broadcasting my liaisons. It won't be a problem to let slip that we've been dating for a while. A few might find it hard to believe that *you* haven't publicised our association, but hopefully we'll convince them that some of my good traits have rubbed off on you.'

She rolled her eyes. 'If I didn't know better I'd think you just attempted a joke.'

His grim lips twitched, but his face remained stoic. 'I'll have my PA email you a list of restaurants I prefer to dine in. If you have any objections, let her know. Please provide her with your training schedule, and I'll try and work around it.'

Rebel supposed she ought to be grateful he was accommodating her needs. But having her time monopolised so completely stuck in her craw. 'You need anything else? Like fingerprints or a sample of DNA?'

His eyes travelled with acute intensity from the top of her head to the tips of her bare toes and back again before he met her gaze with a raised brow. 'Such invasive procedures won't be necessary, but perhaps you'll make an attempt to address your wardrobe issues for the next three months?'

'What wardrobe issues? I thought you preferred me the way I am?'

One corner of his mouth lifted in a shadowed sneer. 'Consider this another minor modification. Skin-tight leather hot pants and see-through tops have their place somewhere on the fashion landscape, I'm sure. My PA will furnish you with a reputable stylist's details. Make use of it.'

'Wow. Do you make a habit of issuing orders like a drill sergeant or am I just special?'

'It seems to be the only way I can get through to you.'

'Really? I don't recall getting the honey treatment, just the rancid-vinegar one.'

He crossed the floor to stand before her. Rebel watched, heart leaping to her throat as he raised his hand. His thumb traced her lower lip as it had done in his office. Except this touch was slower. Deadlier in its intensity.

'You'll get the honey when you deserve it. In the meantime, I'll leave you to practise giving *me* the honey. We're dining out tomorrow night. Make sure you bring your A-game. Remember what's at stake here, Arabella. Fail me and all bets are off.'

She was still slumped against the windowsill when he walked out. Even the firm click of her front door didn't rouse her from the fevered daze rushing over her.

Rebel had no idea of when she finally moved, although she managed a quick call to Contessa begging off her manager's visit, and also to inform her of the change of travel plans. Then she returned her clothes and skis to their rightful place, and made herself a cup of light cocoa.

It was another treat her trainer would no doubt chastise her for, but cocoa had always helped her sleep better. And she needed to sleep.

She needed the escape of slumber to help her *not* think about Draco Angelis. She needed to *not* think about honey or sinful caresses or A-games. Or the dark hunger veiled behind his censure and bitterness.

For one thing, the danger that accompanied the man held a mesmeric quality that spelled doom for any self-preserving creature.

For another, Rebel had always been recklessly attracted to danger.

CHAPTER SIX

THE FLOWERS ARRIVED at eight a.m., just as she was donning her gym gear. Greg, her trainer, who'd arrived at her door five minutes earlier for their run to the gym, raised an eyebrow as he walked in with an armful of the most exquisite arrangement of calla lilies Rebel had ever seen.

Besides the flowers, the black sculptured vase holding the stems was equally breathtaking.

Greg whistled as he set it on her small dining table. 'Flowers from Gilla Rosa. Someone's all out to get your attention.'

Rebel, still taking in the stunning delivery from the florist who only catered to A-list celebrities, attempted a smile. 'I guess so.' Spotting a card, she plucked it, her nerves jangling alarmingly as she opened it.

Château Dessida.
Eight o'clock tonight.
Can't wait.
D

'Château Dessida, huh? I thought you weren't dating anyone?' She started as Greg moved away from where he'd been reading the card over her shoulder.

As her trainer, he was one of a few people who knew how dedicated she was to making the championships. He also knew her occasional outings to nightclubs were coping mechanisms so didn't give her grief about it.

About to confirm that she wasn't actually dating, Rebel bit her lip. There were twelve hours before she had to begin her performance as Draco Angelis' fiancée, but it seemed her acting debut was about to commence. 'I wasn't…until fairly recently.' She dropped the card on the table and propped her foot on a dining chair to finish lacing her trainers. Then she went through her stretching routine.

The six-foot ex–body builder eyed her. 'Don't mean to judge but—is it wise getting involved with anyone so close to the championships?'

Rebel tossed out a laugh that was a million miles from genuine. 'Probably not, but isn't there a cliché about not being able to help who you fall for?'

His dark blond brows spiked. 'It's that serious already?' The brotherly concern in his eyes made her feel a heel for the subterfuge, but Rebel forced herself to remember why she was doing this.

'Cliché number two—I guess when you know, you know?' She grabbed her water bottle and tucked her phone and keys into her pockets.

Greg glanced at the flowers before he followed her out of the door. 'Here are a few more—hard work is its own reward. You've worked hard to get where you are. So don't take your eye off the ball.'

Rebel rolled her eyes, but kept the smile pinned on her face. 'As if there's any chance you'll let me. Besides, you never know. True love might be the extra-special ingredient I need to win this thing.'

She set off before he could reply. Although he caught up with her easily, he refrained from speaking, for which Rebel was grateful. But cranking up her earphones to near maximum didn't stop her mind from reeling at the full assault Draco seemed to have mounted. It was obvious he was setting the scene for their fake relationship to achieve maximum publicity in minimum time, but she would've welcomed a little more time to get used to the idea before being hit over the head with it.

Sadly, the pummelling came at an even more frantic pace the moment she returned from her morning training.

She'd barely stepped out of the shower when her doorbell rang. The courier delivered a five-page document that detailed Draco's schedule for the next fortnight and boxes to tick as to her preferred sources of entertainment. Her mouth dropped open when she read the extensive list and the final bullet point that told her the courier would return in an hour to retrieve the answered document.

Irritated, she started to tick random boxes, but by the next page a cheeky smile twitched at her lips. Crossing out several lines of questions, she scrawled one answer across the page. Then proceeded to do the same on the following pages.

She answered the courier's knock with a smile, which turned into a scowl when she spotted a sleek estate car pulling up behind the courier's van.

The six outfits and matching accessories the stylist delivered fitted perfectly, and the quirky but stylish edge to the designs made them ones she would've picked out for herself, had she come across them in a boutique. With the only exception that the delivered items had featured a designer way out of her price tag.

Deciding going with the flow was better than raising unnecessary hell, she was stepping out of a sleeveless white jumpsuit when her phone buzzed.

She sprawled across her bed to get it. 'Hello?'

'I hope your intention isn't for the next three months to be a tedium of modifications to our agreement.'

Rebel tried to ignore the tingling along her spine that Draco's deep voice elicited. 'Umm, I don't do well with cryptic. What did I do wrong now?'

'Crossing out questions about your personal interests and giving one inappropriate answer isn't acceptable.'

'Oh, right. You don't like pole dancing?' she quipped, tongue firmly in her cheek.

'Or bungee jumping. Or eating blindfolded in a blacked-

out room. Skydiving—with my clothes on—might be a consideration if we had the time. We don't.'

Rebel rolled over and contemplated her black polka-dot
ceiling. 'Are you sure you've got the balls for skydiving?
Not everyone does.'

'Is that a dare?' he growled.

'Maybe. I'll answer the rest of your boring questionnaire
if you agree to skydive with me once the championships are
over. If you have the stones, that is.'

'I don't need my stones to skydive. They're for a specific purpose.'

Rebel was thankful she was on the phone when her face
flamed at his words.

'Yeah, whatever. Do you accept?'

'No, Arabella. I don't accept your invitation. Not everything in life needs to be attacked with adrenaline-fuelled ferocity. And I prefer to see how you fare in the coming week
before I make plans for months down the road.'

The bite in his voice erased any trace of mirth left in
her. Rising, she shifted to the edge of her bed and stared at
the delicate tissue paper and couture boxes strewn on her
bed and floor. Suddenly, the sight of the expensive clothes
produced a whiff of unease inside her. Try as she might,
she couldn't dismiss the insane idea that Draco Angelis
was somehow marking her with an indelible stamp of possession.

'Have I rendered you speechless for once?' he drawled.

Rousing herself, she answered, 'I answered the first page
of your document. I think that should get us through this
first week, don't you?'

'You ticked only one activity that interests you for every
posed question.'

'So I like nightclubs. What's wrong with that?'

A faint growl rumbled down the line. The muscles in her
stomach quivered as an image of a rousing dragon flashed

through her mind. 'We will discuss it further tonight. I'll be there at seven-thirty. Make sure you're ready.'

He hung up before she could reply. Which was just as well since the answer on the tip of her tongue would no doubt have released the fire-breathing monster on her.

Rebel chose to wear the white jumpsuit simply because her afternoon training session overran and it was the only item of clothing that didn't need careful ironing. Slipping her feet into black and gold heels, she accessorised with a long gold necklace and chunky bangles, then caught her hair up in a loose knot before completing the look with gold chandelier earrings and a white clutch.

She was waiting on the kerb by the time Draco drove up in a gleaming black sports car. Pulling the door open, she slid into the soft leather bucket seat. And immediately clocked his tight-jawed irritation.

'Are you in the habit of hanging out on street corners waiting for your dates?'

She took her time to secure her seat belt, which didn't go as smoothly as she wanted because her every cell had grown hyperaware of the powerful and arresting man behind the wheel. He'd swapped yesterday's three-piece suit for a darker set, minus the waistcoat and tie. With the light grey shirt unbuttoned at the neck, she glimpsed a few wisps of dark silky hair that had her quickly averting her gaze.

Once she got the belt's metal housing to click, she drew a breath. Then wished she hadn't when his clean, spicy aftershave attacked her senses. Draco smelling good enough to devour wasn't a thought she intended to dwell on. 'I only came down to save you time. Please don't tell me I've offended your gentlemanly sensibilities?'

His mouth pursed. 'I'd prefer our association not to begin with hints of impropriety.'

'I was standing outside my flat, Draco, not in a red-light part of town.'

He pulled up to a red light and locked cool grey eyes

on her. 'It wouldn't have been too much trouble for me to walk to your door.'

Rebel wasn't sure why his solicitous remark robbed her of breath. Competing in a high-octane sport meant lady-like sensibilities were often mocked. She'd trained herself a long time ago to be one of the boys or risk acquiring a sneering nickname. She'd thought herself immune to need-ing gentle consideration. And yet the thought of Draco treat-ing her with the tiniest deference caused a lump to rise in her throat. Her father had worshipped her mother that way, bending over backwards to grant her smallest wish.

Her mother had grumbled, but she'd always done so with a teasing smile. The memory thickened the lump in her throat, even as the acute lance of pain pierced her heart.

Struggling to retain her composure under Draco's intense stare, she cleared her throat. 'Noted. I'll do better next time.'

Surprise lit his eyes, but he turned away without re-sponse as the light turned green. The rest of the short jour-ney passed in silence.

Château Dessida, located in a side street off the King's Road, was tiny and extremely exclusive. It was renowned for its French fusion-themed dishes, the three-Michelin-starred chef who ran the kitchen rumoured to personally select which customers patronised his establishment. He also reserved the right to publicise who dined in his res-taurant, with famous photos making his millions-strong social-media following green with envy.

Draco tossed his car keys to the waiting valet and guided her through the canopied doorway.

'It's show time,' he murmured in her ear.

Before she could grasp his meaning, he pulled her close and settled a hand over her hip. Despite the layers of cloth-ing separating them, Rebel felt his touch as keenly as if he'd branded her bare skin with a hot iron. Biting back a gasp, she stumbled. Draco's other hand shot out to grasp her waist.

'Steady, *agapita*. You okay?'

Held immobile, she stared up at him, then grew dizzy all over again as his mouth stretched in a dazzling, captivating smile. Rebel knew she was gaping, but for the life of her she couldn't look away from the stunning transformation on Draco's face. Gone was the fire-breathing ogre who seemed to find fault with every word that spilled from her lips.

In his place was an Adonis who oozed charm and attentiveness as the hand on her hip rotated in a slow caress and his other hand gripped her tighter.

'Arabella? Baby, are you okay?'

Absurdly, it was the combination of her name and the endearment that tossed her out of her stupor. Sucking in a long, restorative breath, she summoned a bare-toothed dazzler of her own. Leaning closer, she tiptoed her fingers up his chest.

'Laying it on a bit thick, aren't you, *baby*?' she remarked through clenched teeth.

The hand on her waist drifted up her arm, leaving a trail of goose bumps. 'Your neat little stumble attracted the right attention. We're now the spectacle for a few dozen pairs of eyes to feast on.' With a little too much practised ease, he lifted her faux-fur wrap from her shoulders and handed it to a cloak attendant.

Irritation jerked through her. 'I didn't do it on purpose.'

'Then it's a good thing your lover is here to catch you when you're adorably clumsy, isn't it, sweetheart?' Light fingers framed her cheek, his smile continuing to blind with its fake brilliance.

Rebel was about to snap for him to ease off with the false charm, but her words dried in her throat when Draco's name was boomed from over her shoulder.

François Dessida, a short, wiry man with thick, flowing brown hair, greeted them with a short but effusive torrent of French, which Draco answered flawlessly. Introductions were made, a few Gallic shrugs thrown in the mix, then

François clicked his fingers. As if by magic, the maître d'
appeared with a discreet camera.

Rebel found herself wedged between the two men, Draco's
hand back on her hip as he dragged her close enough for there
to be no doubt as to their intimacy. Resurrecting her smile,
she held her pose through several snaps, then exhaled in relief when François clicked his fingers again.

Wishing them a pleasant evening, he disappeared back
into his domain.

By the time the maître d' showed them to their table,
having stopped at a few tables when Draco returned greet-
ings, Rebel felt as brittle as glass and just as transparent.

Her smile was fracturing at the edges and with each
brush of Draco's hand on her—a gesture he seemed bent on
repeating often in this insane charade—her insides clenched
tight.

The moment they sat down and he'd dismissed the maître d' with their wine order, he leaned forward.

'What's wrong?' he breathed smoothly, but she caught
the steely edge in his voice.

'Can we dial down the touchy-feely stuff, please?' she
whispered.

'The idea is to exhibit that we're utterly besotted with
each other. That involves a degree of contact.'

Thankful they'd been seated at an intimate table away
from the nearest guests, she replied, 'But not three thousand degrees of it. Can we not be a couple who are discreet
about their PDA?'

'To all intents and purposes, I'm about to propose to you
tonight. We're starting what will become one of the most
memorable nights of our lives. And you expect me to keep
my hands off you?'

Her mouth dropped open. 'You're about to propose?'

'That's generally how engagements happen,' he replied.

'No, I meant…you're going to do it *here*?' Her gaze
darted around only to confirm they were still the subject

of great interest. Anxiety clawed up her chest. Which was absurd because all this was make-believe.

'You don't seem pleased about it,' he quipped.

Struggling for composure, she threw on a mock pout. 'I guess because you've ruined the surprise. Now I have to sharpen my acting skills even more.'

He reached across the table and took her left hand. 'I'm sure you'll rise to the occasion admirably.' Raising her hand, he kissed her ring finger.

The flash of a phone camera a second later confirmed the reason for the gesture. But it didn't stop her belly from flipping over with a mixture of anxiety and dread. The moment he set her free, she drew her hand into her lap and curled it into a fist. She was fast becoming aware that she wasn't as immune to Draco Angelis' touch as she'd assured herself she was. The chemistry she'd denied so vehemently last night was alive and well, and growing with each passing second.

Draco's stellar performance continued throughout their appetiser and main courses. He tucked into his plate of braised veal and roasted vegetables soaked in red wine sauce, while she pushed her truffled chicken escalope around her plate, taking the occasional bite when he sent her a speaking look. By the time the course was over, the food had congealed in her stomach.

'Something on your mind?'

'You asked for my A-game. I don't think I can bring it. I'm not sure I can pull this off,' she blurted once their wine glasses had been refilled.

He inhaled sharply, his eyes snapping with displeasure. 'I suggest you find a way to make it happen. We've set the ball rolling on this. It's too late to change your mind now. Even if your father makes a triumphant return and you somehow find yourself with another windfall, you still have an agreement to fulfil.'

The remnants of wine she'd just swallowed turned sour

in her mouth as she twisted the wine-glass stem between her fingers.

The sensation of falling deeper into a bottomless chasm grew. She jumped when Draco leaned closer. 'He hasn't returned, has he?' he enquired.

Pursing her lips, she shook her head. 'No, he hasn't.' Despite her calling him every free moment she'd had today, her phone remained silent.

'Has he done this before? Disappeared without a trace?'

Pain dredged through her. With every fibre of her being, Rebel wished she could answer in the negative. 'Yes, he's done it before.'

Draco's gaze sharpened. 'When?'

'When…when my mother died. After her funeral, he left home. He didn't return for three months.'

He frowned. 'How old were you?'

'I was seventeen.'

'And he left you alone?' The bite was back, the charming façade he'd worn all night slipping to reveal the ruthless man beneath. Absurdly, Rebel felt a tiny bit of relief at seeing the real man, even though this version of Draco remained a formidable force that battered at the foundations of her existence.

Rebel shrugged. 'He had my aunt look in on me every once in a while, but I was pretty much independent by then.'

'And that excuses his actions?' Anger laced his every syllable.

Unable to risk him seeing her guilt, she stared down at her plate. 'He'd just lost the love of his life. He…he was grieving.'

'While he had a responsibility to you? Were you not grieving too?'

Her gaze snapped up. 'Of course I was!' Swallowing, she shook her head and continued. 'But…there's more to the story, Draco.'

His mouth twisted in a cynical grimace. 'Isn't there al-

ways? Sadly, more often than not, *more* is just an excuse
for shirking responsibility or seeking blanket absolution.'

'We all deal with our issues in different ways.'

'Yes. And your father's way seems to be doing a runner
and leaving you with the smoking gun,' he drawled pithily.

'Don't—!'

'More wine, *madamoiselle*? *Monsieur*?'

They both started. Draco recovered first, reaching out to
take the bottle from the waiter and dismissing him. When
she shook her head, he set the bottle down without refill-
ing his own. Silence cloaked them for several minutes, with
Rebel trying hard to stem the tremors charging through
her body.

She couldn't believe she'd spilled her guts to Draco, given
him further ammunition against her and her father.

'You gave me your word. You will not back out of this,'
he stated with unmistakable gravity.

For myriad reasons, she wanted to take back her prom-
ise. But each and every reason that tumbled through her
head was a selfish one. And they all centred around how
Draco Angelis made her *feel*. Unbalanced. Apprehensive.
An all-encompassing excitement each time he touched her.
A craving for more of that touch.

But her feelings didn't matter here. Winning the championship in order to keep her mother's memory alive and
ensuring she found a way back to her father were the two
most important reasons to stick with this. She couldn't do
either from a prison cell.

After a brave sip of wine, she set her glass down. 'I won't
back out. From this moment, I'm all in.'

CHAPTER SEVEN

DRACO EXHALED THE BREATH locked in his chest and nodded. He refused to acknowledge the anxiety that slowly seeped out of him as he stared at Arabella. 'And I have your assurance that this is the last time I'll have to deal with a change of heart?'

A shrug lifted her smooth, bare shoulder. 'I'll try not to make a habit of it, but I reserve the right to throw a mini wobbly if this charade gets a little too much. I'm human after all, not a robot.'

Had she been a robot, she would've earned the title of sexiest robot created. Her gold accessories highlighted her perfect, vibrant skin, drawing his gaze to her slim neck, delicate collarbones and the delectable shadows between her breasts. The spark that had started in his groin when he'd pulled her close at the door surged into a flame. He shifted in his seat, his trousers growing uncomfortably tight as she lifted her water glass and drank from it.

Setting it down, she sent him a furtive glance.

'This is really important to you, isn't it?' she probed.

Draco guessed that this was her attempt to steer the conversation away from her father. And while residual fury burned in his blood at the realisation that the man whose integrity and hard work he'd relied on for the past five years had turned out to be untrustworthy to the extent of abandoning his own family when he'd been needed most, Draco was content to let the matter rest. For now.

He took his time to answer, relaying their coffee orders to the waiter before he responded, 'Yes, it's important.'

She continued to toy with the crystal goblet. 'Why? And

before you say so, I think I can accurately guess it's not about the money.'

He tensed, debated for a moment how much to divulge. Maria's privacy was of the utmost importance to him. As long as he had breath in his body, his sister wouldn't know the slightest pang of further suffering. He hadn't been able to protect her when it counted. But he intended to do everything he could to ease her tiniest worry.

'No, it's not about the money, although, as a businessman, it's in my interest to protect my and my clients' assets.'

'Of course, but there's more.' It wasn't a question. It was a statement of unwavering certainty.

Normally, prying from his date was a turn-off. But he found himself answering her, while reminding himself that this wasn't a proper date. This was a charade to get him what he wanted. What Maria wanted.

'Carla Nardozzi and her father are thinking of renewing her contract with Tyson Blackwell for another three years. I intend to make sure that doesn't happen.'

Surprise sparked her blue eyes. 'But Tyson is one of the most highly sought-after trainers out there. I worked with him in a group programme myself a few years ago.'

Renewed fury flamed through him, but he banked it down. He was supposed to play the part of a besotted lover, not an angry one, exhibiting bewildering signs of jealousy. 'I'm aware of that. Why did you part company?'

She shrugged. 'I think he had his eye on bigger fish. Carla Nardozzi, I expect.'

'Consider yourself lucky. He's known to push his trainees beyond their limits.'

She smiled at the waiter who delivered her coffee, before she met his gaze once more. 'And that's a bad thing?'

Regret and bitterness locked a vice around his chest. 'It is when they eventually break.'

Her eyes shadowed with sympathy, an emotion Draco wouldn't have associated with the flighty, self-obsessed creature he knew her to be. 'This happened to someone you know?'

The vice tightened. 'Yes.' He forced the word out.

She nodded, then picked up her coffee and blew gently on it. A different sort of tightening took hold of Draco. He wasn't sure whether to be resentful of the reminder that his libido was alive and kicking or welcome the distraction from trying to grapple with the diverging personalities of the woman sitting across from him. A sympathetic listener and narcissistic thief. Was there such a thing?

'I'm sorry that happened to them. Were you close to this person?' she pressed.

Draco decided that he preferred to tackle the subject of his libido. Discussing matters that ploughed through rough and disturbing memories wasn't what he'd intended for this dinner. And yet the box that resided in his jacket pocket remained there as he lifted and tossed back his double espresso.

'Did you take care of the matter of your other liaisons as you promised?'

Mocking laughter spilled from her lips. 'First of all, I made no such promise. Secondly, where on earth did you get the idea that I had *liaisons*, plural?'

His teeth ground until pain lanced his jaw. 'There have been several photographs of you cavorting with a certain rock band for the last few weeks.'

An emotion flicked through her eyes, one that resembled hurt. 'And that automatically means I'm dating all of them?'

Tension gripped him. 'Are you?'

'No. Cole, the lead singer, used to be into snowboarding when we were younger. I met him again at an event a few weeks ago, and we just hung out for a bit.'

'In the pictures you seem to be hanging out in his lap.' The words emerged in a rumble that thoroughly irritated him.

Arabella shook her head. 'I swear, if I didn't know better, I'd think you were jealous.'

His tension increased, along with the irksome need to probe this subject. 'This is nothing more than due diligence to ensure there are no surprises down the road.'

She held his gaze, hers bold and clear. 'There won't be.'

For the second time in under an hour, tension eased out of Draco. For whatever reason his instinct was to believe her. Or perhaps on a subconscious level he knew this was a minor problem, easily resolved once the world knew she belonged to him. His gaze dropped to her bare fingers, a sudden need sparking through him.

Confirming she'd finished her coffee, he stood and held out his hand.

After a tiny hesitation, she slipped her hand in his and stood. The few diners remaining glanced their way. One or two acquaintances tried to catch his eye, but he avoided them. He'd achieved what he came here for. He wasn't sure why he'd decided to take the next step away from prying eyes but he was tired of being on show.

The maître d' materialised with Arabella's wrap. Draco draped it over her shoulders and caught her faint shiver as his fingers brushed her skin.

He'd effectively debunked her denial of their chemistry at her flat last night. But little had he known that he would be caught in the tangle of chemical reaction so strong that he'd spent the night fighting lurid dreams.

She murmured her thanks and walked beside him, her hand once more clasped in his. He stared down at her profile, forcing himself to stay removed from the ever-growing tendrils of attraction grabbing at him.

A cold, rational part of him insisted that the attraction would make their fake relationship more believable. While the part of his anatomy that refused to remained unstirred urged him to change the parameters of their agreement. To make certain sections of it real.

He suppressed that urge and led Arabella to his car.

Even if he were on the market for a brief dalliance, Arabella Daniels wouldn't be his choice of partner. Her wild, brash approach to life would never gel with his, even for the weeks-long period his affairs usually lasted. Besides, she'd all but admitted to being as unscrupulous and lacking in integrity as her father.

There was no way he could risk exposing such a person to Maria.

Satisfied with his decision, he saw her into the car and slipped behind the wheel. The return journey back to her flat went much faster. When she went to open the door, Draco growled, 'Stay.'

As before, she seemed surprised by his gesture as he rounded the bonnet and opened her door.

'Thank you.'

Taking her by the elbow, he walked her to the front door and waited as she dug through her clutch for her keys.

Another furtive glance at him prompted a twitch of a smile. She was nervous.

'Invite me up.'

Nerves turned to surprise. Then suspicion. 'Why?'

'Because there's one more thing to address before we end the evening.'

Her eyes rounded before she caught his meaning. 'Oh, the engagement ring. I thought you wanted to do that in front of an audience?'

He shrugged. 'We lost our audience while we were discussing…other matters. And I don't intend to place my ring on your finger on the steps of your flat. Invite me up.'

The breath she inhaled was a shaky one. 'Umm…okay.'

She opened her front door and he held it wide for her, then followed her up the flight of stairs to her flat. In her living room, Draco waited as she turned on lamps and straightened cushions. Then watched, bemused, as she twisted her fingers and eyed the entertainment centre.

'You seem nervous.'

She laughed and shrugged. 'Not sure why I am. I guess I've never been genuinely fake-proposed to before.'

The idea that she'd been proposed to at all sent a thin vein of tension through him. He dismissed it and reached into his pocket. As his fingers closed over the velvet box, tension mutated to something else. Something Draco faintly recognised as trepidation for this moment. The kind that ran parallel with monumental tasks he didn't want to fail at. Frowning, he pulled the box from his pocket. There'd been no words to practise because this wasn't a prelude to a love union. They were each playing a finite role with a clear endgame in mind. The moment shouldn't contain as much gravity as was moving through him.

'If you want dramatic music to draw out the suspense, just say the word. I have tons,' Arabella quipped, one perfectly shaped eyebrow raised.

He fisted the box for a brief moment. 'That won't be necessary.'

Striding to where she stood, he held it up and pried it open.

She gasped, then frowned. 'It's real. I mean, I'm not a gem expert, but that looks…real!' Blue eyes met his, alarm swimming in the depths.

His teeth gritted. 'You thought I would supply you with a fake ring?'

'Well…yes. To go with the fake engagement? I don't know why you look so offended, but that would make sense, wouldn't it?'

'It would also announce our engagement as a sham to the whole world.'

Her gaze dropped down to the box. 'But this is probably worth more than I owe you. You're sure you trust me with it?' she murmured. 'What if I lose it?'

'It's insured against loss. And theft.' Draco wasn't sure why he added that. When she raised her gaze and he spotted the hurt she tried to hide, a tiny spark of remorse burst through him. Which was absurd because this situation had come about because of her collusion with her father's duplicity. Brushing aside the feeling, he growled, 'Give me your hand.'

She hesitated for one moment. Then two. At the back of his mind, Draco faintly wondered if this was what the average man felt like when he got down on one knee. If so, then he pitied them. Her unnecessary hesitation was irritating in the extreme. And he wasn't even on one knee. Nor did he intend to be.

'Arabella. Your hand.'

Rebel slowly held out her left hand, nerves eating her alive. 'Damn,' she muttered under her breath.

Draco's gaze rose from where he held the ring poised. 'What's wrong?'

She shrugged. 'If I'd known I'd be sporting a rock like this, I'd have made more of an effort with my nails.' She kept them trimmed short for training, but a little gloss wouldn't have gone amiss. She swallowed as she caught his frown. 'Sorry, I didn't mean to ruin the moment.' Realising she was babbling, she pressed her lips together.

'There isn't a moment to ruin,' he rasped. Rebel felt the cold tug of platinum over her knuckle. Then the ring slid into place. 'And your nails are fine.'

The rectangular-cut diamond was flanked by baguette diamonds, which connected to the platinum band. In the low lights of her flat, the ring glinted and flashed as her fingers trembled. It was a perfect fit. Just how he'd achieved that was a mystery, but Rebel couldn't take her eyes off the ring's sheer perfection. Nor could she divorce her mind from wandering down a senseless road of how she would've felt if this moment were real.

Not that the man she'd have chosen would've been Draco Angelis. He was far too arrogant and domineering for her to even consider him as—

'Is it my turn to ask whether we need melodramatic music? Or do you not like the ring?' Draco drawled with a slight edge in his tone.

'It's…' *beautiful*. Wondering why the word stuck in her throat, why so many different emotions darted through her, Rebel dragged her gaze from the stunning ring. 'It's fine. It'll probably get the job of convincing Nardozzi to back off done all on its own.'

His mouth twisted. 'I think you need to put in more personal effort than that.'

Before she could answer, his phone buzzed. Slipping it from his pocket, he stared at the screen for a moment, a hint of satisfaction flitting over his features. 'Dessida has done what I requested of him.'

Why was she surprised that Draco could get men with bloated egos like François Dessida to bend to his will? 'Great,' she responded, even though an added ball of uncertainty churned in her stomach. 'We're all set, then.'

'Not quite.' He stared down at his screen for a few more seconds before his steely gaze pierced hers. 'Your body language needs a little work.'

'Excuse me?'

He turned the phone towards her. The chef had posted a picture of them on his social-media site. 'This doesn't quite do the trick.'

She flicked a glance at the picture, suddenly unwilling to look closely at it. 'Our picture has already had over half a million views. I fail to see what the problem is.'

'The problem is we're supposed to be lovers. Your posture indicates otherwise.'

Rebel forced herself to look past Draco's firm, proprietary hand on her hip. Or the fact that it sparked a fizz of unwanted sensation through her. Clinically, she perused her slightly stiff posture and the neutral expression she'd forced her features into in reaction to Draco's touch. Her gaze slid to the dominating presence beside her.

'You could've done with cracking a smile too, don't you think?' she countered.

He slid the phone back into his pocket. 'The next time we're seen together in public you'll be my fiancée. Your performance needs to be stellar.'

'Fine. I promise to fawn all over you.'

He shook his head. 'No, I'm not risking you going overboard either.'

She threw up her hands. 'What, then? You should know, I'm not the here's-a-cute-selfie-of-us-cuddling-while-walking-our-dog type.'

'Neither am I. But we need to achieve the right balance.'

'And how do you suggest we do that? Take a compatibility test?'

'Of sorts.'

He stepped forward and gripped her waist. The unexpected move, and the blistering heat from his touch, made her whole body clench tight. 'What are you doing?' Her voice rose several octaves higher than it'd been a moment ago.

'You just tensed up. If you do that every time I touch you, we might as well declare this thing a failure.'

'You surprised me, that's all,' she replied, her voice still unlike her own.

He dragged her closer and her tension mounted. 'Arabella, relax,' he rasped, his voice deep and frighteningly hypnotic.

'Said the snake charmer to the snake.'

One corner of his mouth lifted in a shadow of a smile. Then the pads of his thumbs pressed into her hip bones.

Electric sensation blasted through her. The secret place between her legs tingled wildly before singeing her with a fiery need that robbed her of breath. Draco stared at her as his thumbs continued to play over her covered skin, the direct gaze adding a potent layer of awareness to the one already blanketing her.

Just when she thought she couldn't stand it any more, his gaze dropped to her mouth. A rough sound rumbled from his chest, but she was too caught up in what was happening to her body to pay it much heed.

But she heeded the unrelenting descent of his head, and the mouth that took hers a second later.

Every single atom in her body strained to that point of contact, to the pressure that teased at first, then turned into a deeper, more breath-stealing exploration.

Rebel had been kissed before, but the expertise Draco brought to his kiss, even mere seconds into the act, melted her senses. Warm, firm lips bruised hers, the feeling of being devoured drenching her before she succumbed to it.

His hand strayed from her hip to the small of her back, compelled her closer still. Her arms moved, almost of their own accord, twined around his neck. Silky hair teased the back of her hands and Rebel gave in to the temptation to slide her fingers through his hair.

His tongue breached her mouth, the bold swipe as he shamelessly tasted her knocking the strength from her knees. Desire blistered her, tightening over her skin until her breasts ached and her nipples were needy little buds straining against her bra. Needing to relieve the ache, she rubbed herself against him.

A groan erupted from him. Lost in sensation, Rebel barely acknowledged being lifted off her feet. Or laid down on the sofa. Every frantic heartbeat begged for more of what she was experiencing. The kiss. The man. The potent smell of him that filled her nostrils and the hands moulding her body. She wanted it all with a desperation that defied logic.

When he gripped her leg and angled it over his hip, she twisted to accommodate him, the move settling him snugly between her thighs.

The unmistakable power of his erection brushed her clothed core. Lightning zapped at the contact, electrifying and so strong, they both froze. She opened her eyes to find grey eyes, dark with volatile hunger, staring into hers.

Hunger that had no place whatsoever inside the parameters of what she'd agreed to.

With a shocked, garbled cry, Rebel wrenched her mouth from his. Disengaging the fists locked in his hair, she slammed them on his shoulders and pushed.

'Get off me. Now.' Her voice was a shaky mess, light years from confident, and nowhere near rational.

Draco lifted his imposing body off hers, his control back in place as if that wild hunger she'd seen in his eyes had been a figment of her imagination. 'Calm down, Arabella.'

She jumped up and fled to the other side of the room. One shaky hand sliced through her hair as she noted she'd lost her shoes along the way to insanity. 'God, I can't believe that just happened,' she muttered under her breath.

He took his time to straighten his cuffs, then shrugged. 'We needed to be familiar with each other. Now I know what you taste like, and you won't jump whenever I touch you in public.'

'Not if you're going to paw me like you did a moment ago.'

He raised a mocking brow. 'You reciprocated in kind, *glikia mou*. I'm sure I can locate a claw mark or two on my person should I feel inclined to do so.'

Heat rushed up her face at the reminder of her wanton behaviour. Folding her arms to still her body's betraying tremble, she glared at him. 'Are we quite finished? Only I'd like to get some sleep. I have an early start in the morning.'

He sauntered past her and paused at the door. 'We are for now. Don't forget we do this again tomorrow night. With added public scrutiny thrown in.'

Her heart tripped over itself as unpleasant images of being in a goldfish bowl tore through her mind. 'Are you sure all this is just to save Carla? From where I stand, she seems to be doing just fine.' Rebel hated herself for probing,

but all day she hadn't quite been able to shake the feeling
that there was more to his motives where Carla was concerned than Draco was letting on. And she hated herself
even more that the prime emotion when she thought about
the two of them felt alarmingly like jealousy.

Draco's face hardened into a steel mask. 'I've learned
to look beneath the surface, Arabella. If you bother to do
the same, you'll see that things aren't always as they *seem*.
Goodnight.'

She stayed rooted to the spot as he left her flat. Although
his words echoed through her mind, it was the depth of feeling in his voice and wave of vivid pain that had crossed his
face that stayed with her.

CHAPTER EIGHT

'You're dating Draco Angelis?'

Shock lined every inch of Contessa's face as she stood in Rebel's doorway. Her mop of red hair and electric-blue dress should've clashed horribly, but somehow the ensemble worked. Probably because her unapologetic, no-nonsense attitude dared anyone to criticise her wardrobe style.

Not that Rebel would've done so as her manager brushed past her and headed for the kitchen. She plunked the bottle of champagne in her hand on the breakfast counter and turned to her.

'Your email was a little vague as to why you weren't going to Chamonix any longer, but I'm guessing this new development has something to do with it? Tell me it's not true—' She gasped as her gaze fell on the rock adorning Rebel's finger. Rushing forward, she caught up Rebel's hand. 'What's this?'

'Umm…want to take a wild guess?'

'An engagement ring? You're *engaged*? To Draco?'

Rebel bit her lip and gave a sheepish nod.

A deeper bewilderment etched Contessa's face. 'When? And why? Damn it, what's going on, Rebel? I had no idea you'd even met the guy, never mind were dating him!'

'It sort of just happened.'

'A serious rock like this doesn't *just happen*. You've been evasive these past few weeks.' She dropped Rebel's hand, her green eyes wary and hurt. 'I thought you trusted me?'

'You know I do.'

Contessa's gaze dropped to the ring, then back up. 'Then why won't you tell me what's going on?'

Rebel didn't know Draco well enough to speak with certainty as to how he'd react to her divulging details of their agreement. And she had too much to lose to risk it. 'Because I can't. I'm sorry.'

Contessa's eyes narrowed shrewdly. 'It's something to do with your father, isn't it? And the money he gave you?' She snapped her fingers. 'You wanted me to get it all back but you never said why. Does this Draco thing have something to do with it?'

Shame and anxiety engulfed her. 'Please, I can't really talk about it. And I'm sorry to have to cut this short but Draco will be here in a minute.'

On cue, her door intercom buzzed.

'Why? Doesn't he want you to have friends?' Contessa snapped. 'Or are you suddenly ashamed of me?'

'Don't be absurd. Of course I'm not ashamed of you. I... we're going out, that's all.'

The older woman's gaze drifted over the moss-green beaded dress and platform heels Rebel wore. 'I can see that.' She hitched her stylish tote handbag higher on her shoulder, then sighed. 'Be careful, Rebel. You're more than a client to me. And I'd hate myself if you got hurt. You know he represents Rex Glow now? Have you stopped to think he may have had something to do with them dropping you?'

'Yes, I—'

Contessa shook her head. 'This engagement...well, all I'm saying is, a man like Draco can give you a lot. But he'll take more than you'll want to give.'

Rebel frowned. 'I know exactly what he wants from me. I don't intend to give him more than that.'

'The sport agents' business is a small world. He's discreet, I'll grant him that, but I know a few of the women he's been involved with in the past. They always believe they're incapable of being hurt by him, but things always end the same way. With the women emotionally and professionally shattered, and Angelis walking away without a backward glance.'

'It's a good thing that you're in charge of my career, then, isn't it?' Rebel said with a forced smile.

'What about your heart?'

'I'm fully in control of it. I know you're worried, but please trust that I know what I'm doing,' she replied, choosing not to recall the sleepless night she'd spent thinking about Draco, the kiss they'd shared, and the unfurling heat in her belly each time she relived it. Assuring herself it was a simple chemical reaction and therefore didn't warrant further thought had lost its credibility somewhere between dawn and sunrise. As had telling herself she didn't really want to know the reason behind Draco's anguished look when she'd asked about Carla in the moments before he'd walked out.

Both subjects had stayed with her all day and, the closer the time came for her date with Draco, the more uneasy she'd grown.

The intercom buzzed again, ending with a snap of impatience.

Schooling her features, she smiled at Contessa. She knew her friend and manager wasn't buying her assurances when Contessa stalked past her to the door she'd walked through minutes ago. Collecting her black purse from her bedroom, Rebel rushed after her, cursing as she stopped to lock her front door.

She caught up with Contessa as she was pulling the main door open.

Contessa and a just-arrived, smartly dressed Draco eyed each other. Despite her warning, Rebel watched her friend's eyes widen a little as she took in the full impact of the man before her. A second later, Draco glanced past her to capture Rebel's gaze.

'Good evening, Arabella.'

The sensual curl of her name from his lips sparked a higher charge in her belly. Doing her best to ignore it, she came down the last few steps and stood next to Contessa.

'Are you going to introduce me to your friend, *glikia mou*?' he asked, his voice deep and low.

The endearment reminded Rebel of Draco's Greek origin, reminded her that she knew next to nothing about him besides the circumstances surrounding the situation they found themselves in. And even then, Draco was hiding far more than he'd divulged.

Making a note to do something about it, she summoned a smile. 'This is my manager, Contessa Stanley. Contessa, meet Draco Angelis.'

Draco held out his hand. 'A pleasure to meet you.'

'Good to meet you,' Contessa replied, then her sharp looked morphed into glazed astonishment when Draco smiled. Witnessing the transformation from a few feet back, Rebel couldn't stop herself from staring at the dazzling effect of his smile. It took several moments for Contessa to regain her composure. 'I believe congratulations are in order.'

'Thank you,' he drawled. 'I'm a very lucky man.' The heated, adoring look he sent Rebel could've knocked her off her feet, had she not known it was an act.

Contessa stared at him for another long second, before she cleared her throat and turned to Rebel. 'I'll call you tomorrow. Have a good evening.'

Without another glance at Draco, she headed to the white hybrid parked in front of Draco's sports car.

Draco watched her depart with a faintly amused expression. 'Any reason why she doesn't like me?'

Rebel shut the front door and fell into step beside him, cautioning herself against walking too close. 'She's a sport manager. She suspects you were involved with my sponsors walking. She also believes the women you get involved with end up on the used and discarded heap, both professionally and emotionally.'

Any semblance of amusement vanished from Draco's face. He caught her wrist and glared down at her. 'You didn't tell her about our agreement, did you?'

'Of course not.' She pulled her hand away. 'Although I trust her implicitly,' she added.

'Be that as it may, I'd prefer it if this thing remained between only you and me,' he commanded.

'I'm not stupid, Draco. I don't want this to get out any more than you do.'

He observed her for a moment, grey eyes narrow and intense. 'Good.'

Striding to his car, he held the door open for her, his movements tense as he rounded the bonnet and slid behind the wheel.

After several minutes of silence, she glanced at him, unable to smother the question that had been bubbling at the back of her mind. 'Why *did* you talk Rex Glow into dropping me?'

She'd told herself she didn't care. That she was better off without the demanding apparel and footwear sponsor. But she held her breath as she waited for Draco to answer.

His jaw flexed for a moment. 'I didn't. They'd already made the decision to drop several athletes by the time I joined their board. Yours was just a name on the list.'

Rebel knew it was true because Contessa had informed her of others who'd been dropped. 'And you did nothing to stop it?'

Draco shrugged. 'I didn't know you. And you weren't exactly trying very hard to convince them of your dedication to your sport. You switched disciplines from cross-country to ski jumping after almost five years. Since then you haven't risen above fifth in the rankings.'

'I know you think I'm whimsical about my career, but I'm not. It wasn't an easy decision, especially with the intense training involved.'

He switched lanes suddenly, and her eyes were drawn to his powerful thighs. Recalling them cradled between hers, she turned her heating face to the window.

'Did you grow up skiing?' he asked after a few minutes.

She answered only because talking took her mind off the lurid images unreeling through her head. And perhaps because she wanted him to know that she was more than the superficial pleasure seeker he thought her to be?

'Yes. My mother was a ski jumper. She never made it past the juniors but she excelled in amateur tournaments. She taught me how to jump when I was ten. I loved it but I was stronger in cross-country skiing so it was a natural choice to do that professionally.'

'That makes sense. Less so is why you changed disciplines.'

'I stopped loving cross-country.'

'I'm guessing the reason behind is more emotional than professional?'

She wanted to hate him for the cynical edge to his observation, but how could she when it was the truth? Pain slammed through her as she glanced at his profile and replied, 'Does my mother passing away count?'

He exhaled, a look of regret lining his features. 'It counts. Unfortunately death and tragedy arrive before clarity lights our paths,' he murmured, then seemed to slip into deep thought. Expertly handling the powerful vehicle, he didn't speak until they were a few streets from the restaurant. 'But you didn't change disciplines until a few years after you lost your mother. And yet you won more cross-country competitions in that time.' The statement held a ton of questions. Questions that, should she answer, would expose the state of her hidden anguish to a man whose ruthlessness she was very much privy to.

But not answering would risk leaving him with the belief that she was shallow. Wondering why that mattered so much to her, Rebel decided on a not too revealing answer. 'I was trying to prove a point.'

'To who?'

'To myself. To my father.'

His mouth compressed, disapproval back in full force.

'You disapprove? No matter what everyone else thinks, an athlete needs a better support system than just agents and trainers. I thought I could function without one, and, yes, I was at the top of my game during that time, but in the long run it didn't work for me. So I chose to do something different. It probably doesn't mean anything to you, but I found more fulfilment in jumping.'

Draco parked the car on a quiet lamplit street in Fulham amid several late-model sports cars and SUVs. The restaurant he'd chosen tonight was another exclusive one, frequented by the crème de la crème of celebrities. A discreet security presence ensured the patrons could dine without intrusive media presence, although somehow information usually leaked out.

He helped her out, but held onto her as he shut the door. After clicking the lock, he stood in front of her, effectively pinning her against the car.

Tensing, Rebel tilted her face to look at him, expecting more of the disapproval that had bristled from him. Instead, she read a jagged understanding in his eyes. He looked almost uncomfortable as he stared down at her.

'I understand the need to find fulfilment in what you do. But I believe that it should go hand in hand with attempting to be the best you can be. You have the potential to be number one again, but you've let your emotions and superficial things get in the way of that goal for far too long.'

Draco's view of her might have altered slightly, but he still believed she wasn't committed enough to what she'd dedicated the past five years of her life to. The pang that accompanied the observation triggered alarm. How could the view of a man she hadn't known three days matter so much?

'You should really stop thinking you know all there is to know about me,' she replied.

His eyes dropped from hers, his gaze roving her face before locking on her lips. 'Everything you've told me so far has only confirmed my opinion of you.'

She swallowed, wishing the hurt in her chest and the sudden tingling of her mouth away. Forcing lightness to her voice, she said, 'Whereas I know next to nothing about the man who I'm supposed to be madly in love with. Perhaps we should rectify that before I slip up and commit a faux pas?'

'We will do that over dinner,' he replied. Then his gaze dropped past her shoulders to the unsteady rise and fall of her chest. Pushing back from the car, he completed a full scrutiny before he trapped her hand again. Lifting her ring finger to his mouth, he kissed the knuckle above the stone. 'You look incredible, by the way.'

Her breath caught, her heart tripping over itself before slamming hard against her ribs. 'Thank you. You don't look so bad yourself.' She made a show of perusing him from head to foot, secretly revelling in the freedom to look her fill of the lean masculinity that inhabited the dark suit and black silk shirt. Having experienced the power of that body up close, she found her breathing was decidedly unsteady by the time her gaze rose to meet his.

His smile wasn't as show-stopping as it'd been when he'd unleashed his charms on Contessa. But it had more genuine depth, making it even more dangerous to her equilibrium as she found herself smiling back, her senses singing as his eyes warmed and his thumb rubbed over her knuckles.

'Now that we've established our appreciation of each other's dress sense, let's go eat.'

He linked his fingers through hers and walked her into the modern decor of the Italian restaurant. Unlike before, there wasn't a chef to fawn over them or pose for pictures, for which she was glad. Although their presence wasn't brazenly acknowledged, Rebel caught a few discreet glances as they ate their first course.

But even that small disturbance disappeared as Draco furnished her with his history. His flawless English had made her think he'd been brought up in England despite his Greek name. Finding out he'd only relocated from Athens to England five years ago came as a surprise. But not as much a surprise as discovering he, like her, had lost his mother during his teens. And that he'd been a champion cross-country skier.

Rebel frowned. 'I know the name of every skier who's won a major competition for the last fifty years.'

One sleek eyebrow rose, giving him a rakish look that she strenuously resisted gawping at. 'Are you accusing me of lying?'

Lowering her gaze to the less interesting subject of her water glass, she shrugged. 'I know what I know.' And she definitely would've remembered him.

'I competed under my mother's maiden name of Christou.'

Her head snapped up. 'The only Christou I remember— you're Drakos Christou! Five-time world champion?' Rebel wasn't aware she'd grabbed his hand until he traced his thumb over hers. She started to pull away but he held her tight. And because she liked it, she stayed.

'Yes.' A lopsided smile accompanied the acknowledgement.

Knowing she was risking fan-girling over him, she reined herself in. 'Wow. You look…different.' He'd sported longer hair and a full beard during his competitions years, and although his build had been leaner, more streamlined, it had suited the sport he'd excelled in. No wonder she hadn't recognised him, despite the faint feeling of familiarity she'd experienced in his office when they'd first met. 'Why the change of name?'

The air thickened, sucking dry the easy banter that had eased their preceding courses. 'My father disapproved of my chosen career. He would've preferred it if I'd joined the family real-estate business and succeeded him. He made it clear I wasn't his son until I came to my senses and gave up skiing.'

'But you didn't give it up.'

His features tightened. 'Not until I was forced to anyway.'

With the realisation of just who Draco Angelis was, the worldwide sensation that had surrounded his departure from cross-country skiing came flooding back. 'You trained yourself for the last competition, but your knee blew out before you could win your sixth trophy.'

The hand now curled around hers tightened. 'Discovering that my trainer had been pushing me past my limits just so he could gamble on my winning the tournament left me no choice.'

A soft gasp left her lips. 'No way. What happened to him?'

His nostrils flared as he dragged in a breath vibrating with quiet fury. 'He faced game throwing and other charges, but by the time the case went to trial and the extent of the gambling ring was discovered, it was too late.'

Sympathy welled through her. 'Your knee injury ended your career.'

His lashes swept down to their joined hands. Slowly his grip loosened and he withdrew from her. Rebel missed the contact with an acuteness that stunned her. Drawing her hand from the table, she lowered it to her lap and balled it.

'Amongst other things. But the most important lesson I learned was to always look beneath the surface. I knew things weren't right, but I chose to ignore them because I was determined to win that final championship.' His words held raw self-condemnation that struck a vulnerable place inside her.

Self-condemnation was an emotion she'd lived with and knew well. But Draco's case was different. He hadn't rushed recklessly into a situation through selfishness. He'd been deceived by someone he'd believed he could trust.

The urge to comfort him snowballed through her, but the rigid control once more clamping his features dissuaded her.

The rest of the meal passed in near silence, and Rebel was thankful when Draco asked for the bill.

She was sliding back into his car when her phone started pinging. Digging it out, she read the congratulatory emails flooding her inbox, almost all of them from people she barely knew.

It wasn't until she clicked an attachment that she saw the first headline.

Super-Agent and Sports Star Engaged!

Rebel didn't bother to read the article, knowing this time round the carefully crafted story within was from source. About to click off her phone, she stopped as another picture from a social-media account lit up her screen, along with the history of how many times it'd been viewed.

She gasped.

'Is something wrong?' Draco asked, his gaze spearing her as he paused in the act of securing his seat belt.

She showed him the picture taken of them earlier, as he'd kissed her hand outside the restaurant. The quality of the photo was much too good to have been taken with a discreet phone camera. 'Did you know the paparazzo was there?'

Shrugging, he pressed the ignition and the car roared to life. 'Of course. That was the whole point of the act, wasn't it?'

For a moment, Rebel couldn't speak. Her hand trembled as she tucked her phone back in her bag. She called herself a thousand kinds of fool for each dart of hurt that lanced her. She'd dropped her guard for a handful of moments. So what?

If the figures were to be believed, the public were lapping up the image of a loved-up 'Drabella'.

'Yes, I guess it was,' she replied quietly.

'Then we'll chalk up the night as a success. Put on your seat belt, Arabella.'

Woodenly she complied, then lapsed into silence. After all, what else was there to be said?

Draco left her at her door with instructions to be ready for his chauffeur on Saturday. The announcement that they would be travelling via his private jet to Tuscany was carelessly thrown over his shoulder as he returned to his car. He seemed in a hurry to get away, so Rebel nodded through it all, then hurried inside.

Keeping a tight leash on the ball of emotions that had lodged in her chest, she climbed the stairs to her flat. Her feet froze on the last step as she saw the figure standing in her doorway.

Time and age had taken their toll on the man whose profile was visible in the hallway light, but Rebel would've recognised him anywhere. 'Dad?'

He jerked upright from his slumped position. The eyes her mother had insisted were the exact shade of her own widened a touch before dimming with wariness.

'Arabella.'

Her avid gaze sprinted over him, took in the pertinent details of weight loss pronounced by his baggy clothes, his thinning hair and unshaven face, before meeting his shadowed eyes.

'What...what are you doing here?' Considering she'd been frantically calling him every day for the past two weeks, the question was absurd, but the shock of seeing him again after so many years battered her thought processes.

'I came because of this.' He held up a copy of the latest edition of the evening newspaper. The picture on her phone was blown up on the broadsheet. Rebel's gaze darted away from the picture of her face as Draco bent over her hand, and took a step closer, her insides clenching with hurt as she stared at her father.

'I call you every day for weeks and you don't answer, but you turn up because of a picture in the paper?'

'It's not just any picture, though, is it?' he replied, that trace of condemnation she'd prayed never to hear again underlining his words. 'You need to end whatever this is, Arabella. Now.'

Shakily, she approached him and indicated the door. When he moved away, she inserted the key, opened it and thrust it wide.

She went inside, then didn't breathe until she heard his footsteps behind her.

Looking over her shoulder, she asked, 'Would you like a cup of tea?'

'Arabella—'

'I'm going to boil the kettle. You're already here. You might as well stay for tea.'

She hurried to the kitchen, kicked off her shoes and turned on the kettle. Her father walked in a few seconds later. After giving the room a once-over, he dropped the newspaper on the counter, pulled out a stool at the breakfast bar and sat down.

Struggling to contain her anxiety, Rebel got busy fetching mugs. Once the kettle boiled, she made the tea and slid a cup to him. 'Can I get you anything with it? Biscuits? A sandwich?'

He cradled his cup but made no move to drink it. 'You can tell me what this is about.' He indicated the paper.

'Can we forget about that for a minute, please?' Before he could respond, she rushed on. 'Where have you been? *How* have you been?'

'Away. Fine.' He continued to avoid her gaze, and with each second that ticked by Rebel's heart broke all over again.

'I'm sorry, Dad,' she whispered. 'I don't know how many more times I can say it.'

His breath shuddered on a deep exhale. 'The apology doesn't matter, Arabella. It never did. You're my child. Forgiving you was never a problem.' He pointed to the picture.

'But this is a problem. We spoke a few days ago, then overnight you go and do this?'

Her fingers clenched around her mug. 'You make it sound as if we have long talks on a regular basis. You may have known where I was and what I was doing, but I had no idea where you were. Until two weeks ago, I hadn't heard from you in *years*! And when I did try to talk to you after that, you barely said a handful of words to me. So, no, it hasn't been overnight for me, Dad, but years. Years during which you've watched over me, apparently. How else would you have known I'd been dropped by my sponsors?'

His fingers clenched around the mug. 'I had to.'

Pain clawed deeper. 'Because it was your *duty*? That's what you said in your letter, wasn't it? Was it your duty to deposit stolen money in my account?'

His head jerked up. 'You know?'

'Of course I know. According to Draco you didn't do a great job of hiding your tracks.'

He pushed away the tea and stood. 'Is he threatening you? Is that what this *engagement* is about?' He lurched towards the door. 'I'll turn myself in.'

Slamming her own cup down, she launched herself in the doorway. 'You can't!'

He frowned at her. 'Why not?'

'Because…it's too late. I've used the money and Draco knows it. If you go down, so do I.'

'But you didn't know it was stolen.'

'That doesn't matter. If Draco decides to press charges, I'll automatically become an accessory.'

Her father's throat worked as he swallowed. His head bent forward, and she glimpsed weariness in each movement.

Hesitantly, she placed a hand on his arm. 'Why did you take the money, Dad?' she asked, because deep down she knew he hadn't really changed from the upright, hard-working man she'd grown up admiring. 'Surely you must have known you wouldn't get away with it? That I'd be in the frame too if you were caught?'

He veered away from her, heading back to the stool. His rejection cut deeper but she stood her ground.

'I wasn't…' He stopped and shook his head. 'I wasn't thinking straight. I thought I could sell our old house and replace the money before he found out.'

'Why? Why was this so important to you?' she demanded, desperate for some indication that this hadn't been just duty for him.

'I promised your mother I'd look after you. It was one of the last things I said to her before…' He stopped again.

Rebel swallowed the sob that stemmed from her soul. 'She's gone, Dad. But I'm still here.'

Her father's head slowly rose from its heavy slump, then he speared her with haunted eyes. 'You took her from me. Then you began to turn into an exact copy of her.'

Her heart shrank. 'You hate me for that, don't you?'

He shook his head, his blue eyes swimming with sorrow, sharp and ocean-deep, even after all these years. 'I don't hate you. I could never hate you. But…I can't stand to look at you. Not when you were twenty and we fought constantly until you left home. And not now.'

The stark declaration wrenched a sob free as a part of her died.

'Where do we go from here, Dad?'

'I don't know. You've always known how I feel about your skiing. I always knew it wouldn't end well. And it didn't, did it?'

'Dad—'

'You don't need to talk me round. I know you'll do as you please, like always. But I know this thing you're doing with Angelis isn't the answer. The man is a predator.'

She wanted to refute the allegation. But really, what evidence had she apart from one evening's conversation where a small part of his life's story had tugged at her heartstrings? Draco had reverted to type soon enough.

Besides, she had even less of a choice now. After seeing her father still locked in grief after all this time there was no way she could stand by while he suffered for something he'd felt compelled to do because of her.

Heart in her throat, she shook her head. 'I can't, Dad. Like I said, it's too late.'

A full minute passed before he stood. He paused beside her by the kitchen door, but made no move to touch or even look at her. 'Goodbye, Arabella.'

Her tears came thick and fast long before he shut the door. And it was only through sheer exhaustion that sleep finally overtook her in the early hours.

CHAPTER NINE

THEY LANDED AT Pisa Airport mid-morning, before being flown by helicopter to Olivio Nardozzi's estate in northern Tuscany.

Draco alighted first before helping Rebel down. Guiding her beneath the rotating blades, he draped his arm around her waist and steered her to the path that led up to the sprawling mid-twentieth-century villa.

Although her mint-green sundress and matching sweater did nothing to alleviate the deep sizzling sensation his touch sent through her body, Rebel was too numb to do more than stay at his side as they approached the wide terrace that overlooked an aqua-tiled Olympic-sized pool.

She'd woken up raw and aching, unable to relive the conversation with her father without experiencing a hopeless, consuming pain at the thought that there could be no easy reconciliation. Not if her father couldn't look at her without—

'Whatever is wrong with you, Arabella, I suggest you get it under control right now,' Draco slashed in a fierce undertone. 'Now is *not* the time to drift into a trance.'

Rebel dragged herself back from the edge of the abyss, thankful that the unseasonably warm weather provided her with the perfect cover of her sunglasses as she blinked back rising tears.

'Not even a love trance with you in the starring role?'

He sent her a glance filled with combative censure, and a touch of disappointment. Reaching down, he plucked the sunglasses from her face and tucked them into his tailored trousers.

'We both know I've been far from your mind since you

boarded my plane in London this morning. I don't expect to be the subject of your thoughts night and day, but I expect you to be both physically and *mentally* present for this to work.' His voice was a low, hard throb so they wouldn't be overheard, but each word held unmistakable warning.

'Cool your jets, Draco. I haven't suddenly taken leave of my senses,' she whispered. Then in a pseudo Marilyn Monroe voice, she added, 'I'm still besotted with love for you and can't wait to tell our hosts what a lucky woman I am to have captured your elusive heart.'

They rounded another sun-dappled terrace and came face-to-face with Carla Nardozzi. Dressed in a pale yellow, clinging sundress, she stood next to an older man Rebel guessed to be her father, Olivio. Judging from their frozen expressions, it was clear her last words had carried. Before embarrassment could kick her hard, Draco strode to the middle of the terrace, where their hosts waited.

'Olivio, good to see you again.' He clasped the older man's hand in a firm greeting, then turned to his daughter. 'Carla, a pleasure, as always.' Draco's smile was warm as he leaned down and kissed the stunning, model-thin figure skater on both cheeks.

Rebel fought the acid-tipped spears that attacked her insides as she watched the scene.

Carla Nardozzi's limpid green eyes stayed on Draco for a second longer than Rebel thought was necessary before both father and daughter turned to her.

Returning to her side, Draco caught her hand in his. 'Allow me to introduce Arabella Daniels.'

Olivio was the first to greet her, eyes a shade lighter than espresso measuring her shrewdly. 'Welcome to my home, Miss Daniels. I look forward to making your further acquaintance,' he said in a thick accent.

'Thanks. And I'm sorry if you overheard me just then.'

'Nonsense. A woman should shout her love for her man from the rooftops. If it is genuine, that is,' Olivio declared.

His eyes dropped to her engagement ring, his scrutiny long and intense before he smiled at her.

Rebel forced her own smile wider. 'Oh, I'm glad you think so. Not everyone approves of public displays of affection.'

Carla came forward, her hand outstretched. Her caramel-streaked, chocolate-brown hair was pulled up into a severe chignon, the effect showing off the sleek lines of her jaw and neck. 'A pleasure to meet you.'

Rebel shook her cool hand, but before she could reply, Carla continued, 'So, it's true, then, what the papers are saying? You two are really engaged?' Her eyes drifted briefly over Rebel before they returned to Draco. Seeing the almost imploring look in the other woman's gaze, a boulder wedged in Rebel's midriff.

'Yes, it's true. I've finally succumbed to my heart's desire.' Molten grey eyes met Rebel's in a look designed to fool the most hardened heart.

Feeling him about to lift their linked hands and kiss hers as he had on Wednesday night, Rebel tensed her arm. Moving closer, she draped her hand on his chest and rose to kiss his cheek. His muted exhalation was the only exhibition of surprise at her move.

'But…didn't you two meet only recently?' Carla pressed, her eyes darting searchingly between them.

Rebel laughed and shook her head. 'We only chose not to make our relationship public before now since Draco is a *monster* when it comes to his privacy.'

Carla's smile was a little stiff. '*Sì*, I haven't forgotten.'

The boulder in Rebel's chest grew. 'Anyway, it's all out in the open now. Which is just as well because from the moment I met Draco, I knew my life would never be the same again. Fortunately, he felt the same and now doesn't mind shouting it to the world. In fact, he wouldn't leave my flat earlier this week until I'd accepted his ring and everyone knew I belonged to him. Isn't that right, darling?' She let her gaze drift over his face, stopping to linger at his mouth before meeting his eyes.

His eyes gleamed without a trace of mockery as his head angled towards hers. 'Only because my heart insisted you were mine, and I wasn't about to let you get away.'

A delicate throat-clearing fractured the moment. And yet Rebel couldn't look away from Draco, despite the astonishing evidence of his superb acting skills.

He broke the connection first. Rebel slowly sucked in a restorative breath before facing their hosts.

'Apologies for being sceptical. We wanted to be sure the media wasn't playing tricks on us,' Olivio stated. 'But now that you have confirmed this news, we must celebrate.' He snapped his fingers and a member of his staff rolled forward a serving trolley. At Olivio's nod, the server plucked a bottle of vintage Pol Roger champagne from a silver ice bucket and popped the cork.

'Not for me, thank you,' Carla said when she was offered a glass. 'I have another training session in an hour.'

'Ah, *sì*.' Olivio smiled indulgently. 'My daughter, she's the ultimate perfectionist. Never resting until the gold crown is on her head. And then she gets to work again the very next day.'

Carla paled slightly, a trace of anxiety passing over her face before she regained her composure.

Beside her, Draco tensed and a momentary trace of anger pursed his lips. But he lifted his glass at Olivio's prompt.

'To your future union. May it last for as long as there are stars in the sky.'

Carla excused herself as soon as the toasts were done, walking away with a painfully erect posture. As soon as he'd finished his drink, Olivio summoned another member of staff.

'This is Stefano, your personal butler. He will show you to your rooms and give you a tour of the grounds and facilities when you're ready. I have a few more guests arriving today, but tonight we're doing things a little informally. Food and drinks will be ready whenever you are out here on the terrace. There's nothing more special than dining al fresco on a cool Tuscan night.' Although he smiled, the warmth didn't quite reach his eyes.

The men shook hands, and Draco steered her out of the room.

The interior of the villa was opulence personified, with marble the dominant feature gleaming on the floors and walls. Followed a close second by Carla. Her pictures and trophies were displayed proudly on every surface. On the walls, several portraits and pictures with world leaders and dignitaries documented her from childhood to womanhood. It was clear Olivio regarded his daughter as his prized possession.

Rebel batted away the desperate envy she felt towards the other woman as the memory of the scene with her own father threatened to cut her off at the knees. Locking it away at the back of her mind once more, Rebel focused instead on the endless stream of Carla-mania, experiencing a touch of unease as she realised how extensive the displays were.

She was forcing herself not to think about the more disturbing interaction between Draco and Carla when she entered their designated suite and stumbled to a halt. Peripherally, she heard Draco dismiss Stefano and shut the door behind him, but she couldn't look away from the bed.

It was huge. Set on a pedestal made for lovers. With no other bed or divan in sight.

'Staring in horror at the bed won't let it magically dissolve into twin beds, *glikia mou*,' Draco drawled as he walked past her, pulling his shirt from his trousers as he crossed to what she assumed was a dressing room.

She stared, dry-mouthed, as he unbuttoned his shirt and shrugged it off. Discarding it on the centre island, he toed off his shoes as he went to a shelf and selected a white polo shirt. Barefooted, he strutted back into the room, then paused, one eyebrow raised at her.

'Are you staring at me in horror now because you want *me* to disappear?'

Rebel knew she was gaping at his contoured chest. The expanse of golden, vibrant skin made her tingle from head to toe. Which was bad. Really, really bad.

'I…we didn't discuss sleeping arrangements,' she blurted.

'Because it was inevitable that we would have to share a room with one bed in it for obvious reasons.'

The fever that had gripped her spiked. 'Well, you should've told me so I was better prepared, seeing as I'm not as well-versed in fake engagements as you seem to be.'

'Keep your voice down,' he warned as he sauntered towards her.

'Oh, please. You don't really think Olivio's skulking outside, eavesdropping on us, do you?'

He stopped in front of her. Still shirtless. More devastating to her senses. 'You tell me. Do you think our performance convinced him?'

'I don't think anything convinces Olivio that he can't hold physically in his hand.'

Grey eyes narrowed at her. 'What makes you say that?'

'Most people keep their trophies in a cabinet in a special room. He keeps Carla's trophies and pictures within easy view and reach, as if he needs a visual reminder of his and her success. I bet he's framed every endorsement he's negotiated on her behalf too. So I guess you were right about this.' She wriggled her ring finger. 'If nothing else, the fat diamond should work for us. Can you put your shirt on?' she snapped, forcing her knees to lock so she didn't retreat from the sinful temptation that was his bare torso. Or worse, lunge at him!

Both his eyebrows arched and a wolfish grin curved his lips. 'Why, Arabella, you'd think you'd never seen a half-naked man before.'

'Whether I have or not isn't the question here. It is whether the visual…situation is my choice, or whether it's imposed on me.'

'I see you've regained your smart mouth. If nothing else, I suppose it's better than your sullen mood this morning.'

Draco watched her eyes dim as if a switch had been turned off. For the first time in his life, he wanted to curse himself for stating a truth when discretion would've been the better part of valour. Truth be told, he hadn't enjoyed sharing space with a silent Arabella. He hadn't on Wednesday night either on the drive back from dinner. But *then*, he'd been reflecting on their dinner conversation, a part of him wondering whether he'd taken leave of his senses somewhere between the first and second courses. No other explanation made sense as to why he'd divulged intimate details known only to his closest family. Even the trial he'd mentioned had been held behind closed doors to protect Maria.

He'd eventually reasoned his behaviour away as a necessary evil in the task he'd undertaken. In the grand scheme of things, what did it matter if Arabella knew a few more details about him than he was comfortable with? He seriously doubted that she would step out of line with the threat of criminal charges hanging over her head.

He'd expected things to resume as planned, only to be met with a woman who, while he'd felt a modicum of satisfaction that she wasn't jumping at his touch any more, didn't seem inclined to engage with him on any level whatsoever.

And that had been before he'd seen the heavy traces of anguish shadowing her eyes this morning. He'd spotted the evidence of tears beneath her cleverly applied make-up the moment she'd stepped on the plane that not even the sunglasses had been able to disguise. Her mournful posture when she didn't think she was being observed had added to the mounting evidence that something had happened between Wednesday night and this morning.

'Arabella? Is something wrong?' he prompted when she remained silent.

A burst of laughter tripped from her lips but her gaze refused to meet his. 'Right at this moment, nothing that a quick chat about our sleeping arrangements won't fix.'

She was being evasive, but, short of shaking the truth out of her, Draco had no choice but to bite down on his frustration. 'You're that concerned about sharing?' He glanced at the bed. 'The bed is big enough for two. Or are you afraid you'll attack me in the middle of the night?'

She shrugged. 'I already have a few black marks against me. I'd rather leave grievous bodily harm off my list of sins.' Her tone was light but held a brittle edge that sliced at him. He searched her expression, his fingers itching to catch her chin and make her look at him so he could see beneath the snarky surface.

Draco wasn't entirely sure why he didn't. Perhaps he was wary of exposing a different set of problems. Where Arabella was afraid of close contact with him, was he craving it with her? More than that, was he craving more of the closeness he'd felt when he'd opened up to her about his past?

He stepped back abruptly. The questions were absurd in and of themselves. They were both playing a part. Closeness was a given. But not to be mistaken for anything he needed, never mind craved.

'If you're that worried about it, you take the bed. There's a living room through there with a comfortable enough sofa.'

He tugged his polo shirt over his head and returned to the dressing room to don his loafers.

'Do you want a tour of the training facilities?'

Her nod held relief. 'If you hang on a sec, I'll change into my trainers.'

When she joined him a few minutes later, she'd tied her hair into a ponytail. Stefano showed them where several golf buggies were parked in a neat row after Draco refused a personal escort.

He took the path that curved west of the villa, then aimed the buggy towards the domed building that sat atop a small hill. 'You seem to know your way around.' Her tone was neutral, as if she didn't care whether he answered or not.

When he glanced her way, her face was angled away from him.

His jaw clenched for a tight second. 'Yes. I've been here a few times. I advised Olivio during the training-facility build five years ago.'

She frowned. 'That implies a friendship. But you don't react to each other as friends do.'

'Probably because over the years we haven't seen eye to eye on a few issues.'

Her gaze flitted to him, speculated, then drifted away. 'But he still wants you to marry his daughter.'

Draco shrugged. 'Purely for dynastic reasons.'

Her mouth firmed and minutes ticked by as they crawled up the hill.

Bringing the buggy to a halt before large studio doors, he stopped her as she went to get out. 'I don't like it when you're quiet. If there's something on your mind, spit it out.'

Dull blue eyes met his. 'I thought you didn't like it when I used my smart mouth?'

His gaze dropped to the plump lips in question and heat dredged through him. 'I'm finding that I prefer it to your silence.'

She froze. They stared at each other for several charged seconds, the atmosphere growing thick and sultry, until she broke the connection and jumped from the buggy. 'Be careful what you wish for or I may never shut up again,' she said over her shoulder.

Deciding that it wasn't a scenario he was completely dissatisfied with, Draco followed her into the facility. The main feature was the enormous ice rink, around which several specialist gyms and sports-health centres had been installed. He found Arabella in the weights room, inspecting the state-of-the-art equipment.

She looked up as he entered. 'I'm in charge of my own training this weekend so the bench press is out of the question.'

'What are you swapping it with?'

'Free weights.'

He shook his head. 'You can't switch this far into the training.'

'It's only for this weekend. I talked it over with my trainer.'

'A small change can go a long way to hurt you. If you don't need to change it, don't. I'll spot you.'

Her eyes widened. 'Don't you have other stuff to attend to?'

'They will be dealt with. But not at the risk of neglecting your training.'

She blinked at him, her mouth dropping open to form responses that never emerged. Again he felt the gravity of unspoken words.

When minutes ticked by, he gritted his teeth. 'Are you happy with that?'

A shrug lifted her shoulders. 'Sure. If you want.'

As they left the gym the sound of blades cutting across ice filled the hall below. They both paused and watched as Carla, dressed in a white leotard, glided across the frozen surface.

She moved with effortless grace, years of practice making her fearless as she executed jumps and pirouettes that had seen her rise to the top of her game.

As he watched her, the wretched pain that came with wondering what Maria could've been slammed into him. Gripping the railing, he stared at the figure below and saw the image of his sister, her wide, infectious smile lighting her face as she did the only thing she'd ever dreamt of doing.

'She's breathtaking.'

He heard the voice from afar, lost as he was in tormenting memories. 'Yes, she is,' he breathed, still unable to
take his eyes off the figure. Draco wasn't sure how long
he stood there, wishing he could change the past. Knowing he couldn't.

When he resurfaced, Arabella had moved a short distance away, facing away from the railing with her arms
folded. Her face was averted, but he caught the pain etched
deep into her profile.

About to call her name, demand that she tell him what
was wrong once and for all, he froze as a dark tingling
seized his nape. A door slammed shut at the far side of
the rink and he watched a figure glide to where Carla had
stopped in the middle of the ice.

Every nerve in Draco's body tightened as he recognised
the man.

'Draco?' Rebel's voice came from a tunnel of darkness.

'Hmm?'

'Are you okay?'

'No,' he bit out.

'What's going on?'

'That man Carla's talking to. That's Tyson Blackwell.'

Arabella turned around, glanced down at the ice. 'Did
you know he was going to be here?'

'No. Olivio chose not to inform me of that fact.' His grip
tightened around the smooth railing, the urge to rip it from
its moorings clawing at him.

'Right. As devious as that sounds, unless you intend to
stare Tyson to death, can we get out of here, please?' Her
voice trembled, her features pinched in misery.

Without waiting for an answer, she vaulted out of the
door and rushed down the stairs.

He emerged into sunlight, fury still burning in his chest.
Draco had never felt inclined to cause bodily harm. Not
when his trainer had sent him down a path that had ruined

his dream. Not even when he'd surfaced from his nightmares to find his sister's life equally ruined.

But seeing Blackwell here, preparing to sink his teeth into yet another victim, Draco had to fight hard to resist the urge to march back in and rip the man to pieces.

Instead, he forced one foot in front of the other. Reaching the buggy, he slammed on the ignition, wishing he had an engine far more powerful than a battery-packed one.

Beside him, Arabella sat in silence once again, her hands folded in her lap, her features remote. The volatile emotions churned harder inside him. A roar mounted in his head.

With no outlet, hopelessness closed over him, dark and devastating. In that moment, Draco knew his only choice was to drive. So he let the silence reign.

CHAPTER TEN

'COME THIS WAY. I know a back way to the suite,' Draco said, his voice a gruff command.

From the moment she'd seen his face as he watched Carla skate, Rebel's world had turned dark and her misery had bloomed. Like toxic smoke, it'd sped through her veins, insidious and inescapable, until her body was steeped in it.

Up until that moment, she hadn't realised she'd been using Draco as a balm against the gaping wound of her father's rejection since she'd stepped on his plane this morning. It didn't matter that the man was often times cold and ruthless, or cutting and dismissive. It didn't even matter that, when it came right down to it, she was an unwitting criminal, who dangled between jail and freedom at the sole discretion of the man she was relying on to drag her from her nightmares.

All she'd cared about was that she was with him, and not at her flat, reliving each word her father had said. She'd been sure it was why the thought of a history between Draco and Carla chafed as much as it did.

Draco's face as he'd watched Carla glide over the ice had hammered home a different truth—her reasons for relying on Draco weren't wholly for the sake of avoiding thinking about her father.

The level of her misery had forced her to acknowledge another truth. Draco obviously cared for Carla beyond platonic or business interests.

'The sight of Carla with that man upsets you that much?' she forced herself to ask, because she couldn't *not* know.

'Yes, it does,' he grated as they mounted stairs that ended in two wraparound terraces.

Her heart dipped, along with her ability to think straight. She followed almost robot-like as he took the left wrap-around terrace, which brought them to a set of French doors. He thrust it open and they entered the hallway that led to their suite.

She stepped in front of him as he was about to head to the living room.

'Carla means more to you than just getting her away from Tyson Blackwell, doesn't she?' she challenged, absently wondering why she couldn't stop herself from probing a point that seemed to lance her with arrows of bewildering pain.

Draco frowned. 'Of course. You think I'd go through all this for someone I didn't care about?'

Rebel's hand shook as she lifted it to her temple. 'Sorry, I'm confused. You care enough about her to want to save her from Tyson, but it's just the marrying her that you're against?'

'I'm against being manipulated, period,' he snarled. 'Somewhere along the line, Olivio has obviously concluded he can leverage my private life to suit him. That's not going to happen. Now if you're done with your questions, I'd appreciate not being interrogated further about this. You know your role. Just play it and we'll be fine.'

He went to the drinks cabinet. Grabbing a bottle of single-malt whisky, he pulled the cork and poured two fingers into a crystal tumbler.

He knocked it back in one clean swallow. Then he slammed the glass down and clenched both hands in his hair.

Several Greek curses fell from his lips as he paced the floor.

Chest tight with emotions she refused to name, she eyed him. 'You do realise that if you insist on continuing this fa-çade and you don't do anything about the state you're in, you're going to blow this charade wide open, don't you?'

He paused mid-stride. 'Why do you think I'm in here knocking back drinks instead of out there, punching Blackwell's face in?' he growled.

Rebel flinched. She needed to walk away, leave him alone to handle this on his own. She wasn't equipped to deal with anyone's emotional fallout; not when she was actively hiding from her own. But she'd also never seen anyone care this deeply…not since witnessing the unstinting adoration between her parents. She'd deeply missed the overflow of warmth from that special bond. So even though a physical ache lodged in her chest as she watched Draco try to wrestle his emotions under control, she remained rooted to the floor beside the armchair.

'Are you going to talk to Carla about this?'

'I'll have to. I can't let this go any further. Olivio might not listen, but I hope she will.'

He dropped his hands from the back of his neck and then stared at his trembling fingers. He seemed fascinated with his body's reaction. Then slowly he clenched his fists and exhaled. Although his body calmed, the Draco who walked past her with a curt, 'I need a shower,' possessed eyes so bleak they were almost black.

She instinctively reached out and grasped his arm. He jerked to a stop, his gaze going to where she held him, then back to her face.

'Arabella, I'm not thinking very rationally right now,' he rasped. Residual fury vibrated off him, emotional aftershocks that threatened to bury her the longer she stayed this close.

'I know, and I'll be quick. I just wanted to say, if you can help it, don't let this eat you up too much.'

'As long as that bastard is sniffing around her, it'll eat me up.'

'But—'

His hand shot out to grip her arm, the other coming up to hover over her mouth. His thumb slid across her mouth.

'Enough, *glikia mou*. I don't want to think about Black-well any more. So enough. Okay?' Bleak eyes searched hers, pleading.

At her nod, he dropped his hand. And replaced it with his mouth. Shock held her still long enough for him to delve between her lips. Then pure, unadulterated sensation took over. Her moan rose up from her soul, excavating every yearning she'd tried to suppress since Wednesday night. Her hands gripped his bare arms, the fierce joy of touch-ing him somewhere else besides his nape and face piercing her. She strained up, plastering her needy, super-charged body against his, and earning herself an answering groan in return. One hand trailed the length of her back to her be-hind, then splayed open to drag her even closer. She ground against his erection, her nerves tingling, the secret place be-tween her legs dampening, readying itself for this man...

This man who didn't belong to her.

He nipped at the corner of her bottom lip just as she jerked away from him. They parted and she was left with a coppery taste in her mouth. Draco's eyes zeroed in on the spot, a hiss issuing from his lips. 'Arabella *mou*...your lip.' He reached out. She danced out of his way.

'It's okay, I'm fine.' She licked at the spot again, and he groaned.

'Sweetheart, let me—'

'No. You can't do this, Draco.'

He stared at her for a frozen second, his breath shudder-ing in and out. With another curse, he threw his head back and closed his eyes for a brief moment. Exhaling one last time, he stared straight at her. 'No. I guess not. But next time, tell me which body part you want me to cry on before I go thinking everything is available to me.'

'How about we agree right now that *none* of it is avail-able to you?'

His gaze dropped to her mouth. 'So I get your *words* and nothing else?'

'Wasn't that what you wanted?' she replied.

A stiff smile twitched one corner of his mouth. 'Thanks for the reminder.'

He strode out of the room with long, angry strides. Rebel waited till she heard the faint sound of running water before she hurried to the dressing room. She swapped her trainers for heels that would elevate her attire back to smart casual. Combing out her hair, she sprayed perfume on her wrists before grabbing her bag and slipping out onto the terrace. She reclined on the shaded lounger, willing her racing pulse to subside as she plucked her phone and earphones from her bag. Cranking up the music, she tucked up her legs to her chest.

Much as she'd have liked to escape the suite totally, she didn't want to risk running into Olivio or any of his guests without Draco in case the agitation bubbling beneath her skin showed. If Draco wanted to stay, he would need his acting skills to get them *both* through tonight and tomorrow.

Rebel grew drowsy as her pulse finally calmed and her thundering heartbeat stopped roaring in time to the music.

The feeling of a soft blanket being draped over her roused her from sleep. Draco sat on the twin lounger, his eyes a lot less volatile than they'd been. In fact, he looked downright solemn and perhaps even a touch contrite.

'How long have I been asleep?' she asked around a dry mouth.

He handed her a cool drink, which she accepted and sipped gratefully. 'Long enough for your cycle of crazy music to play three times.'

So just over two hours. 'It's not crazy music. It calms me down.' She bit her lip as she said it, wondering if she would unwittingly set him off.

But he remained seated, his gaze steady on her. 'I owe you an apology. You were trying to help and I…took advantage.'

A knot she hadn't acknowledged unravelled inside her.

'You warned me you weren't thinking rationally. I should've let you go, not insisted on saying my piece.'

His mouth twisted. 'Your piece, brief as it was, was very welcome. It saved the shower wall from getting a pounding.'

'Yikes. Not sure you'd have come off without serious battle scars, what with *all* that marble.'

He grinned, then sobered after a few seconds. 'While you were asleep, I spoke to Olivio. He won't discuss his business with Blackwell, but it turns out he's not staying at the villa. I guess Olivio wasn't prepared to risk one of us walking out.'

'Did you get a chance to talk to Carla?' she asked.

He shook his head. 'She was resting after her training.'

Rebel twirled the straw through her drink. 'So what now?'

'We can go down to dinner. Or we can stay here and have dinner brought up to us. We are newly engaged, after all.'

The thought of not having to put on a show in front of strangers was hugely appealing. She'd fallen asleep before she'd worked things through and now the events of the afternoon came flooding back.

Setting her half-empty glass down, she braced her elbows on her knees and massaged her temples.

He frowned. 'Are you all right?'

'I'm trying to wrap my mind around all this.'

Draco sighed, a wave of cold misery rushing over his face before he schooled his features. Then he released a breath. 'Perhaps a further explanation would help?'

'Please,' she murmured.

For almost a minute, his jaw clenched tight. 'After my knee blew out and my career ended, I shut everyone out. I was angry with myself for not seeing what Larson and his team were up to. I just gave my statement to the police and let them handle it. What I didn't know was that they'd missed one crucial member of the team. Larson's nephew.'

Her heart leapt into her throat as she made the connection. 'Tyson Blackwell?'

Draco nodded grimly. 'He was in charge of my sister's training.'

'Your *sister*?'

'Yes.' He blew out a ragged breath. 'Maria was a figure skater. She and Carla are best friends. They don't see each other as regularly any more, but she idolises Carla. Watching Carla's videos was the only thing that pulled her from the brink after the accident.'

'What happened to Maria?'

'What always happens when Blackwell's in charge. He pushed her past her limit. She was doing a quadruple rotation she was woefully unprepared for when she fell and hit her head on the ice. She fractured her third vertebrae and lost the use of her arms and legs.'

A sob strangled Rebel's chest. 'No!'

'By the time I got my head on straight after my own accident, Blackwell had covered his tracks. He stood trial but he only got an eighteen-month ban for two of his trainees missing doping tests. He got off scot-free for what he did to Maria.' Bitterness and anger twisted his face.

The same expressions he'd exhibited this afternoon as he'd watched Carla skating...

Had she got it wrong? Had she attributed a different spin on Draco's feelings for Carla? The pressure eased in her chest. Surely he wouldn't have gone to the trouble of engineering a fake engagement to put off a woman he could have had if he felt so inclined? From the first, it'd been Olivio's manipulation and Tyson Blackwell's presence in Carla's life that had enraged Draco.

Relief punched through her, startling a laugh from her throat.

'What?' Draco demanded.

'I...nothing.' She sobered and reached out, curling her hand around his jaw before the action fully registered. 'I know it's hard to believe, but what happened to your sister wasn't your fault.'

He shook his head. 'It was. Larson didn't broadcast it but I knew he had a nephew. I was so focused on my career, I didn't pay attention to the team my father had hired for Maria. If I'd been around more, I would've noticed that things weren't right.'

'Sorry to break it to you, but if you couldn't see it in your own team, how would you have noticed it in your sister's team?'

Raw anguish propelled him to his feet. 'I was her older brother. I was supposed to look after her!'

The weight of her own guilt crushed down on her. 'Blind spots when it comes to our family are dangerously common.'

He stopped and stared down at her. 'Your father?'

She shrugged, her chest clamped in a steel vice. 'Me. My mother. We all have our faults. Some are a little more unforgivable than others.'

Exhaling sharply, Draco strode to the terrace railing a few feet away and gripped it hard. The muscles in his back bunched as tension gripped him harder. 'I had you investigated—I'm sure you understand why. Your mother died in a skiing accident. You weren't responsible for her death.'

The blood drained from her face, and her lungs closed up. Dropping her head forward, she desperately tried to get her blood pumping again.

Sound faded in and out as she tried to breathe.

'Arabella!'

A moment later, Draco swung her into his arms and strode back into the suite. The sofa was the closest comfortable surface. He placed her there and drew the blanket over her and crouched before her. 'I shouldn't have left you in the sun for so long.'

'I'm fine.'

'You're not. You didn't eat on the plane and you haven't

eaten since we got here,' he huffed. Rising, he headed for the door. Rebel heard him issuing instructions to Stefano before he returned to the living room.

Despite the guilt eating her alive, she couldn't look away from him as he sat on the coffee table and leaned towards her. Brushing her hair from her face, he tucked a strand behind her ear. The side of his finger smoothed over her cheek to her jaw before repeating the caress.

The gesture was so sweet, she wanted to relive it over and over. 'Are you going soft on me, Draco?' she murmured.

'Only until you're back on your feet,' he murmured back. 'Then it'll be all-out war again.'

She sighed. 'War is exhausting.'

'Who have you been fighting, *glikia mou*? Besides me, that is?' he asked, his voice a gentle rumble that lulled her from the secret place she'd inhabited for far too long.

'My father.'

'You've seen him?'

Her gaze clashed with his. 'Will you hate me if I say yes?'

He stilled, his finger dangerously close to her pulse. 'Family is complicated, I get that. Besides, I gave my word that if you fulfilled your part of the agreement, I'd forgive the debt.'

Relief flooded her. 'All right, then. He was waiting for me when I got in on Wednesday night.'

Draco frowned. 'At your flat?'

'Yes. He'd seen the news of our engagement in the paper.'

One brow rose. 'Let me guess—he came to warn you off me?'

She nodded. 'He's not a fan of yours.'

His mouth twisted. 'I don't have many of those these days who aren't contracted to me in some fashion or other.'

Her eyelids felt heavy again, but she fought them open. 'I was your fan way before you turned into Draco the Dragon.'

'*Efkharisto*, Arabella.'

'I love the way that sounds.'

'What?'

'The Greek...and my name.'

She stared up at him, her breath catching all over again at the sheer dynamic beauty of his face. Then she shut her eyes when his image swam. 'Why am I drowsy again?'

'Probably because you haven't slept well recently.'

'Hmm. You're bad for my health.'

His mouth twitched. 'You were telling me about your father.'

'Yes. He offered to turn himself in so I wouldn't be engaged to you any longer. I refused.'

She wasn't sure whether the sharp exhalation came from him or her, but she pressed on. 'I told him it was too late. I'd given you my word. Besides, I don't think prison dungarees would suit me, do you?'

'You'd look good in anything, but perhaps prison gear shouldn't be on anyone's wish list.'

'I agree. Anyway, he accepted that there was nothing he could do so...' She tried to shrug, but couldn't quite pull it off. Sorrow clawed at her, her father's words still fresh, and deep, and anchored into her heart. Tears brimmed and rolled down her temples.

This time Draco's hiss was audible. 'What did he say to you?'

'I asked when I'd see him again. He said he...he couldn't look at me without seeing my mother...and that it hurt too much that she's no longer alive, so he intends to stay away.'

He surged to his feet. '*Thee mou.* What sort of man is he?' he raged.

Rebel struggled up. When he tried to stay her, she grabbed his hand. 'You don't understand, Draco. He loved my mother. I mean *really* loved her. It shattered him completely when she died.' Another tear rolled down her face. She swiped at it with her free hand.

'It still doesn't excuse his treatment of you.'

Her heart ached that she couldn't tell Draco the last piece

of her life's puzzle. But after hearing him condemn himself and anyone who'd been responsible for his sister's injuries, Rebel knew he would never forgive her for causing her mother's death. 'Does it hurt? Sure. But I don't want him to be in pain because of me. If he can find some peace away from me, then…'

Draco made a rough sound at the back of his throat. Raising her head, she met his laser-sharp gaze. 'You'd sacrifice that? A lifetime's relationship just so he could be happy?'

Her tiredness was receding. But with more clarity came harrowing pain. 'As opposed to him being miserable with me? Yes, I would.'

'You're…extraordinary,' he husked out.

She raised one eyebrow. 'You seem surprised.'

The knock on the suite door stopped their conversation. Draco stared down at her for several heartbeats before he called out for Stefano to enter.

The trolley was heaving with meats and sausages from the barbecue going on by the poolside, Stefano informed them. Warm focaccia bread, with olive oil and garlic sauces, and an assortment of salads were unearthed from beneath domed dishes.

Dismissing Stefano, Draco heaped a plate with food and set her tray down on her lap. After seeing to his own, he sat down next to her. They ate in companionable silence, for once at ease with each other's company.

Her insides clenched momentarily at the thought of the tight secret lodged inside her. She'd thrown caution to the wind and told him as much as she could about her relationship with her father. Despite Draco's harsh views, she knew he wouldn't go after her father as long as she kept up her end of the bargain.

She was used to flying through the air without a safety harness or a net to break her fall. Ski jumping was one of the riskiest sports out there, and yet she'd thrown herself into it without a backward glance.

She glanced at Draco and found his gaze, direct and intense, on her.

Perhaps it was time to take a different, equally exhilarating, risk.

CHAPTER ELEVEN

THE SOUND OF the door shutting woke Rebel in the early hours. She'd said goodnight to Draco shortly after their meal last night with an arrangement to head out to the gym at five a.m.

Turning over in bed, she stretched her limbs, groaning with relief at the most restful sleep she'd had since her father's letter had brought her nightmares about losing her mother surging back. She hadn't even needed her earphones to drown out the demons.

Glancing at the clock, she noticed it was only four-fifteen. Had Draco headed out to get his own training in before he trained with her? Pushing aside the covers, she sprang out of bed. On the off-chance she was mistaken, she peeked into the living room. The sofa bed had been tucked away and the sheets folded up.

Deciding to join him, Rebel changed into her exercise gear, caught up her phone and earphones, and left the suite. Knowing she would get lost if she tried the shortcut, she went through the villa, unease striking all over again at the gratuitous display of Carla Nardozzi's pictures and trophies.

She stepped out into the crisp air, thankful that the whole estate was well lit. After stretching her arms and legs, she placed her earphones in and struck out in the direction of the facility.

The studio door stood ajar when she reached it. She slipped in and muted her music.

The cry from the direction of the ice rink froze her steps.

Changing direction, she entered the room to witness the tail end of an argument between Carla and Tyson Blackwell.

He had her gripped by the arms, Carla's whimper echoing across the room.

'You want to win another glitzy trophy? Then do what I tell you to do!'

'A triple axel into a death spiral sounds insane!'

'Damn it, maybe I am wasting my time with you. All your competitors are doing it. Fail to master it and you can kiss your career goodbye.'

He flung her away from him. Carla tried to catch herself but went sprawling onto the ice.

Rebel stepped into the light. 'Hey, you can't talk to her like that!'

Tyson whirled from his fallen victim. 'Who the hell are you?'

'Someone who can see that you're pushing her way too hard.'

He shooed her away. 'The way I run my training programme is none of your business. Now, I suggest you clear off.'

'I'm not going anywhere. Unless Mr Nardozzi decides to throw me out, of course.' From the corner of her eye, she saw Carla drag herself up and totter on her blades.

Turning, shock slammed through Rebel at the full blast of the younger girl's glare before Carla carefully schooled her features.

'She's my father's guest. She's here with Draco Angelis.'

Even from several dozen feet away, Rebel saw malicious interest spark in his eyes. Leaving Carla's side, he slid across the ice to her.

'So you're Angelis' little piece on the side I've heard so much about this past week.' His head tilted. 'You look familiar. Do I know you?' A suggestive leer draped his face.

'Yeah, in your dreams.'

The leer evaporated. 'This is a training session, not a spectator event. Please leave.'

Rebel looked past him to where Carla stood, a forlorn

figure in the centre of the ice rink. About to call out to her, she spun at the sound of thundering footsteps.

'Arabella!'

The urgency in Draco's deep voice sent a delicious spark down her spine. 'In here,' she called out.

He surged into the room a second later, his eyes narrowing as they zeroed in on her. 'You were supposed to wait for me—' He froze as he spotted Tyson Blackwell. Then he looked past him to where Carla was poised.

When Draco's eyes clashed with Rebel's, his rage had quadrupled. 'What the hell's going on here?'

'I'm conducting a training session. Have you been out of the game so long you've forgotten even the basics, Angelis?' Tyson sneered.

Draco ignored him. Striding to the edge of the ring, he called out, 'Carla. Come here.'

'Hey, what the hell—? Stay where you are, girl,' Tyson countered.

After a moment's hesitation, Carla skated to Draco. This close, the finger marks where Tyson had gripped her were visible against her pearly skin.

Fury flared through Draco's nostrils. 'Did he do this to you?' he grated out.

Hesitantly, Carla nodded. Draco pointed a finger at Tyson. 'You're finished. If you know what's good for you, find a deep dark hole and disappear inside. If I see you around one more skater, the only place you'll be heading to is jail to join your bastard uncle.'

'You have no authority here, Angelis. I have Olivio's full support. If you think you're going to change that, forget it,' he snarled. Glancing at Carla, he added, 'We'll pick this up later.' Tyson rolled back to the other end of the ice rink, kicked off his blades and stormed out via another entrance.

Holding out his hand, Draco helped Carla down. 'Take off your blades. I'll take you back to the villa.'

With a dazzling smile at Draco, Carla replaced her blades with heeled boots and tucked her hand through his arm.

Despite choosing to believe that there was nothing romantic between Draco and Carla, Rebel's stomach still contracted with irrational envy as she watched them disappear through the door.

'Right. Guess I'll see you when I see you,' she muttered, unprepared for the renewed misery snaking through her. Just as she was unprepared for Draco to suddenly reappear as she mounted the stairs to the weight room.

'What do you think you're doing?' he snapped.

She paused on the second step. 'Umm…going training?'

'Not without me, you're not.' Taking her arm, he walked her out and sat her on the remaining unoccupied passenger seat of the buggy, which happened to be behind a less-than-happy-looking Carla.

Draco walked Carla to the villa door once they arrived, his low murmuring voice eliciting several nods from her before she went in and shut the door behind her.

His demeanour changed as he strode back to the buggy. Sliding behind the wheel, he flicked her a glance. 'Get in the front.'

She complied, simply because she wanted to be closer to him. She was barely seated when the buggy surged forward. The five-minute journey felt like hours, the easy silence they'd shared last night a smoky figment of her imagination.

As they crested the hill she cleared her throat. 'Are you upset with me?'

His jaw clenched hard before he spoke. 'Damn right. You were supposed to wait for me. Instead I returned to find you gone.'

'I woke up early and thought you were here, at the facility.'

'I'd just gone to get a drink of coffee. We agreed to come here together. At five. Instead I found you here, in the cross hairs of a man I wouldn't trust with my goldfish.'

'Then we should be thankful I'm more substantial than a goldfish, shouldn't we? And for the record, I pack a hell of a punch when threatened.'

His eyes narrowed. 'Is that jibe aimed at me?'

'Unless you plan to attack me, no.'

His hand slashed through the air. 'I don't like this. In case you've forgotten we're still playing a role. One Olivio is keeping a close eye on.'

'Being engaged doesn't mean we're joined at the hip. You were worried about overcooking things. You not letting me out of your sight runs the risk of doing just that. You can frown all you want, but it's the truth.'

'I hardly think not wanting to be parted from you sends that message. Certainly not at four o'clock in the morning when you should be in bed with me.'

Rebel sighed. 'You found me, Draco. I'm okay. Let's chalk it up to a win because my getting here early stopped Tyson from manhandling Carla more than he did.'

Fury detonated. The vibrations from him threatened to flatten her. 'What if you'd been on your own with him?' he seethed.

'I wasn't,' she stated simply.

He fisted his hair for a charged second before he jerked out of the buggy. 'You wanted to train so badly? Let's get to it, then.'

Rebel followed him in, her senses surging higher as she followed his ruggedly lean body up the stairs to the weights room.

Over the next hour, he set a blistering place, his commands bullet fast and relentless.

'Faster!' he shouted over the sound of the treadmill.

'Lower!' he boomed from behind her as she sank into another excruciating squat.

'Damn it, lock your elbows.'

'Damn it, they *are* locked!'

He leaned over the weight bar vibrating with the tension in her triceps. 'Are you being smart with me?' he snarled.

'I don't have a single smart left in me, Drill Sergeant,' she ground out.

Their eyes met. Battled. Then his stormy grey eyes moved over her sweat-drenched body as she lowered the bar and pressed it back up.

'Ten,' he rasped, without taking his eyes off her bare midriff. 'Nine,' he supplied helpfully after another shredding lift.

'Draco...'

'Eight.'

'Stop,' she gasped.

'Seven. Stop counting?'

'Stop...staring.'

'No.' His gaze moved to her breasts and his breathing altered. 'Six.'

'Grrruuuugh!'

'Is that even English? Five.'

'I hate you!'

'I hate you back. Four.' He squatted and brushed back the wet tendrils at her temple. 'Three.'

'You're...touching me, Draco. You want me to fail,' she panted.

'Never. Almost there, *glikia mou*. Two.'

Pain rippled through her body as lactic acid surged through her system. 'One!' she shouted.

He stood over her and took the weight from her trembling grip.

Rebel stood and shook her hands, relief pouring through her wrists and biceps as her pumping heart settled. 'Piece of cake.'

Draco came up behind her, and held a bottle of water to her lips. She drank thirstily, then, just because she could, she relaxed against him, rubbed her back against his front.

His breath hissed in her ear. 'Why do you drive me crazy like this?'

'Umm…you make it too damn easy?'

Dropping the bottle, he flipped her round. '*Thee mou*, your mouth!'

'Is all the workout you need?'

With a pained grunt he smashed his mouth on hers. Strong arms banded her waist and she linked her arms around his neck as he picked her up and walked forward to the martial arts area. Her body hit the mat none too gently, but Rebel didn't care. Draco was kissing her and her senses were on fire. This time when he parted her legs, she welcomed him, holding her breath until he rolled his hips against her.

'Oh!' She thrilled to the shudder that rolled through her.

'Damn, you're so responsive,' he groaned against her mouth.

'Complaint?'

'Compliment.'

'Okay. Proceed.'

He consumed her, each lick, bite and pinch twisting them higher, until they broke apart, desperate for the sweet sustenance of oxygen. Weaving her fingers through his hair, Rebel just gloried in the weight of him and the hand sliding up and down her calf.

'Arabella?'

'Drill Sergeant?'

His mouth stretched against her cheek. Her heart flipped over at the thought that she'd made him smile. Turning her head, she stole a kiss. He groaned again. 'We can't do this here.'

'In this room, this villa, or this country?'

'Definitely not in this room. I'd prefer a different bed and a different villa to one owned by Olivio Nardozzi. How would you feel about leaving a day early and switching to a different country?'

'What about Olivio?'

A hard smile curved his lips. 'My wanting to be alone with you away from this place should serve as a further convincer.'

Her breath shuddered. 'And do you?'

He fused his mouth to hers in a hard kiss. 'Enough to put my pilot on standby to leave immediately after the gala tonight.'

'So…where would you take me?'

His nostrils flared as his eyes darkened. 'I have homes in most of the major sports-orientated cities around the world. But wherever you want to go, I can make it happen.' He leaned down and brushed his growing stubble against her cheek before placing an open-mouthed kiss on the racing pulse at her throat.

'Do all your homes have what I need to train?'

'Of course,' he murmured.

'What about Greg?'

His head jerked up, blazing eyes piercing hers. 'Who's Greg?'

'My trainer.'

He relaxed a touch. 'Get him to send me your training schedule. I'll take care of you until your dry-land drills are over. He can take over again when we get to Verbier.'

Her heart leapt. 'You're coming to the championships?'

'You're my fiancée. How would it look if I'm not there by your side?'

Rebel told herself the lurching of her heart was a good reminder that all of this wasn't real. That what they were doing had a coldly calculated purpose and a finite conclusion, no matter that she'd decided to risk making it a little bit more than the platonic undertaking they'd agreed.

Mentally shaking off the voice that probed the wisdom of changing the parameters of their agreement, she grimaced at him. 'I'm not sure I want you as my trainer if every training session is going to be like this.'

'It's not going to be like this,' he returned. 'It's going to be worse.'

Her eyebrow shot up. 'Worse?'

'I've seen what you're capable of. You protest at every drill, yet you can easily achieve so much more.' A frown locked between his eyebrows. 'It's almost as if you don't want to achieve your full potential.'

Her gaze dropped from his probing look.

He caught her chin in his hand. 'Arabella?'

'I…it's not that. I want to win this championship. More than anything.'

'But?'

'But I'm afraid after that there'll be nothing else. Nothing to strive for. My father is gone, Draco. I don't know if I'll ever see him again. Once the championships are over, I'll have nothing.'

His frown dissolved, but his jaw clenched. 'Why were you doing it in the first place?'

'Mostly for my mother. I want to honour her memory.'

'But not with a win? How is coming fifth when you can be champion truly honouring her?'

'It wasn't so much the winning, as just participating in the sport she loved.'

He shook his head. 'I don't buy that. And I don't think you do either. This still has to do with your father, doesn't it? What is it?'

She swallowed the rock that lodged in her throat. 'He didn't want me to become a professional skier. Like your father, he wanted me to do something else. My mother and I talked him around with…with a promise that I'd give up once I won a major championship.'

Fury roared through his eyes. 'So you've been deliberately holding yourself back because of a promise you made when you were…how old?'

'I was fifteen.'

'You were a child!'

'But old enough to understand what promises meant.'

A scalding curse ripped through the room. He levered himself off her and stood glaring down at her.

'So that's what you're going to do for the rest of your life, always achieving a little less than your potential because of a father who doesn't have a problem betraying you?'

Pain bit deeper. 'Draco...'

'What would your mother have wanted for you?'

She closed her eyes, her insides a churning river of sorrow. 'For me to compete. And win.'

He crouched down and lifted her to her feet. 'And what do *you* want, Arabella?'

Sharp tears prickled the backs of her eyes. 'I want everything. To keep my promise to my father. To honour my mother. And to win multiple championships.'

He shook his head, a tinge of bleakness in his eyes. 'You're realistic enough to know that we never get everything we want. And by fruitlessly hanging onto one dream, you're jeopardising everything else.' He let go of her and took several steps back.

Rebel wasn't sure why that deliberate withdrawal sent a wave of panic through her. 'Draco?' She reached for him, but he stepped farther away.

'Choose, Arabella. Either you're in this all the way or you're not.'

Her hand balled into a fist, the vein of shame she'd always felt when she'd held back instead of going all in during competitions thickening uncomfortably. 'Why? What is it to you?'

'I'm not asking you to choose for me. I'm asking you to choose for yourself.' He paced in front of her but still kept out of reach. 'Imagine yourself thirty years down the line. Is this the legacy you'd want to leave? That you deliberately fell short of reaching for your goals?'

'No.' The word charged out of her, fired from a place she'd deliberately closed off because the desires that resided there were too painful to dream about. Being forced to confront them sent a wave of sadness through her. Because in order to achieve what she truly yearned for, she would be throwing away any chances of reconciliation with her father. But then what were the guarantees that they would reconcile when he'd stated plainly that the very sight of her wrecked him? Was she in danger of throwing out one dream to follow another that might never come true?

The memory of her mother pierced her thoughts, of her beautiful smile and ecstatic cheering when Rebel had won her first junior championship. All the way home Susie Daniels had babbled her pride and hopes for her daughter's future to anyone who would listen. That day had been one of the happiest days of Rebel's life. She wanted to relive that day again. And again. She wanted that memory of her mother to never fade. Never cease to inspire her. With a shaky breath, she looked at Draco. 'No, I don't want that.'

He breached the gap between them and caught her face in his hands. His eyes glowed with a fire she wanted to believe was pride. But then he angled his head and kissed her, and her every sense coalesced into pleasure. He didn't let up until the need to breathe drove them apart.

This time the look in his eyes when their gazes met was one of pure predatory hunger. Sliding his hand down her arm, he laced their fingers and tugged her to the door.

'Come. Let's go and get this day over with so I can begin kicking your ass into gear,' he drawled with unabashed relish.

'Just remember, I kick back.'

He laughed. 'How soon you forget yourself. Insubordination of any kind will only make things worse for you.'

'How did I know you'll try to get your way with threats?'

'Those aren't threats, *glikia mou*. They're golden promises.'

REBEL WAS STILL hiding a smile that threatened to split her face when they returned to their suite. The look in Draco's eyes as she walked away to take her shower could've buckled steel.

All through the day as they mingled with guests whose names she forgot almost as soon as Olivio made introductions, she felt the weight of Draco's hungry stare. Not that he left her side for more than a few minutes at a time. By the time they returned to their suite to get ready for the gala, Rebel was sure she would spontaneously combust if he glanced at her one more time.

But he did more than glance at her when she emerged from the dressing room at a few minutes to eight.

'I'm good to go,' she addressed a tuxedoed Draco, who was nursing a small whisky as he gazed out into the Tuscan night.

He turned. He froze. His scrutiny was thorough, taking in every inch of her white Greek-style gown, cinched in at the waist and collared at the throat with gold metal. At her wrists her favourite gold bangles clinked as she moved nervously beneath his intense…increasingly frowning gaze.

'Draco…?'

'*Thee mou*, you look breathtaking,' he rasped.

'Maybe next time, lead with that, instead of the frown?' she suggested with a nervous but pleased laugh.

He discarded his drink on a nearby surface and came towards her, the frown still in place. 'I've seen the guest list. More than half of them are male sports stars with overblown egos and the impression that they can have anything, or anyone, they want.' He captured her hand, his grip tight. 'Just remember, you're my fiancée. I'll kill anyone who dares to make a pass at you.'

Rebel had ceased trying to fight the insane chemical thrill that his touch and his words brought. She was firmly immersed in whatever was happening between them. So what if a part of her had taken more than a moment or two during the day to wonder what it would be like to be truly engaged to Draco? *That* was the part of her she needed to control.

Now that she'd decided to fight all out for her dreams, she couldn't afford to get emotionally tangled with Draco. Walking away from this charade without emotional loss was imperative. The physical side, the potent chemistry that wrapped them in its own formidable force field, she could handle. And as she'd seen with so many of her friends and acquaintances, the chemistry didn't last for anyone, once explored.

'Well, I hope you'll keep the bloodletting at a distance. I don't want my gown ruined,' she replied.

Exhaling, he muttered something under his breath about her mouth, then tugged her after him to the door.

The ballroom holding the gala was themed like the rest of the villa—an exhibition of marble and Carla Nardozzi. The event, purportedly to raise money for children's sports in Third World countries, was in danger of being overshadowed by the Olivio and Carla Nardozzi Show.

The woman in question, dressed in a white and silver gown that moulded every inch of her skin from throat to feet, her face impeccably made up and her hair caught up in her signature chignon, glided forward on her father's arm to greet them. Compliments were exchanged, but Rebel noticed Carla's gaze barely stayed on her before it returned to Draco. And this time there was no disguising the keen interest in the younger woman's eyes. An unpleasant sensation coiled inside Rebel.

'Carla told me what you did this morning,' Olivio said,

his gaze on Draco. 'She was lucky to have you there to intervene for what I'm sure was just a misunderstanding with Tyson. But I owe you my thanks nevertheless.'

Draco's gaze hardened. 'It wasn't a misunderstanding. And Arabella was there too. In fact, she stopped the situation from escalating.'

Carla laughed. 'Hardly. I had things under control.'

Shock froze Rebel for a second. 'He was manhandling you, and trying to force you to do a dangerous move you weren't ready for!'

Carla's mouth pursed. 'You were there for only a few minutes, Miss Daniels. I only meant I wasn't prepared to do that move at that time of the morning when I'd barely warmed up.'

'A dangerous move is a dangerous move, no matter the time of day it's performed,' Draco inserted with unmistakable gravity. Although his bleak expression cleared a moment later, Rebel's heart squeezed at the naked pain and guilt he carried for what had happened to his sister.

'Then you'll be pleased to know I succeeded in my attempt this afternoon,' Carla said.

Olivio smiled with smug satisfaction. 'Now that we've cleared that up, perhaps we can get on with the evening? Draco, Carla has a few people she's dying for you to meet. I promise to take care of your beloved while you're away.'

Short of offending their host—a move she didn't doubt Olivio would hold against Draco—she had no choice but to slide her hand through Olivio's proffered arm.

Draco's gaze dropped to the point of contact, his nostrils flaring slightly. Olivio's laughter held a touch of edgy mockery. 'She's only going across the room, not to the ends of the earth.'

When Draco's eyes gleamed dangerously, Rebel smiled, thinking it wise to defuse the situation.

'He told me before we left our suite that he'll kill any man who strays too close to me tonight. Perhaps I ought to level the playing field by stating that I'll gut any woman who looks at him the wrong way. Does that help, darling?'

Draco's gaze caught hers, the promise of retribution echoing clearly, before dropping to her mouth. 'It helps.'

'Such passion,' Olivio drawled.

Rebel placed her tongue firmly in her cheek. 'You don't know the half of it.'

Carla slipped *both* her hands through Draco's bent arm, her gaze daring as it met Rebel's. 'Come on. It's almost time for us to take our seats and I may not have time later.'

Rebel walked away, the smile pinned on her face hopefully disguising the fact that her insides were still knotted with an unhealthy mix of anger and jealousy. Draco might not have romantic intentions towards Carla, but the younger woman clearly had other ideas.

'So when is the big day?' Olivio enquired in between playing the attentive host to his mingling guests.

Rebel frowned, dragging her eyes from where Carla was plastered to Draco's side as they chatted with a basketball star and his wife across the room. 'Big day?'

'The wedding. Surely that's what every woman thinks about the moment she's proposed to?' His brown eyes drilled into hers, as if hoping to catch her in a lie.

'A wedding takes time to plan. Besides, I have a championship to think of before we get round to setting wedding dates.'

'Ah, yes. I understand you dabble in cross-country. Or is it jumping?' His teeth were bared in a semblance of a smile, but his eyes were slowly hardening, a hint of a sneer in the espresso depths.

Rebel tossed her head. 'I'm sorry, is there an insult in there somewhere? Only I despise insinuation.'

Another guest approached. Olivio slipped into charming host mode, chatting and smiling until they were once again alone. Then he turned so his back was to the room.

'My Carla needs a man like Draco in her camp to keep her at the top of the game.'

'Isn't she already at the top? And isn't Draco's offer of representation going to achieve what you want?'

'The sort of contract he's offering is one that can be broken at any time. What I need from him is a firmer commitment.'

Rebel arranged her features into fake astonishment. 'What are you saying? That you want me to give up the man I love to your daughter?' Her voice caught, her whole body clenching hard with a stormy sensation that had nothing to do with the role she'd agreed to play.

'I'm in a position to make sure it's worth your while.'

Struggling with the sudden pounding of her heart, she lifted her hand to her throat in a dramatic pose. 'And how much is ripping out one's own heart and throwing it under a bus worth these days?'

Olivio assessed her shrewdly. 'Will a million euros do it?'

Over his shoulder she spotted Draco and Carla, now standing alone. His head was bent towards her shorter form as she murmured in his ear. Rebel couldn't dismiss the evidence that they made a striking couple.

Looking away from them, she stared at Olivio. 'Sadly, I don't think you've thought this through properly. You want me to walk away from a dynamic, wildly successful man, whose net worth I'm guessing eclipses yours many times over, and who I also happen to be in love with, for a mere million euros?' She injected as much sarcasm into her voice as possible. 'And even if I was crazy enough to consider your offer, you forget, there's nothing between Carla and Draco.'

Olivio made a dismissive gesture. 'Romance just needs the right circumstances to be rekindled.'

Rebel's breath locked in her lungs. *Rekindled?*

His superior smile widened. 'I see he chose not to tell you.'

'Perhaps he didn't think it important enough,' she replied, although her voice lacked the conviction she'd been able to project thus far.

'Or perhaps his male pride still smarts from the fact that I put a stop to their dating three years ago because my Carla was too young for that kind of intensity and didn't need the distraction. I don't apologise for looking out for her best interests. But Draco should be made to see he's letting his bruised ego get in the way of a perfect union.'

The poisoned knife that seemed to have impaled her sternum wasn't easing up, no matter how much she tried to breathe through it. In fact, with every second that passed, numbness spread through her body. 'Again, I don't see how any of this interests me. Draco put his ring on my finger. I need a little more than a second-hand tale of infatuation to discard it.'

The soft background music that had accompanied the pre-dinner drinks faded and the lights blinked, indicating it was time to take their seats. Rebel saw Draco and Carla head their way.

'You don't want to make an enemy of me, Arabella,' Olivio warned.

'Oh, I don't know if that'll make a difference, Olivio. This one seems to take pride in collecting enemies,' an intruding voice suggested.

She tensed as Tyson Blackwell stopped beside them, a glass of champagne in his hand. From across the room, Draco's face contorted with barely contained fury as he swiftly headed back towards her.

'What can I say? Meek and mild have never been friends of mine. And I find it hard to bite my tongue at the best of times when someone is being mistreated right in front of my eyes.'

'Maybe you should learn,' Tyson ground out.

'Where's the fun in that?' she fired back.

'Everything okay here?' Draco's icy voice joined the

conversation. In the light of what Olivio had just imparted, Rebel found she couldn't look at him. Not without betraying herself. And now more than ever, knowing how much she wanted to win the championship—ironically thanks to Draco helping her admit the truth she'd been hiding from— she couldn't afford to let her mask slip.

Tyson smiled indulgently at Carla before he shrugged. 'Your girl seems to need convincing about what she saw this morning. As I explained to Olivio, I get passionate every now and then in my quest for excellence. Carla knows she has nothing to fear from me, don't you, *bella*?'

The look that passed between them made Rebel wonder if they were sleeping together, but the younger woman's gaze immediately returned to Draco. With the knowledge of their full history, she could no longer stop the arrows that pierced her heart as she watched them. With a heavy buzzing in her head, she took in Draco's almost protective shielding of the figure skater from her trainer, and Carla's proprietorial hold on his arm.

Pain lanced sharper her as the lights blinked again.

'We need to take our seats,' Carla said without answering Tyson's allegation.

The trainer's face hardened. Glancing away, Rebel caught Draco's enquiring gaze. Unable to deal with it, and not wanting to, she turned away, and followed the usher who stood ready to guide them to their table.

Her breath caught painfully as Draco took over pulling out her chair. 'Arabella?'

'Everything's fine,' she said lightly, flashing an empty smile before reaching for her water glass. Expecting him to take the seat next to her, she glanced up to find him walking away.

Discovering she'd been placed as far away as possible from him with Carla and Olivio on either side of him shouldn't have come as a surprise. Inhaling shakily, she summoned a smile for the tennis star and his expectant wife to her left and introduced herself to the soccer star on her right. Beyond him, Tyson Blackwell smirked at her as he took his seat.

As the courses were served and practised speeches given, Rebel picked at her meal and tried to make conversation, even as a part of her was staggered at how drastically different the evening had turned out from how she'd imagined when they'd left their suite. Just from the simple disclosing of one small fact she hadn't been privy to.

A fact Draco had deliberately neglected to mention.

As if compelled, her gaze lifted from her plate. Across the table, steel-sharp eyes met hers, and, despite the charming smile gracing his lips as he nodded at something Carla was saying, Rebel saw the unyielding questions lurking and the grim warning wrapped around each of them.

Tyson Blackwell laughed loudly at a joke and Draco's jaw tightened. Rebel didn't doubt that Draco's motivation for wanting Tyson Blackwell banned from training was genuine. The man was dangerous. For that reason alone, she had to keep this up. As to why Draco had kept his prior relationship with Carla from her...

She vowed to ask him the moment they were alone.

Looking up, she caught his gaze again, the deeper warning in his eyes tensing her spine.

He didn't need to remind her they were playing a role. Letting go of her glass, she tucked her hand beneath her chin. Allowing her gaze to grow languid, she puckered her lips and blew him a kiss.

His smile evaporated. His fist tightened around his poised knife until his knuckles gleamed white.

Beside her, the tennis star's wife laughed. 'That certainly caught his attention.'

Rebel forced a giggle. 'You think so? A girl has to use whatever weapons she has in her arsenal these days.'

The pregnant woman leaned in closer and nodded. 'I hear ya. Especially when there are shameless predators around who feel they have more rights to your man than you do,' she whispered conspiratorially.

Rebel swallowed, wincing inwardly as the words struck bone. Humming in agreement, she battled her way through further conversation, making sure not to glance Draco's way again.

At the stroke of midnight, the gala ended with a closing speech from father and daughter.

Rebel was saying goodbye to the tennis couple when Draco arrived at her side. 'Arabella, we need to—'

'Draco? You said you wanted to talk to me after the gala?' Carla joined them, expertly insinuating herself between them. 'I've done my bit for the night, so I'm all yours.'

'Carla, I'll come and find you in a while—' He stopped as she shook her head.

'It's been a long day and I want to get to bed soon,' she said softly, her eyes wide and limpid. 'And since you insist on leaving right away, I hope you don't mind if we talk now or I risk falling asleep mid-sentence.' Her smile was wide and perfect.

Draco responded to her smile with one of his own, but Rebel saw the tension that gripped his shoulders when he turned to her.

She pre-empted him with a fake smile and a hand on his chest. His muscles contracted and she dropped her hand. 'It's fine, darling. I'll go and take a shower, and warm your side of the bed. I know how much you love that.'

The look Carla sent her could've shattered granite. Rebel walked away before her smile slipped, holding her head high and avoiding eye contact with the guests drifting out of the ballroom.

She made it to the suite with only Stefano approaching to ask if she needed anything. Thanking and dismissing him, she shut the door behind her, relief mingled with a heavy dose of raw trepidation welling inside her.

Rebel didn't think she'd lost sight of what she was doing

at any point in the shockingly brief time since she'd crashed into Draco's world. So how had she arrived here, deeply unsettled by emotions she could barely explain?

She was in lust with him, that she couldn't deny. But why did her heart ache this much at the thought of Draco having dated Carla? Putting it down to anger over the deliberate trap Draco had let her walk into with Olivio earlier, she lurched from the door, tugging off her shoes as she entered the dressing room. Their cases had been packed and stood neatly by the centre island.

Realising she couldn't shower without having to repack, she left her shoes by the cases and went into the living room. The urge to pour herself a drink and numb the disquieting emotions surging beneath her skin was strong. But stepping up her training meant no alcohol, even for emotional-crutch purposes.

Snorting beneath her breath, she plunked down on the sofa, only to jump up again as Draco's scent curled around her. Heart leaping in her throat, she crossed the living room and sank into the armchair. Grabbing the remote, she turned on the TV.

She was channel-surfing, ignoring the antique fireplace clock that announced that Draco had been gone for an hour, when the door opened.

'Arabella.' Her name was a curt demand.

She muted the TV and stood, cursing the renewed anxiety swirling in her stomach. 'In here.'

He entered the room. Every cell in her body felt as if it'd been zapped with liquid nitrogen when she took in his dishevelled state.

'Wow. You know you can't forcibly save her if she doesn't think she needs saving, don't you?'

A muscle in his jaw flexed. 'What are you talking about?'

She walked to him, caught the betraying scent oozing from him and her heart dropped further.

Keep walking.

She went to the dressing room. Tugging on the handle of her case, she dragged it behind her, only to stop short when he filled the doorway.

'What are you doing?'

'I assume this charade is over, since you stink of her perfume, your hair's all over the place and your jaw is covered in peach lipstick—seriously, though, that "lipstick on the collar" thing is so last-century soap opera. Anyway, I'm guessing either your talk was wildly successful or she refused to take you up on your role as saviour. Judging from your scowl I'm guessing it was the latter.'

'Arabella—'

'By the way, thanks for making me look like a fool tonight. You told me you were trying to get her father to drop his matchmaking. You never said anything about the daughter being head over heels in love with you.'

His scowl deepened. 'Carla has had a crush on me since she was a teenager. It's nothing.'

'Oh, believe me, it's something. A very big something. Especially since you two *dated*.'

He looked momentarily disconcerted, then he shrugged. 'I took her out a few times when she lived in London a few years ago. So what?'

She laughed. 'Only a man like you would ask that ridiculous question.'

'What's that supposed to mean?'

She sighed. 'Never mind, Draco.' She moved forward, expecting him to get out of her way. He didn't. 'Oh, right. I guess you want this back.' Letting go of her case, she tugged the ring off and held it out to him.

'What the hell do you think you're doing?' he growled, his voice jagged ice chips.

'Come on, you can't surely want to prolong this farce! You're wearing another woman's lipstick on your skin, for heaven's sake. Stay. Leave. Do whatever you want. But here's where I step off this crazy train.'

She stepped forward, intending to shove the ring in his pocket. He caught her wrist, trapping it against his chest in a tight grip. Underneath her fist, his heart slammed hard and fierce.

'Put the ring back on,' he sliced at her.

She jerked at her hand. He held on tight.

'God, what do you want, Draco?' she railed, knowing she was inches away from losing control.

'You, Arabella. I want you.'

CHAPTER THIRTEEN

'EVER SINCE I walked in on you performing that ridiculous yoga pose, I've thought of little else but having you beneath me in my bed. Did I not make that perfectly clear this morning?'

Rebel clawed at the strands of sanity blissfully fleeing her mind. 'Again. The lipstick on your face tells a *very* different story.'

With a thick curse, Draco released her, but kicked the door shut. 'Stay here. If you walk out that door I'll make you regret it.'

'Oh…charming.'

He stalked to his case and flung it open. Extracting a fresh pair of trousers and a clean shirt, he slammed it shut.

Rebel stared in disbelief as he jerked his tuxedo jacket off, followed by the dress shirt and trousers. Her mouth dropped open at the sight of him in his black briefs, a picture of ripped, bristling, male perfection, using the shirt balled in his fist to swipe at the lipstick on his face. Stunning was a woefully inadequate description of Draco Angelis' male stature, his perfectly proportioned body overlaid with smooth dark olive skin that just begged to be touched. Worshipped.

From somewhere she regained the use of her vocal cords. 'Umm… Draco—'

He flung the shirt away. 'Shut your mouth and listen for once in your life. I didn't kiss Carla. She kissed me.'

Rebel let her rolling eyes speak for her.

'And before you call it a convenient excuse, no, I didn't see it coming.'

'So you spent the last hour fighting her off?'

He glared pure fire at her. 'I spent the last hour *talking* to her. This—' he flicked impatient fingers at his face '—happened as I was leaving her.'

'Okay, if you say so.'

He glared harder. 'I do say so,' he ground out.

Her stomach quivered. 'And?'

He pulled his clean clothes on, then spiked his fingers through his hair. The silky strands settled, but not by much. He still wore a tumbled-out-of-bed look that was at once heart-throbbingly perfect and deliciously indecent. Snapping up the suitcase, he crossed to her and took her bag. 'She knows what she stands to lose if she carries on using Tyson Blackwell as her trainer. The ball is now in her court. I just hope she doesn't take too long to make her stand.'

A harrowing bleakness threaded the edge in his voice. Her hand on the door, Rebel glanced back at him. 'You tried. Isn't that enough?'

His eyes were a raw, turbulent gunmetal; the skin around his mouth was pinched. 'No, it isn't. Should Maria see on the news one day soon that a tragedy has happened to Carla and I hadn't done everything I could to stop it, it'll finish her. And with Blackwell in charge, it's not a case of if but when. I can't let that happen to either of them.'

Rebel let out a shaky breath. 'So…this engagement *is* really about helping Carla through forcing her father's hand, and not a male-pride thing to get back at Olivio because he stopped you from dating her three years ago?'

Already dark brows clenched in a thunderous frown. 'I see Olivio has filled your head with nonsense. Open the door, Arabella. We're leaving. I can't stand to stay in this place another minute. The moment we're on my plane, you'll tell me what else that bastard filled your head with. I didn't think it was possible, but you've grown even more insufferable since the damned gala.'

Purely for self-preservation purposes, she opened the door and walked out of the suite. Stefano waited in the hallway and took charge of their bags. The walk to the helipad was swift and they were lifting off within minutes.

They boarded Draco's plane and took off with Rebel having no clue where they were going since Draco had disappeared to take a shower. On his return, he clamped the phone to his ear, and conducted several conversations in rapid-fire Greek. A solid hour after take-off he finally hung up and flung his phone on the table between them.

He dragged his hands down his face, but she thought the look he levelled at her was a little less incandescent.

'Is it safe to ask where we're going now?'

He blinked at her, then his gaze dropped to the ring, which had somehow found its way back onto her finger. 'I was going to take you to my water villa in the Maldives. It's secluded and beautiful and rainbow-coloured fish swim up to you to say hello. But after the stunt you pulled tonight—'

'Which stunt are we talking about?'

Narrowed eyes sizzled at her. 'The getting-your-head-filled-with-lies part, followed by the part where you tried to dump me.'

'Oh. Right.'

'Yes. Right. You don't deserve the Maldives. And I don't want to be stuck on a plane for half a day with a woman who drives me insane, and yet who I want to make love to more than I want to breathe.'

Rebel was glad she was seated. His powerful, enthralling words buffeted her like a freak storm, raising her heart rate and melting her insides. 'I guess that's completely rational. So do I get a destination?'

'No. You'll find out when we get there. Tell me what else Olivio told you,' he commanded.

She told him, leaving nothing out. Draco shook his head once and uttered a curse. She grimaced. 'Sorry. But on a positive note, now he thinks I'm not going to step aside easily or be bought off, he might rethink his plans?'

'I doubt it. Men like Olivio rarely change their ways. But

I have to try something. Maria will never forgive me if I don't,' he said grimly.

'Surely you understand that you don't have total control over this?'

He didn't reply and several minutes passed before she asked, 'So, what now?'

His gaze rested on her, scrutinising her from face to midriff and back again. 'I have my investigators digging deeper for anything they can find on Blackwell. Come here.'

Temperature spiking from an infusion of wicked excitement, she rose and rounded the table.

He drew back and patted his lap. 'Sit.'

She hitched her gown up and swung one leg over his thighs. His breath hitched as she lowered herself and settled onto him. Shaking his head, he gave a low, deep laugh. 'I should've known better than to expect you to sit side-saddle with your legs daintily crossed,' he teased.

Face flaming with embarrassment, Rebel drew back. 'Sorry, I'm fresh out of dainty,' she quipped. Bracing her hand on the table, she started to rise.

He clamped his hand on her hips. 'Stay. How is it that your relentless mouth hasn't seen you thrown into an institution long before now?'

Heat rose higher, but this time from the blatant presence of his arousal between her legs. 'Umm...I'm nice to little old ladies and I don't walk under ladders?'

His hands slowly travelled up to shackle her waist. Leaning forward, he stopped a hair's breadth from her lips. 'I want you like crazy, Arabella Daniels.' His voice was a warm, whispered rumble over her lips. 'Nothing has changed since this morning. So tell me you want me too.'

'I want you too,' she delivered, although she couldn't accept that nothing had changed. Tonight's events had unleashed emotions she didn't want to brave uncovering just yet. Hell, she might leave that box sealed for ever.

He stared at her for endless seconds. One hand came up

and teased the hoop that formed the neckline of her dress. When it reached her pulse, he traced it, a light, delicate touch that lit a flame on every nerve ending and concentrated it at her core.

His touch, still light, still tormenting, drifted up to her eyebrows, her cheek, then over her lips. A pained groan ripped from his throat.

'I want to kiss you. *Thee mou*, I want to kiss you so badly.'

'And you're holding back because…?'

His hand dropped back to her waist and his head jerked back to the headrest. 'We're landing in three minutes.'

Cutting disappointment warred with the need to know where they were. Knowing she could do nothing about one and maybe something about the other, she looked out of the window onto a black, inky landscape with only a set of runway lights breaking the vastness.

'You've brought me to the middle of nowhere?'

'Indeed. No one can reach us unless I want them to, or they're prepared to swim a hundred miles in every direction.'

'We're in the middle of the ocean?'

'On my island in the Aegean.'

'How long are we staying?'

'That depends entirely on you. Play nice and I won't fly us north and dump you in a Gulag.'

He rose with her in his arms and walked them to the sofa. Setting her down, he secured her seat belt, then settled down away from her. Glancing at him, she witnessed the strain in his features and bit her lip against a smart quip as his fists bunched on his thighs.

The second they touched down he released his belt and hers, then stood with her.

'Arabella?'

'Yes, Drill Sergeant?' she responded, trying her utmost to stem the anxiety flooding her.

'I'm going to have you. The moment we're alone again, I intend to make you mine. Speak up now if that isn't what you want because you won't be using that smart mouth for talking later.'

Every sharp retort evaporated from her head as erotic images flooded her. 'I want it. I want you.'

His breath shuddered out and he nodded once before moving to the door. An SUV stood a short distance away and he guided her to it before sliding behind the wheel. More lights than she'd seen from above lit their path, but all she could see was vegetation and a profusion of flowers.

'You'll get the grand tour tomorrow after your training,' he rasped, his gaze not moving from the road ahead.

Two long roads and corners later, Rebel sat forward in her seat, her widening gaze on the villa ahead. It was built into the side of the hill, with multi-layers she stopped counting after five. In the dark, welcoming golden lights lit up the vast property, pitching it against the night sky like a wonderful masterpiece.

'Draco, it's stunning.' She craned her neck to see more of it as they neared.

'It's not the Maldives, but it's one of my favourite homes.'

'Water villas and brightly coloured fish are overrated.'

He drove past a pillared entrance with double doors, and through a giant, arched trellis. He stopped before a square wooden gate and entered a code. The gate glided back on a smooth rail and they drove along a narrower drive that led to another pillared entrance. It wasn't until Draco parked and she alighted that her gaze was drawn upward. 'That's a pool. A see-through pool,' she blurted, blown clean away.

His mouth curved. 'You get to have your water villa after all.' He walked round to her, swung her up in his arms and whispered in her ear, 'You can swim naked in there if you want to. In fact, I insist on it.'

He was striding forward as she fought her way through a blush. Codes were entered along the way, a lift accessed that shot them up and spat them out on an upper level. Then they were in Draco's bedroom. He slid her down his body, slowly, torturously, not bothering to hide the thick evidence of his arousal. It nudged her belly as he tugged her even closer. The hands that had shackled her on the plane were twice as hard, twice as demanding, as Draco finally unleashed the ferocious hunger that screamed for satisfaction. He devoured her mouth, muttering words in Greek she didn't understand in between long, ardent kisses. Their groans mingled as each kiss fed the hunger and need for a greater assuaging.

He fisted her hair, his fingers holding her tight as he trailed his tongue over her jaw to the pulse racing at her throat. He lapped at it, his moan deep and primeval. '*Thee mou*, you taste like paradise. And sin. And every forbidden thing in between.'

Her hands, frantically exploring his covered back, bit into his flesh as he nipped at her collarbone. Never having imagined that area to be an erogenous zone, she felt her knees threaten to buckle as Draco explored her. Her eyes grew heavy, drawing half closed as sensation arrowed south and pooled between her thighs. Desperate to discover as much of him as she could before her faculties melted beneath the fierce onslaught of desire, Rebel pulled his shirt up and dragged her nails over his heated skin.

The hiss that heated her cleavage was followed by another savage curse. He dragged his head upward. 'You mean to torment me, don't you?' he rasped thickly.

Slightly shocked by the allegation, she blurted, 'I'm only touching you. You want me to stop?'

His laugh was darkly amused. 'Not even on pain of death would I wish that.'

Stepping back, he yanked his shirt over his head. The chest she'd glimpsed from across the dressing room was now within reach. Rebel's ability to breathe became severely compromised as she glided her hand over his pectoral muscles. As she felt them quiver lightly under her touch a bold, feminine power filled her. She explored south, hesitated, then went lower and grasped him.

Her mouth parted on a silent gasp as the full thickness of him registered.

'Arabella.'

She heard her name from afar, her senses completely overcome by the power and heat of him.

'Arabella.' His voice was more strained, almost guttural as he captured her hand in his.

A sound erupted from her throat that sounded very much like a whimper. 'Draco…'

He spun her round and trapped her with one hand on her abdomen. The other slowly gathered up her gown, the slide of hot silk against her skin delicious, decadent torture. 'Play with me all you want later. But I need to take you…be inside you, right now, before I lose my head.'

She shuddered at the inflamed words. Then shuddered some more, when his clever fingers brushed her naked hip and skated along the edge of her panties. Her legs sagged and parted, the hunger between her thighs desperate for satiation.

A cry ripped from her throat when his fingers finally found her. Pulling aside the wet lace, he caressed her, muttering earthy words that drew her deeper into a sensual stupor.

He toyed with for her several minutes, then one finger slipped inside her, testing her, tormenting her. 'So wet, *glikia mou*. And mine,' he growled.

The hand on her belly tugged open her belt before reaching up to tackle the neck fastening. When it came open, Draco pulled away and spun her around. Rebel gasped at the sheer magnificence of the passion stamped across his face.

Keeping his gaze locked on hers, he pulled the dress off her shoulders. It pooled at her feet, leaving her exposed in her strapless bra and panties. Still trapping her gaze, he reached round and unclipped her bra.

Cool air hit her breasts, puckering the tight tips to harder points. Rebel wanted to cover herself, gain back a little of the control that had long fled.

At the same time she wanted Draco to look at her, drown in her as she was drowning in him. So she kept her hands down.

His eyes dropped. He made a sound that could've been her name or a curse. She didn't care because he reached out and touched her. Specifically her panties, which were torn from her body between one breath and the next. Then the world blurred as he lifted her and tossed her on the bed. The primitiveness behind the act had her shuddering wildly. She was struggling for breath when he fully undressed and prowled closer.

Anxieties she'd pushed to the back of her mind flooded forth. She'd never viewed her virginity with the sacred awe some women did, but Rebel couldn't dismiss the profundity that gripped her as she stared at the magnificent man who would be her first lover. Nor could she ignore the physical evidence of his manhood.

He was impressive. Almost a little too impressive. Apprehension clawed higher. She bit her lip to keep it down as he reached into the bedside drawer and extracted a condom.

Stretching out beside her, he glided his hand from her neck to her midriff. She arched into his touch, forcing her mind away from the power between his legs.

'I didn't desire smart talk, but I admit to being disconcerted by your complete silence.'

She bit her lip harder. 'Hmm.'

He raised his head. 'Was that English?'

Her breath burst from her lungs. 'Draco…please?'

'Begging, Arabella?' His head dipped, and his mouth grazed one nipple. He rotated the bud between his lips before flicking his tongue against it. 'Whatever next?'

When she didn't answer, he raised his head.

She blew out a shaky breath. 'Okay…fine… I'm worried. You're big…I think?'

'You think? I guess there's only one way to find out.'

She gasped as he performed the same decadent torture on her twin nipple. Unable to stand it any longer, she tugged her fingers through his hair. He continued to suckle on her even as she faintly registered the rip of foil.

Pressing her back against the bed, he levered himself over her and took her mouth with his. The thrust of his tongue was a precursor to the thick head that breached her core. She gripped his neck as he probed deeper, then withdrew. Strong arms stretched her legs wider and Draco raised his head.

Grey eyes locked on hers, he thrust inside her.

The deep flash of pain ripped a cry from her lips and drove her nails into his flesh. With her shaky gaze on his, Rebel first witnessed puzzlement, then shock, before fury glazed his eyes. 'You think…' he seethed as understanding dawned. *'You think?'*

'I…know?' she supplied on a gasp, her flesh struggling to contain his thick girth as new, delicious sensations flowed through her.

He moved, perhaps to withdraw. The drugging sensation heightened. She moaned, her fingers digging in deeper.

'Thee mou. Arabella—' he muttered as she rotated her hips, chasing more of the feeling. She tried it again. With a thick curse, he slid one arm behind her back, grabbed her waist and held her still. 'Why…?' He stopped to breathe. 'You didn't tell me you were a virgin. Why?'

'Because it was no big deal. Until it literally was.' Her hips twitched, the need to move consuming her. 'Please, Draco, if you still want me, then take me.'

'If I—' He exhaled in disbelief, his eyes squeezing shut for a long tense moment. Then he released her waist. He let her experiment for a scant minute before he took over.

Eyes pinned on her face, gauging her every reaction, he set a steady rhythm, the tension slowly draining out of him as helpless moans spilled from her lips.

Pleasure as she'd never known exploded through her as Draco filled her, stretched her to her limit, over and over. Her back arched with each thrust, an alien storm raging deep inside.

The earthy scent of their union rose to mingle with all the different, wondrous sensations. Lost in delirium, Rebel didn't know whether she was dying or being reborn.

'Arabella, look at me.'

The rough, fierce command fused her back to him, to see the look in his eyes raw and unashamedly carnal. He let her see how she affected him, let her hear each hoarse gasp and guttural groan as he took her higher until she was consumed by the need to jump off the edge of the precipice.

'Oh, God… Draco!'

'Now, Arabella. Let go.'

Rebel soared as she'd never done before, her world unfurling in a white-hot blaze that wrapped her soul in pure joy. Time stood still, granting her the gift of basking in the breathtaking experience. But eventually, her senses returned to her, albeit on a soft haziness that could only absorb the sound of the man whose thickness still registered deep inside her.

Draco watched her eyelashes lift, an indescribable feeling striking him as he traced the flush of pleasure staining her skin. The fervent need for release gnawed at him, but he held it back. He wanted to stretch out this moment for a while longer. Why, he wasn't exactly sure.

His gaze roved over Arabella's face once more. She was breathtaking.

And she'd been a virgin.

The feeling he'd been holding at bay rushed over him again. Stronger. Heavier.

She'd been a virgin. And she'd chosen him to be her first.

Was he that primitive that it turned him on more than he'd ever thought possible?

He felt himself thicken even further inside her in answer. Her eyes widened as he stretched her. Unable to deny himself any longer, he pushed deeper inside her. Her slick channel welcomed him in a tight embrace. Her back arched, presenting her perfect breasts for him to feast on. He gave himself over to sensation, the new and mind-numbing bliss sweeter than anything he'd ever experienced.

Soft, feminine arms slid around him, holding him through the buffeting storm he never wanted to subside. Inevitably it did.

Burying his face in her neck, he inhaled her sweet scent, then rolled them over. Her hand splayed on his chest.

'How long do I have before the Gulag train gets here?'

The sound of her voice sent another unfamiliar thrill through him. Draco lay there, unable to believe he was perfectly content to engage in post-sex banter. Normally, he would be dressed and out of the door before the hint of familiarity approached anywhere near contempt.

But he wasn't even thinking of drawing away now as his arms tightened around her.

'They can wait. I haven't had my fill of you yet.'

'Ah, reprieve.'

He reversed their positions, tucking her beneath him once more. 'No, not total reprieve. You didn't tell me about Olivio's attempts to bribe you until I demanded it, and you neglected to mention your virginity. Don't hold back anything that important from me again. Are we clear?'

Her eyelids dropped and she swallowed.

Unease trickled down his spine.

A moment later, she blinked. Then smiled. 'Yes, Drill Sergeant.'

Her familiar snark was lacking its signature bite. Draco tried to push away the disquieting sensation that she was hiding something else, but it lingered, cautioning him not to revel in this moment too long. Nirvana could become addictive.

Dropping his guard was foolish. This was just sex, a side bargain struck with his libido as the sole benefactor.

He would move on once his goal was attained.

CHAPTER FOURTEEN

REBEL FELT AS if she'd been asleep for only minutes before being woken up. Probably because she had. They hadn't made love again after the first time last night, but dawn light had already been tingeing the skies as they'd gone to sleep.

'Move it, Arabella. You don't want the sun to get any hotter before your run.'

She dragged her head from the pillow. Draco stood beside the bed, a tray in one hand and her gym gear in the other. He was dressed in running shorts and a body-hugging T-shirt. The sight of his body—the body she'd had the freedom to touch at will last night—sent a pulse of heat through her. Dry-mouthed, she tried to divert her gaze elsewhere as she sat up and accepted the tray. She needed to get her thoughts to coalesce so she could say something that didn't sound completely embarrassing.

But her gaze climbed his frame, lovingly exploring it until she reached his face. And the arrogant smile that graced it.

'You ogling me so hungrily isn't going to get you out of training. In fact for every minute you stay in bed, you get to do another vertical jump.'

Since vertical jumps were her favourite of the exercises, Rebel contemplated staying put. One look at his face told her it was the wrong move.

He set the bowl of muesli in her lap. 'Eat your breakfast. I'll be back in ten minutes.'

He was back in five, just as she was about to get out of bed. She froze. 'Can you…turn around, please?'

'No.' He shook out her training gear. 'You get to wear

this while you train. The rest of the time clothes won't be necessary. You might as well get used to it now.'

She bit her lip and frowned. 'If I'd known your island doubled as a nudist colony, I'd have taken my chances with the Gulag.'

He grinned, then dropped the clothes next to her. 'You'll wish you hadn't said that by the time I'm finished with you. Up.'

She'd made love with him—was still not quite sure how she'd survived that transcendental experience—and yet the thought of him seeing her naked made her whole body flame with self-awareness.

Gritting her teeth, she flung the sheets back and stood. About to reach for her shorts, she gasped when he caught her wrist and yanked her close.

His grin had disappeared, his face a taut mask of hunger and desire as his sizzling gaze burned down her body. 'First, you need to greet me properly,' he commanded.

Rebel told herself it was unwise to give in so easily, to reach so greedily for what she wanted. But she was already surging close, curling her arms around his neck and raising herself on tiptoe to reach his mouth. His slanted across hers the moment they touched, his ravenous possession of her mouth making her senses sing. He fisted her hair, angled her head for a deeper exploration, while his other hand moulded her bottom.

They were both groaning, their breathing harsh, when they parted. Rebel licked her lower lip, already mourning the loss of his kiss. 'Good morning, Drill Sergeant,' she husked out.

'Good morning, Arabella *mou*,' he replied, his face an unsmiling mask reflecting all her cravings. 'Now you can get dressed.'

A full-body tremble raking her, she turned, picked up the shorts and stepped into them. She was sliding them up when she felt his gentle touch on her lower back, just above her right buttock.

Rebel froze. She'd forgotten about her scar.

'What happened here?' he murmured.

She kept her face averted. 'An accident,' she replied, injecting as much lightness into her voice as possible.

'During training?' She heard the frown in his voice. She knew why. The scar wasn't extensive, but the wound had been deep, the scar tissue pronounced. But far deeper was the secret scar she carried on her heart. The one she couldn't tell him about because he would hate her, condemn her as no better than someone like Tyson Blackwell.

'No, it was a long time ago.' Hurriedly she snapped the waistband into place and reached for the top. Yanking it on, she schooled her features and turned. 'I'm ready. You can do your worst now.'

The eyes that met hers held lingering questions. Rebel's breath caught in her lungs; she was hoping against hope he'd let it go. She wasn't ready for the sheer magic she'd discovered last night with him to be over. And it would be if he forced the secret out of her.

After another contemplative look, one corner of his mouth lifted. 'That invitation is way too hard to ignore.' Grabbing her hand, he marched her into the lift, and pressed the button for Level Three.

Rebel read the buttons on the panel. 'There are seven levels?'

He nodded, then pushed her back against the lift wall, his hand bracketing her. 'Guess what's on the seventh level?' he murmured, his lips brushing her temple.

It felt like the most natural thing in the world to slide her hands around his tight, trim waist. 'Umm… Draco the Dragon's lair?'

His mouth twitched. 'Close. I look forward to showing you.'

The lift stopped and they stepped out onto a wraparound

terrace wide enough to fit her Chelsea flat four times over. Her breath caught as she saw the view for the first time. The Aegean glistened like a moving jewelled tapestry, meeting a sky of unmarred blue. Perfectly framing it was the white beach below and the red cliffs that formed the foundations of Draco's villa.

'It's so beautiful.'

He smiled and nodded as he guided her across the vast terrace to stone steps that meandered out of view. 'This is where I come to get away from the world. I had it built seven years ago.'

'Before your accident?'

He trotted down the stairs and she followed. 'Yes. I wanted a private place to train when I didn't need to be on the sports sites. This was the perfect place. When I became an agent, this part of the property became a good place to decompress. The other side of the villa is where I entertain.'

'How big is the island?'

He reached the bottom of the stairs and stretched. While he waited for her to do the same, he adjusted the timer on his watch. 'Four kilometres across. Which you will run twice with three minutes shaved off your usual average. Go.'

He set off through an archway of trellised bougainvillea, disappearing out of sight before she'd taken the first step. She caught up and managed to keep up by the skin of her teeth. Sweat poured off her body by the time they finished the second course, the sun hot on her face as she rehydrated. Her gaze caught Draco's as she swallowed the last drop, and she almost choked at the heat that blazed from his eyes.

'Let's get you inside,' was all he said as he took the bottle from her and disposed of it.

The seventh level was just as she'd suspected. A vast area, twice the size of a basketball court, held gleaming exercise machines in all shapes and sizes. There was even a boxing ring tucked into one corner.

Rebel turned a full circle. 'I was wrong. This is more like Dante's seventh circle of hell.'

He smiled and led her to an exercise mat. 'Hell is good. It helps you appreciate heaven more.'

She found out just how much he relished putting her through hell over the next three hours. He upped her regime by thirty per cent, then grunted with satisfaction each time she achieved her target.

Pride burned in her chest as she pushed her body to the limit. And just for the hell of it, when he called time, she did another ten vertical jumps more than he'd instructed her to.

'Fine, you've made your point. Don't get cocky,' he growled.

She laughed and swiped at the sweat pouring off her temples. 'Yes, Drill Sergeant.'

Turning, she braced her foot against the wall and stretched her arches. She was about to step back when she sensed him behind her. All through training she'd seen the banked hunger in his eyes. Even without looking at him now, Rebel knew he'd finally released the tight grip on his restraint.

'Keep your hands on the wall.' His voice was a deep, primitive rumble that took complete control of every nerve in her body. She shook just from the power of it.

She felt him drop into a squat behind her. A moment later, he grasped one ankle and took her trainer and sock off, then did the same to the other. Standing, he slipped his hands into the waistband of her shorts and peeled them down her legs.

'Draco,' she murmured hesitantly as he widened her stance.

'Yes?'

She shut her eyes with a tiny grimace. 'I'm sweaty.'

'Yes, you are,' he agreed with a decadent relish that tightened her skin and increased the tempo beating at her core.

His hands slid up to her breasts and he lowered the

front zip of her top. Leaving it hanging open, he cupped her breasts on a deep groan.

She shuddered as he tweaked her nipples, her whole body a receptive vessel eagerly absorbing the expert attention being lavished on it. Several mindless minutes later, she felt him drop low again.

Rebel wasn't prepared for the sensation that blazed through her next.

'Draco!' Her eyes flew open and she glanced down to see the source of her pleasure. Molten eyes met hers as his tongue lapped at her nether lips. The view alone was enough to send her into orbit. He grounded her with a firm hand on one thigh, then parted her flesh with his other hand to reach the bundle of nerves that ripped a scream from her the moment he flicked his tongue against it.

He might have caressed her for seconds. Or hours. Time ceased to exist or matter. All she could process was the encroaching tide of bliss that rushed over her and pulled her under.

She resurfaced to find herself still upright but caught in his arms.

'You're exquisite, Arabella *mou*. Truly exquisite,' he rasped against her ear. 'And all mine. Why did you let me believe all those things said about you in the media?' he added gruffly, his tone holding a touch of contrition.

Senses still swimming, she tried to find the right words to reply. 'Umm…you seemed blissfully wedded to the idea that I was a wild, wicked siren. But it was just the…white noise I needed to…to forget.' She bit her lip, wondering if she'd gone too far. Rushing on, she added, 'I told you, you didn't know everything about me.'

He grunted, his hand cupping her core in a shockingly possessive hold. 'From now on *I* will be your white noise. You get to be the wild, wicked siren only with me. And no more hiding important stuff from me. You'll be straight with me on everything. Understood?'

Her heart lurched. 'Draco...I...'

His hand moved between her thighs, melting away the apprehension and budding guilt, and leaving nothing but fevered anticipation behind.

When he picked her up, and walked over to the weight bench, Rebel gave up trying to formulate a single thought.

He arranged her over the bench. The rasp of the condom being ripped open barely registered against her buzzing senses before he was once more in control of her, his hands on her waist, his power at her throbbing centre. He took her higher than he had last night, almost rough in his possession as he drew every ounce of pleasure from her. His guttural shout as he followed her into bliss echoed in her ears as she lost her mind to sensation once more.

For the next three weeks they fell into a rigid routine. Intense training twice a day, six days a week. In between training, they made love, picnicked at various spots on the island, or ate their meals on whichever breathtaking level of Dante's villa took their fancy. On her first rest day, he took her out on a launch to his yacht moored on the other side of the villa. Rebel had seen the impressive vessel on their morning runs, but nothing had prepared her for the beauty of the *Angelis*.

Draco had smiled indulgently as she rhapsodised over the vessel, then let her take the wheel as they sailed around the island.

By some unspoken agreement, their conversation didn't stray into too personal territories, as if they were both emotionally wary, having bared their innermost cores to each other in the first week of meeting.

Of course, Draco didn't know of the last layer, the one she feared would be uncovered each time his gaze lingered on her scar and she pretended not to notice. Or when he kissed it during lovemaking and she felt the question on her skin.

Although, more and more, an equally insidious fear

trickled through her each time her gaze caught her engagement ring. The craving for everything happening between
them to be real had taken permanent root in her heart. She
couldn't shake it off, and with each day that passed it em-
bedded itself deeper into her heart.

It was there, silently clamouring for attention, when she
woke from an afternoon nap on their last week on the island and went in search of Draco. His expansive office was
located on Level Two. It was the only place in the private
villa besides the gym that she went into with clothes on,
having refused point-blank to risk entering a room while
Draco was on one of his many videoconferences.

She heard his dark, smoky voice now as the lift doors
parted, and heard his deep laugh before she saw him, the
sound so beautiful her footsteps slowed. In contrast her
heart leapt, then filled with a powerful emotion that threatened to knock her to her knees.

She stepped into the sunlight as he threw back his head
and laughed again. The clear joy in his face caught her
breath as a certain knowledge pounded through her.

She had no time to process it because Draco turned his
head and saw her. She expected him to wave her to the sofa
at the far end of the room where she usually waited for him
to finish; her eyes widened as he held out his arm to her.

Warily, she stepped forward, then gasped when he
jerked her into his lap. Face flaming, she glanced at the
wide screen.

The woman bore a striking resemblance to Draco, her
dramatically beautiful face and the headrest of what could
only be wheelchair announcing who she was.

'Maria?'

She smiled. 'So I finally get to meet my brother's fake
fiancée.'

Rebel's gaze flew to Draco's. He shrugged. 'Maria and I
don't have secrets. Not any more.' A hint of regret washed

over his face, but it was gone a moment later when his sister replied.

'Enough of that, brother. So we had to learn our lesson the hard way. We got through it,' she admonished gently. Then her gaze swung to Rebel. 'But he still didn't tell me about you until the story hit the papers.'

Draco's hand curled over Rebel's hip as he peered at his sister. 'I was trying to protect you.'

Maria rolled her eyes. 'I live in an ivory tower, Draco, guarded twenty-four-seven by security and private physicians. A scandal or two wouldn't hurt to get the blood pumping.'

Rebel laughed. 'I tell him that all the time.'

'And let me guess, he does the "dragon breathing fire" thing—yep, there it is.'

They both turned to see the deep scowl marring Draco's face, and dissolved into laughter.

He reached up and tucked a strand of hair behind Rebel's ear before cupping her nape in a possessive hold. 'Very funny.'

'He makes it so easy, doesn't he?' Rebel chuckled.

Maria sighed. 'Almost too easy.'

'Enough from you two.' He pointed at his sister. 'I'll see you next week.'

Her grey eyes softened. 'I can't wait. And I know you're doing your best with Carla, but please remember that not everyone who needs help necessarily wants it. I love you no matter what.'

Beneath her, Draco tensed for a second. Then a weight seemed to lift off his shoulders. The smile he sent Maria positively glowed. 'You stay out of trouble.'

Maria rolled her eyes again before her gaze swung to Rebel. 'It was nice to meet the reason for my brother's bigger smile. I hope we meet in person one day.'

She signed off and the screen went blank. Draco turned his monitor off and an awkward silence descended.

Unable to stand it, Rebel cleared her throat. 'I'm the reason for your bigger smile? Does that mean I get an extra half hour's sleep tomorrow morning?' she teased, praying her heart's wild leaps wouldn't show on her face.

Draco snorted. 'In your dreams. Maria's a hopeless romantic who sees hearts and happy ever after in every cloud.' His grip tightened. 'You want an extra half hour's sleep? You *earn* it.'

She managed to keep her expression composed, despite the hollow that caved in her stomach. 'And how do I go about earning my sleep? Scrubbing all seven levels of your villa?'

'The only manual labour I require from you besides your training is on my person,' he replied.

Like a flame on gasoline, the air erupted with desire. The hand around her nape caressed with rough insistence. Then he pushed her off him. 'Take off that dress,' he growled.

She took it off, but before he could grab her she dropped to her knees. Draco froze, giving her the precious time she needed. Before her nerves could get the better of her, she reached for his waistband and lowered his zipper. A hiss erupted from his lips but he raised himself up to help her ease off his shorts and briefs.

She grasped him, emitting a soft gasp as the power and steel of him sent a thrill through her. She caressed him from root to tip and back, lazily, worshipping him. Then she took him in her mouth. Quickly learning what pleased him most, she teased and sucked with just the right amount of pressure for the vocal sounds of his pleasure to fill the room.

At some point his fingers fisted her hair. For an alarming second, she feared he'd pull her away. Her gaze raced up to find his locked on her, his face a tortured mask of brutal hunger. Whatever he read in her face made him nod. Absorbing every expression on his face, feminine power roaring through her, she revelled in owning him as he succumbed greedily to her ministrations.

Afterwards, he caught her beneath her arms and tucked

her up into his lap. Depositing an almost reverent kiss on her temple, he said gruffly, 'For that, *glikia mou*, you can have a whole extra hour in bed tomorrow.'

Draco watched Arabella sleep the next morning, thankful for the reprieve of not having to keep his guard up. He wasn't even sure what he was guarding. The emotions crowding through him had snuck up on him, slipped in and taken up residence while he'd been busy making love to Arabella. Or had it been when she'd met and exceeded his expectations each time he'd set her a physical challenge? Or the times when he'd found himself living for her fearless, smart mouth to draw laughter from him?

However it'd happened didn't even matter.

Maria's observation about his obvious contentment had rocked him, planted the evidence firmly in his lap, before she'd signed off, blissfully unaware of the wreck she'd left him with. But it was a wreck shrouded in fog on a black night of lies. He knew in his gut Arabella was hiding something big from him. She tensed and evaded him far too often for that not to be the case.

He despised himself for not confronting it head-on, for giving himself leave for one more day with the excuse that the investigative report he'd done on her had provided him with enough pertinent details about her. Everything else she'd revealed so far had been harmless.

She couldn't hurt Maria, and that had been enough.

But she could hurt you. His chest tightened, and he pushed the thought away. He could only be hurt if he let this thing spin out longer than their agreed time.

So far his investigators had found nothing on Tyson he could use and Olivio remained intransigent. Draco hated to rely on no news being good news, but more and more he was accepting that the choice might not be his as to whether Carla remained out of danger. She might have been partly responsible for his sister turning a corner during the bleak years after her accident, but Maria was much stronger than he'd ever given her credit for.

He would protect Carla as much as he could, but Draco was beginning to realise that some things were indeed out of his hands.

Arabella rolled over in her sleep, straight into his arms. He was pulling her close even before caution kicked in. She opened her stunning blue eyes and smiled, and he kicked caution to the kerb.

Sliding her arms around his neck, she stretched against him. 'Thank you for my extra hour. It was *heavenly*.'

'You're welcome. Now let's see if this is equally heavenly.'

He lowered his head, took what was his and silenced the clamouring of his instincts.

CHAPTER FIFTEEN

THE PACE CHANGED drastically over the next three weeks. Although she was fully installed in Draco's chalet in Verbier, Rebel barely saw him. Her training had stepped up another gear with Greg and a team Draco had hired now in charge of her on-site drills.

She hadn't realised how much she'd missed the snow until she stood at the top of the ramp on the first day. Breathing in the frigid air, she felt peace settle over her as her mother's smiling face wove into her mind. She suffered a moment's regret for the years she'd wasted being less than she could've been. How could she have ever believed she could go through life like that?

'Ready?' Greg's voice piped from behind her.

'Ready.' She adjusted her goggles a final time and planted her skis, the sheer joy of being here, doing what she loved, firing through her.

Greg counted down and sounded the klaxon. She grimaced as she pushed off a millisecond later than she'd intended.

She could already imagine the conversation with Draco later that night in her head.

Blocking it out, she poised her body for the lift-off. Exhilaration burst through her as her feet left the ramp. The elation her mother had felt and passed down to her wrapped around her as she soared.

Her mother had loved her beyond her own life. Rebel knew that had she survived the accident that had claimed her life, she would've forgiven Rebel's part in it.

It was time to forgive herself. Time to come clean to

Draco. If for nothing else, for the chance to take the risk of baring her heart to see if there was a future for them.

Although things had remained the same on the surface, Rebel had felt a shift in Draco the day after she'd met Maria via video link. He hadn't smiled as widely at her jokes, nor lingered in bed with her when they'd both had a little time on their hands. By the time they'd left the island, the only time she'd felt fully connected to him was when they'd made love.

She couldn't let it carry on. He'd helped her achieve life-changing clarity, the least she could do was give him the complete truth about herself in return. What he chose to do with it was up to him.

Her heart squeezed as the ground rushed up to her. Bending her knees, she executed a perfect landing and skied to the bottom of the hill.

'You know you're going to hear about that take-off, don't you?' Greg said via the mic in her ear.

She grimaced and made a face at the camera that was recording all her jumps for Draco to review later.

'I'm not scared of the dragon,' she quipped, lying through her teeth.

Greg laughed. 'You're in the minority, then.'

Grinning, she skied to the edge of the enclosure, toed off her skis and got back on the escalator for another test jump. She had three days before the championships began, and Draco had found less and less to criticise her about as she'd perfected her jump.

She didn't doubt that he would chew her out for the millisecond delay. But he would be doing so while in the same room with her. And after four days without him, she didn't care if he berated her for half the night. As long as she got to spend the other half in his arms.

She was showered and in bed, anticipating Draco's arrival, when her phone rang. She saw his number, and her heart sank.

'Unless you're calling me from the living room, consider your entire accumulation of brownie points docked.'

'I'm calling you from the emergency room,' Draco replied, tersely.

She jerked upright, her heart slamming hard against her ribs. 'Are you okay?'

'I'm fine, Arabella. Unfortunately, Carla isn't. She's in intensive care as we speak.'

'No! What happened?'

'She fell, hit her head. She hasn't suffered any spinal injuries, but the doctors aren't taking chances. The air ambulance brought her to Rome from Tuscany this morning.'

Rebel's hand tightened around the phone. 'How is Maria taking it?'

'She's being exceptionally strong,' he responded, his voice reflecting a quiet pride. 'I flew her down this afternoon.'

'I'm glad she's there with Carla.'

'Yes. Arabella, I don't know when I'll be able to come to Verbier.'

Her stomach hollowed, bringing with it a tinge of shame for her selfishness. 'It's fine,' she mustered with as much grace as she could. Then, remembering her vow this morning, she added, 'When you do get here, though, we need to talk.'

Tense silence greeted her. Wondering whether the line had dropped, she glanced at her phone. She was still connected. 'Draco?'

'I'm here. We will talk as you wish.' Voices murmured in the background. 'I have to go.'

'Umm…okay—'

He hung up before she could stumble through telling him she'd missed him. Or, even more, that she loved him.

Because she did.

She'd agreed to stage a flawless performance of make-believe love. Instead she'd fallen in love for real.

The irony didn't escape her as the phone dropped from her numb fingers into her lap. Looking down, she caught sight of her engagement ring. Her heart cracked open at the real possibility that she might have to take it off in the very near future. After all, even if Draco saw past her role in her mother's death and forgave her, she had no guarantee that he would want to be with her, never mind on a permanent basis.

Her heart shuddered at the phantom loss even as it contemplated the real one. Desperate to flee the bleakness snaking through her, she grabbed the remote and flicked on the TV.

Every channel carried the news of Carla Nardozzi's accident, with the blame laid firmly at Tyson Blackwell's feet. Footage of the moments before the accident had been leaked to the media, and the trainer had been arrested.

Relief for Draco and Maria for the delayed justice and closure surged through her. Turning the TV off, she lay back in bed, sending up a silent prayer that she and Draco would be granted a chance for a fresh start.

Carla Nardozzi was put into a medical coma the day before the opening ceremony of the Verbier Ski Championships.

Draco called with another terse apology—one that was becoming a common occurrence. And one that Rebel brushed off with a light tone and a heavy heart.

Her first competition took place that afternoon. With Greg and Contessa and the rest of her team in her camp, Rebel should've been ecstatic when she placed second by the end of the first day. Instead she kept her phone on her lap all through dinner with the team, her heart jumping each time she felt a ring that turned out to be her imagination. Tuesday and Wednesday were even better days. By Thursday she was leading the women's ski-jump category, with her name suddenly on every sports commentator's lips. Contessa excitedly booked interviews and negotiated with new sponsors who wanted to be associated with the new and improved Rebel Daniels. Rebel nodded and smiled through it all, but inside she was dead with complete misery.

She was getting ready for her final afternoon session on Friday when Greg walked into the recreation room. 'I've just had a note that there's someone wanting to see you in the VIP hospitality box.' His dark frown spelled his displeasure. 'They won't tell me who it is and I can't bring them back here. I'm going to have to come with you.'

Her heart leapt into her throat, her whole body revving into invigorating life as she jumped up. Draco had arrived!

'It's fine. I have my personal official here with me.' Rebel waved at Greta, the woman who'd been assigned to her.

Greg's lips pursed as he handed over the note. 'Are you sure?'

'I'm sure,' she insisted, rushing towards the door.

Rebel asked Greta to point her in the direction of VIP box number sixteen. The older woman struggled to keep up as Rebel sprinted ahead. The box was at the far end of the luxurious championship course, directly overlooking the ski-jump platform. Slightly out of breath, she entered the semi-lit room, leaving Greta in the hallway. Spotting the figure looking out to the course, she hurried towards him.

'Drac—Dad!' she amended as her father faced her.

'Hello, Arabella.'

'What are you doing here?' The question emerged like an accusation.

She was happy to see him, of course she was, but the scything disappointment of not finding Draco here raked her raw without the numbness to protect her.

'I'm sorry for the cloak-and-dagger stuff. But I wasn't sure you'd want to see me. Not after the way we parted.'

Pain she'd thought she'd grappled under control fired through her. 'You were the one who didn't want to see me any more, remember?'

He sighed. 'I should never have said that.'

'Why not, if you meant it?'

'I didn't *mean* it. It was wrong, but that was just my grief talking.'

Weariness weighted her shoulders. 'It's okay, Dad. I get it now.'

His light blue eyes widened. 'You do?'

'Yes, I do.'

We need to talk.

Draco had lost count of the number of ways he'd dissected those four words, hoping to disembowel every worst-case scenario they might represent. Each time, a new one had reared up stronger, more venomous than before.

What good thing had ever come from those words? Hell, weren't those same words his own lead-in to a break-up with a girlfriend who suddenly grew too clingy? Or an underperforming employee who needed to be kicked into touch or kicked out? He'd never been at the receiving end of them, of course.

Until now.

He read the box numbers as they flashed past, the location Greg had given him stuck in his brain. He wanted to reach his destination yet he dreaded what would happen when he got there. That dread was partly why he'd stayed away. Sure, Olivio Nardozzi had finally wised up to the fact that the daughter he'd viewed as little more than an asset he'd kept too tight a grip on was in danger of slipping away from him and had begged for Draco's help. But everything he'd done for them could've been done from his Verbier chalet, within touching distance of Arabella.

Except he hadn't been sure Arabella would wish to be at his side.

The *not* knowing had finally got to him. He needed to know where he stood, whether her request to talk was a precursor to her walking away from him.

He neared box sixteen and flashed his Access All Areas card at the stout woman guarding the hallway. A few steps away from the door he froze at the sound of Arabella's voice.

'You lost the love of your life because of me.'

'Arabella, don't—'

'No. Don't try to mince your words. If I hadn't disobeyed you both and gone out skiing on my own, she'd still be alive today. She'd be here with you and we'd still be a family.'

Horror clawed up Draco's spine.

'We tell everyone it was an accident, but it wasn't, Dad, and we both know it. I rebelled against my parents. You warned me not to go skiing when there was a blizzard warning. I waited until you'd gone to the village to do the grocery shopping, then snuck out. I wanted what I wanted and it ended up killing her.'

A ragged breath echoed out into the hallway. 'You'll never know what coming back to see the note that she'd gone after you did to me. To have never got the chance to say goodbye...'

'Because of me. I know, Dad. You'll never know how much I wish I hadn't—'

Draco didn't realise his feet had moved until he was standing in the room. Twin pairs of blue eyes swung his way, one narrowing in wary dislike, and the other rounding with the same horror spiralling through him.

'You had a direct hand in your mother's accident?' he rasped, blinding rage eclipsing everything else.

She swallowed, her eyes pools of dark horror. 'Draco... I...'

'After agreeing we'd be up front with each other, you didn't think to tell me you selfishly and irresponsibly put your own mother's life in danger?'

'Draco—'

He waved her silent, her voice a bleak implication he didn't want ringing in his ears. Shaking his head, he laughed. 'But then you didn't exactly agree to the *up-front* part, did you? I was too caught up in…other things to recognise that you avoided that particular stipulation.'

She stepped towards him. 'I wanted to tell you. Draco, please believe me—'

He silenced her with a slash of his hand. 'I let you into Maria's life. She already thinks you're the most incredible woman to walk the earth. And you've turned out to be no better than the man who put her in the wheelchair.'

She gasped.

Nathan Daniels stepped forward. 'Now hang on there, Angelis—'

'Save it. I have no time for either of you. If I never see either one of you again in this lifetime, it'll be too soon.'

Rebel watched Draco walk out, her ashen world turning a soulless, all-encompassing black. From far away, she heard her father call her name. She probably responded, because the worried look in his eyes receded.

'I know this probably wasn't the best timing, but I didn't want to do it after the fact.'

Struggling to think past the pain slashing at her heart, she frowned. 'Do what?'

'Tell you that your mother would be proud of you and what you've achieved. Whether you win today or not, we're *both* proud of you. And I sold our old house. I'm sure you'll agree we need to make new memories?'

Her breath shuddered. 'Yes.'

'I'm seeing a grief counsellor. And I also intend to pay back the money, Arabella. I don't care how long it takes, I'll make things right.'

Tears welled in her eyes. 'Dad—'

'Miss Daniels, it's time to go,' Greta said from the doorway.

She glanced at her father. He nodded. 'We have a lot to talk about, I know. But you need to go and see all your hard work pay off.'

She blinked the tears away. 'Will...will you come and watch me?'

He swallowed hard before he nodded. 'Yes, I will.'

She walked back with Greta, picked up her skis and made her way to the waiting area. She was the first to jump, which helped because once again blocking everything and keeping her mind blank were imperative.

This time it wasn't just her mother's face that spurred her on. Her father's solemn eyes and quiet pride flashed too. Her timing was laser-perfect, and she soared higher than she ever had. But as the snow-white ground rushed up to meet her, a piercing realisation lanced through her.

It's not enough. I want love too.

Unbidden, Draco's words from weeks ago when he'd made her realise she was holding herself back from winning popped into her mind.

We never get everything we want.

Her feet crashed to the ground and she cartwheeled into the barrier. A collective gasp rushed through the frigid air. Officials nearby rushed to her aid, but Rebel was already struggling to her feet.

Draco might believe they never got what they wanted, but she had proved otherwise.

She wanted him. She loved him. She'd never got the chance to tell him. No way was she willing to accept what had happened in the VIP room as her fate until she'd stared him in the eye and said her piece.

She was toeing off her skis when an excited Greg and Contessa rushed towards her. 'Did you see?' Contessa screeched. 'You jumped two *metres* farther than the world-record holder!'

'My God, Rebel, what happened up there?'

I got my heart smashed into a million pieces.

She smiled and shrugged. They waited in the pen for the remaining competitors to jump. With each one that didn't make it as far, Greg and Contessa squealed. If they noticed she wasn't as excited, they refrained from commenting.

Then her name erupted in lights as the winner. Tears welled and her whole body shuddered as she imagined the spirit of her mother wrapped around her in a warm, comforting glow.

Half an hour later, Rebel stood on the podium and waved to the crowd, an even harder determination burning in her chest. Returning to the dressing room, she entrusted her trophy to Contessa and her skis to Greg, then hurried into the shower, with a promise to meet up later.

Slipping on jeans and a long-sleeved top and layering it with a hoodie and beanie to finish off her disguise, she left the grounds and walked to a taxi stand. Whether Draco had left Switzerland or not she still had to collect her belongings from his chalet. But she prayed he would be there. She pulled her phone from her bag and brought up the text app.

When I said we needed to talk I actually meant that I would talk and you would listen. So you owe me another 'We need to talk' minus the fire-breathing antics. Where are you?

She pressed *'send'* with her heart in her throat, and waited.

An answer pinged a second later.

Behind you.

Rebel whirled, her foot slipping on the ice before she righted herself. A black limo crept towards her, its back window slowly winding down as it neared.

Draco's molten grey eyes pierced hers as the car drew to a stop. He alighted and held the door open for her.

She stayed on the pavement. 'You were creeping behind me on the off-chance that I would text you?'

'No, Arabella. My hopes have dropped to nil where you're concerned.'

Her heart stumbled, but she'd come this far. She needed to see this through. 'I need to get my things from your place.'

His eyes shadowed, but he nodded. 'I'll take you. You can talk on the way.'

She slid into the plush interior and retreated to the far side. He regained his seat and slammed the door, sealing them in semi-dark silence.

They travelled a mile with Rebel trying to find her nerve. 'You missed my victory dance on the podium.'

'No, I didn't.'

Her breath caught. 'You were there.'

'I couldn't leave.'

'Too many potential clients to schmooze?'

'The farthest thing from my mind.'

She bit her lip and looked out of the window. When she saw how close they were to Draco's chalet, she cleared her throat. 'Everything you heard me say to my father I'd planned to tell you. Yes, I should've told you when you asked me about my scar, or afterwards. But I'm not perfect. I made a mistake.'

He exhaled. 'Arabella—'

'No, I'm not quite finished. What I did in my past doesn't give you the right to act like an ass. I made a horrible mistake when I was only seventeen that tortured me and which I was still paying for when I met you. But you know what? I've learned to forgive myself, ironically, thanks to you.' She pointed a finger at him. 'But you decided to heap on me anyway—why, because you think I haven't suffered enough?'

A wave of regret washed over his face. 'No. You've suffered more than enough.'

She sagged back in her seat, bewilderment and pain eating at her. 'Then why?'

'I knew what you were keeping from me was big. I just didn't realise how I would feel to know you had a secret like that you couldn't trust me with. I despise secrets and knowing something this monumental had happened in your life and you were hiding it from me… I lashed out without thinking.' He turned suddenly and lunged for her hand. 'Everything I said in that room was inexcusable. I'd braced myself for something else—'

'What?'

'You, breaking up with me. And not the fake engagement either. You said we needed to talk—'

'And you immediately slid into complete-bastard mode?'

'I'd had too much time to dwell on a few worst-case scenarios.'

She didn't want to get her hopes up, not when his words still stung so deeply. 'And the worst was me breaking up with you?'

He slashed a hand through his hair, his breathing ragged. 'I'm in love with you, Arabella. Deeply. Completely. The past few weeks have been hell when each time I wanted to say it, I knew you were keeping something from me. Something that might mean the end of us. Going along with the charade just to keep you close felt like the safest option, but I hated it, and so I overreacted when I finally heard the truth.'

With supreme effort, Rebel regained her power of speech. 'You're…in love with me.' Parts of her were coming alive that she wanted to send back to sleep. Until she was completely certain she wasn't dreaming this.

'You forgot the deeply, completely part.'

She shook her head. 'I still don't understand why you were so mean to me. As for my father…what he did was inexcusable, I know, but he intends to make amends. He did what he did because he loves me. He lost his way for a while, but I think he deserves a chance to make reparations.'

Draco nodded. 'He does, and I intend to give him one. We've already agreed a payment plan for the money he took.'

Her eyes widened. '*What?* When?'

'I went back to the VIP room to beg you to let me take back my words. He was still there. We talked. Then we watched you win together.'

Her hand flew to her mouth as she choked back a sob. 'That does not touch me in any way.'

A hint of an arrogant smile curved his mouth. Then his face turned solemn again. 'I will do better, if you give me a chance. Please, Arabella.'

'You really love me?' The words shook out of her.

He cupped her face, his gaze contrite and direct, and filled with an emotion that caught at her hard. 'Deeply. Completely. You challenge me, you make me feel alive. I give you hell and you laugh in my face. I want that every day for the rest of my life.'

Rebel leaned into him, unable to be this close and not want more of the man she loved more than life itself.

'I hope you realise I'm going to live off this grovelling for the next sixty years?'

He tensed but replied, 'And I will fall at your feet every time and beg forgiveness.'

'Wow. Okay, that sounds like a plan.'

'Does that mean what I think it means?'

'You're in love with me. I'm in love with every infuriating inch of you. I hate you for breaking my heart and making me sad on the day I won my major trophy, but I love you for agreeing to be mine for the rest of our lives.'

He squeezed his eyes shut and dropped his forehead to hers. '*Thee mou.* You wreck me, Arabella. I love you.'

When they reached the chalet, he dragged her inside, then sealed his lips to hers in a fervent reminder of what had brought them together and what was in store for them.

Finally letting go of the fear and letting joy in, she closed the gap between them and slid her arms around his neck. 'I love you, too. Oh, and don't bother getting yourself fixed. I plan on wrecking you every day for as long as we both live.'

* * * * *

ILLICIT NIGHT
WITH THE GREEK

SUSANNA CARR

CHAPTER ONE

TENSION GRIPPED STERGIOS ANTONIOU as he stood alone on the balcony that jutted out from his cousin's mansion. He ignored the iconic view of the Parthenon against the blue September sky as he scowled at the blonde woman at the garden party below.

Jodie Little. His stepsister. His darkest secret.

Burning hot fury ate away at him as he watched Jodie glide through the crowd of Athens's high society. She looked different. She had cut and straightened the long mop of curls. Her hair now fell into soft waves that reached her pointed chin. The yellow floral dress was modest as it skimmed her slender figure. Her bold red lipstick was at odds with her delicate appearance.

He knew the presentable image was false. It was a masquerade, a shield. It had been years since he'd last seen her but he knew time couldn't have tamed her true nature.

"There you are," his mother said as she stood beside him. "When did you get here? Come join the party."

Stergios didn't look away from Jodie. "How long has she been in Greece?" he asked.

Mairi Antoniou sighed. She rested her forearms against the ornate balustrade as she watched her step-daughter charm a guileless shipping heiress. "She let her father know she was at a nearby hotel about two days ago. If she thought she would be welcomed with open arms, she is going to be extremely disappointed."

"Why has she returned?"

"Something about missing her father."

Stergios studied Jodie intently. The seductress didn't understand the meaning of family. She had been absent from her father's life for four years and she suddenly wanted a reunion. "What do you think is the real reason?"

"I don't know," she replied softly. "Gregory doesn't have money of his own."

"And Jodie recently inherited a fortune," he murmured. He tore his gaze away from Jodie and scanned the sophisticated crowd for her father. Stergios spotted the tall, well-dressed man on the other side of the lush garden.

Gregory Little had a talent for marrying wealthy women. His only goals were to keep his powerful wife happy and live in the luxury she provided. Stergios knew his stepfather was a benign presence in their lives, unlike his daughter.

"Gregory didn't know she was coming for a visit," Mairi insisted. "They've been in contact after her mother died earlier this year, but he didn't invite her."

Stergios's stepfather was given a generous allowance. The man knew what was expected of him if he wanted to keep the money flowing, but having a wealthy daughter meant another stream of revenue. "Do you believe him?"

"Of course. Jodie has caused him nothing but trouble and embarrassment." His mother's voice was brittle with anger. "That girl almost caused a rift in our family because she couldn't keep her legs closed."

The blood pounded hard in Stergios's veins as he remembered. Jodie knew how to create problems with minimum effort. It could be uttering an explosive comment at a formal dinner or creating a public spectacle at Athens's most popular nightclub. But none of that compared to seducing his cousin Dimos. If she had succeeded, it would have destroyed a bright and promising future for the Antoniou family.

"She shouldn't be here," he declared gruffly. Why had she shown up this week of all weeks? "Does Dimos know that she's around?"

Mairi stiffened. "I asked him to put Jodie on the invitation list for this party," she reluctantly admitted.

Stergios cursed as he pushed away from the balustrade. He scanned the guests at the party but he didn't see his cousin. That alone was suspicious. Dimos had always gravitated toward Jodie.

"What happened between them is in the past," his mother argued. "Dimos was in a rebellious stage and was easily misled. He was no match for a determined whore."

Jodie had entranced Dimos almost instantly, yet his cousin had not been an innocent victim. Stergios knew his mother refused to believe that. She'd like to think that an Antoniou man had better standards.

"It took us too long to realize that she was a manipulative liar," his mother declared. "When she said you'd followed her into the wine cellar that night... Well, no one was going to believe that."

Stergios closed his eyes briefly. Everyone in the family knew about his aversion to dark and confined spaces. But he had pushed past the reluctance that night because of Jodie. Because of her special brand of trouble.

"Of course she couldn't bewitch you, but Dimos was unworldly back then," his mother continued. "Just remembering everything she has done makes me—"

"It's too much of a coincidence that Jodie has returned when we need this alliance with the Volakis family. She's out for revenge."

His mother scoffed at the idea. "She's not the type who would follow the financial news or understand your long-term plans for the Antoniou Group. Jodie is not that smart. For goodness' sake, she's a finishing school dropout."

"Jodie wasn't kicked out of all those schools because of her academic performance," he reminded her.

"She has no interest in destroying us," his mother said. "She wants to *be* one of us."

"Sometimes the enemy is within the family."

Silence pulsed between them. Stergios inhaled sharply as he firmly pushed back the memories. He sensed his mother turning to face him. Stergios mastered his troubled thoughts and didn't flinch when she tentatively placed her hand against his shoulder.

"You don't need to protect us against Jodie." Concern wavered in her voice.

His mother was wrong. He must always remain alert. Build enough power and wealth that nothing could touch them. He didn't want anyone in his family to know the bleak and cruel world he had experienced.

"She's a problem but we've dealt with worse. In fact, we won't need to do anything," Mairi said brightly, dropping her hand before she turned away. "Jodie can't pretend to be demure and innocent for long. Her true colors will show. They always do."

"And while we wait, she'll seduce Dimos and stop the wedding," he predicted.

His mother gasped. "No, Dimos won't betray us like that."

"Dimos will bed Jodie the first chance he gets," he countered. He knew his cousin would view Jodie as the one who got away.

"He won't," she argued. "He knows how important this merger is to the family."

That didn't stop Dimos four years ago, Stergios thought grimly. If anything, the need to claim Jodie was more imperative to his cousin now. But Mairi Antoniou had a blind spot when it came to family. It was his duty to recognize and eliminate any threats.

"Jodie knows the importance, as well," he warned as he grasped his mother's elbow and guided her back to the party. "She has returned because she has some unfinished business and the money to fund it. She's a real threat to the Antoniou-Volakis marriage. We need this alliance and I won't let Jodie Little destroy it."

Some things never change, Jodie told herself. She flashed a friendly smile at one of the older Antoniou women. The curmudgeon in unrelieved black didn't reciprocate as she drew the lovely heiress away to the other side of the garden. It was as if this family believed Jodie could corrupt the young woman with just her presence.

She strolled along the garden, sipping from her water glass as if she didn't feel all eyes on her. Jodie knew she was being paranoid. Many of the relatives had been indifferent to her when she had lived in Athens. Yet no one seemed happy that she had returned.

Jodie sensed a strange undercurrent that hung in the late summer breeze. These people were convinced she was going to make a mistake or cause a scandal. It was as if the Antoniou family was waiting for disaster and bracing themselves for impact.

They were in for a long wait. Jodie locked her smile into place. That was the old Jodie. She was wiser now, and more in control of her emotions. This time she was determined to fit in. She straightened her shoulders and took a deep breath, inhaling the fragrant garden flowers. This time she would belong.

"Jodie?"

She gave a start when she recognized the male voice. She whirled around and saw her cousin Dimos Antoniou. Jodie instinctively took a step back and wished she hadn't shown any sign of weakness. She corrected herself and welcomed him with a smile before he embraced her with a strong hug.

"It has been so long," Dimos said as he kissed both her cheeks.

"It has," she agreed, not allowing his touch to linger. He looked exactly as she remembered, with his long face, lanky build and black hair that flopped over his forehead. "Thank you for inviting me to your new home. It's beautiful."

"Zoi's family gave it to us as a wedding present."

"I think you and your fiancée will be very happy here."

He thrust his hands in his pockets and rocked back on his feet. "Can you imagine me getting married?" he asked.

She silently shook her head. Dimos was three years older and she had been grateful for his friendship, but he had always seemed immature for his age. "And you're a vice president with the Antoniou Group."

He ducked his head. "That won't be official until I come back from my honeymoon."

"Your family is very proud of you and they want you to have the best of everything. You deserve it," she said huskily as the words caught in her throat. Dimos had understood the rules very early on and, more importantly, had followed them. In return, he was rewarded handsomely.

She wondered what it was like to be loved and accepted by family. She wanted that now more than ever. Jodie had yearned for a wisp of connection with her parents but she had waited for them to make the first move. She now regretted her lack of action when her mother had died suddenly of a heart attack several months ago. Jodie knew she had to do something immediately if she wanted to have a relationship with her father, her only living relative. She would have to be the first to apologize, to yield, to change.

But what kind of sacrifices would she have to make to have her father accept her? How much would she have to hide about herself to be considered lovable?

Dimos's smile dipped as the light dimmed from his eyes. "That's very kind of you, Jodie. Especially after what happened between us."

Shock washed over her and she fought for a mildly interested expression. She hadn't been prepared for Dimos—for any Antoniou—to mention that night. Jodie wanted to cross her arms and back away but she was immobile. The only thing she felt was the pressure of her fingertips as they pressed against the cool surface of her water glass.

Dimos shoved his hand in his hair and looked away. "I did not handle the situation well," he confessed in a low tone.

She fought the urge to find a quick getaway. "No one did," she mumbled. She had been branded a Jezebel, a woman determined to snag an Antoniou man for a husband and ruin any potential marriages that had been carefully orchestrated. After that night she had been considered extremely dangerous to the Antoniou family's future.

"I didn't know that one of the maids had seen us."

Jodie blinked. That was what he was apologizing for? That they had been caught? Interrupted? She pressed her lips together before she said anything. It was tempting to give a scathing reply but she had to be on her best behavior.

"I couldn't believe that maid went and told Stergios." Bitter anger bloomed in Dimos's voice. "What had she been thinking?"

Jodie wondered if she might bite her tongue off as she

fought back the words. The maid had known exactly what Dimos's intentions had been. Jodie wished she had figured it out earlier. She had seen Dimos as a cousin who helped her navigate a big family, not as a viable lover.

"And I know this is years too late, but I should have spoken up." Dimos splayed out his hands. "I didn't realize you would have been severely punished."

She was wrong, Jodie decided. Dimos was still immature for his age. Her jaw hurt as she fought to remain silent and took a small sip from her water glass. She wanted to point out that she had never encouraged him, or that it was never too late to right a wrong. He could have protected her from the fallout at any time. But that wouldn't have served him.

And if there was something she had learned over the years, especially after that infamous night, it was that men didn't understand the meaning of honor, respect or protection. They pursued, they took what they could get and they got out fast.

"So, how long are you planning to stay in Greece?" Dimos asked with a puzzled expression when she didn't respond.

She darted a glance at her father standing among the older Antoniou men. Her first goal was to ask for forgiveness for her past behavior but she didn't know if her father would give her the chance. "I'm not sure," she murmured. "My plans aren't set in stone."

"Then you must come to my wedding," he said, his eyes widening with enthusiasm.

Jodie raised her hand to halt that line of thinking. "I don't want to intrude."

"Intrude?" Dimos laughed. "That's not possible. You're family."

She wished it were true. She wished she didn't have this need to belong somewhere. To belong with someone. She had always been the outsider. The burden. She was used to it, and at times wore the label like a badge of honor, but everything changed after her mother's death. She wanted to be loved, accepted and part of a family.

"You must agree," Dimos insisted.

"Jodie must agree to what?"

She went still when she heard the low, masculine voice. Stergios Antoniou was here. She swallowed hard. He was standing next to her. Her pulse began to gallop as her stomach made a sickening turn. Her skin went hot and then cold but she refused to look in his direction.

"I invited her to my wedding," Dimos said with a touch of defiance.

"I doubt there's space," Stergios responded.

"I can make space," Dimos promised Jodie. "It's going to be on an island that Zoi's family owns. It's small, but not that small."

She nervously licked her lips as the panic swelled inside her. It pressed against her skin, ready to burst free. Every instinct told her to run but she stood as still as a statue. "I wouldn't want to cause any inconvenience for you or your bride," she explained huskily.

"You won't," Dimos said with a lopsided smile. "I'll go ask Zoi right now."

She watched helplessly as Dimos strode toward his fiancée. She wanted to run and hide but knew she had to be brave. At least appear fearless. From the corner of her eye, she saw Stergios's crisp white linen suit. She forced herself to turn. Jodie looked straight ahead at his pale blue shirt. She tried to ignore how it emphasized the breadth of his powerful chest before she jerked her gaze to his face.

Her breath snagged in her throat as her heartbeat roared in her ears. She stared at Stergios's luxuriant black hair that fell past his chin. The shadow of a dark beard almost diminished the whitened scar on his upper lip.

This was not the Stergios she'd known. She blinked several times, noting the bold lines of his cheekbones and nose, the slash of his mouth and his warm golden skin. She recalled how he'd once kept his hair ruthlessly short and had shaved twice a day. Now it looked as if he could no longer contain the wildness that rumbled through him.

His dark brown eyes were cold as he callously assessed her and immediately found her lacking. "I don't know what you're trying to achieve—"

"I wasn't asking for an invite," she bit out. "He offered and wouldn't take no for an answer."

"Perhaps he didn't understand what you were saying." His gaze drifted to her mouth. "You're not good at saying no to any man."

She swallowed the gasp of outrage and fought the driving need to fling the contents of her glass into his face. Damn it, her new and improved image was already slipping. She was never in control when she was around her stepbrother. She had to get away from Stergios or risk making a scene. That wouldn't help her gain forgiveness from her father.

"Don't confuse me with the women you associate with." Jodie turned on her heel.

"Running away already?"

She whipped around, wobbling to a standstill as she glared at him. Stergios had sounded disinterested and bored while she was a jittery mass of nerves. It wasn't fair. "I don't run away. That's your signature move, stepbrother dear."

The muscle bunching in his cheek was the only indication that her barb had hit its target. "You know how to create a disaster and leave without a trace while everyone else deals with the aftermath. The merger had fallen apart after that night because Dimos suddenly didn't want to get married. It has taken me years just to get the Antoniou-Volakis wedding to this point."

"I was banished." She wanted to stamp her feet. This was bad. It was as if her hard-earned poise had disintegrated into nothing. "There's a difference."

"Banished?" Stergios repeated with skepticism. "You've always been dramatic."

And you've always been cold and hateful. No, she realized that wasn't true. Stergios had been tolerant the first time she'd moved in with the Antoniou family. He had been her only companion, her one true confidant. But gradually he had become distant.

The more he was around her, the more he knew and learned about her, the more hostile he became. It had been a relief and yet agony when he missed her eighteenth birthday to work overseas on a project. He had returned a few months later but her joy had been brief and misplaced. It had become obvious that Stergios couldn't stand being in the same room with her.

"If you were banished, why are you working so hard to return to the family fold?" His tone was casual but he watched her with open suspicion. "You're not the type to forgive."

Stergios knew her too well. Having one person understand her should bring comfort, but this man would use that knowledge against her. "I am here," she said slowly, emphasizing each word, "to repair my relationship with my father."

"And that's all?"

No, this time she wanted Gregory Little's concern and interest. She wanted to be a priority. She'd always wanted that from her father but she had tried to gain it the wrong way when she had been a teenager.

Jodie lifted her head when she suddenly understood Stergios's question. "Oh...you think I'm here to get revenge or to cause trouble. To stop this merger that you need so badly. I hate to disappoint you, but the Antoniou family isn't worth my time."

One winged eyebrow arched at her statement. As if he couldn't believe his family wasn't everyone's top interest. "You returned just when Dimos and Zoi are about to marry."

"I'm sorry I didn't get the family newsletter," she said with exaggerated sweetness, "or I would have timed my visit better."

She was about to flounce away but Stergios easily read her next move. He grabbed her arm, his large fingers biting into her pale flesh as he held her still. Her skin went hot as she remembered the last time he touched her. She knew better than to look at him or she would betray her conflicted emotions.

"I don't trust you." His voice was low against her ear.

She shivered from his nearness. "I don't care."

Stergios's grasp tightened. "Stay away from Dimos."

"With pleasure," she said in a hiss and forced herself to look into his dark eyes. "Now let go of me."

Jodie saw the turbulent emotions chasing across his face before he abruptly released her. She was uncomfortably aware how her skin tingled from his touch. "I have no interest in Dimos," she continued. "I didn't seduce him back then and I'm not pursuing him now."

"Why should I believe you? You're a liar."

Her anger flashed wildly. Yes, she had lied in the past, but it had been a stupid and instinctual attempt to protect Stergios that night. She had made a sacrifice for him and he couldn't see it, couldn't appreciate it. The hurt and the injustice of it all rolled inside her. "And if I wanted to seduce Dimos, there is nothing you could do about it," she slung at him.

"I'm warning you, Jodie." His voice was low and menacing.

She pressed her lips together. Why did she say that? Why was she provoking Stergios? She knew better but she was unable to stop. "I could have had him in my bed like that." She gave a satisfying snap with her fingers. "I certainly wouldn't have picked a cold wall in a dark wine cellar."

They stared at each other, instantly trapped in the inconvenient memories. She shifted, her spine aching as she remembered the rough brick against her back. Jodie swallowed as she recalled how she had laved her tongue against Stergios's warm skin. She felt her cheeks flush as the echoes of their mingled gasps and incoherent words reverberated in her mind.

She couldn't think about that. Not now, not here, not ever. "I could have contacted Dimos any time over the years," she declared in a rush. "And he would have dropped everything for the chance to have sex with me."

Stergios sneered with disgust. "So you know the power you have over him."

She did now, not when she had been eighteen. "I know the power I have over all men," she said loftily. "Dimos is more susceptible than most."

"And why do you think that is?"

No doubt he saw it as her fault. "I haven't encouraged him at all, but warn me off again," she said in a growl as she glared at him, "and all bets are off."

Stergios braced his legs as if he was preparing for battle. "You dare to threaten me?"

"There is very little I wouldn't dare," she told him boldly as her legs shook. "I am here to be with my father. If you block that in any way, I will do everything in my power to stop the Antoniou-Volakis merger."

His expression went blank. There was no anger or repulsion. It was like a mask and that unsettled Jodie more than his cold fury.

"It wouldn't take much." She knew she had to stop talking and yet she pursed her lips and made a show of looking around the party. "All I have to do is crook my finger and Dimos will—"

"You have always been a destructive force." His voice was just a rasp. "But I won't allow you to destroy this family."

"I don't care about the Antonious." The family was simply an obstacle to her goal. She had to play nice with them if she wanted even a tenuous bond with her father.

Stergios set his hands on his lean hips. "You need to leave and never return."

Jodie regretted saying anything to Stergios. He could prevent her from getting what she wanted. She wished she had planned a better strategy to meet with her father. She had been too impulsive, too impatient and too scared of getting rejected again. But she couldn't show her uncertainty or Stergios would use it against her. She lifted her chin and met his gaze. "That is out of your control."

His smile chilled her to the bone. "It's foolish of you to think that."

Dread trickled down Jodie's spine. It was foolish for her to go toe to toe with Stergios. He was a dangerous animal who lashed out if he felt threatened or cornered. "I have every right to be here."

"And I have a right—a duty—to protect my family at all cost."

She'd always known that. It was one of his traits she had admired and it used to hurt that his protection hadn't included her. "According to Dimos, I am family."

Stergios's eyes narrowed into slits. "I have *never* considered you family."

Those words would have slayed her when she was fifteen but now they slid right off her. "It's easier for you to think that, isn't it?" Jodie leaned closer, refusing to show how his words, his presence, had shaken her. "Helps you sleep better at night."

The mask fell away and exposed Stergios's wrath. A ruddy color seeped beneath his golden skin. His eyes glittered as he hunched his shoulders, ready to pounce. Jodie's chest seized as she watched his upper lip curl, pulling tightly at his scar.

"After all—" her voice trembled "—the great and virtuous Stergios Antoniou is supposed to be trustworthy and do what is right. He strives for excellence and discipline. Why, he would never have sex with a virgin without marrying her."

His jaw clenched and she knew his restraint was slipping. She had just made her most dangerous enemy very angry. She knew she should retreat and hide—no, she should beg for mercy, but the words kept spilling from her mouth.

"He would never have sex with his eighteen-year-old stepsister, right? And then walk away without a backward glance." The rejection had swamped her that night but she didn't stumble over the words now. "Discard her and throw her to the wolves."

She saw the pure hate glowing from his eyes and she wanted to recoil. Did he hate her for reminding him of his moment of weakness? Or was it something more? Did he hate her because she continued to show him what kind of man he truly was?

"But I know the real Stergios Antoniou," she confessed, driven to finish what she'd started. "I saw it that night four years ago. You're like every other man I've met. Threaten me all you want, stepbrother dear, but I'll take my chances."

CHAPTER TWO

"Jodie, would you care for some more coffee?" Mairi Antoniou asked.

"No, thank you," she replied as she studied her father and stepmother from across the breakfast table. What should have been an intimate meal was more of a grueling interview. She had been prepared for that. Jodie wished she could spend some time with her father in private but getting him alone was proving difficult.

She was, however, making progress. Jodie couldn't believe she was back in the Antoniou family home. She'd never considered it a possibility. Yet, two days after she had been invited to Dimos's housewarming party, she was eating a late breakfast with her father and stepmother while a maid was unpacking her suitcases.

She should be celebrating. Relieved that the reunion with her father was going this smoothly, this quickly. Her instincts told her not to trust it and Jodie tried to ignore the negative voice in her head.

Looking around the breakfast room, Jodie noticed it was still fussy and formal. She always found the ivory chairs uncomfortable and the large white floral arrangements overwhelming. She studied one of the many portraits of Mairi's ancestors that covered the sea-foam-green walls. Once again, she decided that Stergios did not get his stunning masculine beauty from his mother's side.

Jodie's gaze rested on a portrait of her stepmother. She

wondered what it would be like to be surrounded by family and tradition. Some of the younger Antoniou generation found the family customs constricting but she would have found comfort and privilege in continuing traditions.

Jodie looked down at her gold-rimmed china plate that had been passed down from generation to generation. Only a guest unfamiliar with the Antoniou household would think the breakfast had been planned as a feast to celebrate the return of the prodigal stepdaughter. But the family always had pastries, olives, cheese and *tiganites* in the morning. The small pancakes had been her favorite and she would often drown them with grape molasses, much to her stepmother's horror. Today she avoided the *tiganites* and had been the epitome of good behavior.

"I hope you will find your room satisfactory," Mairi said.

"Thank you." It was the same room she had stayed in years ago. In the corner on a separate floor from the rest of the family. But that didn't matter. She was going to accept what was offered and pass every test they gave. She would win the approval and love of her only living relative.

"What are your plans for today?" her father asked as he set down his paper and rose from his chair.

"I need to find a wedding present for Dimos and Zoi." It had to be appropriate but impersonal. She didn't want her gift to cause any speculation or a lecture from Stergios. Jodie winced. She wasn't going to allow her stepbrother to influence her in any way.

"And perhaps some clothes for the wedding?" Mairi suggested as she gave a pointed glance to Jodie's bright green dress. "It will be very...conservative."

Jodie nodded. Mairi had shown remarkable restraint not commenting on her short hem or towering heels. What was considered understated in New York City was dif-

-ferent than her stepmother's opinions. She had to make some adjustments. "I understand."

"I'm sorry we have to leave just when you've arrived," Mairi said as Gregory helped her out of her chair, "but your father and I have some business to attend to in the city."

"Please don't feel like you need to entertain me." She didn't want to be the center of attention. She wanted to show her father that she could seamlessly be part of his life without any trouble or work.

"Make yourself at home," her father said as he gave an awkward pat on her shoulder before he trailed after Mairi.

Home. She grimaced as she felt a pang in her chest. This stately mansion had never been her home. She had arrived here the first time when she was fifteen after she had been kicked out of another boarding school. Jodie had felt as if she'd been on probation the moment she had first entered the vestibule. But it hadn't mattered if she had behaved or caused trouble. She was always going to be sent away to another school, another country.

Now her actions would make a difference. For better or for worse. One mistake and her father would disown her for good.

Jodie rose from her seat and strolled into the entrance hall. She barely glanced at the marble grand staircase or the carved limestone walls. It was the silence that grabbed her attention. She forgot how quiet it was in this place even though Mairi liked having her extended family live under one roof.

She linked her hands behind her back and walked outside onto the shadowy portico. Her eyes widened with pleasure as she surveyed the bold colors of the grounds, the scent of the exotic flowers and the sounds of a gurgling fountain in the distance. She sighed as the tension ebbed from her shoulders. It felt as if she had paradise all to herself.

Jodie remembered spending many hours following the web of gravel paths to escape the house. She had frequently skinny-dipped in the large lake until her stepmother found out and put a stop to it. She also climbed the trees in the wooded area, daring to go as high as she could, often ignoring Stergios's exasperation and words of warning.

Jodie descended the terrace and noticed the garden had thrived in her absence. It took her several moments to recognize the changes in the landscaping. She suspected they were made in favor of the high-tech security features. Mairi could have hidden the cameras and emergency call buttons but the Antonious always needed to see what protective measures were being taken around them.

She left the terrace and wondered if there was a new piece of sculpture or work of art. Walking past the formal flower garden, she remembered how exploring the grounds had been one of her many solitary diversions.

When she had first moved here, she'd thought having many relatives would be a blessing. For an only child who had lived in boarding schools since she was six years old, the idea of a big family was as tantalizing as it was foreign. It had ultimately been a disappointment. It wasn't easy being an outsider in a close-knit family.

It was only after Jodie had been banished that she'd realized the Antoniou home was more than a showpiece. She paused and brushed her fingertips against the velvety petals of a flower. The house and the grounds were part of the family's fortress. Mairi only felt safe when she was at home and surrounded by loved ones.

The Antonious didn't trust any outsider with the exception of Gregory. Jodie understood why. They had placed their trust in one of their own and paid the cost.

They may never recover from being blindsided decades ago when Stergios was kidnapped as a child.

Jodie closed her eyes as the wave of sympathy washed over her. She had only collected bits and pieces of the story since everyone seemed to follow a pact of not discussing it. She knew Mairi and her ex-husband had been in an ugly custody dispute and that Stergios's father had hired a team to kidnap his son. Stergios had only been seven years old.

Jodie blinked away the sting of unshed tears as she imagined a young and vulnerable Stergios. Mairi was a tigress when it came to her only child but she didn't find him until he was nine. Stergios had lived on the run and in horrible conditions. He had emerged scarred, malnourished and tormented from the experience.

From the day Stergios had been taken, the house and grounds became impenetrable. So had the Antoniou family. Jodie accepted the fact and she knew their wariness wasn't entirely personal.

Jodie sighed and slowly retraced her steps, returning to the portico. She saw a flash of movement in the corner of her eye and turned to see Stergios. He emerged from the wooded area, the gravel crunching under his running shoes as he jogged toward the house with a punishing pace. The fight-or-flight response swirled in her chest. She cast a quick glance in the direction of the formal garden, her heart skipping a beat as her hands bunched into fists.

It was too late to disappear, Jodie decided as she watched Stergios get closer. She tried not to notice that he only wore a dark pair of running shorts, or the way his golden skin glistened. Her gaze darted to his broad shoulders and then to his muscular arms. Jodie felt a spurt of heat low in her belly and she wasn't sure where to look.

She focused on his chest and followed the path of his dark hair. Her attention rested on his V-cut abs.

He didn't break his rhythm as he jogged onto the terrace and then stepped onto the portico. He passed her as if he wasn't going to acknowledge her presence.

"I didn't know you were still living here," she blurted out.

Stergios stopped without turning around. "I don't." Sweat ran down his spine but he didn't sound out of breath. He placed his hands on his lean hips and stretched. She was mesmerized by the play of muscles and the faint crisscross of scars that ran down his back. "I have a home of my own but I stay here when I'm in Athens."

Jodie stepped in front of him, blocking his way. It was irritating that he wouldn't deign to look at her. She inhaled his scent and went still. It was hot, sweaty and male. A blush crept up her neck and into her face. She didn't know why it left her flustered.

"How long are you planning to stay?" Jodie asked. His nearness was almost her undoing. Her breasts felt heavy and tight and she crossed her arms against her chest.

"For as long as you are, *pethi mou*," he said. "I'm only here to keep an eye on you."

"What?" Jodie's lips parted as a thought occurred to her. "Is that why I was invited to the family home? To make surveillance more convenient for you?"

His eyes glittered with amusement. "It was thoughtful of you to accept."

Jodie abruptly looked away and stared at the door that led to the house. She should have known it hadn't been her father's idea. Her intuition had been correct. She shouldn't trust this act of hospitality.

She wasn't going to let this get her down. Jodie clenched her teeth as she encouraged the flicker of determination to catch fire. It didn't matter why she was invited. She was here and she was going to make the most of it.

"Going to go pack?" he asked in a drawl.

Her arms tightened around her as if she was holding herself together. "Why would I?" she asked as she slowly met his gaze. "I'm getting what I want."

"Are you sure? Dimos doesn't live here."

"Wonderful," she declared. "Now you don't have follow him like a guard dog and save him from predatory women. That must free up so much time for you."

There was a heavy beat of silence. "That wasn't the only reason I stopped Dimos."

"Of course it was. If Dimos had sex with me, a woman supposedly under the protection of the Antoniou family, he would have been stuck marrying me instead of the heiress of your choice." She paused, not sure if she should say anything more. "Do you even know why we were down in the wine cellar that night? We were going to break into the good stuff while everyone was out of the house."

"It didn't look that way when I tore you two apart."

Jodie glared at him. When Stergios had intervened, Dimos had her in a tight hold and had been sticking his tongue down her throat. She hadn't been trying to get closer to Dimos—she had been pushing him away! "I was never interested in him. There was no way we were going to have sex!"

Stergios lifted an eyebrow. "Then how do you explain what happened between us?"

She felt her face turn bright red. It had been different with Stergios. When Jodie had returned from her last finishing school fiasco, she had become violently aware of her stepbrother's sexual allure. It didn't matter that he was eight years older or that he was too intense for someone like her.

But Jodie didn't want anyone to notice how much

power Stergios had over her. She had some pride! The man hated her and yet she wanted to get closer to him. She had become an expert at hiding her attraction. Or so she thought. Now she knew why she'd always bickered with Stergios. Why they'd always seemed to get under each other's skin.

When Stergios had shoved Dimos up the stairs that night, she had launched into an argument with her step-brother that felt as though it had been simmering for weeks. Vicious words had been exchanged and nothing had been held back.

To this day Jodie wasn't sure what had happened next. What had been the trigger? Had she made the first move or had he? All she knew was that her mouth had slammed against his. His kiss, his touch, had set her free. It was as if they had exploded out of their cages. She'd clawed and bit as he ruthlessly made his claim. She'd encouraged him to give her everything he had. Their coupling had been fast and feral.

She hadn't experienced anything like it since. Even now her heart pumped hard and her skin felt scorched as she remembered the way he took her against the wall.

"I looked for you after that night," Stergios confessed.

She jerked back as the memories splintered. "No, you didn't," she said softly. "You left like a bat out of hell. Where did you go?"

He speared his hands in his long hair and gave a guttural sigh. "It doesn't matter."

It had mattered to her. She had felt rejected and abandoned. Used.

"You'd left Greece by the time I returned," Stergios said, staring blindly at the garden. "I went to America to find you. I assumed you went to your mother's but you had already left by the time I arrived in New York. Your mother wasn't helpful in how to contact you."

She gave an awkward nod. Carla Little had not been a motherly, nurturing kind of woman who needed to know what her daughter was doing. "Mom was in the middle of a business deal that would have determined her legacy," she mumbled. "She couldn't afford any distraction."

"I kept looking for you," he admitted with great reluctance before he returned his piercing gaze on her. "No one seemed to know where you were."

Her parents hadn't been interested in finding out. While her friends were envious of her independence, the lack of parental concern had always embarrassed Jodie. "I knew how to take care of myself," she said. "Why was it so urgent to find me?"

"I wanted to check on you."

Jodie drew her head back. She wasn't sure what to say. Of all the people who had been part of that night, he had been the only one who tried to contact her. Even though he had made it clear how much he didn't like her, how little she meant to him.

Stergios watched her with an intensity that pinned her to the spot. "You were a virgin and I was…rough."

Jodie frowned when she saw his stony expression. Stergios had been beating himself up about that night when she'd savored the primal and naked responses. It had been everything she had hoped for with the man who had starred in her secret fantasies.

And why did he have to bring up her inexperience? Her eyes widened with surprise. "Wait…were you going to insist on *marriage*?" she asked. She knew how the Antoniou males thought. They had very old-fashioned views. The men married the virgins and had affairs with experienced women.

"I didn't use protection that night," he said stiffly, as if the oversight went against his personal code of honor. "I needed to know if there were consequences."

Oh. He wasn't worried about her as much as he was concerned about an illegitimate child. Disappointment crashed through her. She wanted to hunch her shoulders and curl into herself as if she could contain the pain. "There weren't," she said in a whisper.

Stergios gave a sharp nod. "I knew I had to seek you out because you wouldn't have volunteered that information with me."

Not necessarily. He always assumed the worst in her. "If you thought that, why did you give up looking for me? We're talking about your child, the Antoniou heir," she said grandly as she spread her hands up high in the air. "You would have searched the world if you thought that was a possibility."

"I stopped looking a few months later." His features hardened as he gave her an unforgiving look. "There was a picture of you online and you were definitely not pregnant."

She frowned. "What picture?"

Stergios sneered from the memory. "You were on a yacht in the Caribbean with that royal playboy." He spat out the last word as if it was a curse.

Jodie wanted to cringe. The prince had been a mistake. She had been looking for love. She had been desperate to *be* loved and found a playboy instead. Unfortunately, she had found a few playboys on her search for love before she wised up.

"I see," she said calmly as she watched Stergios's lip curl with disgust. "And suddenly it no longer mattered that I was a virgin or eighteen."

He shrugged. "I might have been your first, but then you threw yourself at the next man who showed any interest," he declared as he turned away. "You were no longer my problem."

No longer my problem. The words echoed in her mind

as she dazedly watched Stergios stride into the house. Once he'd decided that she "belonged" to another man, she had no longer existed.

Jodie hissed air between her clenched teeth as the pain ricocheted. He had ruthlessly cleaved her out of his life. He had moved on without missing a step. It was a fear she struggled with constantly. The fear of becoming invisible. Forgotten.

But she had no idea it was that easy.

She needed to work harder to become unforgettable to those who mattered. It was an impossible task, Jodie decided as she took the steps back to the garden, intent on getting away from the house, from Stergios. As she marched along the path she gradually realized what she had to do. She was going to use her wealth to become an indispensible member of the family. She might be unlovable now, but money could change anything.

CHAPTER THREE

HE HAD UNDERESTIMATED JODIE, Stergios decided later that night. He considered what he had seen at the family dinner a few moments ago and scowled. Not only had she gained her father's attention with the mention of an expensive gift for his upcoming birthday, but Jodie had also excelled in the area that had consistently been her downfall. She had been the quintessential dinner companion, delighting the surliest of his uncles and making fast friends with the younger wives and fiancées.

Stergios reluctantly admired Jodie's strategy. She had approached the outer circle of his family and was slowly gaining allies. He couldn't have this.

He leaned against the marble newel post as he watched Jodie descend the staircase like a regal queen. She had reapplied her bright red lipstick after dinner and he found it difficult to look away from her mouth. He couldn't fault her long-sleeved black dress. It should have been modest but it clung lovingly to her thighs. The white stripe zigzagging from her shoulder to her waist and hips was pure Jodie. Despite her attempts to blend in with the crowd she couldn't wear anything that might have her fade into the background.

"You gave a worthy performance at dinner tonight," he said as she drew closer.

She cast him a haughty look. "I don't know what you're talking about."

"You were very proper." He should have appreciated the charade. Stergios remembered the family dinners she'd attended in the past. At times he hadn't known if she'd been intentionally provocative or if she'd been unable to control her tongue. "You're playing it safe. That's not like you."

She stood on the last step and met his gaze. "I know what is expected of me."

"Especially if a wrong move will harm your chances with this family." She wasn't going to make a mistake soon. Jodie was using all of her knowledge from her past visits to dazzle and deceive. "What is it you want from us? Status? A favor?"

"As I have said before, I no longer want to be estranged from my father."

She was sticking to that story but Stergios knew there had to be something more. What had happened that would cause this change of heart? What did her father have that she wanted? "Why?"

She frowned. "He's my father."

"He's also the one who threw you out of this home." And to someone like Jodie, that act would have been unforgiveable.

The corner of her mouth dipped before she looked away. "Emotions ran high that night," she said quietly. "We said and did things we later regretted. It's time to forgive and move on."

Stergios raised an eyebrow at her practiced answer. "You think Gregory regretted his actions? That he wants forgiveness?"

She hesitated and glanced at the music room where her father was chatting with guests. "I can only speak for myself," she replied in a faraway voice.

"You didn't think the timing of that night had been suspicious?" He crossed his arms as he watched her closely. "He cast you out of his life when you were eigh-teen."

Jodie's head jerked and she gave him a cold stare. "Mairi kicked me out," she corrected him. "This is her house and my father was obligated to agree with her."

"And Gregory was no longer receiving child support from your mother." His quiet tone didn't soften the blow.

She pressed her lips before she spoke. "You think my father only tolerated me because of the money?"

There were many times when he had believed that. Gregory may have won full custody of Jodie, but he had constantly sent her overseas to any school that would take her. When she was away, it was as if Gregory forgot her existence. Each time Jodie had been expelled from a school and came here to live, Gregory had made it clear that the living arrangements would be temporary.

"He didn't get rid of me the moment he could. I hadn't just turned eighteen," she reminded him. "If that had been his reason, he would have kicked me out months before."

Stergios knew he had wounded her. Her rigid stance and cool tone didn't give her away. It was in the way she tried to give a scornful smile. Her tremulous lips ruined the effect.

He had dug in and exposed a fear that had settled deep in her heart. It gave him no pleasure. But Stergios knew he couldn't hold back if he wanted her to leave. He had to go in for the kill.

"It's common knowledge that Gregory wanted to be-come a father so he could eventually live off the child support."

Her forced smile tightened. "Yes, I've heard what was said during the divorce proceedings. That was one law-yer's argument and it doesn't make it true." She took the last step and headed for the music room to join the others.

"Why would you want a relationship with a man who only showed an interest in you for the money?" he called after her.

"Perhaps you should ask your mother that question." She whirled around. There was restrained anger in her movement but her expression was coldly polite. "My father married Mairi for money. She married him because he's a respectable escort. He's not a danger to her fortune or family like your father was."

Stergios's head snapped back. No one discussed Elias Pagonis in this house. In front of him. *No one.* Stergios had shed his father's name years ago but he couldn't rid himself of the memories and the damage Pagonis had created.

Jodie took a step closer as if she wasn't aware of the emotional grenade she'd just lobbed. "Mairi and my father have been married for ten years and they have grown fond of each other. Is it really outside the realm of possibility that my father can grow to love his only child?"

Stergios struggled to focus as old anger swelled inside him. He wouldn't allow Jodie to distract him with the mention of Pagonis. "Are you going to buy Gregory's love with your inheritance and hope it becomes the real thing one day?"

"Do you think that's the only way I can get love? By paying for it?"

Stergios heard the crack in her voice and the weak sound pulled at him. "Be careful with this plan," he said roughly as he fought for control over his emotions. "You'll soon run out of money. And when that happens, Gregory will have no use for you."

"Why are you giving me advice, Stergios? I can't believe it's from the goodness of your black, withered heart. If my father loses interest in me, that will suit your purposes."

"Because I don't believe that's why you're here." Rejection was the one thing Jodie Little couldn't excuse. "You can't accept that Gregory got rid of you."

"He didn't get rid of me." She leaned forward and he noticed the suspicious moisture in her blue eyes. "He had to make a choice between his wife and his daughter."

"And he'll make the same choice over and over again." Stergios almost missed the flicker of pain before she blinked. "You have money now but it's nothing compared to what we have. We have more money, influence and power. You can't compete."

"I'm not trying to take him away from your mother." Her voice was rough with annoyance.

"*Oxi*, it's worse. You're trying to become part of this family." He viewed her plan as an invasion and he would use all of his resources to prevent that. "Do you actually believe we're going to lower our guard and let you in?"

"No, of course not. It didn't happen before. Why should it now?" She shook her head as if she was suddenly weary. "I am not the enemy, Stergios. I don't have the power to hurt anyone."

Stergios wanted to scoff at that declaration. "I disagree. I've seen the damage you cause without even trying."

Jodie set her mouth into a grim line. "Don't put all the blame on me."

"You have always been trouble." He raked his hand through his hair. "If you weren't causing me headaches, you were destroying everything important to me. I can't have you anywhere near Dimos's wedding."

Jodie stared at him silently for a moment before she raised her chin. "Sorry to hear nothing is going your way, Stergios," she said with a dismissive wave of her hand. "You better get used to it while I'm around."

The woman didn't understand, Stergios decided. His

gaze rested on the sway of her hips as she strutted to the music room. Jodie assumed he played fair but when it came to protecting his family, he wasn't constrained by a gentleman's code of conduct. He had learned early in life what it took to fight to the death. He followed the law of the jungle and always won. Always.

Stergios wandered into the music room a few minutes later. It had taken some time to purge the thought of Pagonis and rein in his emotions. Jodie had hit her mark and it appeared she had done so without any strategy. It was as though she could see through him however much he tried to dissemble.

He stood by the door as he watched one of the guests, yet another heiress and family friend, play his mother's favorite sonata on the piano. Everyone seemed spellbound by the display of technical precision but the music didn't reach him. Rarely did anything pierce through his armor these days. Just Jodie Little. Stergios frowned at that troubling thought.

"Stergios?" He turned and saw Zoi Volakis. He wasn't sure how long she had been standing there. She was a petite woman with dramatic features who dressed just like every other female in his social circle. "I've been meaning to ask. What exactly is Jodie to this family?"

"She is Gregory's daughter from his first marriage," Stergios answered. He refused to say she was part of the family. Legally she was a relative but her actions proved otherwise. She wouldn't think twice about destroying his family.

"She doesn't look anything like him," Zoi decided. "And they act like strangers."

So he wasn't the only one who noticed that. "They're Americans. New Yorkers."

She gave a wry chuckle. "That must explain it. How long does Jodie plan to stay?"

Her casual tone hit a wrong note and Stergios went on alert. "She hasn't said. Why?"

Zoi hesitated, as if she was reluctant to say anything. "Jodie is very close to Dimos."

He looked around the music room for his cousin. Frustration and something dark and dangerous bloomed inside him when he saw Dimos and Jodie standing by the windows, apart from the other guests. "They grew up as cousins in the same house."

Stergios recognized Dimos's awestruck look. He had seen that expression on his cousin's face in a picture four years ago. Mairi had sent him a picture of a family event when he had been working on an assignment overseas. It was more than infatuation. He had known at that moment that Dimos wanted to claim Jodie.

And Stergios returned home immediately after seeing that picture. He had done everything in his power to keep Dimos and Jodie from getting together. Stergios could tell himself it was to protect the merger but there had been darker, more primal reasons he hadn't wanted to explore.

"Is there anything I should know?" Zoi asked.

"No, of course not," Stergios replied smoothly. "Dimos wants to marry you."

She nodded her head but she didn't appear relieved by his answer. "Dimos and I do not have a love match, but I take this commitment seriously," Zoi said. "I'm getting married because it's my duty to my family."

Stergios tensed when he heard the warning underneath Zoi's polite tone. He didn't need this. Not now. "Dimos knows how important this merger is for both our families."

"Good, but I am not as self-sacrificing as you may think." She cast another glance in Dimos's direction before she lifted her chin with injured pride. "I had tolerated the delays and setbacks before we got engaged, but I will not be humiliated by my husband's wandering eye."

Stergios gritted his teeth as he watched Zoi walk out of the music room. They were so close to getting this merger settled but it could all fall apart in the next few days. He took part of the blame. He had pushed Jodie too far and had hurt her feelings. She retaliated the only way she knew how.

He strode toward his cousin and Jodie. They seemed to be in a world of their own with their heads tilted close to each other. Dimos must have caught a glimpse of him. His forehead was creased with worry as he cautiously approached Stergios. "What's wrong?"

"Stay away from Jodie," he warned in a low, fierce tone.

Dimos flushed as he glowered at him. "Why? You can hate her all you want but—"

"She isn't going to share her body or her bed with you." Stergios watched with satisfaction as Jodie slipped out of the music room and hurried to the grand staircase. She wouldn't be a concern for the rest of the night.

His cousin continued to splutter with outrage. "What the—"

"She's leading you on because I told her not to," Stergios said with brutal honesty. "Haven't you learned anything about this woman?"

"You have no—"

Stergios leaned forward and watched with satisfaction as his cousin took a cautious step back. "And if this wedding doesn't happen, if you try anything with Jodie, I will cut you out of this family."

Dimos's jaw went slack before his eyes glittered with hate.

"You're supposed to be engaged," he said as the anger flashed hot inside him. "Act like it. Go find your fiancée and pretend Jodie Little doesn't exist."

Stergios turned his back on his cousin and forced a genial expression before he mingled with the guests. Now if only he could afford the same luxury and act as if the threat of Jodie Little didn't loom over his family.

Just a couple more days, Jodie thought as she rested her head against the soft leather chair. It was almost over and yet the knowledge didn't relieve the coiling tension inside her. Dimos's wedding was to be held the following evening and she would have finally proven to Stergios that she had no plans of revenge or destruction. But intuition told her that he wasn't going to stop. He was going to find a way to push her out for good.

Jodie shifted in her seat and tried to relax. The ride in Stergios's private helicopter was loud but she wore a headset to communicate. She had found the all-white interior and luxurious touches more intimidating than comfortable. It was just another reminder that the Antonious had more money and power than she.

She glanced at Stergios. He sat in the chair next to her and read his tablet. He was dressed more for a funeral than a wedding in his black designer suit and black silk tie. He had been moody since they had left the house and she had done her best to ignore him.

Jodie crossed her arms and tapped the pointed toe of her black stiletto heels against the floor. "I still don't understand why I had to arrive at the wedding with you."

He didn't look up from the screen. "It's a matter of logistics."

She made a face. "You have a thousand relatives and not one could include me in their travel plans?"

"Not one."

"And it has nothing to do with the fact that you won't let me out of your sight until Dimos gets married?"

He swiped his fingers against the touch screen. "That is correct, *pethi mou*," he murmured distractedly.

He had been her shadow for the past few days and she had been unable to shake him off. It didn't matter if she talked nonstop or gave him the silent treatment. He didn't care if she wanted to have a private moment with her father or get lost in a crowded party. He had always been at her side.

Jodie pointedly looked away from him and nervously peered through the window. She didn't like the way the dark gray clouds filled the sky or how the choppy waves crashed against each other in the Aegean Sea. She hoped they landed soon before the weather got rougher.

Just as she was going to ask how much longer the trip would last, Jodie saw the island as the helicopter pilot started his descent. Her lips parted with surprise when she saw the rolling hills covered with fat, leafy trees. After meeting Zoi and her family, she had expected one big amusement park filled with pristine beaches, golf courses and all the amenities. This looked like an uninhabited island.

As the helicopter set down on the landing pad, Jodie caught a glimpse of a house. It was white and modern with clean lines and a flat roof. It wasn't a mansion and she assumed it wasn't the main residence. It probably belonged to one of the islanders.

She scrambled out of the helicopter inelegantly in her form-fitting orange dress and sky-high heels but she refused Stergios's assistance. She stood at the edge of the helipad as she watched him confer with the pilot.

"Where is your suitcase?" Jodie asked as he walked past her, effortlessly carrying her bags.

"Everything I need is here," he said, patting his briefcase.

She didn't doubt it. The man was outrageously sexy

and didn't have to primp or make any effort to look good. It really wasn't fair.

Jodie followed him along the gravel path, falling behind thanks to her spindly heels. She heard the whine of the helicopter behind her as it ascended. "It's very quiet here," she commented as she brushed her hair away from her face.

"Not for much longer, I'm sure."

There was no music or the sound of conversation. What kind of event was this going to be? A wedding should have a festive tone, even if it was arranged.

"The way Zoi had talked about her wedding, I thought there'd be more decorations," she said as she tried to walk faster. "I'm not saying she'd line the helipad with flowers but I wouldn't put it past her."

Stergios didn't say anything as he waited for her to catch up.

Jodie stopped next to him and placed her hands on her hips as she looked around. It was strange that no one had met them. "Where is everyone?"

His mouth settled into a harsh line. "At the Volakis Island, I assume."

Jodie frowned with confusion. "Wait. What?" She shook her head as she tried to make sense of what he said. "Isn't this the Volakis Island?"

"*Oxi*, this is my home," he replied in a resigned tone.

She glanced around again at the white sand beach and leafy trees. The island was unspoiled and isolated. Free from any distraction. It suited Stergios.

"Why did we have to stop here?" She whirled around and watched the helicopter fade into the gray sky. "Why didn't you ask the pilot to wait?"

"He'll be back in three days."

"What?" Her heel skidded against the path. She grabbed

his sleeve but her hand barely wrapped around his muscular arm. "I don't understand what is going on."

His eyes were cold and wintry when she met his gaze. "You didn't leave when you had a chance," he said in a clipped tone. "You didn't stay away from Dimos. You left me no choice."

Her mouth parted as the shock and confusion crashed inside her. "What are you saying?"

"You're not going to the wedding," he announced. "You're stuck here with me until I decide it's safe to let you go."

CHAPTER FOUR

"You can't do that!" She looked around the island, the scent of the briny ocean and the promise of rain suddenly overwhelming. Her head began to spin as she took deep gulps of air. "I did not agree to this. My father is expecting me at this wedding. It will embarrass him if I unexpectedly don't show up."

"You have no choice in the matter. I suggest you get inside before the storm hits."

She waved her hands in the air as she spluttered with outrage. "Do you honestly believe that I will just follow you? Only because you say so?" She reached inside her purse and grabbed her phone. "You forget that I'm not an Antoniou who mindlessly obeys your orders."

"Put that away," Stergios replied. "You're not going to reach anyone. There is no internet or phone connection on this island."

She refused to believe him. A man as important and powerful as Stergios Antoniou would have all of the latest technology. But as she held up her phone she saw he was telling the truth. Maybe she was in a bad range. Maybe she had to go higher on the island.

"People are going to worry if we don't show up." She hated how her voice escalated as she took short, choppy breaths. "Especially you. You have to be at the wedding. You've been part of it every step of the way. Will it still go on if you don't manage every moment of it?"

"One of my assistants is calling my mother to let her know we've been detained because of mechanical problems."

He sounded indifferent. She hated it. Hated him. "You thought of everything. How long have you been planning this?"

"It came to me this morning. Does it matter?" He gave a shrug before glanced at the darkening sky. "We need to go inside."

"No." She looked around wildly, her heart pumping. There had to be a boat around here. A Jet Ski. Something. She would find a way to escape if she had to comb through every inch of this island.

"Come along, *pethi mou*," he said with a bite of impatience. "The caretaker is away but you are safe with me. After all, you are my guest."

She scoffed and cast him a look of disbelief. "I am your hostage."

Stergios flinched. He went pale as his expression turned blank. "What did you say?" His voice was a rasp.

"You heard me." Jodie didn't like how the air suddenly crackled between them. Alarm trickled down her spine. "You have kidnapped me. *You*, of all people."

He dropped the suitcases on the ground as if his fingers went slack. "You don't know what you're talking about." His hand sliced through the air. "This is not a kidnapping."

"You are detaining me against my will." Her voice faded as he approached her. It took all of her courage to stand her ground.

"Did I take you by force?" he asked through clenched teeth. "Are you in chains?"

Jodie saw the haunted look in his eyes and she knew he was wrestling with old memories. But she couldn't afford to show him any sympathy. "What are you saying?

That I'm not your prisoner because I had a comfortable ride over here?"

He stabbed his finger in the direction of the house behind him. "You will have a room of your own and plenty of food. You will have comfort and privacy. I will make sure every one of your needs are met."

"As long as I do what you tell me?" She flung her hands high in the air. "Forget it. I'm not going into that house. How do I know that you won't lock me in the room?"

"There are no bars on the windows. You can come and go as you please."

"As long as I stay on the island," Jodie added. "That still makes me a prisoner."

He closed his eyes and drew in air between his teeth. His hands clenched and unclenched at his side. "This is not a kidnapping."

She crossed her arms and glared at him. "Then get me off this island right now."

He paused as the tension radiated from his body. Just when she thought Stergios was going to explode, he opened his eyes and took a step back. "*Oxi*. No."

His answer was so quiet and calm. He didn't care what he did or to whom. "I should have expected this." She shook her head in disgust. "This is why you intimidate everyone. They can sense that you aren't the gentleman you pretend to be. They know there's a wild animal just underneath ready to pounce."

"I'm going inside." Stergios walked away and grabbed the luggage. "You can do whatever you please."

She stamped her foot as the fury ripped through her. "What have I done to deserve this?" she called out to him. "Why do you hate me so much?"

Stergios slowly turned around. His eyes were cold and his mouth was curved in a stern frown. She couldn't tell what he was thinking or feeling. He was back in control. "Hate you?" he asked. "Jodie, I don't give a damn about you."

"You're lying," she yelled. "You wish you could forget me. You hate how I make you feel."

The corner of his mouth hitched. "Dream on."

"I could tell that night in the wine cellar," she blurted out. "That's why you ran away. You were ashamed that I had that much power over you." *Ashamed that, of all women, it had been me.*

Stergios's harsh features tightened as he hunched his shoulders. She could tell she struck a nerve. He was trying to hold himself back before he retaliated.

Jodie pressed her fingertips against her lips. She had to curb her tongue. She was already vulnerable to this man. She didn't need Stergios to figure out how he made her feel. She was the one who lost control when they were together. He was the one who had power over her.

"I'm going to make you regret this," Jodie said in a hiss as she turned around and went back up the steps. "And you will have no one to blame but yourself."

Stergios paced along the windows that overlooked the beach. He had discarded his jacket hours ago and had rolled up the sleeves of his white shirt. It was turning dark and the rain was still coming down hard. Jodie had not made an attempt to find shelter.

He paused and looked for a flash of the bright orange designer dress. He had seen the pop of color every once in a while as she searched the island for an escape. Stergios now spotted her sitting on the wet sand near the house. Her blond hair was plastered against her head and her soaked dress clung to her body as the ocean waves lapped against her bare feet. With her slumped shoulders and outstretched legs, she appeared weary. Defeated.

Kidnapped.

Stergios hissed and rubbed his hands over his face. Jodie always knew what to say to pierce his armor. She would do anything to get a reaction. But it wasn't going to work. This was not a kidnapping.

He knew what a kidnapping felt like. It was a constant state of fear and of not knowing. It was howling pain punctuated with numbness. At times he hadn't felt human. He had been a pawn, a package. His childhood, his innocence, had been stripped from him in an instant. Worst of all, he had discovered what he was capable of and how far he would go to find freedom.

He understood what it felt like to be taken. And still… Stergios stared at Jodie. He replayed his actions in his mind and it had been strangely familiar. The truth suddenly cracked his resistance wide open. It was as if jagged shards dug deep in his chest and he couldn't breathe.

He had made the same decision his father had made years ago.

Stergios took a shallow breath as the pain scored through him. This hadn't been a delay or a detour. He had kidnapped someone. He had followed his instincts and had snatched Jodie in broad daylight.

He rested his forehead against the windowpane and struggled to remain standing as a cold sweat prickled his skin. The idea to abduct Jodie had come naturally and he hadn't questioned it.

Stergios closed his eyes as the nausea swept through him. After all these years of fighting the possibility, blood will out. He thought he had been protecting his family by keeping Jodie away. Instead, he had uncovered one of his deepest fears. He had always pushed himself to be a better man than his father. To distance himself from everything the man had represented.

But every time he looked in the mirror, he was reminded of his father. Despite his achievements and milestones, nothing could cover up the fact that he was Elias Pagonis's son.

Stergios stepped away from the window. He thrust his hands in his hair, but he didn't feel the sting of his fingers dragging along his scalp. He had to fix this. Redeem himself. Find a way to erase his actions.

He glanced up at the sky and noticed how the trees swayed against the wind. There was no way they could leave the island tonight in this weather. And could he allow Jodie to attend the wedding? Was he willing to take that risk?

Stergios would consider the consequences later. Right now she was his obligation. He couldn't let anything happen to her while she was here.

He strode out of the house, the door banging against the wall, and marched through the sand. Jodie's eyes widened as she caught a glimpse of him. She scooped up her shoes as she struggled to stand up.

"You are so stubborn," he called out over the roar of the storm.

She scurried back, poised to run. "Don't talk to me! I'm furious with you."

"Are you going to stay out here all night?" The wind whipped his hair as the cold sheet of rain stung his bare skin.

"Yes," she spat out. "I'd rather catch pneumonia than be your prisoner."

"You always pick the wrong choice," he said in a growl as he rubbed the water from his eyes. "Instead of showing common sense, you have to make some dramatic statement."

"This from a man who thought kidnapping was the only option."

He had had enough. Stergios lunged forward and

grabbed Jodie. She screamed as he gathered her in his arms. She fought for her release, kicking and slapping, demanding that he set her down.

"Keep that up and I'll drop you," he warned as he walked across the beach.

"Try it and I'll take you down with me."

He entered the house and walked through the living area, past the welcoming heat of the fire he had built in the fireplace. "There are two bedrooms," he told her as he approached the door. "Mine is on the other side of the house. This one is yours. You can stay here for as long as you like."

"I bet you'd like that," Jodie said as she kicked wildly in the air. "You want me to hide in here. Stay out of the way so you can forget what you've done."

He was finished with dramatic, impertinent women who brought nothing but disruption into his life. All he wanted was peace. A sense of security. Anything that blunted the tension inside him.

Stergios carefully set Jodie onto the floor. "Your bathroom is through there," he said, nodding in the direction of one of the doors. "Your suitcase is in the closet."

"That's it?" She stood before him barefoot and in a sodden dress, but she didn't appear small or vulnerable. "That's all you have to say to me?"

He wiped the dripping water from his forehead with the back of his hand. "You do not want to know what is going through my mind right now."

"Bringing me here was a mistake," she said with a snarl. "You assumed I was a threat to the Antoniou-Volakis marriage and you thought you were so clever to keep me away. But the truth is I'm a threat to you. I'm the only person who's cracked you. I see you—the real you."

"You're not so special," he said as he stepped over the threshold. "You're the only one who has yet to realize that you should be afraid of the real me." He quietly closed the door behind him and strode away.

An hour later, Jodie wrenched open her bedroom door and entered the main room of the house. She could have stayed in the hot shower all night but the last thing she would do was hide in her room. As much as she wanted to avoid Stergios, she wasn't going make herself invisible.

She tightened the belt around her robe, wishing she had something heavier than the ivory silk one that didn't reach her knees. With any luck, Stergios would be in his room.

Jodie took a moment to look around. It wasn't a surprise that Stergios's island getaway was light, airy and luxurious. He had always surrounded himself with exquisite beauty.

There were large windows that offered a panoramic view of the ocean. The cathedral ceiling's exposed rafters and the stone floors seemed to reflect the island environment. The modern fireplace in the center of the main room was a showpiece. She was tempted to curl up on one of the white couches and get warmed by the dying fire.

Jodie pressed her hand against her growling stomach and decided she needed to get something to eat first. She went in search for the kitchen and found that the large room was casual and inviting. Jodie skidded to a stop when she saw Stergios sitting at the kitchen table.

Her heart banged hard against her chest when she saw him sprawled on a heavy wood chair. Stergios had discarded his business suit for a long-sleeve blue T-shirt and faded jeans. His large feet were bare and his damp hair was slicked back.

There was a clear liquor bottle and a shot glass resting by his hand. She caught a scent of the strong alcohol and suspected it was Tsipouro. Only Stergios would take a drink made for social gatherings and treat it as a solitary event.

Stergios didn't glance up. "Go away, Jodie."

She jerked, unaware that he had seen her. Jodie grabbed the collar of her robe closer as she fought for courage. "I wish I could, but my movements are extremely limited."

He lifted his head and silently glared at her.

"Anyway, I'm hungry," she announced as she padded barefoot to the large refrigerator. "Do you have anything for the prisoner? Maybe some bread and water?"

"Go back to your room," he said as he returned his attention to his shot glass. "I am not in the mood for company."

Jodie closed the refrigerator door and studied him. She hadn't seen him in this kind of mood. It was stormy and unpredictable. "Then just ignore me. You're a pro at it."

He gave a huff of a laugh and slumped against his chair. "You refuse to be ignored. You know how to get attention. You can't help it."

"I don't like being invisible," she admitted.

"I could never accuse you of that." He poured another shot and held it out for her.

She crossed her arms and leaned against the kitchen counter. "No, thanks. I don't drink."

"Liar," he said huskily. "It was one of the top three reasons you got kicked out of school. Boys, alcohol and cheating. And didn't you say you snuck into the wine cellar with Dimos to find alcohol?"

"Reason enough to give it up, don't you think?"

He gave her a mocking salute with the shot glass. Downing it one gulp, he set the glass down with a thud.

"I've never seen you like this, Stergios," she murmured. He often moved with fluid grace. Tonight he seemed uncoordinated. "Are you drunk?"

"I'm working on it." He pushed the shot glass away as he grimaced. There was a beat of tense silence before he spoke again. "You were right about me. I am my father's son."

"I didn't say that," Jodie insisted. She didn't know much about Elias Pagonis but she knew his actions had been reprehensible.

"You didn't have to. I...kidnapped you," he said with an odd hitch in his voice. "I can't remove all traces of my actions but I will make it right. A helicopter will be here first thing in the morning and it'll take you to the wedding. I will remain here."

She stared at him. There had to be a catch. Why was he allowing her to attend the wedding? Stergios Antoniou never admitted defeat.

He dragged his gaze to meet hers. His dark eyes were troubled and filled with remorse. "I'm sorry that I frightened you."

Jodie drew her head back at the surprising apology. "You don't make me scared. You make me angry," she clarified.

He gave a harsh bark of laughter. "Typical. You don't even know when to be worried. I should warn you that I'm in a very dangerous mood."

"Stergios..." she said as she approached him.

"You know what I'm capable of when I'm sober." Stergios rubbed his hand against the dark stubble on his jaw. "You should go hide in your room."

Jodie ignored the trepidation curling deep in her belly. "No, you can't just send me away and act like I don't exist."

"You don't understand." His voice was strained. "I am feeling volatile."

"You usually do when I'm around."

He went still and gave her a sidelong look. "Careful, *pethi mou*."

"And you carry around this guilt about what happened between us in the wine cellar. Why? I take equal responsibility for that."

"You feel guilty, too," he decided. "Guilty for going too far. For surrendering to me."

She felt her skin heat as she remembered the glorious moment she had yielded to him. "I don't feel guilty."

"Then why did you lie?" He sat up straight in his chair. "That's what I can't figure out. Why did you tell everyone that we didn't have sex that night?"

"No one would have believed me." It wasn't the full truth but it was a reason Stergios could accept. "Your family acts like you are a god who can do no wrong. They treated me like I was a plague that kept returning."

He shook his head. "You lied because you were ashamed."

"No, I wasn't. I'm not." She had been fascinated with Stergios. She had been infatuated him with the wild abandon of someone who had never felt that way before. The only thing she was ashamed about was how much he meant to her when she meant nothing to him.

"You could have saved yourself that night," Stergios said. "If you had told them that I had taken advantage of you then—"

"Taken advantage? I was with you every step of the way." Her voice rose. "Why would I make that kind of accusation? I don't want anyone to think that about you. That's why I stuck by my story. I lied to protect you."

He leaned forward, resting his arms against his legs. "Protect me?" His voice flicked like the tip of a whip.

"I could tell that you were ashamed of what happened that night. You hated yourself because of it. Why would I advertise that?"

"I don't need your protection," he said in a withering tone as he stood. "You are the one who needs protection from me."

"No, I don't."

"I had lost control that night, but so did you," Stergios said in a low, gravelly voice as he approached her. "I had unleashed something wild. I felt it when I was deep inside you."

She tried to appear unaffected by his statement but she couldn't hide her reaction. The way her pulse fluttered at the base of her throat. The kick of lust that made her gasp. The delicious heaviness that settled in her pelvis.

"And I can do it again." His voice was thick as his hooded eyes focused on her mouth. "One touch and you will come apart."

Jodie's lips stung with awareness. "You killed anything I felt for you when you walked away that night."

"Which just makes it worse, doesn't it?" He rested his big hands on the kitchen counter, trapping her. "You don't want to desire me," he said in a mesmerizing tone as he leaned in. "I'm the one who can tear down your masquerade and I'm the one who drives you wild. You're ashamed that you respond to me."

She swallowed hard as she fought the urge to draw him closer. "That's not true," she whispered.

"It's okay, Jodie." Stergios dipped his head and his mouth brushed her ear. Her breath hitched in her throat as she inhaled his scent, his heat. She was surrounded by him. "That's how I feel when I'm with you. And I still can't stop myself. I don't want to."

He slid his hands in her hair, his fingers gripping the back of her head. She flattened her hands against his chest, determined to push him away when he claimed her mouth with his. She gasped as the raw pleasure tore through her.

Stergios tilted her head and drove his tongue into her mouth. His rough jaw scratched her skin and her lips stung under his forceful kiss. Jodie clawed at his shirt as she drew him in deeper. She shivered when she heard Stergios's groan of pleasure.

He bunched her hair in his hands as he devoured her with a ferocious hunger. Hot excitement crawled up her chest as she went wild under his touch. Jodie clung to his shoulders, bucking her hip against him.

Stergios suddenly wrenched away from her. He looked stunned as he gulped for air. Shell-shocked. Just like the last time, Jodie thought miserably as the throbbing lust tormented her.

She didn't want him to stop and yet she didn't have the courage to reach out for him. Her legs trembled and she stared at his face that tightened with anger and primal need. Stergios Antoniou was bad for her. He didn't care about her. He felt no respect. He was ashamed of this attraction. But right now she didn't care. She knew she would later.

Stergios turned away. "Go back to your room," he said hoarsely as he walked back to the kitchen table, his movements stiff and reluctant. "And lock the door."

CHAPTER FIVE

THE NEXT MORNING Stergios stood by the windows as he gripped the satellite phone in his hand. He watched the storm with a sense of resignation as he considered his options. There were none. He had been caught in his own net. He was being punished for what he had done.

Pain throbbed in his head and his eyes felt gritty. It had been so long since he had a hangover and it had been reckless to dull his senses around Jodie. Instead of drinking himself into a stupor, he had wasted no time in kissing her.

Stergios tensed when he heard the wheels of Jodie's suitcase drag along the stone floor. He was ready to deal with her. Last night he had pulled himself from the brink of disaster. If he hadn't pulled back, he would have taken Jodie to bed.

"I'm ready to leave," she announced as she stood next to the door.

He turned and saw Jodie in high heels and an aquamarine sheath dress. She was the epitome of cool elegance. Her beauty captured his imagination and yet it was too careful. Too perfect. He yearned to see the spark in her blue eyes. It had often given him a kick of anticipation because he'd known she was about to do something daring.

"We have a problem," he said and watched her shoulders tense as if she was ready to argue. "The weather is too severe for travel."

Jodie's eyes narrowed. "I don't believe you."

Stergios clenched his jaw. He was unaccustomed to anyone questioning his word. He gestured at the window. "Look outside."

She glanced out the window. "It's not that bad. You're making this up. You will stop at nothing to keep me away from your family."

"I want nothing more than to get you out of my home, *pethi mou*." He rubbed his hands over his eyes. "I would swim to the Volakis Island if it meant getting you out of here, but we are just going to have to suffer each other's company."

She crossed her arms and looked away. "For how long?"

"Possibly until tonight." *If they were fortunate.* "I promised I will get you to the wedding and I will."

"I've decided not to go to the wedding," she said quietly. "I want to return to Athens and then go back to New York."

"Why?" She had been insistent that she needed to attend the wedding. She had been in a panic when he had delayed her. "What has changed?"

"Nothing." Jodie walked over to the fireplace and perched on the sofa's armrest.

"I was right," he said as he followed her. "You had been out for revenge. But this detour ruined your plans."

Jodie rolled her eyes. "You are obsessed with this idea of revenge. Why do you think I want revenge on your family? Because of how I have been treated?"

There was some truth to that. He was not proud of how his family behaved. Jodie had been young and vulnerable and they made her feel unwanted. If he had been in the same position, he would have wanted some payback. "Your father didn't shield you. Instead of revenge you want to repair your relationship with him. It doesn't make sense to me."

"I was never close to my parents and I've been estranged from my father for four years. My mother wasn't able to bond with me from the beginning." Jodie looked at the floor, her cheeks turning bright red as she revealed the truth. "I thought I had come to accept that this is the way our family interacted. But then Mom died unexpectedly of a heart attack."

"And you felt the loss of what could have been," he murmured. He had those unguarded moments after his father died in prison.

She gave a sharp nod. "I'm twenty-two and I know it's too late to get the parents I needed when I was a child. But I wanted some family connection before it was too late."

"Gregory Little doesn't know how to be a father," Stergios decided.

"I know," Jodie said as she idly swung her foot. "But it would mean a lot to me if my father was interested in what was happening in my life. If he called or visited me. Included me in a family celebration." Her foot stopped as she exhaled sharply. "Anything that would make me feel like I'm not alone and forgotten."

Stergios frowned. "That's all you want?"

"You wouldn't understand." She blinked rapidly and dabbed her fingertips against the corner of her eye. "You are surrounded by family. They are involved in every part of your life, whether you want it or not. They care about you and, in return, you protect them. That's what I want."

"You want my family to take care of you? Protect you?" Had his mother been right? Did Jodie secretly want to be an Antoniou?

"No, no, no," Jodie said with a small smile. "I don't want to be part of your family. I want to be part of *mine*."

"Going to New York won't make that happen."

"It's not going to happen wherever I am. I ambushed my father and he's on guard." She tilted her head back and gave a groan of regret. "I approached the so-called reunion the wrong way and I can't repair it."

"Your plan is to walk away and act as if Gregory doesn't exist?" That didn't sound like something Jodie would do. She was the most tenacious person he knew.

"Yes, it's finally time to admit defeat." She dropped her hands and slowly stood up. She took a deep breath and set her mouth in a determined smile. "Look on the bright side, Stergios. After tonight, we will never cross paths again."

This was what he wanted. Needed. Yet Stergios fought back the bleakness as he imagined a future without Jodie. Instead of the peace he craved, his world was colorless and deathly quiet.

Stergios shook his head, ridding himself of the image. That didn't make sense. Life would return to normal once Jodie was gone. It would be better. He silently walked back to the window, knowing that the pilot couldn't get here fast enough.

Jodie's head jerked up as the lights flickered. She checked her watch for the hundredth time. Night had fallen and there was no update from the pilot.

She nervously bit her lip and stared at the flames dancing in the fireplace. The helicopter had to show up and take her away. She wasn't going to be stuck here for another night. Alone with Stergios.

As Jodie watched him through her lashes, Stergios prowled around the room, glaring at the crashing waves and torrential rains. Throughout the day the tension between them had ebbed and flowed. One moment they could talk easily and share a laugh. And then, quite suddenly, the atmosphere would change. The tension between them now stretched until she swore it shook.

Jodie rubbed her thumb against her lips. She shouldn't have let that kiss happen but she couldn't resist another taste of the passion she'd experienced long ago. She had found her response alarming and she had been on edge all day.

Stergios probably thought she responded that way with every man. But she had been celibate for a long time and no man intrigued her enough to take him to her bed. She was determined to wait for a man who cared about her. A man she could trust with her body and heart.

Stergios wasn't that man, Jodie decided as she fought with the weight of disappointment. She watched him lean his shoulder against the window. He had proven it that night four years ago.

"Where did you go after you left the wine cellar?" Jodie cringed as the words spilled from her mouth. She knew better than to bring up that night.

He stared broodingly through the window. "As far away as I could."

It suddenly occurred to her and she looked around. "You came here, didn't you?"

Stergios hesitated. "Why would you think that?"

She burrowed deeper into the couch and stared at the fire. "This is your getaway. Your sanctuary."

"Doesn't feel like it," he muttered.

"It's isolated here. Secluded. With all communication cut off, this is the only place you will find solitude. That's why you didn't know I was banished until it was too late," Jodie said with a sigh as the truth hit her. Stergios wouldn't have abandoned her like that if he had known.

"I should have stayed and protected you." His voice was heavy with regret.

Jodie wished he had stayed but she'd instinctively understood that he had been fighting demons of his own. That was why she had lied to protect him. It had been her turn to take care of him. "What did you do while you were here?"

"Went quietly insane," he said softly.

She frowned at his serious tone. "Why?"

He gave her an incredulous look. "Do I have to spell it out? I had taken advantage of a vulnerable girl. A virgin. My stepsister. What kind of man does that?"

She raised her hand to stop that train of thought. "Okay, first of all, I was an adult at the time. A woman. And I was not vulnerable."

"I took your virginity," he said in a growl. "I'm not proud of that."

His words shouldn't hurt so much. That moment had been life-changing and he wanted to forget it. Erase that night completely. "You didn't take it," she argued hotly. "I gave it to you."

He pushed away from the window. "You had no say in the matter."

"Yes, I did!" she said as she leaned forward. "You were the one I wanted. I had lusted after you."

He stopped in his tracks as his gaze sharpened.

"That's right. I lusted after you." It had been thrilling, scary and all-consuming. "It was not a crush. Not a passing interest. It was an obsession. I tried to hide it because I knew you would reject me."

"You hid it very well." He tilted his head back and closed his eyes. "It's good I didn't know."

She blinked when the lights flickered again. "Why?"

"You had become a temptation," he said as he dragged his hands down his face. "I had done everything I could to deny myself. I left home…"

Jodie gasped. "That was why you went abroad? Because of me?"

Stergios crossed his arms as if he was holding himself back. "I knew I had to get out before I did something."

"You were only gone for a couple of months." She had been overjoyed when he had returned to Greece that summer. She hadn't questioned why he came back so soon. "What happened?"

His gaze darkened. "I came to realize that Dimos wanted you and it was only a matter of time before he made his claim. I couldn't let that happen."

"It was never going to happen because I had no interest in him." She remembered what Stergios had said about that night. *That wasn't the only reason I stopped Dimos.* Jodie's heart began to race as she made the connection. "You weren't protecting Dimos or the merger that night. You were protecting your property."

Stergios remained silent as a ruddy color stained his high cheekbones. She saw the possessive gleam in his eyes and something wicked and primal flared deep inside her.

"I did not belong to you!" she insisted. "I belong to no man!"

"*Oxi*, you belonged to hundreds."

She flinched from his cold statement. "You couldn't bear to look at me after we had sex. And what? I was supposed to wait around in case you changed your mind and wanted to bed me again?" She shook her head when she realized that was exactly what he had expected. "I moved on, Stergios, just like you did. Just because you were my first doesn't mean you own me."

Stergios clenched his jaw and she felt the anger pulse from him. The tense silence plucked at her nerves and all she could hear was the crackle of the fire. She knew she was getting into dangerous territory.

Jodie cleared her throat. "I don't think the pilot is coming for a while and I'm getting hungry." She bolted from her seat and hurried to the kitchen.

She felt Stergios was right behind her. It was as if she was being pursued. Cornered. Her skin tingled as her stomach clenched. Why wasn't he giving her space? Why didn't he stay in his separate corner now, when she needed some distance?

"You *gave* your virginity to me?" he asked hoarsely. "Why would you do that?"

She turned around suddenly and collided into his hard, muscular chest. Jodie jumped back and crossed her arms against her chest. It was a flimsy barrier against such a man.

"I shouldn't have put it that way," she said. "It makes it sound like it was a gift. Like there is some obligation or responsibility attached to it."

"There is," he said roughly.

She didn't agree with his outdated view but she knew it was useless to argue. "If that's how you felt about it, why did you give up looking for me? Why didn't you ask me to marry you?"

"Would you have accepted?" he shot back.

"It's hard to say." Jodie fought for an inscrutable expression. She would have accepted. Without question or hesitation. She wouldn't have cared that he didn't respect her or love her. Knowing that, it was a good thing he had stopped looking for me. "You didn't answer my question," she said huskily.

She watched the muscles twitch in his cheek. "Any marriage with you would have been disaster!"

"You weren't thinking about our compatibility," she said as the hurt bled through her. "You thought you deserved a woman better than me. You weren't going to settle for me when you wanted a woman who shared your heritage and your status."

"My marriage will be a strategic alliance," Stergios said with no apology. "It will give my family and me unlimited power and influence. And when that happens, nothing and no one could ever harm us again."

"So it doesn't matter what kind of woman you marry?" She didn't believe it. Stergios would want a "good girl" for a bride. Someone sweet and obedient.

"I need a wife who doesn't cause trouble," he said harshly. "A woman who can create a peaceful—"

The lights flickered and extinguished, plunging them into complete darkness.

Jodie gave a startled jump. She automatically reached out and curled her hand against his forearm. She felt his soaring tension under her fingertips. "Stergios?"

"The generator should kick on," he said in a strained voice.

She waited a few moments but the darkness remained. The wind howled outside and she heard Stergio's labored breathing. "I don't think it will," Jodie whispered.

"It has to."

He said it as a prayer. Her fingers clenched against his arm. "Or what?"

The beat of silence stretched before Stergios responded. "You don't want to know."

CHAPTER SIX

HE WAS INSTANTLY transported to the time he had been held captive. It was dark and he was shivering. The metal cuffs chafed at his wrists. Blood trickled from his mouth as fear pulsed inside him.

Jodie's fingers flexed against his arm. "Uh…Stergios?" Her voice sounded far away. "I have a confession to make. I…um… I don't do well in the dark."

Join the club, he thought as the memory dimmed. But her admission didn't sound right. He recalled how often she frolicked around the gardens at night when she didn't think anyone was watching. She had been fearless and free.

"Is it okay if I hold on to you?" she asked as she curled her arm around his.

"If you have to." Turmoil churned inside him as he broke out into a cold sweat. He didn't want to be touched. He needed to keep his distance but he couldn't deny Jodie's request.

"It's kind of dark in this kitchen, don't you think?" Jodie carefully turned them toward the door. "Can you take me back to the main room? I would feel better sitting by the fire."

He remembered the campfire his captors had gathered around every night. It was the only thing that held back the dark wilderness. But he had always been far away from the campfire and didn't get to enjoy the heat or the light.

Stergios silently walked Jodie to the main room. He was very aware of how her body brushed against his arm. Only she wasn't leaning against him. She felt strong and confident.

"I guess my problems with the dark—with nighttime, really—happened early on." Jodie's voice was soft and soothing. "I think it started at my first boarding school. It was an eerie place and the older girls told us ghost stories."

Jodie's voice went in and out but her hold on his arm remained firm. His tension diminished when he saw the glow from the fire. There were still too many shadows and dark corners, but he was able to guide Jodie to one of the sofas.

"Thank you. Would you sit with me?" she asked as she patted the cushion next to her. "It would make me feel safer."

He reluctantly sat with Jodie even though he knew it was a bad idea. She didn't know what he was like in the darkness. It could take some time before the lights came back on.

"I got kicked out of that school a few years later," she continued as she curled up on the sofa, her dress riding up her thighs as she tucked her legs underneath her. "They had given me several chances but I wasted them all. The next school I went to was horrible. I didn't last long. Maybe a month?"

Stergios didn't look at her. He silently watched the fire as he tried to push the memories away. It had happened years ago. Some of his recollections were blurry and some were just an intense, overwhelming feeling. But there had been some moments that were razor sharp no matter how much he tried to forget.

"The school in South Africa was nice and I made some great friends there. Now, looking back, I should have tried harder to adapt."

She fell into silence. He didn't like that. He wasn't following every word but he clung to the gentle rhythm of her voice.

"You purposely got kicked out of every boarding school," he said gruffly. "Why?"

Jodie shifted uncomfortably in her seat as if she was embarrassed. "The letters and phone calls from home had stopped," she told him. "I didn't see either of my parents during the school breaks. I was being left behind and I couldn't let that happen."

The woman was so afraid of becoming invisible. He didn't understand it. She grabbed attention wherever she went. She hadn't been in Athens for years and yet her name was still on everyone's tongue. "So you did everything you could to get your parents' attention."

"I broke every rule I could think of. I cheated on tests even when I knew the answers. I snuck boys in my room just to get caught and I planted liquor bottles where they could be found. I did whatever would require a call to my parents. Or better yet, be sent home."

"It didn't work," he murmured. Her stays at the Antoniou estate were brief and rare.

"No, it didn't. My actions had the opposite effect." There was a hint of regret in her voice. "The more stunts I pulled, the less my parents wanted anything to do with me. They sent me to places so far away that I couldn't visit home. It was as if they didn't know what to do with me. I felt abandoned."

Rejected, Stergios thought. So she pulled stunts that would create more attention.

Jodie was lost in her thoughts as she stared at the fire. "I often wondered what would have happened if I had run away from one of those schools. Would my parents have looked for me?"

"Of course they would." His response was automatic.

"You would assume that, Stergios," she said with a soft chuckle as she patted his shoulder. "But your family was different than mine. They always wanted to keep you close," she said with a longing sigh. "You knew all your relatives would do everything in their power to find you."

"True. I taunted my captors with the knowledge all the time. That the wrath of the Antoniou family was going to rain down on them." A vengeful smile tugged at the corner of his mouth. "And it did."

"And now you protect them with the same drive." Her eyes shone with admiration. "You take care of every relative no matter how faint the blood connection."

"Not Pagonis. He may have been my biological father but he had me kidnapped. All to get my mother's fortune." Stergios felt the bile rise as he thought of the man. Pagonis hadn't considered how it would traumatize his son. "He deserved to die in prison."

She rested her head against the back of the sofa and watched the flames dance in the fireplace. "I suspect you never told anyone what happened during your ordeal. You needed to spare them the details."

He gave her a startled look. Jodie understood him too well. His silence had been his way of protecting his family from the unpalatable truth. "The less they know, the better."

She stroked his clenched hand. "What happened that made you hate the dark?"

"I know the dangers that the night holds." He had overcome every one of them. "But it's nothing to what the darkness had revealed inside me."

"I don't understand."

The truth pressed against him, ready to break free, but he had learned to keep it to himself. "Everything I knew and believed in changed in one night." He spoke slowly as the words did not come easily. "We often camped in the wilderness. I had been left outdoors, chained and caged."

He remembered the metal rattle of his prison. His kidnappers liked to drag their weapons against the bars. The overwhelming clatter reverberated in his ears and he was stuck in that time and place until Jodie squeezed his hand.

"One of my captors…" Stergios paused as he tried to purge the face from his memory. "He thought I was easy prey. I was young and trapped. But I fought back."

"You had no choice," Jodie said.

The memories started to collide. It had happened quickly and he had no time to think or strategize. It had all been instinctual. "I almost killed him. I probably would have if his coconspirators hadn't stepped in."

"It was self-defense." Jodie didn't look horrified or shocked. She didn't draw back in fear. Instead she leaned closer. "You were just a child and he wanted to hurt you."

"I saw how much damage I could cause at a young age." Stergios could still feel the warm blood and hear the echoing screams. "I didn't know there was so much violence and rage inside me. That night I discovered what I could do when I am cornered."

"Why do you let people think you're afraid of the dark? It's not true."

"There's some truth in it. I avoid being in a position where I can't see potential threats. But it's easier for them to accept that I hate the dark. They don't want to dig deeper and I don't want them to know that the darkness is a trigger. It reminds me what I had to do to survive."

Their gaze connected and she didn't look away. He was caught in the depths of her blue eyes. He didn't move, didn't speak. For one infinitesimal moment, he found the peace he had been searching for.

"What happened after you fought back and wounded that man?" Jodie asked. "Your captors must have punished you."

"*Ne*, it's how I got this scar." He gestured at his mouth.

Jodie moved closer and brushed her thumb against his lip. "It didn't stop you from fighting back again, did it?" she whispered.

Her touch broke the spell. "Careful, *pethi mou*." He wrapped his fingers around her wrist but he didn't pull her hand away. "I am no gentleman. I am an animal. I am red in tooth and claw."

There was no fear in her eyes. Jodie didn't listen to his warning. Didn't care. The tenderness in her gaze left him unsettled. He slowly set her hand away from him.

"Don't worry, Stergios. Your secret is safe with me," she promised.

He leaned forward and rested his arms on his knees. "I shouldn't have said anything."

"Why not?" she asked as she drew back. "You had to tell someone. It's not something you want to share with your family. They already feel so guilty they couldn't protect you during that time."

"I don't know why I told you." He knew it was a moment of weakness that he was going to regret.

"Because you don't see me as family," Jodie said as she rose from the sofa. "You don't need to protect me."

He gave a humorless laugh. "*Ne*, I do. You're not smart enough to be cautious around me. At times you bait me, wanting a reaction. Now you know better."

"I can take care of myself," she said as she walked to the kitchen. "And you."

Stergios scowled. That was the last thing he wanted. He did not want to rely on Jodie Little. She was unpredictable and seductive. Trouble. He was safer on his own.

* * *

Stergios woke up abruptly. He jackknifed up and looked around. He was on a sofa in the main room. There were ashes in the fireplace and light was blazing from the lamps. He glanced outside and saw that it was night. He heard the downpour outside but he didn't hear the whistle of the trees in the storm.

Checking his wristwatch, he saw it was past midnight. Stergios sat forward and rubbed his hands over his face. He didn't feel refreshed from his nap. He was mentally exhausted and on edge.

The lights must have woken him. He remembered Jodie went to bed a few hours ago after she gave up on talking with him. He had been defensive and uncommunicative. He had shared something personal, something he wouldn't have shared with anyone, and now he was waiting for the backlash.

He rose stiffly from the sofa and stretched. The way his shirt was creased, he guessed his sleep had been troubled. It usually was if he thought too much about his time in captivity.

Stergios needed to move around. Think about something else and the memories would vanish for a while. Grabbing the dirty dinner plates from the side table, Stergios walked into the kitchen. He went still when he saw Jodie by the sink.

The ivory slip she wore was innocent and seductive. It looked delicate, as if it would fall apart under his touch. Stergios swallowed hard as he noticed how the silk clung to her curves and angles. Lust smashed into him as his gaze followed the lace edge that emphasized her cleavage.

"Oh, you're awake," she said as she drank water from a glass.

His hands gripped the plates so tightly that he thought

they would crack. "What the hell are you wearing?" His voice lashed in the electric atmosphere.

She glanced down. "What's wrong with it?"

He strode to the sink and tossed in the dishes. From the corner of his eyes, he saw Jodie flinch from the loud clang. "You were going to wear that at Dimos's wedding?"

"Well, not at the ceremony." Jodie set her glass in the sink. "When I was in my room and sleeping. Alone."

He didn't believe it. That was the kind of lingerie a woman wore when she had seduction in mind. "A woman does not wear that when she's sleeping alone."

"That's enough, Stergios." She gave a tired sigh and held her hands up to stop him. "You no longer think I had my eyes on Dimos, so what gives? Are you trying to start an argument?"

He was and he hated that Jodie had called him on it. He felt exposed. To Jodie, who knew his secrets and his dreams. She knew how to hurt him and worse, how to make him feel stronger. She had the ability to be his most dangerous enemy, and the one person who stood her ground when others would retreat. He had to create some distance.

Stergios towered over her. "You think you know me, but you don't."

Instead of backing down, Jodie rose on her tiptoes and met his gaze. "From what I understand, you have a problem with what I sleep in."

"I do." His gaze flicked along the low-cut nightie. His skin burned as he imagined trailing his fingers down the valley between her breasts. "What man bought it for you?"

She settled back on her feet, obviously surprised by his question. "I bought it because I like it."

"You were thinking about a man when you bought it." Jealousy, hot and corrosive, bled through him. No other man should have the privilege to see her like this.

She gave a huff of exasperation and gestured at the ivory silk. "What is it about this nightie that you find so offensive?"

"That you're in it," he bit out.

He saw the angry spark in her eyes. She set her hands on her hips and the silk pulled at her curves. His tongue cleaved to the roof of his mouth as he stared at the outline of her hard nipples. He was tempted to snap the thin straps with his fingers and watch the silk glide off her body and pool at her feet.

"Would you like me to take it off?" she asked sweetly. "Right here, right now?"

His stomach clenched as he imagined her striptease. "It's that attitude that got you banished from the Antoniou family."

Her chin jerked up. "Is that right?"

"Gregory has always been embarrassed by your sexual behavior," he told her as the lust pounded through his veins. "How many schools kicked you out because of boys? Do you think your father was proud of that?"

Her eyelashes fluttered. She wasn't prepared for these accusations and line of questioning. "But only you know that I didn't do anything with them."

"And your father wasn't surprised when you were accused of trying to seduce two men in the wine cellar," he pointed out. The anger and desire clashed inside him. "He didn't stand up for you. He knew what you were."

Her cheeks went pink. "Why is it a problem for me to have sex?" she asked.

"Have as much sex as you want." He remembered how he had claimed her in the wine cellar. Stergios's arousal was painfully swift. The sex had been unforgettable and he was never able to recapture that feeling. "In marriage. With your husband, not a revolving door of lovers."

She glared at him. "Your double standards exhaust me. Is it wrong that I liked having sex with you?"

"*Ne!* Yes!" he said through clenched teeth. His nostrils flared as he remembered how Jodie's orgasm had gone on and on. She had held nothing back.

She was telling him this because she wanted him to remember. She knew he was on edge and his good behavior could easily snap. He shouldn't have told Jodie anything about himself. She was using the information to her advantage.

"Despite what your family thinks, I am not a whore," she said as she walked past him. "I am a healthy woman with a healthy appetite for sex. Deal with it."

He watched her strut away and fought the urge to follow. To hunt. Stergios's muscles locked as he fought to remain where he stood. He was not an animal. He was not—

Stergios chased Jodie before he even realized it, his footsteps quiet as raw need ate away at him. When he grabbed her arm, he knew he was already past the point of no return. Whirling Jodie around, Stergios slammed his mouth against hers.

CHAPTER SEVEN

His kiss was hard and punishing. Jodie tried to resist as he forced her lips open with his tongue. Stergios's hand spanned against her breast as he invaded her mouth. His possessive touch nearly undid her. Her nipple tightened as she imagined his rough hand and his inquisitive tongue roaming against her bare skin.

"No," she whispered.

"Ne," he said in a hiss before he nipped her bottom lip with the edge of his teeth.

She gasped as the bite sent stinging hot sensations throughout her body. Jodie jerked her head to the side. Her rejection didn't stop him from dragging the tip of his tongue along the curve of her throat.

Jodie pushed against his shoulders. "No, Stergios. This isn't going to happen." Her strong words were undermined by her breathless tone.

Stergios's large fingers slid against her hips. She sensed he wanted to crush her silk slip in his hands. Desire pooled between her legs as he grabbed her bottom with a rough urgency that excited her. She couldn't stop the whimper from escaping her tight throat.

He chuckled as his lips pressed against her collarbone. Her fluttering pulse beat against his mouth. "You want it as much as I do," he said triumphantly.

She squeezed her eyes shut but she couldn't ignore the truth. She *did* want this. She wanted him more than anything else. Jodie knew she should be ashamed. She desired a man who couldn't stand the sight of her.

Stergios thrust his knee between her trembling legs and she bucked against his hard, muscular thigh. Jodie held back a sob of pleasure. She was weak against him. She didn't care what Stergios thought. She needed him deep inside her.

"You don't want this," she said in one last-ditch effort to stop this madness. "You just want to display your dominance over me." She shivered with anticipation as she imagined how he would take her. It wouldn't be making love. It would be a primal mating. "I won't let you."

"You will, *pethi mou*," he predicted as he rocked her hips harder against his thigh. "You will beg me."

No, she wouldn't. She couldn't! It was humiliating that she was hot and ready for him in an instant. She needed to salvage some of her pride. "You're doing this because you revealed too much to me," she shot back. "You don't want anyone to know you, least of all me!"

Stergios gripped the back of her head. "Open your mouth for me," he said in a rasp before he lowered his head.

She pressed her lips together but Stergios would not be denied. His kiss ignited the ferocity inside her. He knew just how to touch and excite her. Stergios had set the standard for her and no other man had made her feel like this.

Jodie wanted to go wild in his arms. She wanted all he had to offer but she was afraid. This man had almost destroyed her after the last time they were together.

"We can't do this," she said against his mouth. "We shouldn't!"

"I know." His hands clenched her waist and he suddenly lifted her up. Jodie clung to his shoulders as he wrapped her bare legs around his lean waist. She saw the raw passion in his dark eyes as he carried her to his room.

The overhead lights blazed in the master bedroom. She only caught a glimpse of the stark and modern decor before he tossed her onto his bed. The mattress was wide and low to the ground. She barely noticed the cool white sheets against her back before he tumbled on top of her. He reached for her hands, lacing his fingers with hers, and stretched her arms above her head.

She twisted underneath him. "You're going to regret this," she warned.

"You are to blame," he decided as he burrowed his face against her neck.

She stiffened. "Me?"

He let go of her hands and palmed her breasts. His touch was urgent and demanding. "You can't tolerate the idea of being invisible," he muttered as if he were in a trance.

She arched her spine as his hands rubbed her sensitive nipples. "Shut up." She shouldn't have made that confession to him.

"You used to wear the most provocative clothes at home." His voice thickened and his words began to slur as he slid his hands against her rib cage. "The boldest colors. Anything that would capture my attention. My imagination."

Her face burned hot. It was true. Had she been that obvious years ago? And she had fallen in the same pattern tonight without recognizing it. Jodie shouldn't have taunted him but she wanted him to notice her. Claim her. She had always needed to be the center of his attention. To be the most important person in his life.

But she couldn't be. She was everything he didn't want in a woman. In a wife.

"You had me in agony for years," he confessed as he shoved the hem of her slip above her hips. "When you walked into a room, I had to leave."

Her hands clenched the pillow beneath her head. What was he saying? She couldn't concentrate when he stared at her with such intensity.

He bunched the silk in his hands and revealed her abdomen. He bent down and pressed his mouth against her clenching stomach. His warm breath wafted over her skin and she shivered. "If we were at the dinner table, I had to sit where I couldn't see you."

Her chest rose and fell as he tore the slip off her body. She was splayed out before him. His for the taking. She writhed under his touch, the anticipation overwhelming.

"I found no reprieve," he continued as he took her breast into his mouth.

Jodie tossed her head from side to side as he teased her unmercifully with his tongue. Just when she didn't think she could take it anymore, Stergios bit down on her tight nipple. She cried out as the fiery sensations scorched through her veins.

"You were everywhere," he whispered before he laved his tongue against her tender flesh. "In my home, in my dreams."

He reached for her other breast and pinched her nipple. Jodie arched her spine, her feet digging into the mattress, as he took her to the edge of pleasure and pain.

"But I couldn't have you. I wouldn't allow it. I knew I wouldn't be gentle or careful if I touched you." He paused. "I was right."

"I don't want you to be gentle," she insisted in a gasp. She wanted him to be reckless. She didn't want Stergios to hide any part of himself.

Savage need stretched his golden skin against his sharp cheekbones. "Good," he said in a growl. "Because I can't. Not with you."

Stergios rose from the bed and yanked off his shirt. She sat up and reached for him. She wasn't going to be gentle, either. Jodie pressed her mouth against his V-cut abs and licked his heated skin. She smiled, the sense of power hurtling through her, as his muscles bunched under her touch.

She grasped the zipper of his jeans and dragged the rest of his clothes down his powerful thighs. He looked like a pagan god, his jaw clenched, eyes glittering with lust, as he speared his hands in her hair.

Staring at the glorious male body in front of her, she reverently encircled her fingers against his throbbing erection. He was hot and powerful under her touch. Jodie licked the tip and hummed with appreciation before she covered him with her lips.

She tasted him with a building hunger and he encouraged her in a husky, strained voice. Jodie heard him mumble something about her red lips as she pleasured him. When she drew him deep inside her mouth, Stergios's ragged breath echoed in the bedroom. She gripped him hard when he swelled against her tongue.

Stergios grasped her jaw and stopped her before carefully pulling away. Panic filled her chest. Why was he stopping? Why did he have to come to his senses when she was aching for him? "Wait," she pleaded.

"I can't," he said in a low, driven tone. Stergios grabbed for her and turned her over. Jodie blinked, startled. She was on her hands and knees facing away from him. He slid his finger along the wet folds of her sex. Pleasure rippled through her.

He grabbed her hips, his fingers digging into her skin, and mounted her. Jodie closed her eyes as the low, guttural moan ripped from her throat. She clawed the sheets, heat blooming her skin, as he gave a deep thrust.

Jodie rolled her hips as he stretched and filled her. Stergios withdrew only to thrust harder. She urged him on and he exceeded her most brazen demands. She met his demonic pace as the bed shook beneath them.

Stergios slid his hand beneath her and found her slick clitoris. Jodie surrendered to his touch. Her mind shut down as her climax hit. Her cries of ecstasy echoed in the room as wave after wave of white-hot pleasure swept through her.

Her flesh gripped Stergios and his thrusts grew unpredictable. Unbridled. He banded his arms around her and held her close as he surged deep inside. His chest, slick with sweat, pressed against her spine as he burrowed his face into the crook of her neck.

"Jodie!" he said in a roar as he found his release.

Her knees buckled from the force and she collapsed onto the mattress. Her arms and legs shook as she fell onto her pillow. Jodie's heart felt as if it was going to burst through her skin as she took in big swallows of air.

Every muscle pulsed and twitched. Stergios rolled to his side and silently gathered her in his arms. Jodie weakly closed her eyes as he held her close. She needed his touch but she didn't want to him to see how much the simple gesture affected her.

As she rested her head against his chest, listening to Stergios's thudding heartbeat, she tried to tell herself that this didn't mean anything. It was a moment of madness, never to be repeated.

But she couldn't lie to herself. Tonight meant *everything* to her.

Jodie stood by the bay of windows and looked out onto the beach. It was a cloudy and gray morning. There should be nothing that stood in the way of her getting off this island.

She saw her reflection in the window. Her hot-pink dress was prim with its rounded collar and short sleeves. Her black handbag hung from her forearm as she clasped her hands in front of her. The proper image was a far cry from the carnal woman last night.

Jodie felt her skin go hot as the memories overwhelmed her. She had reached for Stergios during the night and demonstrated exactly how she felt. There had been no limits to her desire. It was as if she had been parched for years and had finally found water to slake her thirst.

But when she had woken in the morning, she had been alone in her bedroom. Tucked into her bed and her torn slip carefully folded on the chair next to her. At some time around dawn Stergios had carried her into her room, as if sharing a bed for the whole night had been too intimate for him.

After she had showered and dressed, she had searched the small house and discovered Stergios was gone. His absence had been like a fist in the stomach. It was just like the last time. He had recognized how far he had fallen and couldn't get away fast enough. Only this time he wasn't able to go very far.

Jodie flinched when she heard his footsteps outside but schooled her features into a cool expression when the front door swung open. She exhaled slowly, bracing herself before she turned around to greet him.

Her heart skipped a beat when she saw him dressed in a casual white tunic and a faded pair of jeans. His hair was tangled and windswept and the stubble on his angular jaw seemed darker. She longed to walk up to him and curl against his chest. Her thought vanished when her gaze clashed with his wintry eyes. The generous lover who had kissed her breathless last night had been replaced with the cold and ruthless man.

"The helicopter will be here in ten minutes," he informed her as he set down the satellite phone. "The pilot has been instructed to take you to Athens."

"Thank you." She gestured at the suitcase by the door. "I'm packed and ready."

The silence stretched between them. Stergios started to

pace the room but kept his distance from her. He couldn't have made it more obvious that he wished she were already gone.

As she watched him prowl the room, Jodie knew she should feel some sense of feminine pride. She could make the great Stergios Antoniou fall to his knees. But she didn't feel victorious. Stergios didn't like her. He wished he didn't want her. He couldn't stand being next to her.

"Are you okay?" she blurted out. "Last night after the power outage…" He cast a scathing look and she stumbled into silence. It was a mistake to mention his moment of vulnerability.

"I'm fine," he said tersely. "And you?"

She gave an abrupt nod. She didn't trust herself to speak.

"You can't be," he decided, his voice a rasp. "I can see the whisker burns on your skin from here.

There were faint scratches all over her body. He had marked her in more ways than one. "And I see a love bite on your neck."

He raked his hands through his long hair. "That's different."

No, it wasn't. Jodie turned her attention back to the beach before she started an argument. He had encouraged her to explore his body in the middle of the night. Nothing she did or said had shocked him. But did he find her desire for him unseemly in the light of day? Should her lust not match his?

She guessed she was supposed to be innocent, passive and fragile. Right now she felt fragile. She felt as if she was going to burst into tears.

Stergios took a few ground-eating strides to reach her. "Give me your cell phone," he said as he stretched out his hand.

She automatically took a step back. "I don't think so," she said as she held her purse close to her body.

His eyebrows rose in surprise and her fingers tightened on the leather. Did Stergios expect unquestioning obedience after she had yielded completely to him last night? "I want to add my number to your contact list."

Jodie stared at him. "Why?"

His lips compressed into a line. "I will need to know if there were any consequences from last night."

"There won't be."

"How can you be so sure? Are you on the pill?"

"Well, no…" There had been no reason for her to have a prescription.

His shoulders hunched as the harsh lines of his face deepened. It looked as if he had the world on his shoulders. Had he felt this way four years ago when they first had made love?

She raised her hands as if she could soothe his troubled thoughts. "You have nothing to worry about."

"You're wrong." There was a bite of anger in his voice. "If you get pregnant, everything I have worked for all these years will disappear."

Jodie went still. It hurt that she was a distraction, a hindrance to his dreams, but how would her presence in his life ruin everything? "What are you talking about?"

"Do you know the fight I would have on my hands if I had a baby out of wedlock? A love child with my stepsister?" His face was ashen. "The board of directors would crucify me. The scandal would damage the Antoniou Group. I would be forced to marry you and I can't let that happen. When I marry, it will be to strengthen my family's power base, not because of a mistake."

Jodie bent her head and stared at the ground. He sought for extraordinary power so no one could harm him and he would use marriage to get it. Jodie wanted him to feel safe even if it meant he had to stay away from her. Peace was the one thing she couldn't give him. She never could.

There was one thing she could do for him. She could leave and never come back. Sever all connections. Jodie winced as she imagined the hole it would leave in her heart. But she had to let go of Stergios so he could find what he needed.

What they both needed, she amended. Because he would marry for power and she would marry for love. Whatever this was that they shared wouldn't last. She wouldn't waste his time or hers anymore.

"I expect you to call me whether or not you're pregnant." His hands were bunched at his sides. "If you don't I will hunt you down and get my answer."

It would be a repeat of what happened last time. Only this time she would know that he was pursuing her. And she'd let him catch her. And if he found her again, they would fall back into bed and the cycle would continue. Jodie twisted her lips. He would be drawn to her and hate the power she had over him. It wouldn't stop him unless he thought she had fallen into bed with another man.

Another man. Jodie lifted her head. What if she said another man had a claim on her? Her pulse started to race. *No, no, no.* She couldn't do it. It would be too painful. The ultimate betrayal in Stergios's eyes. She immediately discarded the idea. If she told that lie, Stergios would cut her out of his life for good.

Which was what she wanted, didn't she? She had to end this relationship before it became an unhealthy obsession that changed the course of their lives. But if she did this, there was no turning back. Stergios would never forgive her.

Which was why she had to go through with it. It was the only way. Her mouth was dry and she nervously licked her lips. "Like I said, you don't have anything to worry about," she said in a whisper. She wasn't sure if she could do this.

He gave an impatient sigh. "How would you know?"

Her heart pumped hard and her stomach twisted. The room tilted and she fought back the nausea. She could do this. All she had to do was lie and make a clean get-away. Just a few words and she could end this madness.

"Jodie?"

She struggled to meet his curious gaze. "Because I'm already pregnant." She forced out the next words as she spread her hands against her stomach. "With another man's child."

CHAPTER EIGHT

"THEN...*KATALAVÉNO*? I don't understand." His mind lagged behind but the pain had been sharp and swift. There was another man in Jodie's life. And she... Stergios refused to believe it. "What did you say?"

"I'm—" her voice hitched "—already pregnant."

Pregnant. She was with child. *Another man's child.* The bitterness cut through him like acid. He studied her slim figure in the hot-pink dress. *"Oxi,"* he said in a whisper. "I don't believe you."

She lifted her chin. "Why would I lie about something like this?"

Stergios couldn't move. He felt as if he'd been hacked down from where he stood. Pregnant. She couldn't be pregnant. No, Jodie was *his.*

A chill settled into his bones. Stergios remembered feeling like this before. The numbness held back the searing pain so he could cope. Survive. The coldness would be temporary and then the ferocious rage would take over. "Who's the father?"

She appeared surprised by the question. "That is none of your business."

"Do you know?" His voice was flat.

She jerked back as if she'd been slapped. "I'm going to ignore that."

"Do. You. Know?" He bared his teeth as he enunciated the words.

She pressed her lips together and crossed her arms.

"You don't know," he said in a stunned breath. How could she do this? Stergios thought he knew Jodie. "Was he a stranger? Or were there a few other candidates at that time?"

She glared at him before she turned away. "I'm so glad I shared this news with you."

Other pieces of the puzzle started to fall into place. The anger and despair swirled and clashed inside him. "This is why you no longer drink," he said in a low voice as he struggled to control his emotions. "And why you suddenly have this interest in family."

She gave a start as if she couldn't believe he had put the pieces together. "It isn't sudden," she said over her shoulder.

Stergios bunched his hands in his hair as his heart thudded against his ribs. "I couldn't understand why you wanted to reconcile with your father," he said as he searched his memory for other signs. "I thought it was for revenge. I couldn't figure it out. I didn't think…"

She refused to look at him. She should be ashamed, he decided. This woman was his. He knew Jodie made no promises to him but this felt like a betrayal. Stergios didn't think she could have hurt him like this. He couldn't forgive her actions.

He dragged his hands down to his sides. "You bitch."

Her spine stiffened but she didn't turn around. "I'm going to wait at the helipad," she announced as she marched to the door.

Stergios watched her. How could she be hard and emotionless now when she had been open and loving last night? "What did your father say?"

Jodie slid to a stop and whirled around. "He doesn't know. No one knows." She pointed at Stergios. "Do not say a word to him."

"Why not?" Why would she hide something like this from Gregory? Would her father disapprove of the man?

"Because…" Jodie spluttered as pink tinged her cheeks. The unfeeling woman was suddenly flustered. "Because it's…customary to wait until the first trimester before you make the announcement."

Something wasn't right. He didn't know if he should trust his instincts but he didn't believe her explanation. "How far along are you?"

She grabbed her suitcase and concentrated on raising the handle. "Not far."

"But you knew you were pregnant. You knew and you spread your legs for me," he said with disgust. "You let me…"

"Stop it, Stergios."

He wasn't going to listen to Jodie's pleas. She had lost that right. The destructive anger flashed inside him before he tamped it down. "If you weren't pregnant, I would…"

"Would what?" she asked, tilting her head as she watched the tremors sweep his body. "No need to hold back, Stergios. What would you do?"

He wasn't sure how he'd respond and that scared him. He would hunt down the mysterious father and destroy him. He would pray that the baby wouldn't inherit Jodie's treachery and manipulation. And Jodie? He would cast her out of his life for good.

Starting now. Stergios ruthlessly controlled the pain threatening to erupt, knowing he had to be emotionless if he was going to retaliate. "I'm grateful that you're pregnant."

Jodie took one step back and watched him as if he was a predatory animal who was ready to go in for the kill. "What do you mean?"

"Because that means you will never have my baby,"

he explained in a disquieting tone. "I'm grateful that my child wouldn't have you for a mother. A whore, a liar and an outcast."

She paled. "Yes, it's a very good thing that you are not the father."

She wasn't fighting back. Stergios wanted her to. He didn't want to see her eyes glistening with unshed tears. He needed answers. "The mother of my child would be—"

"Pure?" she offered. "Compliant?"

"My children deserve a good mother," he said as his gaze raked over her. "A woman they could respect and trust. A woman who could make them proud."

Her eyes darkened but she kept her mouth firmly shut. "Goodbye, Stergios," she finally said and she reached for the door.

"Who's the father?" he said in a roar.

Her shoulders slumped for a moment. And then, as if she had made a decision, she grabbed the doorknob as if it was a lifeline. "The only thing you need to know is that it's not you."

He was suddenly behind her and flattened his hand against the door so she couldn't open it. He wanted her gone and yet he wanted to dole out her punishment. His world was crashing down around him and the woman who destroyed it was walking away without a backward glance.

Jodie kept her head bent. "I hear the helicopter. Please let me leave."

"What do you plan to do? Are you keeping the baby?"

She glanced up at him, horrified. "What are you recommending I do?" Her voice was unsettling and he lowered his hand. "Why wouldn't I keep the baby? Because it's an inconvenience for you? Because it isn't *yours*?"

Did she think he was that kind of monster? His stomach twisted with dread. Jodie had seen him at his worst and this is what she thought of him?

"The sight of you sickens me. Get out," he said in a threatening growl. "Get out of my house and out of my sight. Get the hell out of my life."

"I will, Stergios. As fast as I can."

Jodie leaned back in her chair and looked outside the window of her apartment. She had always enjoyed New York City in the autumn but lately she had struggled to see the beauty. There was a crisp bite to the late October weather and the leaves were turning crimson and gold, but all she wanted to do was hibernate.

"The apartment is just as I remembered."

She turned her attention to her father. He sat across from her at the small table as if he had all the time in the world. *This wasn't happening*, she thought in a daze but his fading blond hair gleamed under the chandelier. She watched numbly as he reached for a scone from the tiered cake stand.

Why was he here? What did he want? She thought cynically. She hadn't been able to hide her astonishment when he had called her in the morning and wanted to drop by.

"You haven't changed a thing from when your mother lived here," he remarked.

"No, I'm not ready to handle that big of a project," Jodie murmured. She had inherited the penthouse apartment months ago but she didn't feel settled. This wasn't home. Growing up, she had always used it as a layover.

"You look pale," Gregory Little said as he took a sip of his tea. "Have you been ill?"

No, she was heartbroken but she didn't dare tell that her father. The man liked to gossip and she didn't want it getting back to Stergios. No one needed to know that she had difficulty eating and sleeping. She couldn't focus. Some days it felt as if time went too fast and other days it dragged on.

It was painful loving someone who didn't love her back. The burden weighed heavily on her like a cloak. She had felt unloved and unwanted many times in her life. She thought she was used to it, but Stergios's disgust and hatred had knocked her back.

"I've been tired since returning from Greece," she admitted as she reached for her teacup. "There were some people sick on the plane. I'm probably fighting off something like a cold."

"That's why you should have your own plane."

She gave a wry smile at his response. Gregory Little had become accustomed to the Antoniou way of life. He would do anything to protect his standard of living.

"Or were you concerned after the helicopter's mechanical problem?" he asked. "That was a rare occurrence. I can't recall it happening before."

Mechanical problem? Jodie frowned until she remembered the lie about why she had missed the wedding. "It does make me hesitate," she said smoothly. "So, have Dimos and Zoi returned from their honeymoon?"

"Yes, Dimos is now vice president but it will be a long adjustment period for him," he predicted. "He doesn't have the stamina to carry the same workload as Stergios."

Jodie flinched when she heard Stergios's name. She clearly remembered the raw fury in his eyes when she had left. That man hated her. She kept trying to tell herself that it was for the best.

"And… Stergios?" She tried to sound casual but she craved for any news or information about him. "How is he?"

Gregory frowned as he took a sip of his tea. "Mairi is worried about him. He has always been a workaholic but it's gotten much worse. But, then, he is finalizing the Antoniou-Volakis merger. I'm sure he will take some time off once that is done."

Stergios had dived right into his work after she'd left. The knowledge wounded her. It was as if their weekend had been a blip in his calendar. He had gone on with his life as if nothing had happened.

"I probably shouldn't tell you since it hasn't been announced," Gregory said as he lowered his voice, "but he's going to get engaged."

Jodie felt her skin go cold as her stomach heaved. Her cup clattered against her saucer. *Engaged.* The word echoed in her mind. Stergios was getting engaged.

"Sorry," she said weakly as she carefully let go of her cup before she broke the delicate handle between her fingers. "That just caught me by surprise. Stergios doesn't strike me as someone who is ready to settle down."

He had met someone special... He belonged to another... He was going to make this woman his wife... A bitter taste filled her mouth and she swallowed roughly.

"He's been playing with the idea of an Antoniou-Diamantopoulos merger for the past year," Gregory Little continued, oblivious to her unnatural stillness.

"Diamantopoulos?" she interrupted.

"Aleka Diamantopoulos," Gregory added. "The shipping heiress."

That didn't narrow it down much for Jodie. She frantically searched her memory until she remembered the quiet woman who played the piano with precision but no passion. Jealousy coiled around her heart and squeezed so hard that she wanted to double over.

"I think I remember her," she murmured. Aleka was sweet and obedient. Young and virginal. Just Stergios's type, she decided uncharitably. "Lovely girl."

"And the alliance between families will make the Antonious very powerful."

"That's...wonderful." Jodie smiled wanly. She folded her hands on her lap as the sense of loss swept through her. Perhaps all of those finishing schools had finally served their purpose. No one would be able to tell that she felt breakable. As if she was going to splinter into a million pieces and she would never be whole again.

Stergios was getting everything he wanted. She should be pleased with the turn of events. He was gaining the power and the security to protect his family. Soon he would find the peace he craved. It was everything she couldn't give him.

She stared at her manicured hands as her mind spun. She had done the right thing when she cut off all connection with Stergios. She had regretted lying to him about being pregnant. So many times she had been tempted to call him and tell him the truth.

But the cycle, the obsession, would have continued. She would have wasted a lifetime wanting to be with a man who didn't think she was worthy of him.

"Jodie?" Her father's voice pierced through her troubled thoughts. "What do you think?"

She jerked her head up and saw Gregory's look of expectation. "I'm sorry?"

Annoyance flickered in her father's blue eyes. "I'm inviting you to come to Greece for Christmas."

Jodie froze as the words replayed in her head. "Why?" she blurted. She gasped with horror and tried again. "I mean—"

He gave an understanding nod. "I shouldn't have allowed this much time to pass between us. I want to make a fresh start. What better time than Christmas?"

"But when I showed up in Athens earlier..." Her voice trailed off. What had changed? Why did he come to this conclusion now when he didn't make any overtures when she last saw him?

"I avoided you." Gregory bent his head and nervously crumbled the scone between his fingers. "You suddenly appeared and we thought you were planning to cause trouble. We should have recognized that you were still grieving the loss of your mother and needed to be around family."

"We?" she asked dully. She should have known her stepmother had a say in this.

"You know, Mairi and me," he explained. "And Stergios."

"Stergios?" She stiffened her spine. She couldn't imagine how he had poisoned her father's opinion of her. "What does he have to do about this?"

"He recommended I drop by and check on you once I finished my trip in Toronto." Gregory Little shrugged. "He acted as if it was urgent but you seem fine."

She didn't understand. How would that punish her? Jodie's head ached as she tried to understand his strategy. Did he think her father would drop by and notice her pregnant belly? Why would he care? Why did he bother? Jodie knew she was dead to him.

"Do you already have plans for Christmas?" her father asked.

"Some invitations have already trickled in but I haven't made any commitments." None of the traditional gatherings had interested her. But the promise of spending the holidays with family? It was something she had yearned for over the past few years and it was too good to pass up. "Who all will be there?"

"All of the family and a few close friends. Shall I expect you?"

Jodie bit her lip, her heart pounding against her chest, as she considered her options. She was afraid to accept.

If she said yes, it meant she would have to see Stergios. But if she said no, she knew her father would not extend this kind of invitation again.

"I would love to, Dad," she said with a smile. "I can't wait."

CHAPTER NINE

Jodie clenched the banister and slowly descended the grand staircase of the Antoniou estate. Holiday decorations swathed the limestone walls and the tallest, fattest Christmas tree sat in the center of the entrance hall. She heard a harp being played in the music room and watched the other guests stand around and chat as they drank the finest champagne.

Her silver dress sparkled under the chandeliers but she wasn't in a festive mood. She pressed her lips as she searched the well-dressed crowd. Her heart stopped and she jolted with surprise when she saw Stergios.

His dark hair was shorn and ruthlessly tamed, emphasizing the sleek shape of his head. Stergios's angular jaw was clean-shaven and his dark suit fitted his sleek, athletic body. He had tamed the wildness within. He was a commanding presence, a man who ruled all he could see.

When his lips tilted in a tender smile, Jodie stared at the transformation on his face. He looked younger. Happy. It took her a moment to realize that look was for the woman next to him. Aleka Diamantopoulos. Jodie's stomach heaved; she watched as the young woman shyly blossomed under Stergios's attention.

He had never smiled like that. Not at her. She hadn't made him that happy or content. Jodie wanted to look away but she couldn't. She took in a reedy breath as her body tensed with jealousy. What was so special about Aleka?

Jodie didn't see an engagement ring on the shipping heiress's finger but she knew it was only a matter of time. She looked away as the dull, aching pain coiled her chest. A giant solitaire representing Stergios's wealth, status and power was probably gift wrapped and tucked in his jacket.

She knew she should have canceled this trip but she didn't want to. She couldn't. Not only would it make it unlikely that she'd get another invitation, but there was something she had to do in person.

She glanced in Stergios's direction again and saw him staring at her. His smile disappeared and she shrank back from his contemptuous gaze. Jodie turned abruptly and regretted it. She squeezed her eyes shut and fought for balance. She knew better than to make sharp turns. Or wear stiletto heels.

Or visit Athens, she thought. The doctor had given her permission to travel, but it was courting disaster. But she had to see Stergios one last time.

Because she was carrying his baby.

Panic fluttered in her veins and she splayed her hand against her stomach. Six weeks ago she had discovered she was pregnant. At first she'd been thrilled and shared the news with her closest friends. But she had been reluctant to inform Stergios.

How could she tell him? She had made such a mess of things. Jodie bowed her head as the tears pricked her eyes. She had lied to Stergios and made claims so he would stay away. Her decisions had turned out to be for the best. Stergios was getting the life he wanted and the wife he needed. An unexpected pregnancy would change all of that.

"Damn, Jodie," Dimos said as he walked by her and stopped. "You look like hell."

"How sweet of you to notice." Her tone was acidic but she knew he spoke the truth. It had been another reason why she had been reluctant to show up at the Antoniou home for Christmas. She didn't want to be remembered like this with her pallor, limp hair and constant tiredness. She had her pride and she wanted Stergios to eat his heart out. Now he was probably thinking he got a clean getaway.

Jodie forced her attention on Dimos and noticed he wasn't looking his best, as well. He looked older with his puffy face and bloodshot eyes. "I understand you've been working around the clock." Concern threaded in her voice. "Doesn't Stergios know you're a newlywed?"

"Let me give you a piece of advice." Dimos swilled his drink. "Consider all of your options before you get married."

Understanding dawned on her. Dimos was staying late at the office so he could avoid going home. "No need to give me advice. I will never marry."

Dimos snorted. "That's what they all say."

"No, seriously. I have no reason to do so. There is no family or financial pressure."

"Lucky you," he said bitterly as he darted a glance in the direction of his wife on the other side of the room. "What about love that you used to spout on about? You had a strong romantic streak in your teen years."

"No, that streak is long gone," she said in a whisper. She used to think she would only marry for love but she had an idealized version of it. Now she knew that love didn't bring her joy or happiness. It didn't fulfil her or give her a sense of purpose. Love brought her confusion and pain. She had the ability to love but she was incapable of being loved. Marriage or a committed relationship was not in her future.

"What guy changed your mind? You'd always talked about having a family."

"It doesn't mean I have to marry or stay with one man." It was what she wanted, but she had to be realistic. Once she had imagined having a loving husband and many children but she needed to modify her definition of family.

Dimos's eyes gleamed with interest. "That's true, monogamy is an outdated and unnatural idea."

Jodie raised her hand. "No, that—"

"Let's hope Zoi doesn't hear you," Stergios said next to Jodie.

Jodie stiffened and her skin tingled at the sound of his husky voice. She wasn't prepared to see Stergios. To be this close without touching him. She tried to remain calm but the agony of what she had lost roiled through her stomach.

Dimos's face turned a deep red. For a moment Jodie thought he was going to launch into a tirade. Instead he closed his mouth with a snap and marched away.

"Do you look for trouble or does it come naturally?" Stergios asked Jodie.

"I didn't say anything about cheating or having affairs."

Stergios looked at his cousin over his shoulder. "Then how did Dimos get that into his head?"

"I have no idea how his mind works."

"Sure you do. He always thinks about sex when you're around." His mouth twisted in displeasure as he noticed how the silver dress hugged her burgeoning curves. "And you were seeing if you still have the sexual allure over him."

"No!"

Stergios's gaze dropped to her stomach. "Have you told him that you're pregnant?"

Her heart stopped and she felt so light-headed she thought she was going to collapse onto the floor. She gave a ragged breath when she remembered that Stergios didn't know the whole truth.

"Probably not," he said with a sneer. "That would change everything. He would run in the other direction and you would have no power over him."

"Don't compare his reaction with yours." She had to tell him about the baby, but how? Where did she start? He wasn't going to believe her and she wasn't up for a battle.

Stergios crossed his arms and studied her. "Why am I the only person you've told?"

She gave an awkward shrug, not sure how to answer that. It did look strange that she had confided in him. "You should be honored."

"You haven't told Gregory and you're past the first trimester."

She gave him a sharp look. "Is that why you manipulated my father into visiting me? So he would see that I was pregnant?"

"Oxi." Surprise flickered in his dark eyes. "No, *pethi mou*," he said quietly. "I had him visit you because you shouldn't be alone at this time in your life."

She blinked, dumbfounded, her lips parting as she watched Stergios walk away. Jodie clasped her hands in front of her as she felt the tears burn behind her eyes. She didn't know why she was getting emotional. She was used to being alone in the world. She just wasn't used to someone noticing her predicament. Or caring. Or reaching out. She had immediately slapped him away, thinking it was a trick.

She was tempted to follow Stergios and apologize. Her heartbeat pounded in her ears. She should tell him everything now before she lost her courage.

Jodie suddenly felt hot stinging needles prick her skin as perspiration blanketed her. She clapped her hand over her mouth, knowing she was going to be sick.

Her bedroom was too far away. Jodie briskly walked to the door that led to the portico. She stepped outside and welcomed the coldness against her skin. Leaning against the heavy stone column, she took in big gulps of the night air.

Her legs felt shaky as she took the steps down to the terrace. She needed to compose herself before she went back inside. No one was going to notice if she was absent. For once, being invisible had its benefits.

The party had drifted into the music room. Stergios searched the crowd that had already broken into the usual groups and cliques. The older generation was on one side of the room while the younger relatives were sitting together and checking their phones.

Servants in black jackets and white gloves were serving champagne and dessert on silver platters. He noticed Aleka was at the grand piano playing traditional Christmas carols. Jodie was nowhere to be found.

Stergios tapped Gregory on the shoulder. "Have you seen Jodie?"

"Hmm? Jodie?" Gregory lifted his head and looked around the room as if he was just now noticing his daughter's absence. "She's somewhere around here. Probably playing billiards," he said, preoccupied, as he motioned for one of the waiters.

"*Oxi*, she's not." He had already checked the billiards room. "I saw her step outside but she hasn't come back."

"She's fine," Gregory studied the desserts on the silver tray the waiter presented. The scent of oranges, cinnamon and cloves wafted in the air. "She's probably walking around the garden. She does that a lot."

Stergios had always thought the man was a lazy father but hadn't Gregory noticed the changes in his daughter? Didn't he care? She was pale, quiet, and the shadows under her eyes suggested she wasn't sleeping. Jodie was trying to hide the symptoms of her pregnancy and Stergios didn't know why she bothered making the attempt.

"It's been twenty minutes since she stepped outside," he said as he checked his watch.

"There's nothing to worry about," Gregory said as he chose a *melomakarona* cookie that always made Stergios think of Christmas. "We have the best security system on the grounds. If she's fallen and hurt herself, she can push one of the security buttons."

Hurt. His chest tightened with dread. Jodie could be hurt and in pain.

Stergios ran out of the room and into the entrance hall. He scanned the area and saw that Jodie still wasn't there. He stepped outside and onto the portico. The cold air slapped at his skin as the darkness enveloped him. Stergios hesitated, his breath caught in his throat, as he pushed away the memories of the pitch-black wilderness.

There were no Christmas lights on the grounds and the moon was hidden behind clouds. Taking the steps two at a time, Stergios stood on the terrace that was streaked with the weak light from the arched windows. He looked around the side garden and didn't see the glimmer of her silver dress.

"Jodie?" he called, his voice echoing in the cold air, but she didn't reply.

Stergios launched down the gravel path, the roar of his blood loud in his ears. He didn't care if there were security cameras and emergency buttons. He knew what the darkness held. He was aware of how a quiet night could turn dangerous.

He surged unseeingly down the path, driven by the memory of being hunted as a little boy and the terror that had overwhelmed him. Stergios flinched when his broad shoulders caught on a branch. He paused and took a deep breath before he continued. Relief and anger swirled inside him when he saw a faint gleam of silver.

Jodie was slumped on the ground, her arms and head resting on a stone bench. She weakly lifted her head when she heard him approach. "Stergios?" she said in a croak.

"You fool," he muttered as he pulled off his jacket in clumsy, urgent moves. His hands were rougher than he intended when he draped it around her shoulders. "What were you thinking?"

"I was sick and wanted to be alone." She gasped when he lifted her into his arms. "Why did you come looking for me?"

"What kind of question is that?" he asked tautly.

"You can't stand the sight of me," she said as she huddled into his warm suit jacket. "I've caused you nothing but trouble."

"Don't remind me." The memories of the wilderness were beginning to swarm and he needed to get back to the house before he couldn't fight them back anymore.

"You searched for me." She reached up and cupped her hand against his cheek. "In the dark?"

"I'm not afraid of the dark," he said in a withering tone as he kept his gaze forward. "I have already explained it."

"You're afraid of what the dark will trigger inside you," she said and dropped her hand before she rested her head against his shoulder. "What I will do to you."

"You don't have that power over me anymore," he said as he held her close. "You killed it the moment you slept with me when you were carrying another man's child."

Jodie gave a long sigh. "Good."

"This is an excessive use of caution, Stergios." Jodie lay back in her hospital bed and looked around the deluxe private suite. "All of the doctors agreed that I was dehydrated from traveling and that's why I got light-headed. Staying overnight for observation is unnecessary."

"You will be discharged when the doctors say it's safe."

No, when you decide it's safe, Jodie silently corrected. Everyone from the patient transporter to the Chief of Medicine had bowed down to Stergios's wishes. She suspected he was a major donor for the hospital. When he had demanded the best room for her, she had not expected this kind of medical care.

Her suite reminded her of a five-star hotel, only this stay would include a private nurse and an in-house chef. When she had been wheeled into the room with Stergios at her side, she had been surprised by the luxurious touches. The room decor was a mix of dark natural wood and a soft green color palette. The bathroom was spacious and the sitting area had sofas, chairs and a kitchenette.

She didn't need this, so why was it important that she was given the VIP treatment? Jodie watched Stergios from beneath her lashes. He was no longer acting like a chieftain on the warpath yet he was on guard for any threat or problems. The color had been restored in his high cheekbones but he still maintained a stony expression.

Stergios wanted her out of his life, so why was he acting like this? He didn't know that she was pregnant with his baby. And why did he insist that he stay with her?

"You should go home," she said gently. There was no way she would sleep if he were here. "I appreciate what you've done but you don't need to watch over me."

He gave her a curt glance. "I've already honored your request and didn't sit in during the physical exam. I am not making any more compromises."

Compromise? The man didn't understand the meaning of the word. It had been a battle getting him to leave her so she could be examined. "I'm allowed some privacy!"

"Privacy?" he repeated incredulously. "I am intimately acquainted with your body. You have nothing to hide from me." He braced his hands against the side of her bed and leaned forward. "Although you are acting suspicious."

Jodie gave him a startled look.

"What's going on?" he asked. He raked his eyes over her. "What did the doctors say? Why are you not taking care of yourself?"

Jodie bristled under his tone. "Don't talk to me like that. I am not neglecting my responsibilities. I am doing everything in my power to have a healthy pregnancy." She was using all of her time, energy and resources to give this child a promising start.

"Calm down, *pethi mou*." He stroked his knuckle against her jaw. "I am not accusing you of anything."

"Your job is done," she said firmly as she jerked her head away, "and you can go home and sleep."

"I will decide when I'm done looking after you."

She saw the determined glint in his dark eyes. "That tone might intimidate your employees, but it just makes me angrier," she informed him in a cool tone. "You are pushing your luck. I will call security and have you removed from this room if necessary."

He arched an eyebrow. "Why are you so uncomfortable having me here?"

"I'm not used to it," she admitted as she nervously plucked the fine linen. She had always wanted someone to care and to worry about her. She needed someone to wonder where she was and if she was okay. But now that she had it, even temporarily, she was afraid that she was going to do something to ruin it.

"You're overwrought and tired. It's time you get some sleep," Stergios ordered as he glanced at his watch. "I'm going to speak to the nurse before I leave."

"Again?" She wearily closed her eyes. "Don't scare her off."

"If she's easily scared, it's best if I know now and have a different nurse assigned to you," he said as he left the room.

Jodie sighed with relief and carefully rolled to her side so she didn't pull at the intravenous tubes. Stergios had been acting strangely overprotective since they'd arrived at the emergency room. Ordinarily she would have hated how he'd taken charge and made demands, but at the time she felt too weak to do it herself. She idly wondered how he'd act if he knew this was his baby.

She needed to tell him the truth but she was unwilling to face the aftermath. He was going to be furious. This child was going to create chaos in his orderly world.

What demands would he make? That she didn't have the baby? That she put it up for adoption? If he tried to coerce her into giving up her baby, he would discover an epic fight on his hands. The best-case scenario was that Stergios would deny the baby's existence and keep it a secret from his family.

Jodie frowned when she heard Stergios's steady footsteps pounding against the corridor floor. She slowly turned onto her back and stared at the open door. It sounded as if he was getting closer.

He knows. Her stomach twisted and she suddenly felt queasy. *He knows about the baby.* She had waited too long to tell him.

Suddenly he was there, clenching the door frame with his hands. She forgot to breathe when her gaze connected with his blistering glare.

"You are not in your second trimester?" His voice was quietly sinister. "Your date of conception was in the last week of September?"

He surged forward and she wanted to launch out of

bed. He got there before she could move. Jodie wished she could curl up in a ball and pretend this wasn't happening.

Stergios flattened his palms against the mattress. He invaded her space and she was trapped. Surrounded. Jodie couldn't look away. She flinched when he spoke in a harsh whisper.

"When were you planning to tell me that the baby is mine?"

CHAPTER TEN

HE WAS GOING to be a father. Stergios stared at Jodie as the thud of his heart echoed in his head. His skin felt cold and clammy as his world slowly tilted. Stergios struggled to remain upright as he drew in a shallow breath. He was bringing an innocent child into this cruel and dangerous world.

Jodie lowered her gaze and turned her head to the side. "I was going to tell you."

He doubted it. If the nurse hadn't mentioned the due date, he may never have known. The possibility sent a chill down his spine. Jodie would have kept him from his child.

"When did you find out?" he asked in a snarl.

She swallowed hard and pressed her lips together. When he thought he was going to have to shake the truth out of her, Jodie quietly responded. "Six weeks ago."

He gripped the side of the bed tighter as the white-hot anger spread inside him. *Six weeks.* The woman had plenty of opportunity to give him the news. She knew he wanted to be informed of any consequences of that night. He had demanded that she add his contact information in her phone. But she had distracted him with a lie that had sent him into a tailspin.

Jodie cautiously glanced up at him when he didn't respond. "I was trying to find the right time," she insisted. "The right words."

"Or were you stalling because you were considering other options? Like getting rid of the child and never telling me."

"No! I wouldn't do that!" She wrapped her arms over her stomach. "I wasn't planning to have this baby but I want it."

His eyes narrowed on her protective gesture. Why was she trying to protect the baby from him? The rage flashed through him, burning hot and destructive, and it hurt to breathe. "Why did you tell me you were pregnant in September?"

Jodie's cheeks turned pink and she slowly lifted her hands as if to placate him. "You have to understand."

"Do you think I'm going to show you mercy because you're pregnant?" His low voice shook as he struggled to remain icy calm. "You had planned to keep my baby from me. It's as good as stealing my child."

"No!" Jodie's eyes filled with tears as if she'd been struck.

"You weren't going to tell me." He drew in a shallow breath as the fury billowed inside him. He often expected the worst in people, but he was stunned by Jodie's treachery. "You were going to let me believe another man was the father."

"No, not exactly." She pressed the heels of her hand against her forehead.

"Trying to keep all your lies straight?"

She slapped her hands on the mattress. "I lied to you when I said I was pregnant. I didn't know I was actually going to have a baby."

Stergios leaned forward, his face inches away from hers as he bared his teeth. "Why did you tell me you were pregnant with another man's child?"

"I knew that we had started up something. It was a sexual obsession that could keep us from what we really wanted. I knew if I told that lie you wouldn't forgive me. You could cast me out of your life and both of us could move on."

Stergios pushed away from the bed. It sickened him that Jodie, of all people, knew how he would react. She had used her intimate knowledge of him against him. "All this time I wondered why you singled me out and told me."

"Listen to me, Stergios," she pleaded.

"I don't want to hear any more lies," he said as he turned away.

"Are you and Aleka engaged?"

He froze and his back went straight. No one knew about those plans. What did Jodie know and how was she going to use it against him? "How do you know about that?"

She dismissed his question with the wave of her hand. "My father mentioned that when he visited me in October. Yes or no, Stergios. Are you engaged?"

"*Oxi.* No." They were finalizing the deal and he would formally ask Aleka in the New Year. He dipped his head. Those plans were ruined. His family would not strengthen their power base because he had to marry the mother of his child. "This does not explain why you lied. Why you were hiding my child from me!"

She took a deep breath. "I thought I was doing you a favor."

"A favor?" The rage pressed against his skin, ready to burst free. "Denying me my child is a favor?"

"We're a burden to you." Her voice cracked as if it hurt to say the words out loud. "You are marrying someone else so you can get everything you want in life."

"Not anymore." Having a baby changed everything. "This child is mine and I want him to know his father."

Only Stergios didn't know the first thing about being a father. His pulse raced at the idea that there was a baby relying on him. He had always known that once he had children, he would be nothing like his father. Now the time had come and he was scared that he would be just like Elias Pagonis. They shared the same blood and the same mannerisms. Hell, he even looked like his father.

His stomach churned. "I'm going to be part of this child's life," he said in a low, harsh tone. "I'm giving him the protection of my name and I'm going to guide him through every milestone. Do not assume that I have no interest in becoming a father."

"I know I am the last woman you'd want to carry your child," she retorted.

He clenched his jaw. "That's not true."

"I remember what you said on the island."

He rubbed his hands over his face, regretting those words of anger. *I'm grateful that my child wouldn't have you for a mother. A whore, a liar and an outcast.* At the time he had meant them. He had said those words to wound, to make Jodie suffer with him.

"You are the mother of my child and how I feel about you is irrelevant," he said coldly as he pushed back the memory of the lancing pain her lies had caused. "All that matters is that we get married."

Her mouth twisted with defiance. "No."

Stergios began to pace around the suite. She would come around. Once she realized all he had to offer to her and the child, she would grab at the engagement ring. He would be the one who had much to lose. The marriage to Jodie would cause a scandal. She was his stepsister and a woman who had encouraged a questionable reputation.

The Diamantopoulos family would be furious and humiliated no matter how much diplomacy and tact he used. They had been important friends of the family and would have been good allies. Now they would become powerful enemies.

"You're not listening to me." Jodie's voice filtered into his troubled thoughts.

And he would have a war on his hands with his board of directors. When news of his hasty wedding and unsuitable bride came out, it would reflect poorly on him and the Antoniou Group.

"Stergios!" Her frustrated tone rang in the suite. "We don't need to get married."

He gradually turned around and glared at Jodie. She should be grateful that he was accepting his responsibility. "We do and we will."

"Let me rephrase it." She flattened her hands against her chest. "*I* don't need to get married. I have my money, a place of my own and the ability to give this child every opportunity."

"This is the heir to the Antoniou fortune," he declared as he thrust his hands in the air. "We have to get married."

"No one needs to know, especially if I live in America and—"

He jerked his head back. "You are going to deny me access to my child."

She blinked hard. "No, we can come to an agreement before the baby is born."

"Fight for custody?" His skin went cold. "You know that I was a pawn in a custody battle between my parents. You know what happened to me and to my family. And now you want me to relive it?"

Her eyes widened. "Stergios, that's not what I said."

He had to get out of here before he said or did something he would regret. "I will not beg for a chance to see my child," he said gruffly as he strode to the door.

"You cannot force me into marriage," she called after him.

"For years I have gathered wealth and power to protect my family." He turned around and captured her gaze.

When she paled, he knew his eyes shone with blood-lust. "I have made choices that an honorable gentleman wouldn't just to keep them safe. You will soon discover that I will use every weapon at my disposal to take care of my child."

Jodie stared listlessly out the window while she lay in bed. She paid little attention to the glorious view of Athens. Her head still ached from her restless night. She had wept until she had succumbed to a fitful sleep.

Stergios had every right to be angry with her. To hate her. She had lied to him, held back information and created a mess in his life. She knew he was ruthless enough to take her baby. He didn't play fair and he would cut her out of the baby's life if he thought she was a threat. She didn't have the power to fight him.

Jodie tensed when she felt as though she was being watched. Studied. Analyzed. She cast a covert glance at the door and her muscles locked when she saw Stergios standing at the threshold. Her pulse began to gallop. The man looked formidable in his dark gray suit and red tie. She was not ready for another onslaught.

"I haven't been discharged by the doctor," she told him.

"I want to apologize about last night," he said stiffly as he clasped his hands behind his back. "I had just been informed that I was going to be a father and my emotions got the best of me. I didn't mean to make those threats."

She knew that wasn't true. Stergios had meant every word. In any other circumstance, he would have kept his thoughts to himself. But the idea of becoming a father had paralyzed him. He was scared that he was going to live through his childhood nightmare.

That was why he wanted an obedient wife, Jodie decided as she studied his carefully blank expression. It was also why he pushed himself to inhuman lengths to amass incredible wealth and power. He needed to protect and rely on himself so he didn't have to trust anyone else.

And he had no reason to trust her. She had lied to him, for him, so many times. That ended now. He may never trust her again but he deserved her honesty. "I'm sorry that you found out this way," she said. "I wish I could make it up to you."

"There is something you can do," he said softly as he entered the room.

Alarm sprinted down her spine. She should have known Stergios would play on her guilt and immediately launch into negotiations. "I'm not marrying you because I'm pregnant."

He shook his head and stepped closer to her bed. "I want you to stay in Greece."

His request took her by surprise. Wouldn't he want to hide her away from his colleagues and family? "For how long?"

Stergios gripped the side of her bed, his knuckles white with tension. "I want the baby to be born here. It's very important to me."

She knew that was an understatement and she wondered why he was downplaying it. Stergios was proud of his heritage and would want to share every aspect of it with his child. She wanted her baby to recognize his home and have an unbreakable sense of belonging. To find comfort in traditions and rituals handed down from his father.

But where would that leave her? This wasn't where she belonged. She had constantly been reminded that this was not her home or her family. If she granted Stergios's request, was it the first step to make her an outsider in her baby's life?

"My...my life is in New York." That was where her friends lived. They were her support system.

"I know that I'm asking a lot." His eyes were watchful as though he could read her every thought. "But if you stay here, I can attend the doctor's visits. I can be part of the pregnancy."

An image wavered in front of her. She saw Stergios's hand curved along her pregnant stomach. His touch was possessive and tender and his eyes were wide with wonder. He shared one of those special smiles with her as their baby kicked against his hand.

She blinked hard and the image disappeared. Jodie shifted against her pillow as she tried to ease the jittery feeling. Why had she imagined that? It was pure fantasy. She shouldn't make a decision based on a dream. "You won't have time to be part of it."

"I will make the time," he promised.

Jodie scoffed at that statement. "I've heard all the excuses before. My mother was obsessed with work just like you. Any family commitments were the first to be broken."

He leaned down, holding her gaze with his. "You need to give me a chance," he insisted in a low, urgent tone.

She knew he was right. It was only fair. He might prove to be an excellent father. The man protected his family and demonstrated loyalty, responsibility and care. He would extend that to his child.

But what about her? Was that why she was afraid to give him a chance? She knew she was being selfish but it was a genuine concern. What if she started to rely on him and he failed her? What if he got bored with the idea of being a father after she made room in her life for him?

She had to take the risk. Her heart beat loudly against her chest wall. She had been pushing people away before they had a chance to discard her. She had to give Stergios a chance. She wanted her baby to have a father he could rely on. That had to start now.

"Okay, Stergios. I will stay in Greece. Just until the baby is born," she added.

Her stomach twisted when she saw the triumph gleam in his eyes before he quickly banked it. The man who promised to care for her and for her baby might be her greatest protector. So why did her instincts tell her that she'd just stepped into a trap?

CHAPTER ELEVEN

JODIE WAS UNNATURALLY silent when they returned to the Antoniou estate later that day. She was deep in thought when he helped her out of her winter coat. He noticed that her brown printed dress and low heels mirrored her subdued nature.

"Is my mother here?" he asked the butler as he gave him the coats.

"She and Kyrios Little are waiting for you in the salon." The butler gave Jodie a commiserating look before he gave a small bow.

They walked into the entrance hall and Jodie hung back, her gaze locked onto the Christmas tree. "I think it would be best if I found my own place in Athens. It wouldn't be right if I stay here."

"They know, *pethi mou*." Stergios curled his arm around her waist. He felt the shock reverberating inside her. "I have informed our parents that you are pregnant."

"You didn't have that right!" she whispered fiercely.

"I have every right." Stergios forcefully bit out the words. "The child is mine."

Jodie's shoulders slumped. "Did you tell them that, as well?"

"Of course. I am not going to hide it."

She closed her eyes as she rubbed her fingertips against her forehead. Jodie appeared pale and Stergios wondered if she should have stayed in the hospital for one more day.

"I can't walk in there," she confessed. "It's going to be a feeding frenzy."

"I won't let that happen," Stergios said as he guided her with his hand splayed possessively against the curve of her hip. "I will take the brunt of it."

"I don't want that, either," she explained. "And you don't have to worry about me. I'm not going to break into pieces because someone thinks I'm a whore."

His mouth pinched. "Don't say that."

"Why?" she asked, walking stiffly to the salon. "You used that word to describe me."

He had and he was not proud of it. "You wanted me to think you were when you made claims of another man, but that is no excuse. I shouldn't have and I won't let anyone else treat you with disrespect."

Jodie pressed her lips together but she didn't argue. "Tell me what I should expect before I walk into the lion's den. How did your mother take the news?" She gave him a knowing look when he hesitated. "You can tell me the truth."

No, he couldn't. Stergios needed to protect Jodie from the vitriol that had spewed from his mother's mouth. "She wants a paternity test as soon as possible."

Jodie nodded. She paused and frowned, her forehead wrinkling. "Why haven't you required it?"

He didn't know why that hadn't been his first priority. It was unlike him. He knew not to trust people until he had absolute proof. Why had he automatically accepted that this child was his when Jodie had lied to him in the past? "The timing fits."

"I know what kind of reputation I have around here but—"

He stopped and cornered her against the carved limestone wall. "Don't."

Jodie straightened to her full height and jutted her chin out. "Don't what?"

"Don't remind me." Stergios curled his finger under her chin and brushed the pad of his thumb against her red lips as if he could wipe away the touch of the other men in her past.

"What I was trying to tell you is that I can take a paternity test but it's not necessary," she said as she pushed his hand away. "I haven't been with a man for a very long time."

Satisfaction rolled through Stergios and he knew she spoke the truth. There had been something in the way she'd touched him during that night. As if she had denied herself for so long and had finally broken free. He rested his forehead against hers as he looked deeply into Jodie's blue eyes. "I was determined to keep you away from Dimos but it wasn't necessary. You were only interested in me. It's always been that way."

She flushed as she scowled at him. "It won't be if you keep gloating about it."

He smiled as he saw the fighting spirit flicker in her eyes. "Come along, *pethi mou*." He offered his hand. "Coffee is about to be served in the salon."

She ignored his gesture and walked ahead of him. "I'm familiar with the schedule in this house."

Stergios grabbed her wrist and forced her to a halt. "We're going into that room as a united front."

Jodie gave him a sidelong look. "Describe *united*."

"It means that you aren't going to fight me, you aren't going to contradict me and you aren't going to stir up trouble." He didn't want his opposition to notice the cracks in his relationship with Jodie. They would use it and he would lose the ground he had already conquered.

"Don't do anything that requires me to fight back."

Jodie paused and was clearly considering her next words. "And don't give them any details about us."

Stergios tilted his head to one side as he released his hold on her. "I'm not one to confide in others."

"No one needs to know that you—" her hands churned as she struggled for the right word "—*detained* me at the island. And they certainly don't need to know what happened four years ago."

"I have no intentions of advertising my lack of judgment. I thought you would at the first opportunity."

Her blue eyes went dull. "Then you don't know me at all."

"Enough of this." He grabbed her hand, lacing his fingers with hers before he led her to the salon. Jodie tried to get out of his grasp.

"United front, Jodie," he reminded her softly.

"That doesn't mean we have to be arm in arm," she said in a hiss.

He gave her hand a squeeze. "You like touching me," he said with a teasing smile. "You definitely like it when I touch you."

"All the more reason not to touch me."

He noticed she didn't deny it, but he also knew she was correct. Stergios couldn't afford any distractions. He reluctantly let go of her hand as they approached the salon but he couldn't break all contact. She needed to know that he was at her side. Placing his hand at the small of her back, he escorted her into the salon.

Stergios immediately saw his mother and Gregory sitting by the fireplace. Tension pulsed in the small, ornate room. He glanced at Jodie as she stood in front of him. He realized she was poised to defend them both. Did she think he wouldn't look after her? Stergios tamped down his displeasure. Jodie needed to trust him.

"Jodie," Gregory said as he rose from his seat and clasped his hands behind his back. "How are you feeling?"

"Better, thank you." Her voice was barely above a whisper.

Stergios noticed that Gregory did not approach his daughter. Jodie immediately took a seat as if she'd known her father's question was out of politeness instead of concern. Stergios had always been aware the two were not demonstrative but it bothered him that Jodie couldn't expect any moral support from her parent.

"The doctor recommended a lot of rest," Stergios said, standing behind Jodie's chair. "More food and liquids."

"And when will it be safe to travel?" Mairi asked.

Stergios recognized the hint of steel underneath his mother's concerned tone. She was already planning Jodie's return flight. "Jodie is staying in Athens for the duration of her pregnancy."

"Why?" Gregory asked. "Her presence will create a scandal."

"I'm aware of that." Stergios gave his stepfather a disapproving look. He should have known Gregory had no sense of anticipation over his grandchild.

"You need to think about this, Stergios." His mother agitatedly twisted her pearl necklace between her fingers. "The Diamantopoulos family are great friends but they have certain expectations for a future son-in-law. They won't tolerate the fact that you have a love child. We need to keep this secret and get Jodie out of here as soon as possible."

He sensed Jodie's tension soar. Did she think he was going to change his mind? Abandon her and their child? "I no longer have plans to marry Aleka," Stergios announced.

Mairi blanched at the news. "Of course you are," she replied in a brittle voice. "Stergios, think of your duty."

"I am." He placed his hand on Jodie's shoulder. "My duty is to Jodie and our child."

Jodie shifted uncomfortably as the room went silent. She seemed fascinated by the faded rug at her feet, but he knew she was not oblivious to the looks of condemnation.

"This merger must happen," Mairi said as she pulled her attention back onto Stergios. "It will give us unlimited power and influence. We are at the final stages of the agreement. There's no turning back."

"Plans change," Stergios said. He was not going to apologize for this decision. He turned to his stepfather. "And, Gregory, I ask for permission to marry your daughter."

Jodie gasped and twisted around to face him. "Stergios!"

He didn't look at Jodie. He watched Gregory squirm as the panic lit his eyes. He didn't need the man's approval, but had been curious to see how his stepfather would respond. The man would not support Stergios's plans of marriage, but neither would he interfere.

Jodie bolted from her seat and pointed accusingly at him. "We have discussed this and I am not marrying you."

"Oh, thank God," his mother muttered with relief.

Stergios saw Jodie turn pale and she wobbled on her feet. "Excuse me," she said, reaching for him. "I'm not feeling well."

He was at her side and silently encouraged her to lean against him. "What's wrong?"

"I stood up too fast." Jodie closed her eyes. "I'm just going to go lie down."

Stergios lifted her in his arms. She felt delicate against him. When Jodie rested her head against his shoulder and sighed, her display of trust and acceptance nearly undid him. He strode out of the salon, ignoring Gregory's blustering and Mairi's cold silence.

"Put me down, Stergios," she ordered when he stepped into the entrance hall. She winced when she saw the butler carrying the coffee service. The older man stopped to gawk at them. "I don't need for us to make a scene."

"Are you really feeling ill?" he asked.

"Why would I lie?"

He held her closer as he carried her up the grand staircase. "To save your father from making a choice."

She looked surprised by his insight. "That's why I interrupted. And you shouldn't have asked him that. What happened to the united front you wanted? Anyway, it doesn't matter what my father would have said. We are not getting married."

"Hush," he said gently as he reached the second floor and turned to the right. "You're unwell. You don't know what you're saying."

"I am pregnant, not an invalid. Just because I disagree with you does not make my opinion unsound." Jodie glanced around the hallway. "Where are you taking me?"

"To my room. It's closer."

Stergios's suite of rooms was not what she had expected. The colors of sand and stone from the sitting room were a blur as he carried her to the adjoining bedroom. The furniture's strong lines and natural wood reminded her of his island getaway. It was nothing like the formality of the rest of the house.

He carefully placed her onto his bed and her pulse skipped a beat. She shouldn't be alone with Stergios. She wouldn't be able to keep her hands off him and it would give him the wrong idea. He would think she was ready to reestablish their relationship.

That couldn't happen. She still wasn't able to give him the life he wanted and he... Her thoughts faded as she watched him remove her shoes. She was so much in love with Stergios that it hurt but he would never love her back. She couldn't take the risk of believing that one day he would reciprocate her feelings.

"I'm going to have your things moved in here," Stergios said as he sat on the edge of the bed.

She bolted up into a sitting position. "Have you lost your mind?" The room tilted and she groaned.

"Lie down." He grasped her shoulders and lowered her onto the mattress.

"I'm serious, Stergios," she said as she laid her head on the pillow. "I am not sharing a room with you. I will find a place of my own. In the meantime, I will stay in a hotel."

"Wherever you go, I go."

She peeked at him from under her lashes. When she saw his determined look and the clench of his jaw she knew she had a battle on her hands. "I said I would stay in Greece. I didn't say I would stay with you."

He stroked her hair away from her face. "You need someone to look after you."

She couldn't argue that after he had caught her from fainting and carried her to the nearest bed. "I'll hire some-one."

Stergios tucked a strand of hair behind her ear. "*Oxi*, I want to be part of this pregnancy."

She rose up and rested against her elbows. "And what will happen if we get married and I have the child? What becomes of me?"

He caressed the length of her throat with the back of his hand as he frowned. "What do you mean?"

Jodie bit down on her tongue. She hadn't planned to voice those concerns but now they were out in the open. "You only want to get married so you have a legal claim on your baby. What happens next?"

"We raise our child."

"Together? I doubt that." She may not be part of Stergios's social stratosphere, but she knew what happened when women married powerful men. "I'm going to be pushed off to the side. I'll be the outsider. You'll send me away and keep the baby."

He gave her an odd, slanted smile. "I won't."

"And it would only be a matter of time before you and the baby forget about me."

"Impossible," he said as his hands rested on the mattress. His arms bracketed her and he lowered his head. "I want our child to have many brothers and sisters."

Hope was a dangerous thing, Jodie thought as a lump formed in her throat. "What?"

"I've never liked being an only child." Stergios pressed his mouth against her cheek. "I know you haven't, either."

She wanted a big family. She had often dreamed of a home that was bursting at the seams with children, laughter and love.

Stergios left a trail of soft kisses along her jaw. "A marriage is meant to protect your property and heirs. I will make you my wife if it means protecting my family but I have no interest in a paper marriage," he said. "Once we marry, you will share my bed and have my children."

His gentle, soothing tone couldn't hide the fierceness behind his words. "How can you make a declaration like that?" she asked as she lay back down. "We aren't even in a relationship."

Stergios hovered above her and she saw the possessive gleam in his eye. "That needs to change immediately."

"Stop." Her heart pounded wildly as she pressed her fingertips against his mouth. "You can't seduce me into marriage."

The challenge flickered in his eyes and she held her breath. What was she doing throwing down the gauntlet like that? She knew she would promise him anything if it meant one more kiss, one more touch.

"I wouldn't dream of it," he said as he captured her hand and kissed her fingertips. "Now go to sleep. You need your rest."

She snatched her hand away. "I mean it, Stergios. I won't live with you and I won't share a bed."

"*Ne*, you will, *pethi mou*. Very soon," he promised as he stood up. "You will give me everything I want and more."

CHAPTER TWELVE

"ARE YOU SURE you want to do this?" Jodie whispered to Stergios as they walked through the cavernous museum to the Antoniou collection. Her black ball gown swished against her legs as they followed the colorful banners that announced the highly anticipated display.

"I have been looking forward to this event," Stergios said as they entered the archway that led to the exclusive party. "The Antoniou family donated historically important artifacts to the museum and it will be on tour for years."

"No, that's not what I meant. I know you want to be here." The pride had shimmered from him as they had entered the prestigious building and she didn't want to do anything to diminish it. "Are you sure you want me to attend. With you?"

He stopped and studied her strained smile. "You're nervous," he said in disbelief.

Of course she was nervous! She didn't want to let him down. Her spine grew rigid when she felt all eyes on her. Jodie swept her gaze along the crowd. They appeared reticent but at least they weren't hostile.

Stergios splayed his hand against her back. The casual touch did little to calm her nerves. She still slept in a separate room. There were some nights when she wished she hadn't drawn a line on their relationship. She was frequently tempted to move into his room and stake her claim but something held her back. She still wasn't sure if Stergios's solicitude was temporary or an attempt to lower her guard.

It didn't help that he was wearing a black tuxedo that accentuated his lean, masculine body. Her mouth had gone dry and a wicked curl of heat had settled low in her pelvis when she had first seen him. His knowing smile had irked her but she still had difficulty dragging her gaze away.

"Just be yourself," he said as he brushed his mouth against her ear. "Stay close to me if you're feeling uncertain."

She gave a choked laugh. "Okay, that's not the advice I usually get." It was usually keep her mouth shut and make herself scarce.

"Why did you want me to attend?" she asked. She felt like she was a curiosity and her presence would detract from the display.

He nodded at someone in the crowd. Everyone seemed to know him but they were too intimidated to draw near. "It's an event that honors my family's history."

"I'm not family. We are not engaged and I'm not marrying you." She was compelled to remind him. During the past few weeks she got the feeling that Stergios was playing a waiting game and believed it was only a matter of time before she acquiesced.

"But you are carrying my child." He lifted her hand and pressed his mouth against her knuckles before he tucked her hand against his elbow. "I want everyone to know that you are under my protection. When your pregnancy is announced, they will know that I claim my child."

"Wouldn't it be better protection if you kept quiet about us?" she asked as she looked around the room and found everyone was openly staring at them. "No one has to know."

He drew his head back and he studied her through hooded eyes. "Are you ashamed that I got you pregnant?"

"No!" She was stunned that he would think that. She wanted Stergios's baby and couldn't imagine sharing this bond with any other man.

His heated gaze drifted down her plunging neckline and leisurely traveled back up until it rested on her necklace. "Is it strange that I want to show you off?"

"Yes!" She looked away when he laughed and she fiddled with her earring.

Jodie immediately put her hand down. She didn't want to damage the jewelry. When Stergios had presented the amethyst earrings and necklace in an old wooden box she knew they were heirlooms. At first she had declined wearing something of such sentimental value but Stergios had insisted.

Brushing her hand along the necklace as if she wanted to make sure it was still there, Jodie couldn't help but stand a little taller while she wore the jewels. Stergios's gesture had honored her. She didn't want to look too deeply into what it meant or whether he'd have allowed her to wear them if she wasn't carrying his child.

"My security team recommended I keep quiet about you," he admitted.

"And you disregarded their suggestion?" Stergios had been very protective of her since she had returned from the hospital. His gestures often left her flustered or inordinately touched. "This event must mean a lot to you."

"In fact, they wish you were inside the Antoniou estate right now so no harm will come to you," he said as a waiter approached them with a tray of drinks.

"And your family wished I was home so I wouldn't cause any trouble." She gave a squeeze to his arm. "Don't worry, I wouldn't do anything to embarrass you."

"I know you won't. Your past antics were designed to

be noticed," he said as he reached for a flute of orange juice and handed it to her. "You didn't want to be forgotten or ignored. You don't have to do that anymore. You have my full attention."

She felt the heat flood her chest and crawl up her neck. She looked away before it flooded her cheeks. Jodie's hectic gaze collided with a familiar pair of brown eyes. She felt the bands of tension release from her rib cage when she saw the friendly face. "There are many people here who will remember my past," she said with a wide smile.

"Recognize anyone?"

"Yes, one of the benefits of attending so many schools around the world is that I probably know someone at any high-society events." She nodded to the brunette who waved excitedly at her. "There is Sofia Xenakis. I haven't seen her since I got kicked out of our boarding school. We never had a chance to meet whenever I was in Athens."

"Is her father Theodoros Xenakis? The media mogul?"

She heard the rare hitch of curiosity in his voice. "Yes, do you know him?"

"Of him," he corrected with a grimace. "I've wanted a meeting with him for years but he's a recluse. He doesn't meet with anyone outside his inner circle."

"Is that so?" She hid her smile against the fluted glass. She may not be part of Athens high society but that didn't make her an impediment for Stergios and his business activities.

His eyes narrowed with suspicion. "Yes, why?"

Her smile grew so wide that her cheeks hurt. "I've been to his house in the Bahamas several times during school vacations. He's a sweetie. Come with me and I'll introduce you to his daughter."

Stergios leaned against the stone museum wall as he typed on his cell phone, replying to an urgent message.

He didn't notice his cousin approaching until the man stood next to him. "Dimos," he said by way of greeting. "I didn't know you were attending. Is Zoi here, too?"

"I don't have to be joined at the hip with my wife," Dimos said with a scowl before he pointed accusingly at the center of the room. "What is she doing here?"

"Jodie is my guest for the evening," he said as he pocketed his cell phone.

"Why?" Dimos broadly gestured at the crowd. "There are too many photographers and journalists here. You're supposed to be courting the Diamantopoulos heiress."

Stergios tried to remember what Aleka Diamantopoulos looked like. It had only been a couple of weeks since he had been pursuing the woman. He had found her docile and ultimately forgettable. He knew Aleka had been raised to marry a powerful man but it had taken a great deal of patience and energy to tamp down his natural aggression when she was around. He couldn't show his true self or it would have frightened her.

Unlike Jodie, he thought as he watched her tilt her head back and give a bawdy laugh that rang in the pretentious museum. The woman had seen him at his worst and she didn't walk away. She wasn't afraid to disagree with him or prove him wrong. Jodie was also under the misguided impression that she needed to protect him. It was during those moments when she'd unwittingly displayed her loyalty.

Dimos winced as everyone looked at Jodie. "The Diamantopoulos family isn't going to be happy that you brought another woman to this important event, even if it is your stepsister. They want to see you pander to their daughter. It's a power play."

"I am no longer pursuing the Antoniou-Diamantopoulos merger." It was strange that he felt no regret. The alliance would have given him everything he wanted. But now his focus was on marrying Jodie. That pursuit filled him with anticipation.

Dimos's shoulders slumped as he gave a sigh of disappointment. "Because you got Jodie pregnant?"

Stergios swung his head around in shock. How did Dimos know about that? Jodie wouldn't divulge that kind of information. He studied his cousin and was immediately on guard. He didn't like the flint of bitterness and envy flashing in the man's eyes.

"Yes, I've heard," Dimos said bluntly. "Your mother is trying to keep the rumors from spreading. It's no use. People are going to find out."

"Good." He had a strategy in place to present Jodie to society in the best light.

"Good?" Dimos repeated before he took a fortifying sip of his drink. "How can you say that? I don't know why you're taking a public stand on this. You know, you're not the first Antoniou man who has had children outside of marriage."

Stergios arched an eyebrow. "Is there something I should know, Dimos?"

His cousin waved away the question. "You don't have to throw out everything we've worked hard for just to acknowledge a child. There is no need to give the kid your name. Why support it when Jodie has money of her own?"

"You wouldn't understand." He would protect his heir even if it meant extending that protection to the mother of his child.

Dimos finished his drink in one gulp as he watched Jodie talk animatedly while she stood among a few socialites. "Oh, hell, no," he said in a low tone as his eyes widened. "Jodie is wearing the Antoniou amethysts?"

Stergios nodded with satisfaction as he watched the violet stones twinkle from her ears and throat. Jodie was made to wear the amethysts.

"Well, there's no hiding it now." His cousin raised his hands in defeat. "No wonder all of high society is flocking around Jodie. Even the reporters will know what this means. You are telling everyone that she will be an Antoniou."

But Jodie didn't know that the jewelry was more than heirlooms. One day he would tell her that the stones were part of family legend and ritual. When he had draped the necklace around her slender throat, he had been declaring Jodie as his intended bride. He claimed Jodie as his own and now everyone knew that she was his.

"Does your mother know that woman is wearing the jewels?"

"Show some respect," Stergios warned in a growl. "*That woman* is going to be my wife and the mother of my child."

"Why are you doing this?" Dimos asked in a hiss. "Is she so good in bed that she's twisted your mind?"

"You'll never know. Is that what's eating you up?"

Dimos cast a vicious glare. "Even I knew as a teenager that Jodie isn't the type of woman you marry," he said. "She's the disposable lover. Try her once or twice and then discard—"

Hot fury flashed through Stergios and he grabbed Dimos by the tie. "Don't."

Dimos grappled at Stergios's hand. "Let go of me," he said weakly, glancing at the interested spectators around them. "People are watching."

"I don't care," he said through clenched teeth.

"I'm not saying anything that hasn't been said before," he choked as his face turned bright red.

"That's going to change," Stergios announced as he let go of his cousin.

Dimos coughed as he loosened his tie. "Are you going to threaten every relative? You'll be popular at the next family dinner."

He didn't need to be liked. He needed Jodie happy and content living in Greece. "I will do whatever is necessary for Jodie to be accepted."

"That's never going to happen," his cousin predicted as he took a cautious step back. "You are going to be the laughingstock of all of Athens if you marry a woman like that. They will shun her."

"Then give them a message from me," he said in a chilling tone. "If you disrespect Jodie, you disrespect me. Hurt her in any way and I will come after you. Got that?"

"You're making a big mistake," Dimos said as he slunk away. "But you'll figure that out soon enough. I just hope you don't take the Antoniou family down with you."

CHAPTER THIRTEEN

A WEEK LATER Stergios cautiously approached Jodie's bedroom as he planned his next move. He felt like he was
flying without a net. What he said or did next could ruin
all of the groundwork he'd covered so far.

The door to her room was ajar. There was a clatter of
something hitting the floor and Jodie's muttered exple-
tive followed. Stergios tapped his knuckles on the door
before he pushed it open.

His eyes lit up with appreciation when he saw Jodie.
Her lime-green tank top and charcoal-gray yoga pants
clung to her curves. She was stretching, extending her arm
as she reached for something at the top of her closet. Wisps
of her blond hair were escaping from her short ponytail. It
took him a moment to notice the open suitcase on her bed.

His chest tightened. "What is this?" he asked in a low,
dangerous tone.

Jodie jumped at the sound of his voice and whirled
around. Her face was red with exertion and her eyes
gleamed with anger. He suspected she could tear up at
any moment.

"What does it look like?" she asked defiantly as she
bundled up a dress and tossed it in the case. "I'm leaving."

Panic flared deep inside him. Suddenly he was at her
side and grasped her arm to stop her. "No, you're not."

"I have to," she insisted as she shook off his hold. "I
swore I wasn't going to live like this again."

"What happened?" He was glad he had followed his instinct and had arrived home early. He couldn't afford the time off but he had felt his relatives' seething anger just under the surface in the breakfast room this morning. He knew the Antonious resented Jodie's presence but he couldn't tell how it affected her.

This was his fault. He had not expected his family to question his choices. They hadn't before but now they felt Jodie had seduced him down a different path. A mutiny was brewing. A week ago he couldn't have imagined any of the Antonious dissecting his decisions. They used to congregate around him like devoted servants wanting to please their master.

Stergios never took their obsequious manner as his due. He knew they only wanted his advice, his help and his money. He had often found it irritating. Maybe that was why he found Jodie's attitude a refreshing challenge.

"I know I'm a burden, just like I was when I was a teenager." Jodie placed her hands on her hips and looked away. "My father is embarrassed by me and he's worried that he's going to be penalized just by being related to me. And Mairi wants me out. Out of the house, the city and their lives. Sound familiar?"

It did. He had thought it would be different this time around. She had him as her ally, her protector. But he was not at home enough to be a physical barrier between Jodie and his family.

"And how do I respond to all this? I'm hiding again." She angrily tossed a pair of shoes into the suitcase. "That had been my strategy when I first came to live here. Then I did the opposite only to find more grief. I'm trying to become invisible because this family refuses to make room for me."

Stergios reached for the suitcase and flipped the lid closed. "You made a promise and I expect you to keep it."

"You made promises to me, as well. You said you would make time for the baby and me. Instead you spend every waking moment at the office." She returned to the closet and snagged a dress off the hanger. "My mother used to do that when she was building an empire of her own. I was alone then and I'm alone now."

"It won't be like this at the office for much longer," he said. He would be home in the evenings once he had taken care of the public relations nightmare. News of getting his stepsister pregnant should have been a six-day wonder, but it didn't help that there was no forthcoming wedding date. It showed his lack of commitment to the mother of his child. It suggested instability in the Antoniou family, not to mention legal ambiguity for his heir.

"I feel trapped," she admitted. "I swore I wasn't going to live like this again and I immediately fall into my old patterns. I stay in my room and out of the way or I'm in the garden."

"You are not leaving."

"I'm staying in Greece. Just not here in this house. I'm moving into a hotel for the short term." She smoothed her hands over her hair and gave a deep sigh. "I should have done it from the beginning. Why did you want me to stay here?"

"This is the safest place for you," he explained. "We have the best security here and no one can get to you."

Jodie lifted her gaze to the ceiling as if she was saying a heartfelt prayer. "You don't have to worry, Stergios. I keep telling you that but you don't listen. I promise you that no one is out to get me."

He gritted his teeth before he informed her of the threats his security team started to receive once they made their first appearance at the museum. It was the usual. They wanted to steal from her or hurt her. They wanted to take her from him.

Stergios was used to the threats being aimed at him. After his kidnapping, he learned to expect the worst in humanity. At times it was white noise and he was numbed to it. But when his security team told him about the first threat against Jodie, his rage had been swift and brutal.

"You are now a public figure," he said. He was not going to tell her about the warnings and threats. Jodie should be allowed to live her life without fear.

"I will be safe in a hotel," she promised.

"You will be safer here," he argued.

Jodie paused and crossed her arms. "Are you trying to protect me or are you trying to keep me from finding out about the scandal?"

He lifted his head as the puzzle pieces started to fall into place. That was why she had this sudden need to leave. She discovered that the scandal was weakening him. His family and colleagues were not standing behind him. His enemies had smelled blood and were circling around him.

Stergios wasn't worried. It was an inconvenience more than anything. At least he knew who his true allies were.

"I found out about it today," she said. "I would have earlier but it's been a while since I've seen a newspaper. Oh, and the internet connection has been under repairs for a week." She arched an eyebrow. "What a coincidence."

He rubbed his hand against the back of his neck. How did she find out? "I don't want you to worry about it. The doctor said to avoid stress."

"Avoid stress," she repeated dully. "How can I when I'm the source of it all?"

Stergios stared at her. He didn't see her that way. She might challenge and frustrate him, but she also brought him joy and light. Jodie was his port in the storm swirling around him.

"You've been through so much in your life. You've

overcome horrific experiences and you were on to great things…" Jodie's eyes filled with tears. "And then I showed up."

He didn't like the sound of defeat in her voice. "Have a little more faith in my abilities, Jodie," he retorted drily. "I have accomplished many things and I've only just begun."

Jodie wasn't listening. "You should have married Aleka," she said softly.

"That ship has sailed," he said in a growl. He had heard that suggestion from everyone, but lately he felt as if he'd dodged a bullet.

She looked at the window. "Maybe I should go back to America." She sounded preoccupied as if she was already making plans. "It would be better for both of us."

"*Oxi!* No!" He moved in front of her, blocking her from the suitcase.

She took a step to the side. "Don't worry, I can be back in time for the birth."

He stretched out his arm to stop her. "That is out of the question."

"The baby will be born in Greece, I promise. You can trust me, Stergios."

"Trust?" he spat out. "Unbelievable. Why should I trust you when you won't give me the same courtesy?"

Her eyes went wide. "I don't understand. What are you talking about?"

"You hide how you feel because you don't trust me. You don't tell me what's worrying you. Why? Do you think I can't fix it?" His anger flashed at the possibility. "That I'm going to ignore your concerns?"

"You don't share your concerns with me, either," she pointed out.

Stergios scoffed. That was different. He was concealing information so she would be happy living here. "It is my job to protect you and the baby. Instead of letting me take care of it, you want to walk away."

"That's not how I see it. You are losing everything you worked hard for because of us. Because of me. And you choose not to tell me."

"Because I didn't want you to grab at the excuse and leave." He gestured wildly as hard, cold fear settled in his stomach. "I am not going to lose you and the baby."

Her shoulders sagged and she sat down on the bed. "Why does it matter if I stay?"

It mattered. Stergios raked his hand in his hair as he took a deep breath. He was already losing her. They didn't share the same room or a bed. She was pushing him away and he couldn't let that happen.

He had to make a compromise. It went against every instinct but he knew if he didn't, Jodie would leave him. "I'm going to be wherever you are." The words came out with great reluctance. "If you don't want to stay in this house, then decide where we're going to live."

She was already shaking her head. "You can't be away from your office. Not now, not when everyone is out for your blood."

Stergios crouched down in front of her. He knew she had some place in mind but she was trying to talk herself out of it. "I will figure something out. Where, Jodie?"

"I want to go back to your home on the island."

He went still. Stergios thought Jodie would associate his home with bad memories. It was where he had kidnapped her, where he had cast her out of his life. "Why there?"

"You're right," she muttered. "It wouldn't work. That's your island getaway. It's not meant for everyday living. It doesn't have a phone line."

"Not anymore." He grasped her hands in his. "After our weekend I made extensive updates on the house. It has the newest technology and a generator that works. But when I found out about the baby, I started making some more changes."

Her face lit up. "Really? You're making room for the baby?" She squeezed his hands. "I want to see. You have to take me there, Stergios. I want to go back to your home as soon as possible."

"Our home," he corrected. "And I'll take you right now."

Jodie felt a sense of peace once she arrived on the island hours later. She inhaled the scent of the ocean and listened to the rustling leaves. She hadn't felt this calm in weeks. She had been tense and on guard while she was at the Antoniou house, but here she knew she could relax and settle in. Maybe even make this place the home she'd always wanted.

"We're almost done with the renovations for this house," Stergios said as he opened the door. "Don't worry about the construction site that you saw when we flew in. It's on the other side of the island. I'm having them build some cottages for the employees."

"Employees?" she asked. It would feel different sharing this paradise with others.

"We will need a cook and a nanny in addition to the caretaker."

Jodie bit her bottom lip to stop her smile. She was surprised that Stergios had time to think about hiring nannies. She liked his growing anticipation and how he was making room in his life for the baby.

Following Stergios into the house, she watched him lift her suitcases and carry them into the main room. Anticipation fluttered low in her belly as she watched the play of muscles under his white button-down shirt. Her gaze drifted to his lean waist and powerful thighs.

Jodie darted her gaze away. She ached to touch him. Hold him. But how could she when she had rejected his advances weeks ago? "What renovations did you have done?" she asked as she walked across the main room.

"The most advanced technology and communication features. I'll show you how the touch screens work later."

Jodie walked to the room she had used before. She blinked when she discovered the guest room was empty. There were no furniture or light fixtures. "Stergios?" she called over her shoulder. "What happened to my room?"

"We've only just finished the renovations and updates," he said. "That can be the nursery. You can decorate it any way you want."

She slowly turned around and found him still in the main room, resting his shoulder against a wall. *Do not make a big deal out of this.* "So there's only one bedroom?"

His pose was casual but he watched her intently. "Yes."

She glanced in the direction of his bedroom and was instantly besieged with erotic memories of the last time she stayed there. Jodie cleared her throat. "I should sleep in the main room," she said hoarsely.

"I would never allow a woman to sleep on a sofa."

She knew from the tone of his voice that he would not be swayed. Jodie walked to the sofas that circled the fireplace. "It's not long enough for you to stretch out on." She gestured at the soft white cushions. "And you're barely getting enough sleep as it is. I can't let you sleep there."

"I won't."

Her pulse skipped a beat. Jodie dragged her gaze back to Stergios. If he wasn't staying in the main room, then that meant…

Stergios grabbed his computer tablet from his briefcase and sat down on the sofa. "It's late and you should get some rest. I'm going to get some work done."

Her heart started to race. They were sharing a bedroom. They were going to share a bed. All night.

She knew she should tell him that under no circumstances were they sharing a room. Instead, Jodie silently grabbed her overnight suitcase and walked to the bedroom with stiff legs. She closed the door and stared at the wide bed. Excitement pulsed inside her.

No, she had nothing to be excited about. Sharing a bed did not mean sex. Even if she was sharing it with the virile Stergios Antoniou. It was not an invitation. She had to remember that. She might want to be intimate and naked with Stergios, but she had made a big mistake when she had refused earlier.

She had told him they weren't resuming their affair because they had no relationship. Instead of arguing, he had granted her wish. He had not made any attempt to get her into bed since.

He was willing to share a bed because he no longer fought the overwhelming need for her. Why? What did she do to kill the attraction? Was it because she was pregnant? Or was it because no woman could hold his interest?

She had to be careful. One word, one move, and she wouldn't be able to keep her hands off him. Her skin heated as she remembered the last time she claimed him. If she had sex with him again, he would discover exactly how she felt about him. And Stergios would ruthlessly use it to his full advantage.

CHAPTER FOURTEEN

"STERGIOS?"

He heard Jodie from far away. Blackness surrounded him and he tried to kick and claw his way to the surface. He had to get to Jodie. She sounded desperate. Afraid.

"Stergios?" Her sharp voice cut through the last barrier. "Wake up."

He was suddenly awake. His heart pounded against his chest as he took big gulps of air. His eyes burned as he checked his surroundings. He was no longer in the loud and chaotic police station where his family had been irrevocably torn apart. He wasn't the vulnerable child who couldn't bear to be touched or held.

He was safe. No one could hurt him. He wasn't alone anymore. Stergios turned his head to the side and saw Jodie leaning over him.

"What happened?" he asked hoarsely through parched lips. His throat hurt. Everything ached.

"You were shouting." Jodie cupped his face with her hands. Her touch was cool to his skin. She wore a light pink slip and one strap fell from her shoulder. Her hair was tousled from sleep and her concern shimmered from her blue eyes. "Are you okay?"

No, he wasn't. His pulse raced and he was bathed in sweat. "I need a shower," he decided, and bolted from the bed.

"Stergios!"

He rushed to the en suite bathroom as if he were being chased by demons. Once he shut and locked the door behind him, Stergios slumped against the wood and discovered that he was shaking all over.

He ignored Jodie's persistent knocking on the door as he stripped from the black pajama bottoms he had reluctantly put on earlier. Striding naked to the shower, he turned the water on full blast before he stepped in.

Stergios braced his arm against the tile wall as he withstood the cold water. It felt like needles but he didn't move away. He rested his head against his forearm, willing his pulse to slow down and the images to disappear.

He didn't know how long he stayed under the water. He was shivering by the time he stepped out of the shower. He dried his body with rough, brutal strokes.

Wrapping the towel around his waist, Stergios went to the adjoining walk-in closet. He probably had something he would wear to bed. He preferred sleeping in the nude and he was reluctant for anything to touch his skin, but he would do it for Jodie's sake.

Donning on a pair of dark blue pajama bottoms, Stergios took a deep, cleansing breath before he reentered the bedroom. All he had to do was act calm and convince Jodie that everything was fine.

He swung the door open. Just as he had expected, Jodie was blocking his way. Her arms were crossed and she tapped her bare foot on the floor as if she had been waiting there the entire time.

"Are you okay now?" she asked. "How often do you get nightmares?"

"Haven't had them in years." He used to get bad dreams if he had been ill or sleep deprived. During those times, it had been as though his body didn't have the strength to hold back the nightmares.

"What was your dream about?"

"I don't remember." His lie was automatic. He didn't discuss his nightmares. Stergios knew the dreams said more about him and his fears than about the ordeal he had suffered.

He felt her watchful gaze on him as he returned to bed. Jodie quietly got in on her side. He tensed as she lay down, knowing she wasn't going to let the matter drop.

Her proximity set him on edge. The mattress was wide but he was extremely aware of her. Her scent, her warmth, and the sound of the silk slip brushing against the cotton sheets. His willpower had been weakened by the nightmares and he knew he would reach out for her without thinking.

"Are you under a great deal of stress?" she asked. "I know about what's going on in your office. Something about the board of directors losing confidence in your judgment because you accidentally got a woman pregnant. Did I get that right?"

Stergios clenched his jaw. He knew where Jodie got that information. "And you say my mother never talks to you. No, I'm not concerned about what's going on at the office. Everyone will fall in line and it will be business as usual."

"Then what triggered the nightmare?"

"I haven't been keeping track." Stergios cringed when he recognized his mistake. He sighed and shook his head. There was no stopping Jodie's inquisition now.

She turned toward him. "So there's been more than one. When was the first?"

"The night I left you at the hospital," he answered reluctantly.

Jodie pressed her hand against his hair-roughened chest. "I'm sorry you found out that way. It must have been such a shock."

"I'm fine." He didn't know why he was sticking to that lie when Jodie could feel the rapid thud of his heart.

"Is it the same nightmare?"

"Good night, Jodie. I apologize for waking you up." He turned off the bedside light and tucked his hands under his head. He was exhausted but he knew he wasn't going to get any more sleep.

Jodie reached out and caressed his chest. He didn't turn away. Stergios needed her soothing touch tonight. The short strokes, back and forth, were surprisingly calming.

"It doesn't matter how I found out about the baby," he eventually said as he stared at the ceiling. "The nightmares would have happened, anyway."

"What do you dream about?" Jodie paused as if she didn't want to encourage more memories. "The kidnappers? The wilderness?"

Exhaustion pulled at his heavy eyelids. *"Oxi,"* he said in a husky voice. "I dream about the day I was rescued."

Jodie's fingers pulled at his curly chest hair. "Why is that a nightmare? Wouldn't that have been a special occasion?"

"It was at first. I was reunited with my family. But my father wasn't there. I had only seen a glimpse of him when I arrived at the police station. And that's when I found out he was the one behind the kidnapping." His voice trailed off as he remembered the overwhelming sense of betrayal.

She continued to stroke his chest. The pattern was hypnotic and the tension binding his ribs relaxed. He found he could breathe easier.

"He had been arrested and gave up the information as part of a deal," Stergios said bitterly. "He would not tell them anything unless he got something out of it. If he hadn't, I don't know how long I would have been missing."

"And you keep having that bad dream since you discovered you're becoming a father," she murmured. "Have you been dreaming the same thing every night?"

He shook his head. But he had awoken from enough nightmares lately that he was having trouble sleeping. It angered him that he was getting the bad dreams. He thought he was over them, that he had moved to the next level of healing and could get on with his life. Instead, it was as if he had a setback once he'd found out that he was going to be a father.

"Tonight was different," he confessed. Stergios clasped Jodie's hand against his chest. "When I dreamed I had seen a glimpse of him, it wasn't his face. It was mine."

Her fingers flexed, her nails scratching his skin as the surprise rolled through her. "You are not going to turn out like your father," she whispered.

"You don't know that." He had inherited many traits from Elias Pagonis. He was ruthless and ambitious just like his father.

"I know what kind of man you are, Stergios. I'm well aware of your flaws but you don't have an ounce of evil in you."

A hardened smile tugged at the corner of his mouth. "Don't be too sure."

"I am sure," she retorted. "I'm also certain that your father had made some choices that took him down a path you wouldn't take. Elias Pagonis had to have made some questionable decisions before the kidnapping."

"He was a cheat and a fraud." He had forgotten about Pagonis's other sins. The kidnapping eclipsed everything. With Jodie's prompting, he remembered some of the actions his father had taken. It was as though he'd been building up to kidnapping and extortion. "There were a lot of questions about his finances."

"You are not your father."

At times he was worse. Stergios let go of Jodie's hand. Elias Pagonis had not been the worst man he'd faced. The more power he had accumulated, the more monsters came crawling out, determined to tear him to pieces.

"Your father was a danger to your family," she pointed out, "but you protect them from the likes of Pagonis."

"You don't know my methods." At times he was just as terrifying as the monsters he battled when it meant keeping his loved ones safe.

"You take care of those who are most vulnerable," she continued, stroking the side of his neck. "You will never allow anyone to harm a child."

And it would destroy him if something happened to their child. Or worse, if he shared more than Pagonis's blood. "I can't do this without you," he said gruffly. "You need to let me know if I'm becoming my father."

Her hands froze. "Stergios, it's not going to happen."

"Promise me, Jodie," he pleaded, his voice raw at the edges. He knew he could trust her. She had the courage to tell him when he was wrong and she was the only person who would care about their child as much as he did.

"I promise," she said with great reluctance. "But you're asking too much of me. I couldn't hurt you like that."

"I'd rather you hurt me than…" The memories started to crowd his mind and he turned away from Jodie. "I can't fail my child."

She pressed her hand against his shoulder. "And that, Stergios," she said softly, "is why you will never be like your father."

Jodie murmured and sighed with contentment as she gradually stirred from her sleep. She was surrounded by heat and wiggled closer. She frowned when she felt Stergios's big hands grasp her arms as the delicious heat faded.

Stergios carefully held her away. "You could tempt a saint, Jodie."

Her eyelashes fluttered as she slowly opened her eyes.

"What's wrong?" she asked, her voice groggy from sleep. The bedroom was dark but she saw the first streaks of dawn filter through the curtains.

"You're too close." He growled in her ear. "I knew this would happen if we shared a bed."

Too close? She blinked a few times and discovered that instead of keeping a safe distance, she was clinging onto Stergios. Her head rested against his bare chest as she listened to the solid beat of his heart. She had draped her arms around him in a loose embrace and her hips were flush with his.

At some point in the night she had gravitated to his warmth and strength. She had turned to Stergios in her sleep because she couldn't stay away. Jodie didn't want to hold back anymore. She knew now that Stergios Antoniou wasn't going to hurt her. He cared for her and for the baby.

Jodie unhooked her bare leg from his muscular thigh. His pajama bottoms hung low on his hips and the thin cotton couldn't hide his thick erection. Heat flashed through her pelvis, her core tightening, as she remembered the masculine power he demonstrated when he had thrust inside her.

"Do you want me to go sleep on the sofa?" Her voice sounded strangled as she rolled back onto her side of the bed.

He flung his arm out and caged her. "Try and I'll bring you back here."

"Careful, Stergios," she teased. "You're on my side of the bed."

"This is not a laughing matter, *pethi mou*. Get any closer and I'm going to touch you." His voice thickened. "Take you. And nothing is going to stop me."

"I'll take my chances," she said in a husky purr.

"You didn't want to share a bed, remember?" She shivered when she heard the shaky restraint in his low, masculine voice. "Because we don't have a relationship, you said."

That had been weeks ago when all they shared was the knowledge that they were going to be parents. She had wanted more from Stergios. Some indication that she was more to him than the mother of his child. Now they were taking the first steps together toward a new life.

"But if you think we're going to have a sexless marriage," he said in a rough tone, "then you are out of your mind."

She felt the flicker of a smile on her mouth. "I thought your interest was fading because I wasn't going to be an easy conquest and just tumble into your bed."

"Fading?" He repeated the word in a choked voice. "Every day I want you more but I don't trust myself around you. I have been in agony all these weeks."

"You hide it well." She curled into him and pressed her mouth against his throat.

She felt him swallow hard as the tension vibrated from his clenched muscles. "Jodie, if I touch you, I won't be gentle."

"The doctors have said it was safe," she reminded him as she curled the tip of her tongue against his skin. "You heard them yourself."

"They don't know how I am around you." His voice wavered.

"But I know you will keep me safe." She arched her spine, pressing her breasts against him. "You will make me ache, Stergios, and you will take me to the edge of pleasure. You will make me surrender until I scream your name, but you will never hurt me."

CHAPTER FIFTEEN

THE ATMOSPHERE CRACKLED between them and Jodie thought he would pounce. That was what she wanted. She needed to feel the lust that was coursing through his veins and colliding with the hard masculine aggression. But Stergios took her by surprise when he claimed her lips with a slow, wet kiss. She moaned as he explored her mouth with the wicked flick of his tongue.

Jodie couldn't contain the growing need pulsating inside her. She caressed his strong body, her touch urgent and greedy. She liked how Stergios's muscles bunched as her fingers swept along his washboard abs. He hissed as her nails raked along his bare back. It was only when she slid her fingertips beneath his waistband that Stergios broke the deeply seductive kiss. She watched the sinful glow of his eyes as she clenched his buttocks.

Stergios's movements were lightning-fast as he grasped her wrists. He held her hands above her head, her fingers knocking against the wood headboard. Excitement tore at her chest as Stergios pinned her to the mattress.

His grasp was firm as he hovered above her. She lifted her head to kiss him but he would not allow it. She whimpered with frustration as she struggled to break free.

"Patience, *pethi mou*," he said with the twist of his lips.

Patience? She had not shared his bed for months. Her lips stung and her skin tingled for his touch. Her breasts felt heavy and full as she began to pant. She rocked her hips to alleviate the insistent throb. Couldn't Stergios sense her raging need? Of course he could.

"Is this payback?" she asked in a stuttering breath as he licked a path to her cleavage. "Because I made you wait?"

She felt his smile against her breast. "Would I do something like that?" he purred.

"Yes!" she said through clenched teeth.

He nipped her skin with his teeth. "I want to bury myself deep into you," he grounded out. "Hard and fast but I won't. I don't want to hurt you."

His words made her shiver with anticipation. She would break his restraint, she decided as she wrested for control. The straps of her slip fell down her shoulders, revealing her breasts, as she tried to pull her wrists from his strong hold. But Stergios would not let go. From the determined gleam in his eye, she knew he would not surrender to the lust stampeding inside him.

Stergios dipped his head and captured her tight nipple with his mouth. Jodie closed her eyes and tipped her head back as she mewled with pleasure. Desire flooded her as he continued this sensual torment. She bucked against Stergios, begging for more.

He readjusted his grip on her wrists and glided one hand along the length of her body. When he cupped her sex she almost came undone at his possessive touch. "Open your eyes." His voice was rough with desire.

Jodie followed his command and her gaze connected with his. He stroked the wet folds of her sex before he dipped his finger inside. Her flesh gripped him tightly. He watched the pleasure chase across her face as he teased her, his eyes darkening with uncontrollable lust when she held nothing back.

He suddenly let go of her wrists and slid down her trembling body. Stergios draped her legs over his shoulders and pleasured her with his mouth. A keening cry escaped her throat as she clenched her thighs against Stergios. Her fingers dug into his hair as she encouraged him closer. His husky moans and her shallow gasps echoed in the room. Jodie went rigid as the ferocious climax stole her breath. Her body shook as the heat scorched through her.

She lay limp beneath Stergios, her lungs aching as she tried to catch her breath. Through heavy eyelids she watched him shove off his pajama bottoms. He gathered Jodie in his arms, his chest hot and damp to the touch, before he rolled over.

Jodie straddled his hips. Anticipation pulsed through her body when she felt his throbbing erection against her. She slowly sat up, dragging her hands down his broad chest.

She smiled when she saw the hungry glitter in Stergios's hooded gaze. His angular features were drawn tight as a ruddy color stained his high cheekbones. He could no longer control the pace.

Jodie reached for the hem of her slip and slowly removed it, inch by inch. His fingers flexed on her thighs as she stretched and rolled her hips. She barely heard Stergios's ragged breath over her pounding heart as she tossed her slip to the side.

Stergios reached up and roughly caressed her body, molding her curves. She grasped his erection and he bucked against her. She stroked him and his growl was low in his throat as he dug his fingers against her hips.

Jodie guided him inside her. She smiled, her heart overflowing, as she felt his shaky restraint. Heat poured from her as he stretched and filled her. She rocked her hips, the pleasure coiling tight inside her. Her rhythm increased as she watched Stergios's face. Words spilled from her mouth unheeded as she rode him harder. Faster.

She cried out when the hot coil of need burst wildly and pleasure radiated from her core, streaming through her body. Stergios sat up and clasped her against him. Her nipples rubbed against his hairy chest as he held her in a tight embrace.

Love poured through her and she whispered against his ear, chanting his name. Stergios went still before he thrust wildly. She laid her head against his shoulder and clung to him before she surrendered completely.

Later that morning Jodie stood on the beach and stared at the ocean. She stuffed her hands in her coat and hunched her shoulders as the wind whipped her hair. She felt the cold through her jeans but she didn't dare go back inside.

What had she said to Stergios? Jodie nervously bit her lip. So many thoughts had chased through her mind. She had felt loved and cherished. She hadn't felt that way before and the sensations had overwhelmed her. But had she said those words out loud? Her stomach twisted with dread. Had she declared her love for Stergios?

She didn't hear him approach until he stood behind her and wrapped his arms around her. Jodie jumped and gave a shriek.

"Don't," he told her as she tried to break free from his embrace.

"Don't what?"

"It has taken me weeks to get you back into my bed." His voice rumbled in her ear. "Don't find an excuse to leave it."

She stood stiffly in his arms. "I'm not."

"You revealed yourself to me, *pethi mou*." Stergios pressed his mouth against the back of her neck. "And now you need to hide."

Jodie clenched her teeth and gathered her courage before she turned to face him. Heat unfurled inside her when she saw his sexy rumpled state. The dark sweater skimmed his lean body and the faded jeans clung to his powerful thighs. The shadow of a beard covering his jaw gave him a rakish edge. But it was his enigmatic brown eyes that made her want to take a step back.

She thrust out her chin. "I don't know what you're talking about."

He captured her gaze and wouldn't let go. "You told me that you love me."

Embarrassment pricked at her skin. Jodie felt the muscles twitching in her face as she tried to maintain an impassive expression. She had almost convinced herself that she hadn't said it out loud because Stergios had shown no reaction. But he had responded. He had gone completely still before he claimed her with a savage wildness.

His restraint had cracked because he knew he had won. He had complete power over her body and her heart. Jodie felt the flush creep up her throat and Stergios watched with a knowing smile as the color flooded her cheeks. She had bared her soul to him and had declared her love. How did she recover from that?

"It doesn't count when you say it while having sex," she said waspishly. "Everyone knows that."

"It counts when you say it."

He knew her very well but that didn't make her feel safe. She felt exposed and she had to get out of there. Jodie turned and trudged through the sand, wanting to get back to the house and get a few walls and doors between them. "Coming here was a mistake. We should return to Athens."

"Why? You weren't happy there," he called out to her. "That's my fault."

She stopped and turned around. "No, it's not. Why would you think that?"

"I thought that since I had included you in the family,

everyone would accept you. I had underestimated how my relatives would react."

"It's not your fault," she insisted. "I can't seem to get along with your family. When I try, it just gets worse."

He splayed out his hands. "Why do you keep trying?"

"I don't know," she said with a shrug. "I always felt like the odd man out. I thought I would eventually win them over. It was a waste of time. It was always going to be me against them."

Stergios strode over to her. "I will always be on your side, Jodie."

Shock ripped through her. "Why?" It didn't make sense. He was an Antoniou. The leader of the family. "What if I'm in the wrong?"

"I'm going to take your side." He stood in front of her. "And you will take mine."

"Oh, now I see the catch." Jodie rolled her eyes and made a face. "But will you take my side when I don't marry you?"

"We're getting married." Satisfaction permeated his voice. "The sooner the better."

She drew her head back. "I haven't agreed to that. I won't."

"You said you wouldn't marry without love." His lips tilted into a smile that made her heart skip a beat. "You love me."

Jodie clenched her hands at her sides as she fought the urge to wipe that smile off his face. "For the last time—"

He raised his eyebrows. "Are you saying you don't love me? Tell me the truth," he warned softly.

She snapped her mouth closed. She had made that promise to herself that she would always tell him the truth. Even if it didn't protect her.

Jodie felt jittery and cornered. She bent her head and walked to the water's edge. Stergios was at her side, quiet but alert. They strolled side by side for a few minutes as she tried to put the words together. "When I said that I would only marry for love, I meant that my husband would reciprocate how I feel. It shouldn't be one-sided."

Stergios gave a long-suffering sigh. "Why are you making this so complicated?"

"You're right. It is complicated," she declared, tossing her hands in the air. "Because if you say you love me, I won't believe you. I'll think it's because you need to get married and this was the quicker way to get results."

They fell into a tense silence as they walked on the sand. He eventually slowed to a stop and she stood beside him. When Stergios turned to her, she lifted her head to meet his inscrutable gaze.

"Jodie, you will get married out of love. I will get married out of duty to my family."

He clenched his jaw and a muscle bunched in his cheek. "You are in love with me but I don't love you. I can't."

Deep down she had always known this but it hurt to hear the words. She exhaled slowly as the pain bloomed inside her.

"I don't allow anyone that close to me. I never could, not since the kidnapping and finding out my father was behind it. However, I can pledge my commitment to you." His voice was low and earnest. "I will put you and our children first. Above all else. Above my relatives and my work."

He was making a vow to always respect and care for her. He promised to make her a priority. She wanted to believe him but she'd had too many promises broken to accept this vow at face value.

He reached for her hand. She found his fingers warm and steady. "I will protect and provide for you and our family. I will be faithful and I won't betray the love and trust you place on me."

She frowned at his solemn tone. Did he see her love as an obligation or a burden?

"And when you marry me, you will give me the same courtesy." His voice took a hard edge. "You will be faithful, you will protect our family, and you will put me and our children first. Do you think you can do that? Can you live that kind of life?"

Heaviness settled in her chest. This man knew her better than anyone else. He could offer commitment, family, protection and attention. Everything but love.

Why couldn't he give that, as well? She knew she was being greedy, but what was holding him back? What was it about her that he couldn't make that leap?

Jodie knew she shouldn't think that way. He was offering her a good deal but the disappointment pulled at her, trying to drag her down. Why was that? After all, when Stergios made a vow, it was unbreakable. How many women had a guarantee that their husband would put them first?

But was she willing to make a lifetime commitment to a man who could not love her? Give her love to her husband knowing that she would not get it in return? Could she enter a loveless marriage for the sake of her child?

"Yes, Stergios." Her mouth trembled as the tears burned her eyes. She had to accept, once and for all, that she was unlovable and nothing would change that. Now was not the time to be greedy. Why hold out for something that she could never have? "Let's get married."

CHAPTER SIXTEEN

STERGIOS STOOD IN the entrance hall of the Antoniou estate. He felt the bite of frustration as he looked for Jodie. Their engagement party was coming to a close and he was eager to have her to himself.

He should have been able to spot her instantly or hear her bold laugh from across the room. Dressed in a purple chiffon gown and wearing the Antoniou amethysts, his fiancée was an intriguing mix of a mischievous pixie and a regal queen.

Fiancée. Finally. There were moments when her stubbornness outmatched his tenacity, but she had accepted his proposal. Triumph and pride flared inside him along with the unfamiliar sense of satisfaction and peace.

Stergios shook his head. Peace was not related to Jodie Little. The woman tested him, pushed him to the limits. He didn't have to wear a mask around her and pretend. And yet, when he was with Jodie, he was the man he wanted to be.

His need for Jodie brought him little comfort. If anything, the knowledge had shaken him to the core. He knew better than to allow anyone that close to him but Jodie had slipped through his defenses. It was a constant struggle to maintain a wall between them when he ached to have her close. Was this what falling in love felt like? If so, he couldn't let that happen. For his own survival, no one should have that kind of power over him.

"Well, thankfully that is over," Mairi Antoniou said as she glided to his side. She wore a black evening gown that was the perfect backdrop to her diamond jewelry. "I hope the wedding happens soon."

"It will," he said as he took the last sip of his champagne. He was looking forward to starting his life with Jodie. Make everything official. He didn't want any delays.

"I don't think you should have given her that diamond ring for your engagement," his mother said from the side of her mouth. "It's an heirloom. It's priceless!"

"The wife of the Antoniou heir wears it. It's tradition." And, more importantly, it meant that he recognized Jodie as family. As an Antoniou. A smile tugged on his mouth as he remembered giving it to Jodie. She had recognized the heirloom and understood the symbolism. She had been deeply honored. From the tears that had clung to her eyelashes when he'd placed it on her finger, the sense of tradition had meant something to her.

"But she'll try to keep the diamond when you two break up," Mairi insisted. "You need to get a written agreement that she gives it back in the divorce."

Sharp coldness invaded Stergios's chest. The more he had stayed on his island getaway, the more he had realized how his family had tried to chip away at his happiness with Jodie.

"I am not divorcing Jodie," he bit out. "She is part of this family—part of me—forever. Get used to the idea, *Mitera*."

She pursed her lips. "I know it's in poor taste to predict the divorce during the engagement party, but you have to agree—"

"If you can't support the idea of Jodie and your only son together, then you will see very little of me or your grandchild," he warned before he walked away.

Stergios ignored his mother's stuttering apology as he walked to the door leading to the garden. He wondered how Jodie had survived living in this house when everyone had expected the worst in her. It was no wonder she had become reluctant to marry into this family. And all this time they thought she was trying to become an Antoniou.

He would protect her from his family, Stergios decided as he walked onto the dark portico. He would demand that Jodie was treated with respect. She deserved no less.

As he stepped onto the portico, he immediately heard Dimos's voice. "How long have you had your eye on Stergios?"

He spotted his cousin standing next to Jodie on the terrace. He was prepared to intervene but something stopped him. He didn't like the confidential tone of Dimos's voice as if they were sharing secrets. He should be the only one who knew Jodie that intimately.

"I was hoping to get a moment of peace before I went back inside," Jodie said wearily. "Where's your wife? You're slurring your words and you should go home."

"I don't want to go home." Dimos's voice rose sharply. "I want to know how you could have chosen him. I had followed you around for years and all that time you wanted Stergios. Why?"

Stergios went still and he found himself waiting for Jodie's answer. He had done things he wasn't proud of but that didn't stop Jodie from loving him. He wanted to know why.

"He's cruel and barbaric," Dimos continued when Jodie didn't respond. "Ruthless. He thinks this is his castle and we are his minions. I don't know what promises he made when he bedded you—"

"Stergios is the best man I've ever known." Jodie's voice cut through Dimos's tirade. "He takes care of his own."

Stergios frowned. He wasn't a good man. At times he was a monster. Jodie knew that firsthand. But he was the best man—the only man for her.

"He is a man of his word," Jodie continued, her voice vibrating with emotion, "and he would do anything for his family. He is going to be an amazing husband and an extraordinary father. He has restored my faith in men and that is saying a lot."

"You could have had me," Dimos said bitterly. "It would have been a wild ride."

Stergios bunched his hands as he saw a mist of red. The idea of Dimos touching Jodie sickened him.

"No, I couldn't," she said in a withering tone. "And do you know why? Because you're right. It was always Stergios. There was no competition."

Dimos's laugh rang out in the dark garden. "You are delusional, Jodie. The man is only marrying you to claim his heir. He's going to get bored with you within a month and then he'll pursue the world's most beautiful women like he used to. A year from now he will dump you and the brat in some apartment far away from here."

"You don't know Stergios." Her voice wavered.

"No, *you* don't," Dimos argued. "He's telling you what you want to hear. You are infatuated with an illusion."

Stergios had heard enough. He didn't need anyone poisoning Jodie's mind. He walked past the stone column. "There you are, Jodie," he said as he watched them both jump guiltily. "It's late and you've been on your feet all day."

Jodie didn't glance at Dimos as she gathered her skirts in her hands and climbed the steps. She reached for Stergios's hand and laced her fingers with his. She didn't say anything as he escorted her inside. As they climbed the grand staircase to his bedroom suite, Stergios asked, "Was he bothering you?"

"He's a pest, nothing more."

"I could always transfer him." His mouth twisted as he thought of a list of unglamorous locations. "Somewhere cold and rainy."

Jodie gave a light chuckle. "It's a tempting offer. I can't believe you thought I was interested in him. He's immature and spoiled."

"He's also closer to your age, handsome and charming." He remembered how he'd considered Dimos a worthy opponent for Jodie's attention. At times it felt as if Jodie preferred his cousin's company. "He's very popular with the women."

"Is he? I'll take your word for it," she murmured as he opened the door to their bedroom suite. She reached for his bow tie and drew him into their room. "You were far too popular with the women at the party."

He liked the possessive quality of her voice. "No, all eyes were on you." Stergios lightly brushed his finger against her ear. "You were made for these stones."

She gave him a questioning look. "What is it about these amethysts? Is there a story behind them?"

"There is." And tonight he would tell her when they were in bed together. Heat flooded him as he imagined Jodie yielding underneath him, wearing only the amethyst earrings and necklace. "Have you heard about the Antoniou legend?" he asked as he kicked the door closed.

Jodie heard the helicopter descend on the island and her smile widened. Stergios was home. She swung the door open and ran lightly on the path. She couldn't wait to tell him how much the baby had kicked during the day. Maybe tonight Stergios would get a chance to feel the baby move.

"Stergios!" Her heart felt as though it was going to expand as she saw him walk down the steps. He was a commanding force in his pinstripe suit and red tie. She met him with a kiss and drew back when his mouth was slack against hers. "What's wrong?"

"I had an emergency meeting with the security team." He looked pale. Shaken. "They've informed me that there's a credible threat against you."

"Impossible," she said. She knew Stergios spent millions on security cameras, safety features and armored cars. He had put a four-guard detail on her whenever she left the island and he had mentioned getting her a body double to distract the aggressive paparazzi. "Why would anyone focus on me?"

He leaned closer and splayed his hand on her rounded belly. "You're carrying my child," he said thickly. "It's the best way to get back at me."

"What are the threats?"

He reluctantly pulled away, as if he wanted to keep shielding his child with his bare hands. "I'm not discussing it with you."

"Not..." Her mouth gaped as she watched him walk to the house. "I'm not delicate, Stergios. I have a right to know."

He held the door for her and ushered her inside. Once he closed the door he went straight to the drink cabinet. She watched him grab a shot glass and the clear bottle of Tsipouro. She knew the threats had gotten under his skin. She had remembered how troubled Stergios had been the last time he had reached for the potent liquor.

Jodie wrapped her arms around herself as she approached him. "Why would someone tell you what they're going to do? That ruins the element of surprise."

"They do it to instill fear." The drink splashed in the shot glass. "It's amazingly effective."

"How long have the threats been going on?" she asked.

He froze, the glass midway to his mouth. She wasn't

sure he was going to answer. "After we made our first public appearance at the museum."

She exhaled slowly. "That long? And this is the first time you tell me?" She struggled to lower her voice. "You lecture me about not trusting you and you were hiding this?"

"I didn't want to worry you," he said before he downed the shot and grimaced.

Jodie shook her head. Stergios seemed to think that his need for security outweighed everything else. "So what are we going to do? Increase security?"

He paused and set the glass down hard as though it was a gavel. "I've decided that you're going back to New York. You will be far away from the threat," Stergios said as he walked to the window. He set his hands on his hips. "I'll have the security team look over your apartment and—"

"You want our baby born in Greece," she reminded him. Why was that no longer important? Her pulse fluttered with panic as she saw his grim face in the reflection. "You want me here."

"This is only temporary."

She tasted fear and swallowed hard. She hated that word. *Temporary.* It was vague. All of her homes had been temporary. She was finally feeling settled. This was becoming her home and now she had to leave. "What if it isn't?"

He was silent. Stergios didn't turn around. He didn't move.

Jodie raised her hand in defeat. "You know what? I'll go back to your mother's house. That place is a fortress."

"You are going back to New York if I have to drag you there."

She'd like to see him try! "What about the wedding?"

He gave a deep sigh and turned around. "We have to postpone it."

The panic that had bubbled inside her was now flowing over. All this time he wanted the security of marriage. Now he had changed his mind. No, she thought bitterly, it was just a postponement. It was *temporary*.

"Stergios, you have wealth, fame and power." She hated how weak her voice sounded. "That is going to attract the good and the bad in people. Once this threat fades, something else is going to replace it. You can't put your life on hold."

"I am not going to allow anything to happen to our child," Stergios said in a fierce growl.

"Neither will I," she promised. "But leaving home because one person made a threat? Why, when this island is well protected?"

Stergios raked his hands in his hair. It was as if he had gone through this argument several times before. "The security team thinks this is the best course."

"I disagree," she said as she clenched her jaw. "I think it's unreasonable. How are you going to conduct business from across the world?"

"The threat isn't focused on me," he said quietly.

Jodie tilted her head. She didn't like his carefully modulated tone. She was missing something. "You just said that this is probably a way to get to you."

His eyes were inscrutable. "I have to stay in Greece."

He wasn't coming with her. He was sending her away. Dimos's words echoed in her head. *He will dump you and the brat in some apartment far away from here.* She tried to block it out as her heartbeat roared in her ears. "I'm not leaving you."

"It's for your own protection."

"Stergios, don't do this, please." Jodie bit her lip. She knew better than to beg. Her fingers ached to grab his clothes and plead her case, but that would only drive him away. "I don't want to go."

He straightened his shoulders and clasped his hands behind his back. "I wish it hadn't come to this."

"I don't want to leave you." She finally found that someone with whom she wanted to share her life. She belonged with him and Stergios belonged with her. "I want to stay here."

"But I want you to go," he said as the harsh lines in his face deepened. "I won't forgive myself if anything happens to you or our child."

I want you to go. The words sliced through her like a jagged knife. He wanted this so-called temporary separation. He wouldn't miss her. Why should he? He didn't love her.

Jodie's legs shook and she thought she would fall into a heap at his feet. "When am I supposed to leave?"

He watched her carefully. It was obvious he didn't trust her flat voice or her sudden acceptance of the situation. "The helicopter pilot is waiting for you."

She felt the tears rolling onto her eyelashes. "Now?" Her voice cracked.

"I don't want to give this guy any opportunity to hurt you."

He was rushing her. Not giving her time to think. He was treating her like an opponent, determined to win before she knew what hit her. "I'm not packed."

"You don't need much. You have an apartment in New York," he reminded her. "And you'll be back soon."

He's telling you what you want to hear. You are infatuated with an illusion. She knew why Dimos's words stuck with her. She had often been guilty of believing what she wanted to be true. How many times had she believed her parents' promises before they had shipped her off to school? They had given her hope because they had been tired of her tears and bargaining. The more she had protested, the more they drew away.

"Are you coming with me? Just to make sure I'm okay?" she asked. She wasn't ready to walk away from Stergios. Maybe she could convince him on the long plane ride that they would do better as a team.

A muscle twitched in his jaw. "It's not a good idea."

She felt like she was bleeding inside. "When will you come visit?"

"I don't know," he admitted in a gravelly voice.

She knew what that meant. He wouldn't visit her. He might contact her. At first there would be a flurry of phone calls and texts. There would be promises to visit soon and proclamations of missing her. And then it would start to taper off. There would be a series of missed calls. Unanswered texts.

Tears burned her eyes and she took short, choppy breaths. Jodie tried to tell herself not to expect the worst. Stergios was not like her parents. He promised a commitment. He promised that she would come first.

So why did it feel as though he was abandoning her? His life would go on while hers was put on pause. She was going to be uprooted and sent away.

Stergios glanced at his wristwatch. "We need to leave as soon as possible. I have a jet waiting for you at the airport."

He wasn't even lingering. She knew the threat scared him. It was like his nightmare coming to life. She needed to respect it and yet…would he send her away if he loved her? Would he insist on this separation if he couldn't live without her?

She didn't know why she was torturing herself with these questions. She needed to accept the truth. He could live without her.

Jodie staggered back as the truth pierced her. She needed to protect herself before she splintered into pieces. "I'll go get my passport."

Stergios's relief was palpable as she walked to the bedroom. She felt stunned and yet she was aware of her surroundings. She heard him reach for his cell phone before he spoke in a low, urgent tone.

Once Jodie closed the bedroom door, she walked to the middle of the room and stopped. She looked down at her engagement ring. It represented hope and commitment. Promises and family. But it had all been an illusion.

The tears clogged her throat as she pulled the ring off and placed it on the table by the bed. If Stergios wanted her back, if he wanted to marry her, then he was going to find her in New York and convince her to return.

Because right now, she was better off on her own.

CHAPTER SEVENTEEN

STERGIOS SAT ALONE in the ornate living room in Jodie's Upper East Side apartment as he waited for her return. He hadn't seen her in over a week and he had been in quiet agony. His life had been in disorder and he wanted his fiancée back.

He wasn't certain of his welcome. On his flight over, he had imagined that she was at home, pining for him. But the surprise was on him. Jodie had plunged back into her full social life as if she had to make up for lost time.

Stergios heard the front door open and he sat up straight in his chair. Anticipation beat wildly inside him when he heard Jodie's familiar voice as she spoke on her cell phone.

"Yes!" Her laugh made his heart take a tumble. "We definitely should meet up, Henry. It's been a long time."

Henry? Hot, bitter jealousy rolled through him and he clenched the armrest with his fingers. Who was Henry? The security team had not mentioned this man. And why did she sound so happy talking to this Henry?

He saw Jodie stride past the door and her cheerful voice faltered. Stergios didn't move as he waited. He kept his steady gaze on the doorway and watched her slowly retrace her steps.

Jodie looked radiant and healthy as she stood at the threshold. Her gray dress acknowledged but didn't accentuate her full breasts and pregnant belly. Her red lips parted open but she didn't smile. Her blue eyes sparkled with surprise and joy but immediately went blank.

"Let me call you back," she said in a trance before she disconnected the call. She lowered her hand and stood as still as a statue. "The security team didn't tell me you were here," she said through bloodless lips. "I guess we know where their loyalties lie."

"Who is Henry?" Stergios winced at his harsh tone. This was not the reunion he had intended.

"An old friend." She tossed her phone on a nearby table and leaned against the door frame. "And what have you done to my butler and my housekeeper?"

"I've given them the day off."

She arched her eyebrow with displeasure. "What brings you to New York?"

"You," he said in a husky purr. He didn't want to spend another day without her.

"Isn't it dangerous to be near me?" She pursed her lips as though she was holding back what she really wanted to say. "Wasn't that why you sent me away?"

He heard the hurt weighing down her voice. "We caught the man who made the threats. He has a history of stalking celebrities and public figures."

"So it's over." She gave a sharp, decisive nod and crossed her arms. "Thanks for letting me know. There was no reason to fly all the way over here. You could have left word with your security team."

She showed no joy or relief like he had when he'd received the news. He had rushed over to America the moment it was safe and she didn't feel the need to cross the room for him. "I'm here to take you back home."

She motioned at the ornate walls and painted ceilings. "I am home."

This was not her home. She didn't stamp her personality anywhere in this four-bedroom penthouse apartment. It was as impersonal as a hotel room.

"You have a nursery to finish and we can get back to our wedding plans. Which reminds me." He reached into the breast pocket of his jacket and held the diamond solitaire between his fingers. "You left this behind."

He had been stunned to discover that Jodie had removed her engagement ring before she left Greece. Panic swelled deep inside him when Jodie stared wordlessly at the ring.

She glanced up and her gaze collided with his. "It no longer belongs to me," she said in a hoarse whisper.

Stergios jumped from his seat and gripped the ring in his hands. "What the hell is that supposed to mean?"

She thrust out her chin. "It means that I'm not returning to Greece and I'm not returning to you."

He was losing her. The diamond bit his palm. Stergios drew in a short breath as alarm squeezed his chest. He had realized how much he needed her when they were apart. Now he couldn't get her back. "Why?"

"Why?" Anger flashed in her blue eyes as she pushed away from the door frame. "How can you ask that? You shipped me off at the first excuse."

"It was not an excuse!"

"If you are going to send me away every time there's a problem, then it's better if I stay here in New York."

"That is not going to happen. You made promises and—"

"So did you," she lashed out and pointed accusingly at him.

He sliced his hands in the air. "We are getting married. The sooner the better." He needed to bind Jodie to him in every possible way.

"No." She waved her hands and took a step back. "I will still give you full access with the baby but not with me. That's over."

"Because I tried to keep you safe?" His voice rose in disbelief.

"Because you cast me off the first chance you got." She glared at him as the hurt shimmered from her eyes. "Because you disregarded my fears in favor of yours."

"That's not what happened." Or had it? He remembered her pleas when he had sent her away. He had wanted to give in and hold her in his arms, but he had known he had to stay strong. This time he hadn't been able to let her have her way.

"Do you think I felt safe when I was sent away and I didn't know for how long?" Her bright red lips trembled. "Am I supposed to feel some sort of security when I'm isolated and I don't hear from you?"

"I didn't call you right away because of security reasons. I didn't want you to be located. And then when I tried to contact you I couldn't reach you."

She hastily wiped her eyes with the back of her hand. "I've heard every excuse when my parents didn't stay in contact with me, but that's a new one."

He splayed his hands out as the anger and frustration billowed inside him. "Do you think I wanted to stay away from you?"

"Yes."

The simple word was like a punch in the stomach. How could she believe that?

"I made the most difficult decision to let you go," he said gruffly. "I didn't know how long it would be until I saw you. I denied myself the pleasure of watching our child grow strong inside you. I knew it was a possibility that I would miss every milestone of this pregnancy and very possibly the birth. But I made that choice because I needed to keep you safe."

"But you didn't allow me a choice," she argued, her eyes flashing with fire. "You didn't give me any information or time to make a decision."

"The less you knew about the threats—"

"No, you don't get to say that. You made these decisions because you knew you had power over me. I have rarely refused you anything and that is my fault. I settled for commitment over love and this is where it got me." A tear tracked down her cheek. "Alone and abandoned."

He was suddenly in front of her. "Jodie," he said in a ragged breath as he reached out and rubbed the tear away. Her pain was ripping him apart. He had hurt her without realizing it. He did this. And he didn't know how to fix it.

"I trusted you but you took advantage of the love I have for you." More tears spilled over her lashes. "You know my history. You know how miserable I was having no family connection, hating how I was forgotten and invisible. And yet you did the same to me as my parents."

"It's not the same," he said as he cupped her face between his hands.

"Why did your fears take precedence over mine?" she whispered.

"The situation was urgent and—"

She pulled away from him. "The situation is always going to be urgent. Each separation will be temporary. That is, until it becomes routine. And eventually, I will be living away, alone and forgotten, because I had put my trust in you."

"I won't let that happen," he promised. Stergios needed another chance to prove that he was worthy of her trust.

"It won't happen because I'm not going to give you that power again. I won't allow you to decide my fate." She rubbed her hands over her face and rolled her shoulders back before she took a deep breath. "I will not marry you. We are co-parents and that's it. That's all you wanted, anyway."

"I want more," he said gruffly. "I want it all."

Her mouth twisted into a bitter smile. "So did I. It didn't work out. Goodbye, Stergios," she said with a hitch in her voice.

The cold fear threatened to break him. Jodie was giving up on him. On them. He couldn't let that happen. "No, I'm staying here."

"Why now?" she asked tearfully. "Why not when I wanted you with me? Never mind. It doesn't matter anymore." She dismissed her questions with the wave of her hand. "New York City is big enough for the both of us."

"I'm staying here with you in your apartment."

She bristled at his commanding tone. "No, you're not!"

"We're co-parents, remember? You won't deny me access to my child." He sounded more confident than he felt. Stergios knew he was taking a big gamble. Jodie could strike back by keeping him away during the rest of her pregnancy. But he didn't think she would do that, no matter how hurt and angry she was with him. It was more important to her that their child had a strong bond with both parents.

"You're right, I won't," she said as her shoulders sagged with defeat. "That is the only reason I'm agreeing to this. I'll have the housekeeper make up a bed for you and you can have the library as your office."

"That's generous of you," he said softly as he watched her with suspicion. He thought he would have to fight tooth and nail for Jodie to make room for him.

"Only because I know it will be temporary," she said as she walked out of the room. "You'll leave and return to your old life once you realize that I'm not marrying you."

* * *

She had to give Stergios credit, Jodie thought as she swept into her penthouse apartment three weeks later. The man was determined to prove her wrong. He had invaded her home, her life and her every waking moment.

She tensed as his hands caressed her bare arms as he removed her coat. Stergios was a charming companion at the breakfast table and a supportive father-to-be at the doctor's office. He was the perfect escort to social events. She flicked her gaze at him, noting how sophisticated and sexy he appeared in his dark suit and tie.

He wasn't leaving, Jodie realized. At first she thought it was simply a battle of wills but now that she had put all the pieces together, she knew he was setting down roots here.

It didn't make sense, she decided as she marched away, her black cocktail dress swishing against her knees. He had other commitments. He couldn't stay in New York.

"You are in a bad mood," Stergios drawled as he followed her into the living room. "What's wrong?"

"I'm not moody," she said through clenched teeth. "I'm pregnant."

"Is it because Henry spent most of the time talking to me?" he teased. Her pulse gave a kick at his dazzling smile. "It's only because he wants another chance to beat me in squash."

"Who would have thought the two of you would have become fast friends?" she muttered. Stergios had made a point of meeting her closest friends during the past few weeks. They adored him and had loudly advised her to marry him before he got away.

Stergios shrugged. "Once I knew Henry wasn't a romantic rival, I could see that he's a good man who I could trust around you."

Jodie felt her nostrils flare as she tamped down her annoyance. "I told you that he was an old friend."

"*Ne*, you did." He slowly turned and was suddenly in front of her. "However, what you didn't tell me was that he was the first boy who was caught in your room at boarding school."

"Oh, he told you that." She felt her cheeks burn under Stergios's possessive gaze. "Nothing happened between Henry and me. We're just friends and we looked out for each other. No big deal."

"He still looks out for you." Stergios paused thoughtfully before he continued. "Which is why I asked him to watch over you while I'm gone."

She flinched and she felt the blood drain from her face. "Gone?"

"I have to go to Athens for a few days." His tone was careful as he cupped her shoulders with his big, warm hands. "I want you to come with me but you've made it clear that you won't leave New York."

Jodie didn't want him to go. What if he chose not to come back? She was suddenly tempted to go on the trip with him but bit her lip before she revealed that to Stergios. "Why are you returning to Greece?"

His fingers flexed. She sensed that he wanted to gather her in his arms but he didn't move. "That's something I want to talk about with you. I'm prepared to step away from my position in the Antoniou Group."

Shock pulsed through her and she jerked out of his hold. "What? Why?"

He slid his hands in his pockets and watched her through hooded eyes. "It's the only way I can stay here with you."

"No, no, no." She raised her hands to stop him from that dangerous train of thought. "You can't do that. I won't let you."

"I can't abandon all of my responsibilities. I will stay on with the Antoniou Group as an advisor."

He wasn't listening to her. Jodie grabbed his arm. "Don't do it. You'll regret it."

He covered her hand with his. "*Oxi*, I won't." His voice was soft but confident.

"Maybe you won't regret it for a month or even a year, but you will one day." Her fingers dug into his sleeve. "You are giving up everything you've worked your entire life for. I can't let you do that."

Stergios's eyes darkened. "I know what I want, Jodie. It's you."

He was wrong. She bent her head as the chaotic emotions rushed through her. Stergios wanted access to the baby. He wanted to create a stable family life for his children. He didn't want *her*.

"Go back to Greece, Stergios." It hurt to say those words. Jodie closed her eyes as the pain tore through her. "Marry the heiress who can give you power. Rule the world. You don't need to stay here. I'll be fine."

"I choose you, Jodie." He wrapped his arm around her waist and drew her closer. "Why does that scare you?"

"You don't understand," she said in a whisper as her body went limp. "I'm not going to be enough for you. I'm not going to meet your expectations. I'm not the wife you need. I'm *keeping* you from what you need. What you really want."

"I need you," he insisted. His fingers spread through her hair and he cupped the back of her head.

"You are so far away from your home. You're not there because of me."

"I choose to live here." He tilted her head back and she had to meet his gaze. "This is where we can protect our relationship and no one with an agenda can tear it down. This is where you are valued and respected."

Tears burned the back of her eyes. "Your family is halfway around the world. You should be with them."

"You are my family." Sincerity rang in his voice. "You and this little one."

"But what about your goal to make the Antonious untouchable?" It had been the one thing that motivated him through his life. He couldn't give that up now.

"I will always provide for you," he promised. "I will protect you no matter what. But I will not spend another day without you," he vowed. "I want to fill my days and nights with you. I want to know our children and I—"

"When did you decide this?"

"When I sent you away to the other side of the world." The lines in his face deepened with misery as he remembered. "It was the wrong choice and I won't do it again. I promise we will face any obstacle, any threat, together."

"Why?" she asked breathlessly.

"I can't live without you. I don't want to anymore." His hand tightened in her hair. "I love you, Jodie."

She had yearned to hear those words and now she was afraid to accept them. If they weren't true, if his love wasn't strong enough to last forever, it would destroy her. "No, you don't," she whispered. "You told me that you would never—"

"I didn't want to believe it. I wanted to protect myself from being vulnerable," he said as he pressed his mouth against her hair. "I don't let anyone close to me, but I let you. Because I know you will protect me like I will protect you."

He loved her. Stergios loved her. Her breath caught in her lungs but she struggled to accept that as truth.

"I've been falling in love with you all this time. It's you. It's always been you," he confessed as he brushed his lip against her cheek. "And I'm going to prove my love to you every day. Just give me another chance."

She wanted to give him a chance but this was the biggest risk she'd ever take. If she took this leap of faith, it required her to be bold. Live and love wildly. She would accept his ring and take his name. She would create a family and a life with this man.

"Please, Jodie." His mouth pressed against her jaw. "Let me show you how much you mean to me. Let me love you."

"Yes, Stergios." She clasped her hands on his cheeks. "I want all of that and more."

EPILOGUE

JODIE SAT ON the stone bench and tilted her head back as the evening breeze carried the heavy scent of flowers. She inhaled deeply and smiled as a sense of peace washed over her. The splendor of the Antoniou estate gardens was lost on her boisterous and inquisitive children, who were now fast asleep in the nursery under the watchful eye of their beloved nanny.

It was a constant source of amazement for Jodie that she was a welcomed guest at the Antoniou home. Over the years the haunted look faded from Stergios's eyes and Mairi had gradually accepted that Jodie was the woman her son needed. Jodie was also beginning to see signs that Mairi and Gregory would be the kind of grandparents she'd hoped for her children.

Rising from the bench, Jodie brushed a leaf from her dinner dress and walked back toward the house. As she took a turn, her heart leaped with joy when she saw her husband striding down the path. Her gaze greedily roamed his body as she noticed how the dark suit emphasized his athletic build.

"There you are," he muttered as he reached for her. His touch was possessive and urgent as he clasped his hands on her hips and pulled her close. "I had back-to-back meetings but you were on my mind all day."

"Stergios!" She frantically pushed at his audacious

hands but he managed to capture her fingers. "Someone will see us."

"I don't care." His voice was low and seductive as and he guided her off the gravel path. "I can't get enough of you."

Her spine bumped against the rough bark of a tree. Anticipation fluttered in Jodie's stomach when she saw the glitter of lust in Stergios's eyes. "Your family will think I'm a bad influence on you."

"They believe you've tamed me. Domesticated me." He raised her arms above her head, holding her wrists against the tree trunk. A slow wicked smile pulled at his lips. "If they only knew the truth…"

Her skin flushed as she remembered how she'd driven him to the height of ecstasy just before dawn. His response had been aggressive and primal as she'd held him spellbound. "Mairi will banish me from this house," Jodie warned as she arched against Stergios.

"I go where you go," he reminded her in a husky growl. Stergios leaned into her and she yielded against his hard, masculine body. He teased her with the featherlight touch of his mouth as she tried to capture his tongue.

"You drive me wild," Jodie confessed as she tore out of his grasp and thrust her hands into his dark hair before she kissed him with a rapidly building hunger.

They had been married for five years and her desire for Stergios burned brighter than on her wedding day. Every intimate touch, heated debate and unguarded moment brought them closer. Jodie trusted this man with her heart, her body and her most private thoughts.

"And to think I had wanted a shy and compliant wife," Stergios murmured as he bunched the hem of her dress in his hands. "A woman who wouldn't distract me."

"You're the one who changed the course of my life.

I didn't know I could be this happy." She hesitated and whispered, "It frightens me sometimes."

Stergios lifted his head. "Because you're afraid it won't last?" he asked as he let go of her crushed dress. "That someone or something will try to steal your happiness and destroy it. Or are you afraid of what you will do to protect your happiness?"

"All of it." Jodie looked away. "Am I that transparent?"

"Only to me." He gently cupped her face with his large hands. Her breath caught in her throat as he held her gaze with his intense brown eyes. "Because I know how you feel. It scares me how much I need you in my life. I will do anything to protect this. To protect us."

"I know." He had proven it to her throughout the years. They both had made choices, sacrifices and compromises in the name of love. "But one day we will be tested."

"Then we will face it together, *pethi mou*. When I'm weak, you will be strong for the both of us. When you're scared, I will protect you. I will be with you during your best and worst moments. And through it all, nothing will stop me from loving you," Stergios vowed before he claimed her mouth with a ravenous kiss. "Nothing."

* * * * *